IRÈNE

PIERRE LEMAITRE

Also by Pierre Lemaitre in English translation

Alex

IRÈNE

PIERRE LEMAITRE

Translated from the French by
Frank Wynne

MacLehose Press
New York • London

MacLehose Press
An imprint of Quercus
New York • London

© 2006 by Pierre Lemaitre et Éditions du Masque, departmente des editions Jean-Claude Lattès
English translation © 2014 by Frank Wynne

Originally published in French as *Travail soigné* by Jean-Claude Lattès in 2006
First published in the United States by Quercus in 2014

ISBN 978-1-62365-800-7

Library of Congress Control Number: 2014951595

Distributed in the United States and Canada by
Hachette Book Group
237 Park Avenue
New York, NY 10017

Manufactured in the United States

10 9 8 7 6 5 4 3 2 1

www.quercus.com

For Pascaline

For my father

The writer is someone who arranges quotes and removes the quotation marks.

Roland Barthes

I

Monday, April 7, 2003

1

"Alice . . . ," he said, looking at what anyone else would have called a young girl.

He used her name as a sign of complicity but could not make the slightest dent in her armor. He looked down at the notes scribbled by Armand during the first interview: Alice Vandenbosch, twenty-four. He tried to imagine what twenty-four-year-old Alice Vandenbosch normally looked like. She was probably a young woman with a long slim face, sandy hair, honest eyes. What he saw when he looked up seemed completely improbable. The girl was nothing like herself: her hair, once blonde, was plastered to her skull and dark at the roots; her face had a sickly pallor, a large purple bruise on her right cheek, thin threads of dried blood at one corner of her mouth . . . all that was human in her wild, frantic eyes was fear, a fear so terrible she was still shivering as though she had gone out on a winter's day without a coat. She clutched the plastic coffee cup with both hands, like a lifeline.

Usually, when Camille Verhœven stepped into a room, even the coolest of customers reacted. Not Alice. Alice was shut away inside herself, trembling.

It was 8:30 a.m.

A few minutes earlier, when he had arrived at the *brigade crimi-nelle*, Camille had felt tired. Dinner the night before had gone on until 1 a.m. People he did not know, friends of Irène. They had talked about television, told stories that Camille might have found quite funny but for the fact that he was sitting opposite a woman who reminded him of his mother. All through the meal he had tried to dispel the image, but it was uncanny: the same stare, the same mouth, the same cigarettes smoked one after the other. Camille had found himself swept back twenty years to a blessed time when his mother would emerge from her studio wearing a smock smeared with paint, a cigarette dangling from her lips, her hair disheveled. A time when he would still go to watch her work. She was an Amazon. Solid and focused, with a furious brushstroke. She lived so much inside her head that sometimes she did not seem to notice his presence. Long, silent periods back when he had loved paint-ing, back when he watched her every movement as though it might be the key to some mystery that concerned him personally. That was before. Before the serried ranks of cigarettes declared open war on her, but long after they caused the fetal hypotrophy that marked Camille's birth. At the time, drawing himself up to his full height—he would never be taller than four foot eleven—Camille did not know which he hated more, the mother whose toxic habit had fashioned him into a kind of pale, slightly less deformed copy of Toulouse-Lautrec, or the meek, powerless father who gazed at his wife with pathetic admiration, as though at his own reflection in a mirror: at sixteen Camille was already a man, though not in stature. While his mother accumulated canvases in her studio and his laconic father worked at the pharmacy, Camille learned what it meant to be short. As he grew older, he stopped desperately trying to stand on tiptoe, got used to looking at others from below, gave up trying to reach shelves without fetching a stool, laid out his personal space like a doll's house. And this diminutive man would survey, without really understanding, the vast canvases his mother had to roll up in order to take them to gallery owners. Sometimes his mother would say, "Camille, come here a minute . . ." Sitting on a stool, she would silently run her fingers through his hair and Camille knew that he loved her; at times he thought he would never love anyone else.

Those were the good times, Camille thought over dinner as he stared at the woman sitting opposite who laughed raucously, drank little, and smoked like a chimney. The time before his mother spent her days kneeling next to her bed, resting her cheek on the blankets, the only position in which the cancer gave her a little respite. Illness had brought her to her knees. And though by now each found the other unfathomable, this was the first time that they could look at each other eye to eye. At the time, Camille had sketched a lot, spending long hours in his mother's now deserted studio. When he decided to go into her room he would find his father, who now also spent half his life on his knees, pressed against his wife, his arm around her shoulders, saying nothing, breathing to the same rhythm as her. Camille was left alone. Camille sketched. Camille killed time and he waited.

By the time he went to law school, his mother weighed as little as one of her paintbrushes. Whenever he came home, his father seemed cloaked in a heavy silence of grief. The whole thing dragged on. And Camille bent his permanently childlike body over his law books and waited for it to end.

It arrived on a May day like any other. The telephone call might almost have been from a stranger. His father said simply, "You should probably come home." And he knew right away that from then on he would have to make his own way in the world, that there would never be anyone else.

At forty, this short, bald man with his long, furrowed face now knew that this was not true, not since Irène had come into his life.

But all these visions from the past had made for an exhausting evening. Besides, game had never really agreed with him.

It was at about the time he was bringing Irène her breakfast on a tray that Alice had been picked up by a squad car on the boulevard Bonne-Nouvelle.

"In ten minutes," said Camille, "I want you to come tell me you've found Marco. And that he's in a bad way."

"Found Marco . . . ?" Armand was puzzled. "Where?"

"What the fuck do I know . . . just make it happen."

With short, swift strides, Camille scurried back to his office.

"So," he said as he came toward Alice, "Let's take it again from the beginning."

He stood facing her: they were almost eye to eye. Alice seemed to wake from her trance. She stared at him as though seeing him for the first time and must have felt more keenly than ever how ridiculous the world was; two hours earlier she had been beaten up, her body was a mass of bruises, and now here she sat in the *brigade criminelle* staring at a man no more than four foot eleven tall who was suggesting they start again from the beginning, as though this nightmare had a beginning.

Camille sat at his desk and automatically picked a pencil from among the dozen or so in the cut-glass desk organizer Irène had given him. He looked at Alice. She was not an ugly girl—rather pretty, in fact. Her delicate, sorrowful features were somewhat gaunt from too many late nights and too little care. A pietà. She looked like a reproduction of a classical statue.

"How long have you been working for Santeny?" he asked, sketching the curve of her face with a single stroke.

"I don't work for him!"

"Okay, let's say two years, then. So you work for him and he supplies you, is that the deal?"

"No."

"And you still think he's in love with you, am I right?"

She glared at him. Camille smiled and looked down at his drawing. There was a long silence. Camille remembered a favorite phrase of his mother's: "It's the artist's heart that beats inside the model's body."

On the sketchpad, with a few deft strokes, a different Alice slowly began to appear, younger than the woman sitting opposite, just as sorrowful but not as bruised. Camille looked at her again and seemed to come to a decision. Alice watched as he pulled a chair up next to her and perched on it like a child, his feet dangling.

"Mind if I smoke?" Alice said.

"Santeny's in deep, deep shit," Camille said as though he hadn't heard. "The world and his brother are gunning for him. But you know that better than anyone, don't you?" he said, gesturing to her bruises. "Not exactly friendly, are they? So it's probably best that we find him first, don't you think?"

Alice seemed to be hypnotized by Camille's shoes, which swung like a two pendulums several inches from the floor.

"He's got no one to turn to, no way out of this. I give him a couple of days at most. But then you haven't got anyone either, have you? They'll track you down . . . Now, where's Santeny?"

A stubborn little pout, like a child who knows she's doing something wrong but does it anyway.

"Okay, never mind . . . you're free to go," said Camille, as though talking to himself. "Next time I see you, I hope it's not at the bottom of a dumpster."

At precisely that moment Armand stepped into the office.

"We've just found Marco. You were right; he's in a terrible way."

Camille looked at Armand in feigned surprise.

"Where was he?"

"His place."

Camille shot his colleague a pitiful look: even with his imagination Armand was tight fisted.

"Okay. Anyway, we can let the girl go," he said, hopping down from the chair.

A little flurry of panic then:

"He's in Rambouiller," muttered Alice under her breath.

"Oh," said Camille, unimpressed.

"Boulevard Delagrange, number 18."

"Eighteen," Camille echoed, as though repeating the number excused him from having to thank the young woman.

Without waiting for permission, Alice took a crumpled cigarette pack from her pocket and lit one.

"Those things will kill you," Camille said.

2

Camille was gesturing to Armand to dispatch a squad to the address when the telephone rang. On the other end, Louis sounded out of breath.

"We've got a clusterfuck out in Courbevoie," he panted.

"Do tell . . . ," Camille said laconically, picking up a pen.

"We received an anonymous tip-off this morning. I'm there right now. It's . . . I don't know how to describe it–"

"Why don't you give it a go," Camille interrupted fractiously. "See what we come up with."

"It's carnage," Louis said in a strangulated voice, struggling to find the words. "It's a bloodbath. But not the usual kind, if you see what I mean . . ."

"I don't see, Louis, not really."

"It's like nothing I've ever seen in my life . . ."

3

Since his extension was engaged, Camille walked to Commissaire Le Guen's office. He knocked curtly but did not wait for an answer. He liked to make an entrance.

Le Guen was a big man who had spent more than twenty years following one diet after another without losing a single ounce. He had acquired a somewhat weary fatalism that was visible in his face, in his whole body. Camille had noticed that, over the years, he had adopted the air of a deposed king, surveying the world with a sullen, disillusioned expression. Hardly had Camille said a word than Le Guen interrupted him purely on principle, explaining that, whatever it was, "he didn't have the time." But when he saw the slim dossier Camille had brought, he decided accompany him to the crime scene nonetheless.

4

On the telephone Louis had said, "It's like nothing I've ever seen in my life . . ." This worried Camille; his assistant was not given to doom mongering. In fact he was exasperatingly optimistic, so Camille expected nothing good of this unexpected call-out. As the Péripherique flashed past, Camille Verhœven could not help but smile thinking about Louis.

Louis Mariani was blond, his hair parted to the side, and he had that unruly tuft genetically bestowed upon children of the privileged classes, a wayward curl constantly flicked back with a jerk of the head or a nonchalant yet practiced hand. Over time, Camille had learned to distinguish the different messages conveyed by the way Louis pushed back his hair, a veritable barometer for gauging his moods. The right-handed variant covered a range of meanings running from "Let's be reasonable" to "That's simply not done." The left-handed variant signaled embarrassment, awkwardness, timidity, or confusion. Looking at Louis, it was easy to imagine him as an altar boy. He still had the youthful looks, the grace, the fragility. In short, Louis was elegant, slim, delicate, and a royal pain in the ass.

To crown it all, Louis was loaded. He had all the trappings of the filthy rich: a certain way of deporting himself, a particular way of speaking, of articulating, of choosing his words, everything in fact that comes from the top-shelf mold marked "Rich spoiled brat." Louis had initially excelled in college (where he had studied a little law, some economics, history of art, aesthetics, psychology), changing courses according to his whims, unfailingly brilliant, treating education as a series of inane achievements. And then something had happened. From what Camille understood, it had to do with Descartes' dark night of the soul and the demon drink—a combination of philosophical intuition and single-malt whiskey. Louis had seen his life stretching out before him, in his perfectly appointed six-room apartment lined with bookshelves full of tomes on art and inlaid cabinets filled with designer crockery, the rents from his various properties rolling in like a civil servant's salary, spending vacations at his mother's place in Vichy, frequenting the same neighborhood restaurants, and he found himself confronted by a personal paradox as sudden as it was strange, a genuine existential crisis that anyone other than Louis would have summed up by saying "What the fuck am I doing here?"

Camille was convinced that, had he been born thirty years earlier, Louis would have become a left-wing revolutionary, but these days ideology no longer offered an alternative. Louis despised sanctimoniousness, and by extension voluntary work and charity. He needed to find something to do with his life, his own living hell. And suddenly it became clear to him: he would join the police. Louis never doubted for a moment that he would be accepted into the *brigade criminelle*—doubt was not a family trait, and Louis's brilliance meant that he was rarely disillusioned. He passed his police exams and joined the force, motivated partly by a desire to serve (not to Protect and Serve, but simply to serve a purpose), partly by the fear that life would soon become entirely solipsistic, and partly, perhaps, out of an imagined debt he felt he owed the working classes for not having been born one of their number. When he passed his detective's exams, Louis found the world utterly different from how he had imagined it: it had nothing of the quaintness of Agatha Christie or the deductive logic of Conan Doyle; instead Louis found himself faced with filthy hovels and battered wives, drug dealers bleeding to death in dumpsters in Barbès, knife fights between junkies, putrid toilets where the addicts who survived the fights OD'd, young male prostitutes selling their asses for a line of coke and johns who refused to pay more than five euros for a blow job after 2 a.m. In the early days, Camille found it entertaining to observe Louis, the blond bangs, the florid vocabulary, his eyes filled with horror but his mind like a steel trap, as he filled out endless reports; Louis imperturbably taking witness statements in echoing, piss-stained stairwells next to the corpse of some thirteen-year-old pimp who had been hacked to death with a machete in front of his mother; Louis heading home at two in the morning to his enormous apartment on the rue Notre-Dame-de-Lorette and collapsing fully dressed on his velvet sofa beneath an engraving by Pavel, between the bookcase of signed first editions and his late father's collection of amethysts.

When Louis first arrived at the *brigade criminelle*, the *commandant* did not immediately take to this smooth, clean-cut young man with the upper-class drawl who seemed unfazed by everything. The other officers on the team, who found it mildly entertaining to spend their days with a golden boy, were ruthless. Within less than two months, Louis had encountered most of the cruel pranks and hazing rituals with which groups humiliate outsiders. Louis accepted his fate without complaint, smiling awkwardly.

Camille noticed earlier than his colleagues that this surprising and intelligent young man had the makings of a good officer, but, perhaps trusting to Darwinian selection, he decided not to intervene. Louis, with his rather British stiff upper lip, was grateful to him for that. One evening, as he was leaving the offices, Camille saw Louis dash to the bar across the road and knock back two or three shots. It reminded him of the fight scene in *Cool Hand Luke* where Paul Newman, battered, dazed, and unable to land a punch, keeps getting up every time he's knocked down until the men watching lose heart; even his opponent loses the will to fight. And indeed, faced with Louis's professional diligence and his surprising ability to appeal to their better nature, the other officers eventually gave up. Over the years, Camille and Louis accepted each other's differences, and since the *commandant* enjoyed an undisputed moral authority over the team, no one was surprised that the rich kid gradually became his closest colleague. Camille always addressed Louis by his first name, as he did everyone on his team. But as time passed and the team changed, he realized that only the longest-serving members called him Camille. These days the team was mostly comprised of rookies, and Camille sometimes felt as though he had usurped a role he had never sought and become patriarch. The rookies addressed him as "*commandant*," though he knew this was less to do with hierarchy than an attempt to compensate for the instinctive embarrassment they felt at his diminutive stature. Louis also addressed him by his surname, but Camille knew that his motivation was different: it was a reflex of his class. The two men had never quite become friends, but they respected each other, and both felt that this was a better basis for a good working relationship.

5

Camille and Armand, with Le Guen trailing behind, arrived at 17 rue Félix-Faure in Courbevoie shortly after 10 a.m. It was an industrial wasteland.

In its center a small derelict factory lay like a dead insect, surrounded by former workshops that were currently being renovated. The four finished units looked as out of place as tiki huts in a snowy landscape. All had white rendering, glass roofs, and aluminum windows with sliding panels, offering a glimpse of their vast interiors. The whole place looked deserted. There were no cars save those of the *brigade criminelle*.

Two steps led up to the warehouse apartment. From behind, Camille saw Louis leaning against a wall, spitting into a plastic bag he kept pressed to his mouth. Camille walked past, followed by Le Guen and two other officers from the team, and stepped into a room lit by the blinding glare of spotlights. When they arrive at a crime scene, rookie officers unconsciously look around for death. Experienced officers look for life. But there was no life here; death had leached into every space, even the bewildered eyes of the living.

Camille had no time to worry about the strange atmosphere that pervaded the room as his gaze was immediately arrested by the head of a woman nailed to the wall.

Hardly had he taken three paces into the room than he found himself faced with a scene he could not have imagined even in his worst nightmares: severed fingers, torrents of clotted blood, the stench of excrement and gutted entrails. Instinctively, he was reminded of Goya's painting *Saturn Devouring His Son*, and for an instant he could see the terrifying face, the bulging eyes, the crimson mouth, the utter madness. Though he was one of the most experienced officers on the scene, Camille felt the urge to turn back to the doorway, where Louis, not meeting anyone's eye, held his plastic bag at arm's length, like a beggar declaring his contempt for the world.

"What the fuck is this . . . ?" Commissaire Le Guen muttered to himself, and his words were swallowed by the void. Only Louis heard him and came over, wiping his eyes.

"I don't know," he said. "I walked in and had to walk straight back out again . . . That's as far as I've got."

Standing in the middle of the room, Armand turned toward the two men, looking dazed. He wiped his clammy hands on his pants and tried to compose himself.

Bergeret, head of the forensics team from *l'identité judiciaire*, went over to Le Guen.

"I'm going to need two teams. This is going to take a while." Then, with uncharacteristic candor, he added: "It's not exactly your usual crime scene."

There was nothing usual about it at all.

"Okay, I'll leave you to it," Le Guen said to Maleval, who had just come into the room and was already racing out, both hands clasped over his mouth.

Camille signaled to his team that it was time to man up.

It was impossible to imagine what the apartment had looked like before . . . this. Because "this" had now ravaged the place, and they did not know which way to turn. To Camille's right, sprawled on the ground, were the remains of a disemboweled body, jagged, broken ribs poking through the stomach and one breast, the other having been hacked off, but it was difficult to say for sure since the body of the woman—that it was a woman was the only thing that seemed certain—was smeared with excrement, which only partially covered countless bite marks. To the left was a head, the eyes burned out. From the gaping mouth snaked pink-and-white veins. Opposite lay a body from which the skin had been partially peeled away; deep gashes lacerated the flesh, and there were yawning wounds, carefully demarcated openings in the belly and vagina, probably made using acid. The head of the second victim had been nailed to the wall through the cheeks. Camille surveyed the scene and took a notebook from his pocket, only to quickly put it back again as though acknowledging that the task was so monstrous that all his methods were useless, every approach doomed to failure. There is no strategy for dealing with atrocity. And yet this was why he was here, staring at the nameless horror.

Before it had clotted, someone had used the victims' blood to daub on the wall in huge letters: I AM BACK. It was obvious from the long drips at their base that a lot of blood had been used. The characters had been scrawled using several fingers, sometimes together, sometimes apart, so that the inscription seemed somehow blurred. Camille stepped over the mangled body of a woman and went to the wall. At the end of the sentence, a finger had been pressed against the plaster with great care. Every ridge and whorl was distinct; it looked just like the old-style ID cards when a duty officer would press your finger against the yellowing cardboard, rolling it carefully from one side to the other.

Dark sprays of blood spattered the walls all the way to the ceiling.

It took several minutes for Camille to compose himself. It would be impossible for him to think rationally in this setting—everything he could see defied reason.

There were about a dozen people now working in the apartment. As in an operating theater, to outsiders the atmosphere at a crime scene can often seem quite relaxed. People are quick to laugh and joke. It was something Camille loathed. Conversation between the crime scene investigators was full of crude jokes and sexual innuendo, as though they needed to prove they were blasé. A common attitude in professions that are predominantly male. To a forensics officer accustomed to dissociating horror from reality, the body of a woman—even when dead—is still a woman's body; a female suicide victim can still be described as "a good-looking woman" even when her face has bloated and turned blue. But the atmosphere in the apartment in Courbevoie was very different. It was neither grieving nor compassionate, but hushed and powerful, as though even the most hard-bitten officers, caught off guard, were wondering how they could possibly make light of a body that had been disemboweled beneath the sightless gaze of a head nailed to the wall. And so, in silence, the forensics team took measurements, collected samples, redirected the spotlights as they snapped photographs, documenting the scene with an almost religious stillness. Though Armand was an experienced officer, his face was deathly pale as he stepped over the crime scene tape with a ritualized slowness, as though fearing that a sudden movement might rouse the furies that still haunted this place. As for Maleval, he was still puking his guts out into a plastic bag; he had twice tried to join his team only to immediately back away, literally suffocated by the stench of excrement and rotting flesh.

The apartment was huge. Despite the mess, it was clear that great care had been taken in decorating it. As in most warehouse apartments of its kind, the front door opened directly onto the living room, a vast space with whitewashed concrete walls. The right-hand wall was filled by an enormous print. You had to step back to get a sense of it. It was an image Camille felt he had seen before. Standing in the doorway, he racked his brains, trying to remember.

"The human genome," Louis said.

That was what it was: a reproduction of the human genome reworked by an artist in ink and charcoal.

A large picture window looked out onto a development of semi-detached houses in the distance, screened by trees that had not yet had time to grow. A faux cowhide was tacked to one wall, a long rectangular piece of leather daubed with distinctive black-and-white markings. Beneath it was a black leather sofa of astonishing proportions, probably a bespoke piece of furniture custom made to the precise dimensions of the wall, but it was impossible to know—this was not a home but a different world, one where people hung giant pictures of the human genome on the wall and hacked young women to pieces after first eviscerating them . . . Lying on the floor beside the sofa was an issue of *GQ* magazine. To the right was a well-stocked bar and to the left a coffee table with a cordless phone and an answering machine. Nearby, on a smoked-glass cabinet, was a large flat-screen television.

Armand was kneeling in front of the unit. Camille, who given his height was usually in no position to do so, laid a hand on his shoulder and, gesturing to the VCR, said, "Let's have a look at what's in there."

The cassette was rewound. The video showed a dog—a German shepherd wearing a baseball cap—peeling an orange gripped between its front paws and eating the segments. It looked like something from one of those TV shows of "hilarious" home videos, the filming amateurish, the framing predictable and crude. In the bottom right-hand corner was a logo for "U.S.-GAG" featuring a smiling cartoon camera.

"Let it run," Camille said. "You never know."

He bent over the answering machine. The music on the outgoing message seemed to have been dictated by the zeitgeist. A few years ago, it would have been Pachelbel's *Canon in D*. Camille thought he recognized "Spring" from Vivaldi's *Four Seasons*.

"'Autumn' . . . ," Louis muttered, staring at the floor. Then, suddenly: "Hello!"—A man's voice, probably forty-something, the accent refined, educated, the diction strangulated—"I'm sorry, but I'm in London right now."—He is clearly reading a prepared text; his voice is high-pitched and nasal—"Please leave a message after the beep . . ."—slightly shrill, sophisticated—gay?—". . . and I'll call you as soon as I get back. Speak soon."

"He's using a vocoder," Camille said.

He headed for the bedroom.

The far wall was taken up by a huge mirrored wardrobe. The bed was also covered in blood and feces. The bloody top sheet had been stripped off and rolled into a ball. An empty Corona bottle lay by the foot of the bed. Next to the head of the bed was a large portable CD player and a number of severed fingers laid out like the petals of a flower. Lying beside the player, crushed by the heel of a shoe, was an empty Traveling Wilburys jewel case. Above the bed—one of those low futons with a hard mattress—was a Japanese silk painting whose composition seemed to be enhanced by the arterial blood spray. There were no clothes except for a pair of suspenders strangely knotted together. Camille glanced into the wardrobe, which the forensics boys had left open: there was nothing but a suitcase.

"Anyone check this?" Camille asked the officers working the scene.

"Not yet" came the impassive answer. *I'm clearly just getting in their way*, thought Camille.

He bent down next to the bed, trying to make out the name in red italics on the black matchbook lying on the floor: *Palio's*.

"Ever heard of the place?"

"No, never."

Camille called over to Maleval, but seeing the young man's ashen face in the doorway, he gestured to him to stay outside. It could wait.

The bathroom was completely white except for one wall, which was covered with a Dalmatian print wallpaper. The bath was covered with bloody smears. At least one of the girls had got in or out of it in a pitiful state. The sink looked as though it had been used to wash something . . . maybe the killer's hands.

Maleval was tasked with tracking down the owner of the apartment, and Camille, Louis, and Armand left the forensics team to finish documenting the scene and taking samples. Louis took out a ciga-rillo. When he was with Camille, he refrained from lighting up at the *brigade criminelle*, in the car, in restaurants—anywhere, in fact, except outdoors.

Standing side by side, the three men silently stared out at the housing project. Freshly emerged from the horrors within, they now found the sinister *Stepford Wives* scene comforting, even vaguely human.

"Armand, I need you to go door-to-door," Camille said at length. "Maleval can go with you as soon as he gets back. And try to keep it discreet, okay? We've got enough shit to deal with as it is."

Armand nodded, though his eyes were fixed on Louis's box of cigarillos. He was bumming his first smoke of the day when Bergeret came out to join them.

"This is going to take a while."

Then he turned on his heel and went back inside. Bergeret had started out in the army. He was clipped and brusque.

"Jean!" Camille called after him.

Bergeret turned. He had the handsome, rather obtuse face of someone who stood his ground against the folly of the world.

"Top priority," said Camille. "You've got two days."

"Yeah, right . . ." Bergeret grunted and turned his back on them.

Camille looked at Louis and shrugged.

"Sometimes it works . . ."

6

The apartment on the rue Félix-Faure had been renovated by a company called SOGEFI, which specialized in real estate investments.

Quai de Valmy, 11:30 a.m. A striking building overlooking the canal, with acres of marble floors, acres of glass, and a receptionist with acres of cleavage. A flash of the badge, a flicker of panic, a quick ride in the elevator, then more acres of marble flooring (the colors reversed this time), the vast double door to the cavernous office of a guy with a face like a slapped ass by the name of Cottet— Please, take a seat—cocksure, this was his turf—how can I help you, bearing in mind I can't spare you much time?

As it turned out, Cottet was a house of cards. He was one of those men who can be unnerved by the slightest thing. He was tall but seemed to inhabit a body he had borrowed. His clothes were clearly bought by his wife, who obviously had her own idea of the kind of man he was—and not a particularly flattering one. She imagined him to be an overbearing company director (the pale-gray suit), decisive (the white shirt with thin blue stripes), and always in a hurry (the Italian leather shoes with pointed toes), but she knew he was simply a middle manager who was brash (the garish tie) and actually a little vulgar (gold signet ring and mismatched cufflinks). Seeing Camille step into his office, he flunked his first test: his eyebrows shot up in surprise; then he quickly composed himself and pretended he hadn't noticed his arrival. It was the worst possible reaction, thought Camille, and he had seen them all.

Cottet was the sort who took life very seriously. There were business propositions that he might describe as "low-hanging fruit," those that required "joined-up thinking," and those clusterfucks that were "learning opportunities." From the look on Camille's face it was clear that the present circumstances did not fit into any of these categories.

In such situations, Louis often took the lead. Louis was patient. Louis could sometimes be a little pedantic.

"We need to know how and under what circumstances the apartment was leased. As you can appreciate, it's somewhat urgent."

"Of course. Which apartment are we talking about?"

"17 rue Félix-Faure, in Courbevoie."

Cottet paled.

"Ah . . ."

Then, silence. Cottet stared at his desk blotter aghast, mouth moving like a fish.

"Monsieur Cottet," Louis began again in his coolest and most careful tone, "I think it would be best for you and for your company if you were to explain things calmly and in their entirety . . . Take your time."

"Yes . . . yes, of course."

Then he stared up at them like a drowning man.

"That particular contract was not exactly . . . how can I put this? . . . it did not quite conform to best practice, if you see what I mean."

"Not really, no," Louis said.

"We were contacted last April. The person in question . . ."

"Name?"

Cottet looked at Camille; then he seemed to stare out of the window as though looking for help, for solace.

"Haynal. His name was Haynal—Jean, I think . . ."

"You *think*?"

"Yes, Jean Haynal. He was inquiring about the apartment in Courbevoie. Cards on table . . . ," Cottet said, regaining a little of his cocksureness, ". . . we're in a bit of a holding pattern with that particular development . . . We've invested a lot in that patch of industrial wasteland, and we have four units finished, but so far the results have not exactly been compelling. Oh, we won't be out of pocket, but . . ."

Camille was irritated by his circumlocutions.

"Cards on table: how many units have you sold?"

"None."

Cottet stared at him as though the word "none" were a death sentence. Camille would have bet that this little gamble had put him and his company in a very parlous position.

"Please . . . ," Louis said encouragingly, "go on . . ."

"Regardless, the gentleman in question wasn't interested in buying; he wanted to rent for three months. He said that he represented a film company. I refused, of course. That's one industry sector we won't touch. Too hard to gain traction, tough margins, tight timescales, you see what I'm saying? Besides, we're in the business of selling developments, not playing at real estate agents."

Cottet spat these last words with a contempt that spoke volumes about the seriousness of the problems that had forced him to become a real estate agent.

"I understand," Louis said.

"But we're all subject to the laws of reality," Cottet added, as though this shaft of wit showed that he was sophisticated. "And the gentleman in question . . ."

"Was willing to pay cash?" suggested Louis.

"Cash, yes, and . . ."

"And prepared to pay over the odds?" Camille added.

"Three times the market."

"What was he like, this man?"

"I didn't really notice," said Cottet. "Most of our dealings were by phone."

"What about his voice?"

"Well spoken."

"So . . . ?"

"He asked if he could visit the property. He wanted to take photos. We arranged a viewing. I met him on-site. That was the point at which I should have been suspicious . . ."

"Of what?" asked Louis.

"The photographer . . . He didn't seem—how can I put it—very professional. He showed up with some sort of Polaroid. He lined up the photos he took neatly on the floor like he was terrified of getting them mixed up. He checked a piece of paper before every shot, as though he were following instructions he didn't understand. Even at the time I thought, that guy's no more a photographer than I am . . ."

"A real estate agent?" ventured Camille.

"If you like," Cottet shot him a black look.

"Can you describe him for us?" Louis tried to distract him.

"Vaguely. I didn't stay on-site long. There was nothing for me to do, and I wasn't about to waste two hours in an empty unit watching some guy take photos . . . I opened up, watched him work for a bit, then left. He left the key in the mailbox on his way out; it was a spare so we didn't need it immediately."

"What was he like?"

"Average . . ."

"By which you mean?" Louis persisted.

"Average." Cottet was becoming heated. "What do you want me to say? Average height, average age—he was average!"

There followed a silence during which the three men seemed to ponder the nondescript nature of the modern world.

"But the fact that this photographer was so unprofessional seemed to you to be another guarantee, didn't it?" said Camille.

"Yes, I admit that's true," said Cottet. "Everything was paid in cash, there was no contract, and I assumed that the film . . . I mean, that with that kind of movie we weren't likely to have any problems with the tenant."

Camille was the first to get to his feet. Cottet walked them back to the elevator.

"You'll have to make a formal statement, obviously," Louis explained, as though talking to a child. "And you may be subpoenaed to appear in court, so . . ."

"So don't touch anything," Camille interrupted. "Don't fiddle your books; don't go near anything. As far as the tax man is concerned, you're on your own. We have two girls hacked to pieces, so right now—even as far as you're concerned—that's all that matters."

Cottet stared at them, his eyes vacant, as though trying to gauge the consequences—no doubt he suspected they would be catastrophic—and suddenly his gaudy tie looked as out of place as a cravat on a death-row prisoner.

"Do you have photographs, blueprints?" asked Camille.

"We put together a top-of-the-range presentation brochure . . ." Cottet began pulling his most dazzling huckster's smile before realizing how inappropriate his smugness sounded and immediately filing it away for later use.

"Have everything sent over to me right away," Camille said, proffering a business card.

Cottet took it gingerly, as though it might burn his fingers.

As they headed back down, Louis commented on the receptionist's "attributes." Camille said that he hadn't noticed.

7

Even with two teams working, *l'identité judiciaire* had to spend every waking hour on-site. The inexorable ballet of squad cars, motorcycles, and vans meant that by late morning a crowd of rubberneckers had gathered. It made you wonder what could have prompted people to come all the way out here. It was like an influx of the living dead from some B movie. The media showed up half an hour later. Not to photograph the crime scene, obviously, nor was there to be a press statement, but within hours leaks had sprung, and by 2 p.m. it seemed better to make a statement than to leave the media to their own devices. Camille phoned Le Guen from his cell and explained his concerns.

"There's been a lot of talk around here, too," Le Guen said.

Camille stepped out of the Courbevoie apartment with only one goal: to say as little as possible.

There were fewer people than he had expected: twenty or so gawkers, fewer than a dozen reporters and—at first glance—no big names, just freelancers and ambulance chasers; it was an unexpected opportunity to defuse the situation and gain a couple of precious days.

There were two good reasons why Camille was both famous and infamous. His expertise had earned him a solid reputation that his height had transformed into notoriety. Though it was difficult for cameramen to frame him, the journalists rushed forward with questions for this diminutive man with his peremptory manner. They found him to be curt but candid.

On certain occasions—cold comfort, given the many drawbacks—Camille's physical appearance had its advantages. Once seen, he was never forgotten. He had already refused to appear on various television programs, knowing he had been invited in the hope that he would deliver the stirring monologue of a man "who has brilliantly triumphed over his physical shortcomings." Clearly, presenters were drooling at the prospect of lead-in footage showing Camille in his mobility vehicle—a car with all the controls on the steering wheel but a police siren on the roof. Camille would have no truck with such publicity—and not just because he hated driving. His superiors were grateful to him for this. Only once had he weakened. A stormy day. An angry day. A day when he would probably have to take the *métro* while people either gawked at him or averted their eyes. He had been invited to participate in a current affairs show on France 3. After the inevitable hand-wringing homily explaining that this was a general-interest report he had a duty to represent, the program researcher had obliquely hinted that Camille stood to gain from it on a personal level, presumably imagining the whole world was desperate for fifteen minutes of fame. This was the day when he had slipped in the bathtub and fallen flat on his face. A miserable day for midgets. He agreed, and his superiors did their best to pretend they were happy for him to appear on the show.

When he arrived at the studios, already depressed at having given in to temptation, he had to take the elevator. A woman juggling an armful of files and tapes got in with him and asked which floor he wanted. With a stoical look, Camille gestured to the button for the fifteenth floor, which was a little beyond his reach. The woman gave him a shy smile, but, reaching for the button, she dropped everything she was carrying. When the lift arrived at its destination, the two of them were still on all fours gathering up papers and stuffing them into files. She thanked him.

"I have the same problem hanging wallpaper," Camille reassured her. "Everything goes wrong."

The woman laughed. She had a lovely laugh.

He had married Irène six months later.

8

The reporters were in a hurry.

"Two victims," Camille began.

"Who are they?"

"We don't know yet. Two women. Young . . ."

"How old?"

"About twenty-five. That's all we can say for now."

"When are they taking the bodies?" a photographer asked.

"In a while. We're running a bit late. Technical problems . . ."

A pause in the questions, the ideal moment to rush in:

"I can't say much right now, but to be honest, the case is nothing out of the ordinary. We've don't have much to go on, that's all. We'll be making a statement tomorrow night. Until then, it's probably best to let the boys from forensics do their work . . ."

"So what do we run with?" said a young blond guy who looked well on his way to liver failure.

"You say: two women who have not yet been identified. You say: murdered in the past forty-eight hours by person or persons unknown, motive and cause of death yet to be determined."

"It's a bit thin!"

"That's what I was trying to tell you."

It would have been hard to say less. There was a moment of confusion in the ranks.

And at that precise moment, what Camille had fervently hoped would not happen, happened. The forensics van, having reversed, found it could not get close enough to the entrance of the building because for some mysterious reason there was a concrete planter in the way. The van driver got out and flung open the rear doors and two forensics officers jumped out. The reporters, who up to that point had been distracted, were suddenly riveted as the door to the warehouse apartment opened to reveal the living room wall completely covered with blood spatter like a Jackson Pollock canvas. As if the reporters needed any further confirmation, the officers meticulously began loading the van with clear sealed bags, tagged and ready to be sent to the morgue.

Reporters are a little like those undertakers who can size up a corpse for a coffin with a single glance. Seeing the bags being piled into the van, they could tell the bodies had been dismembered.

"Shit!" the hacks said in chorus.

Before the officers had time to extend the cordon, the photographers were clicking away furiously. The pack divided into two like a cancerous cell, one half photographing the forensics van and shouting "Over here!" so the grisly removal men would stop and turn to look, the other half grabbing their cell phones and calling for backup.

"Shit!" echoed Camille.

A complete mess. Then he, too, took out his cell and made the calls that would put him in the eye of the hurricane.

9

The boys from *l'identité judiciaire* had done a good job. Two windows had been cracked open to create a through breeze, and the stench of morning had dissipated to the extent that handkerchiefs and surgical masks were no longer necessary.

At this point, crime scenes can be more disturbing than they were before the bodies were removed. It feels as though death has struck a second time, whisking them away.

This particular crime scene was even worse. Only the lab assistants were still there, armed with cameras, rangefinders, tweezers, vials, evidence bags, and luminol, and it now looked as though there had been no bodies, as though death had denied the victims the final dignity of a corpse that had once been living. The forensics teams had taken away the severed fingers, the heads, the entrails. All that remained were traces of blood and shit, and stripped of its stark horror, the apartment now appeared very different. Even to Camille, it looked utterly bizarre. Louis warily eyed his boss, who had a peculiar expression—brow furrowed, eyebrows knitted—as though trying to solve a crossword puzzle.

Louis stepped into the room and headed straight for the TV unit and telephone. Camille went into the bedroom. They explored the space like visitors in an art gallery, eager to discover some detail they had previously overlooked. A little later, still brooding, they ran into each other in the bathroom. Louis headed off to make his own inspection of the bedroom, and Camille stared out of the window while the forensics technicians unplugged the spotlights and rolled up the cables and plastic sheeting, snapped shut cases and toolboxes. As he wandered through the apartment, his mind made keener by Camille's troubled expression, Louis's neurons were firing on all cylinders. And, gradually, he, too, took on a more preoccupied air, as though he were doing mental arithmetic to eight decimal places.

He found Camille in the living room. On the floor was the suitcase from the wardrobe (top-of-the-range, cream leather with protective metal corners like those on flight cases), which the forensics officers had not yet taken away. It contained a suit, a shoehorn, an electric razor, a wallet, a sports watch, and a portable photocopier.

One of the technicians now reappeared and said: "It's not your day, Camille . . . there's a TV crew pulling up outside." He glanced around the room at the blood on the walls and ceiling. "And this is going to be all over the nine o'clock news from now until doomsday."

10

"This was premeditated; it took a lot of careful planning," said Louis.

"I think it's more complicated than that. In fact, there's something about the whole thing that doesn't add up."

"It doesn't add up?"

"No," said Camille. "Almost everything here is brand new—the bed, the carpets, everything. It's hard to imagine someone shelling out all that money just to shoot a porn movie. You'd rent a furnished apartment. Actually, usually they don't rent at all; they find a place they can use for free."

"A snuff movie?"

"The thought had crossed my mind," said Camille. "It's possible..."

But they both knew that the vogue for such films had long passed. Besides, the expensive, carefully arranged décor did not quite fit with that kind of hypothesis.

Camille went on pacing the room.

"The fingerprint on the wall over there was too perfect to have been accidental."

"Nobody would have been able to see anything from outside," Louis followed his train of thought. "The door was closed, the windows covered. No one stumbled upon the crime. Logically, the killer was sending a message to us. He not only premeditated the murders, he claimed them. But I find it difficult to imagine one man creating all this carnage . . ."

"We'll see," said Camille. "But what I find most fascinating is the fact that there's a message on the answering machine."

Louis stared at him for a moment, surprised to find that he had lost the thread.

"Why?"

"What bothers me is that you've got all the equipment—the phone, the answering machine—except for the most important thing: there's no phone line . . ."

"What?" Louis rushed over, tugged on the phone and pulled the low table away from the wall. There was only an electrical socket; the phone was not connected.

"The premeditation is obvious. No one's even tried to hide the fact. It's like everything is right there in plain sight . . . That's a bit much."

Hands in his pockets, Camille walked around the room some more and stopped in front of the human genome.

"Yeah," he said finally. "That really is too much."

11

Louis was the first to arrive, followed by Armand. Once they were joined by Maleval, who had been taking a call on his cell, Camille's team, which some officers referred to deferentially or derisively as the "Verhœven Brigade," were all present and correct. Camille quickly read through his notes, then looked up at his colleagues.

"Any thoughts?

The three men looked at each other.

"The first thing we need to know is how many perpetrators there are," ventured Armand. "The more there are, the better the chance we can track them down."

"One guy can't have pulled off a thing like this on his own," Maleval said. "It's not possible."

"We won't know for sure until we've had the results back from forensics and the autopsy. Louis, bring us up to speed on the rental."

Louis gave a brief account of their visit to SOGEFI. Camille took the time to study Armand and Maleval's reactions.

The two men were polar opposites: one profligate, the other miserly. At twenty-six, Jean-Claude Maleval had a charm that he abused as he abused everything—late nights, pretty girls, his own body. He was the sort of man who is incapable of thrift. The seasons might change, but still his face was drawn and tired. When he thought about Maleval, Camille found himself a little worried and wondered how expensive his colleague's vices were. Maleval had the makings of a bent cop in the way that some children, even in nursery school, are clearly destined to be morons. In fact, it was difficult to tell whether he was squandering his years as a single man like a spendthrift might squander his inheritance, or whether he was already on the slippery slope to addiction. Twice in the past few months, Camille had come upon Maleval talking to Louis. On each occasion, they had seemed embarrassed, as though caught doing something they shouldn't, and Camille was convinced that Maleval was hitting up Louis for cash. But perhaps not regularly. He decided not to get involved and pretended he had seen nothing.

Maleval chain-smoked American cigarettes, liked to make a small bet on the ponies and had a particular predilection for Bowmore single malt. But of his various proclivities, Maleval prized women above all. Maleval was unarguably handsome. Tall, dark haired, with a face that radiated low cunning and a body that even now could win him back the place he once held on the French Olympic judo team.

Camille studied his flip side of the coin for a moment: Armand, poor Armand. Of the twenty years he had been an *inspecteur* at the *brigade criminelle*, he had spent nineteen and a half with the reputation of being the most shameful skinflint the police had ever known. He was ageless, a lanky streak of piss, gaunt, lean, and fretful. Armand was defined by what he lacked. He was indigence incarnate. His stinginess did not have the charm of being a character flaw. It was pathological, profoundly pathological, and was something that Camille had never found amusing. Truth be told, Camille did not give a tinker's curse about Armand's meanness, but having worked with the man for so many years, it pained him to see the depths to which "poor Armand" would sink to avoid spending a red cent, the convoluted subterfuges to which he resorted to avoid paying for a measly cup of coffee. Perhaps it was a legacy of his own handicap, but Camille sometimes experienced these humiliations as though they were his own. What was truly piteous was that Armand was aware of his condition. It troubled him, and as a result he became a sad, lonely man. Armand worked in silence. Armand worked hard. In his way, he may well have been the junior officer in the *brigade*. His tight-fistedness had made him a meticulous, painstaking, scrupulous officer capable of spending days combing through a telephone directory or endless hours on a stakeout in an unmarked car with a faulty heater, capable of interviewing every resident of a street, every member of a profession if it meant—literally—finding a needle in a haystack. Give him a million-piece jigsaw and Armand would take it into his office and spend every waking hour putting it together. The nature of the research was unimportant. He did not care about the subject. His need to accumulate information made any personal preference redundant. More than once it had proved miraculous, and though everyone agreed that on a day-to-day basis Armand was insufferable, those same officers were quick to agree that this diligent, single-minded officer had something most others lacked, some quality of infinite patience that admirably proved that, taken to its logical conclusion, a mindless chore can border on genius. Having worn out every possible joke about his meanness, his fellow officers had eventually stopped ridiculing him. No one found it funny anymore. Everyone was appalled.

"Okay," said Camille, when Louis had finished his report. "Until we get the preliminary reports, let's take things as they come. Armand, Maleval, I want you to go over the physical evidence, everything that was found at the scene. I want to know where everything came from: the furniture, the knickknacks, the clothes, the bed linen . . . Louis, you look into the video, the American TV show, anything that seems a little bizarre—but don't get too sidetracked. If anything comes up, you're in charge of briefing everyone. Any questions?"

There were no questions. Or there were too many; it amounted to the same thing.

12

An anonymous caller had reported the crime to the local police in Courbevoie. Camille decided to drive over and listen to the recording.

"There's been a murder. Rue Félix-Faure. Number 17."

The voice was obviously the same as the one on the answering machine, the same distortion probably made using the same gadget.

Camille spent the next two hours working on forms, affidavits, questionnaires, filling in the blanks with the unknown factors and wondering what the hell it was all about.

When forced to deal with tedious administrative procedures, he often suffered from what he thought of as a mental squint. With his right eye, he dealt with forms in triplicate, yielding to the demands of statisticians and writing out reports in the official style, and all the while the retina of his left eye still lingered on dead bodies sprawled on the floor, on wounds black with dry blood, on faces distorted by grief and by the desperate struggle to stay alive, by that last baffled look when confronted with the surprising finality of death.

And sometimes all these images were superimposed. Camille found himself imagining the severed fingers of the woman laid out like a wreath in the center of the logo of the *police judiciaire* . . . He set his glasses on the desk and gently massaged his temples.

13

A soldier to his very bones, Bergeret, the head of *l'identité judiciaire*, was not a man to hurry things nor to defer to anyone's demands. But Le Guen had clearly used his influence (the idea of a clash between these titans, two immovable objects grappling pathetically, was like a sumo wrestling bout filmed in slow motion). Whatever he had done, by midafternoon, Camille had the preliminary forensic report.

Two young women, age between twenty and thirty, both blonde. The first woman was five foot five, weighed 110 pounds, with a strawberry mark on her left inside knee, healthy teeth, and a generous bust, The second woman was about the same height and weight but had no distinguishing marks; she too had good teeth and a generous bust. Both victims had eaten three to five hours before death: crudités, carpaccio of beef, red wine. For dessert one of the victims had had strawberries, the other a lemon sorbet. A bottle of Moët & Chandon brut and two champagne flutes found under the bed bore their fingerprints. The writing on the wall had been done using the severed fingers. To establish the modus operandi—an expression beloved of all those who never studied Latin—would obviously take considerably more time. In what order had the women been butchered, how had it been done, and with what? Had it required more than one man (or woman)? Had they been sexually assaulted and if so how (or with what)? There were so many unknowns in this grisly equation that Camille was determined to solve.

The most curious detail was that the clear print of an index finger found on the wall was not real, but had been made using a rubber stamp.

Camille had never been a Luddite when it came to computers, but there were days when he could not help but think that these contraptions were evil at heart. No sooner had he received the preliminary forensic reports than the central booking computer offered him a choice between good and bad news. The good news was that the fingerprints of one of the victims were in the system: one Éve-lyne Rouvray, twenty-three, living in Bobigny, known to the police for soliciting. The bad news was that this reinforced the idea they were dealing with a pervert and brought back all of the gruesome imagery Camille had been trying, ineffectually, to dismiss from his mind. The fake fingerprint on the wall was also in the system: it related to a cold case from November 21, 2001. Camille had the file sent up right away.

14

The case file that now landed on his desk was also evil to its core. On this point, everyone was agreed. Only an officer with a death wish would have wanted to take over a case that, in its time, had been the subject of so much media attention. Back then, reporters had speculated wildly about the fake fingerprints in black ink found on the toes of the victim. For several weeks, the papers had trotted out the same details, under new headlines: there was talk of the "Tremblay Butcher," of the "Tragedy on the Landfill," first prize going—as so often—to Le Matin, which had covered the story under the headline DEATH REAPS A MAIDEN.

Camille knew as much about the Tremblay case as anyone—no more, no less—but as he considered the horrific details of the crime, he suddenly felt the eye of the hurricane grow smaller. Reopening the Tremblay case would shed a very different light on things. If this killer had been hacking women to pieces all over the suburbs of Paris, new cases would keep turning up until eventually they arrested him. What sort of guy were they dealing with? Camille picked up the phone, called Le Guen, and told him the news.

"Shit," said Le Guen simply.

"That's one way of putting it, yes."

"The media are going to love this."

"I suspect they're head over heels already."

"What do you mean, 'already'?"

"What do you expect?" said Camille. "The *brigade criminelle* is like a sieve. We had reporters showing up in Courbevoie less than an hour after we got there . . ."

"And . . . ?" Le Guen sounded worried.

"And there was a TV crew . . . ," Camille reluctantly admitted.

Le Guen fell silent for a few seconds, which Camille turned to his advantage.

"I want a psychological profile drawn up on these guys," he said.

"What do you mean, 'these guys'? You mean there's evidence of more than one killer?"

"This guy, these guys . . . what the fuck do I know?"

"Okay The case has been referred to Deschamps as *juge d'instruction*. I'll call her and have her appoint an expert."

Camille had never worked with this investigating magistrate, but from their one or two chance encounters remembered her as a woman of about fifty, slim, elegant and astonishingly ugly. The sort of woman who defies description, with a taste for garish gold jewelry.

"The autopsy is scheduled for tomorrow. If we can get an expert on it quickly, I'll have whoever it is sent over for the preliminary conclusions."

Camille postponed his reading of the Tremblay file. He would take it home. Right now, it was best to focus on the case in hand.

15

Évelyne Rouvray's police record.

Born March 16, 1980, in Bobigny. Mother: Françoise Rouvray. Father: unknown. Left school at fourteen. No known employment. First arrested in 1996 for prostitution, caught in flagrante in a car at the Porte de la Chapelle. At the time, the girl was still a minor; more than anything, it was just a lot of paperwork, and besides, she was bound to show up on the police radar again. Which indeed she did. Three months later—here we go again— little Miss Rouvray is arrested for soliciting on the boulevard des Maréchaux. Once again she is in a car, and again she is in fla- grante. This time the case goes to court, the judge realizes they are destined to meet again, and as a welcome gift the judicial system gives the minor (soon to be major) delinquent an eight-day sus- pended sentence. Curiously, after this point, there is no record of her. This is rare. Usually, the list of arrests for petty offenses gets longer over the years—over the months if the girl is particularly industrious; maybe she has a drug habit, maybe she has AIDS; one way or the other, if she needs the money she'll be turning tricks around the clock. But there's nothing of this in her file. Évelyne gets an eight-day suspended sentence and drops off the map. At least until she is found hacked to death in the warehouse apartment in Courbevoie.

16

Last known address: *cité* Marcel Cachin in Bobigny. A 1970s low-end housing project with smashed-in doors and ransacked mailboxes, adorned from floor to ceiling with graffiti tags. On the third floor, a door with a spyhole. At the words "Police, open up!", the haggard face of Évelyne's mother appears. It is impossible to guess her age.

"Madame Rouvray?"

"We'd like to talk to you about your daughter Évelyne."

"She doesn't live here anymore."

"Where did . . . where does she live?"

"I've no idea. I'm not the police."

"Well, we are the police, so it's in your best interests to help us out here . . . Évelyne's got herself into trouble, serious trouble . . ."

Curious now.

"What sort of trouble?"

"We need an address for her."

She hesitates. Camille and Louis are still standing on the doorstep. They're cautious. They're old hands at this.

"This is important."

"She's at José's place. Rue Fremontel."

The door is about to close.

"José who?"

"I don't know. Just José."

This time, Camille jams his foot in the door. Madame Rouvray isn't interested in her daughter's problems. She's got other fish to fry.

"Évelyne is dead, Madame Rouvray."

In an instant, she is transformed. Her mouth widens into an O, her eyes well with tears; there is no scream, no sigh, just these silent tears, and suddenly, inexplicably, to Camille she seems beautiful. There is something about her face, something he saw in young Alice that morning, though Madame Rouvray's face is not bruised, only her heart. He looks at Louis, then back to her. She is still gripping the door, staring down at the floor. No words, no questions, only silence and tears.

"We'll need you to come down to identify the body . . ."

She is no longer listening. She looks up again and wordlessly lets them know she understands. The door closes quietly. Camille and Louis, relieved that she did not invite them to come inside, turn to leave.

17

José, according to the central computer, is José Riveiro, age twenty-four. A precocious career criminal with a record for car theft and violence, he has been arrested three times. Having spent several months inside for his part in the holdup of a jeweler's in Pantin, he was released six months ago, and there has been no news of him since. With a bit of luck, he won't be home, and if their luck really holds, he'll be on the run: he'll be their man. Neither Louis nor Camille believes this for an instant. From his police record, José Riveiro is not some crazed killer with a taste for the high life. In any case, he answers the door wearing jeans and slippers; he is not particularly tall; his sullen, handsome face wears a worried expression.

"Hello, José. I don't believe we've met."

From the moment they set eyes on each other, it is war between José and Camille. José is a real man. He stares down at this little runt as though he were a piece of dog shit on the pavement.

This time, Camille and Louis immediately step inside. José asks no questions; he lets them pass, his mind probably working overtime trying to think why the police would show up at his place unannounced. This is all he needs. The living room is tiny, with a small sofa and a television. There are a couple of empty beer bottles on the coffee table, a hideous painting hanging on the wall, the stink of sweaty socks: obviously a bachelor pad. Camille steps into the bedroom. It's a pigpen, men's and women's clothes strewn everywhere, the décor is creepy, the duvet cover is fluorescent plush.

José is leaning against the doorframe, tense, looking for a fight, determined not to say anything, to put one over on the feds this time.

"You live on your own, José?"

"What's it got to do with you?"

"We ask the questions, José. So, do you live alone?"

"No. I live with Évelyne, but she's not here right now."

"And what does Évelyne do for a living?"

"She's looking for a job."

"Ah . . . But she can't find one, am I right?"

"She hasn't yet."

Louis says nothing—he waits to see what approach Camille will take. But Camille suddenly feels immensely weary, because this whole thing is predictable, banal; in his profession even dealing with shitheads becomes a formality. He opts for the fastest route; he wants this over with.

"When did you last see her?"

"She left on Saturday."

"And is it normal for her not to come home?"

"Well, no, actually," says José.

And at that moment José realizes they know something he doesn't, that the worst is yet to come and that it will come soon. He glances straight ahead at Louis, and then looks down at Camille. Suddenly Camille is no longer a midget; his is the terrible face of death itself.

"You know where she is, don't you . . ."

"She's been murdered, José. We found her body this morning in an apartment in Courbevoie."

Only now do they realize that young José is genuinely devastated, that while she was alive, Évelyne lived here with him, that he loved her even if she was a prostitute, that she slept here in this room with him. Camille sees the young man's face crumple, etched with the bewilderment and the grief of true tragedy.

"Who did it?" José asks.

"We don't know yet. That's why we're here, José. We need to know what she was doing there."

José shakes his head. He has no idea. An hour later, Camille knows everything there is to know about José and Évelyne and the little working arrangement that led this rather shrewd girl to get herself chopped to pieces by a psychotic stranger.

18

Évelyne Rouvray was *quick on the uptake*. Having been arrested once, she quickly realizes she is on a slippery slope and she has only to look at her mother to know that life is about to go downhill, and fast. As for drugs, though she is a user, she is careful to remain a high-functioning addict. She turns tricks at the Porte de la Chapelle and is savvy enough that when clients offer to pay double to do it without a condom, she tells them to fuck off. A few weeks after her arrest, José breezes into her life. They move into the apartment on the rue Fremontel together and get themselves online. Évelyne spends a couple of hours a day at the computer looking for clients; she only does outcalls, and José always drives her to the meeting place and waits. He plays pinball in the nearest café. José is not really a pimp. He knows that in their little business venture, Évelyne is the boss; she is organized and very careful. Until now. A lot of clients ask to meet up in hotels. This is what happened last week. She met the john at a Mercure hotel. When she came back, she didn't say much about the client other than that he was a friendly guy, not pervy, and stinking rich. In fact, he had suggested they meet up again a couple of days later. A threesome this time; he left it to Évelyne to find the second girl. His only stipulation was that she be about the same height and the same age. And he's got a thing for big tits. So Évelyne phoned Josiane Debeuf, a girl she met down at the Porte de la Chapelle; it's an all-night job, the guy will be alone and he is offering a sizable wad of cash—the equivalent of two days' work. He gave her an address in Courbevoie. José drove the two of them there. As they came into the deserted housing development they felt anxious. To make sure everything was aboveboard, they agreed José would wait in the car until one of them waved to let him know it was all right. He was sitting in the car about twenty yards away when the client opened the door. With the light streaming from inside, he only saw him in silhouette. The man shook hands with the two girls. José waited for twenty minutes until Évelyne came to the window and waved. José was quite happy to leave them to it; he was planning to watch the Paris Saint-Germain match on Canal Plus.

As they left José Riveiro's apartment, Camille asked Louis to put together a file on the second victim, Josiane Debeuf, age twenty-one. It should be easy to find information on her. The working girls on the Périphérique were usually known to the police.

19

Finding Irène hale and healthy, lying on the sofa watching television, her hands resting on her belly, a broad smile on her lips, Camille realized that since morning his mind had been swirling with images of dismembered women.

"Are you okay?" she asked, seeing him appear with a heavy file under his arm.

"Yes . . . I'm fine."

To change the subject, he laid a hand on her stomach and asked, "So, is the baby kicking up a storm in there?"

Hardly had he said the words than the nine o'clock news came on, with footage of the *identité judiciaire* van slowly pulling away from the rue Félix-Faure in Courbevoie.

By the time they showed up, there was precious little for the TV crews to film, so there were shots of the entrance to the apartment from every conceivable angle, closed doors, the last forensics officers leaving the scene, a close-up of the shuttered windows. The accompanying voiceover adopted the solemn tones reserved for national disasters. This alone told Camille that the media had no intention of letting the story drop without good reason. For a split second, he expected a government minister to be formally charged.

There was lengthy footage of the plastic bags. It was not every day that one saw so many of them. The reporter stressed how little was known about the "terrible tragedy at Courbevoie."

Irène said nothing. She looked at her husband, who had just appeared on-screen. Emerging from the apartment at the end of the day, Camille had simply repeated what he had said some hours earlier. But this time he was on film. Surrounded by a circle of boom microphones, he had been shot from above as though to highlight the strangeness of the situation. Thankfully, the story had been late in reaching the news desks.

"They clearly didn't have much time to edit the piece," Irène said in a professional tone.

The images confirmed her evaluation. The footage of Camille was fragmentary; they had kept only the best parts.

"Two young women whose identities have not yet been confirmed have been found dead. We are dealing with a . . . particularly savage crime." ("What was I thinking, saying something so stupid!" Camille wondered.) "Juge Deschamps has been appointed investigating magistrate in the case. That's all I have to say for the moment. I'd be grateful if you could allow us to get on with our work . . ."

"Poor baby," Irène said when the news story was over.

After dinner, Camille pretended to take an interest in what was on television; then he leafed through a couple of magazines before taking some papers from his desk and, pen in hand, glanced through them until finally Irène said, "You'd be better off getting some work done. It might relax you . . ." She smiled. "Will you be late?"

"Not at all—I'll just quickly look over this file and then I'll come to bed."

20

It was 11 p.m. when Camille laid file number 01/12587 on his desk. It was a thick sheaf of paper. He removed his glasses and slowly rubbed his eyelids. It was a gesture he had always enjoyed. Having been blessed as a child with excellent eyesight, he had sometimes been impatient for the day when he, too, would do it. In fact, there were two distinct versions of the gesture. In the first, the glasses were removed with a sweeping gesture of the right hand, the head turning slightly to the right as though to add a finishing touch. The second, a more refined version of the first, was accompanied by an enigmatic smile, and when perfectly executed, the glasses were removed, with understated awkwardness, by the left hand so that the right could be held out to the visitor for whom the gesture had been made, like an artistic performance intended as a greeting. In this second version, the left hand removed the glasses and set them down within reach, then massaged the bridge of the nose between thumb and middle finger with the index pressed lightly against the forehead. In this version the eyes remained closed. The gesture was intended to be interpreted as a moment of relief after a long period of intense concentration (a brief sigh could be added if desired). It was the sign of an intellectual gradually—very gradually—growing old.

Long experience of reports, court records, and witness statements had taught Camille to quickly navigate unwieldy case files.

This case had begun with an anonymous call. Camille flicked to the relevant statement: "There's been a murder. Tremblay-en-France. The landfill on the rue Garnier." The killer clearly had his little tics. It's amazing how quickly people develop a routine.

The repetition was clearly as significant as the words themselves. The formulation was simple, calculated, purely informative, making it clear there was no confusion, no panic, no effect whatsoever. And the fact that this formulation had been repeated was not inadvertent. In fact, it spoke volumes about the self-control—whether real or imagined—of the murderer acting as emissary for his own crimes.

The victim in the Tremblay case had soon been identified as Manuela Constanza, a twenty-four-year-old prostitute of Spanish origin who turned tricks in a seedy hotel on the corner of the rue Blondl. Her pimp, Henri Lambert, known as Lard-Ass Lambert—fifty-one years old, with seventeen arrests and four convictions, two of them for living off immoral earnings—had immediately been taken into custody. Lard-Ass Lambert did some rapid calculations and decided to confess to being involved in the robbery of a shopping center in Toulouse on November 21, 2001, which cost him eight months without parole but gave him a solid alibi for the time of the murder. Camille went on leafing through the file.

A series of extraordinarily detailed black-and-white photographs, then suddenly: a young woman, her body cut in half at the waist.

First photograph: the naked lower half of the mutilated body. The legs splayed. A large hunk of flesh has been ripped from the left thigh and a long gash, the blood already black, extends from the waist to the genitals. From their position, it is clear that both legs have been broken above the knee. A close-up of one toe shows a fingerprint in black ink made using a rubber stamp. The killer's signature. Exactly the same as the one at the apartment in Courbevoie.

Second photograph: the upper half of the body. The breasts are covered with cigarette burns. The right breast has been sliced, attached to the body only by a few shreds of skin. The tip of the left breast has been slashed. The wounds on both breasts cut to the bone. It is clear that the young woman was trussed up. The deep marks and burns caused by thick ropes are still visible.

Third photograph: a close up of the head. It is hideous. The face is little more than a gaping wound, the nose is deeply embedded in the skull, the mouth has been slashed from ear to ear with a razor. The face seems to stare out, grinning hideously. The teeth are broken. All that remains is this perverse mockery of a smile. Camille can hardly bear to look. The girl had dark hair of the kind writers like to describe as raven black.

Camille is gasping for breath. He feels a wave of nausea. He looks up, studies the room around him, then bends once more to study the photo. He feels a certain closeness to this young woman who has been hacked in two. He remembers a phrase used by one of the reporters: "This grinning rictus was the ultimate atrocity." The razor cuts begin precisely at the corners of the mouth and extend in a curve to just beneath the earlobes.

Camille puts down the photos, opens the window, and for a long moment he stares out at the rooftops and the street below. The Tremblay murder was committed seventeen months ago, but there is nothing to suggest that it was the first. Or that it will be the last. The question now was, how many more victims might come to light? Camille was caught between relief and anxiety.

From a technical point of view, there was something reassuring about the way in which the victims had been killed. It neatly corresponded to the classic profile of a psychopath, which was a bonus for the investigation. What was most worrying about the Courbevoie murders was the crime scene itself. Though the killings had clearly been premeditated, there were too many incongruous details: expensive objects left behind, the curious staging of the crime scene, a rather American exoticism, the telephone with no line out . . . Camille began to delve through the various reports in the file.

An hour later, his worry had found reason to grow and blossom. The murder in Tremblay-en-France had also been characterized by a number of unknowns, and he mentally began to make a list. There was no shortage of strange details. It was immediately apparent that the hair of the victim, Manuela Constanza, was extraordinarily clean. Forensics indicated that it had been washed using a commonly available apple-scented shampoo about two hours before the body was discovered and consequently *post mortem*, since the girl had been dead for at least eight hours. But it was difficult to imagine a murderer mutilating a young girl, hacking her body in two, and then taking the trouble to wash her hair. Several of her internal organs were missing. There was no trace of the intestines, liver, stomach, or gallbladder. Camille felt that this rather fetishistic aspect of collecting trophies did not quite square with the initial profile of the psychopath. He would have to wait until tomorrow and the autopsy results on the Courbevoie murders to know whether on this occasion there were organs missing, too.

The presence of the fake fingerprint in both cases meant there could be little doubt that they were dealing with the same man.

There was one discrepancy: there were no signs that the Tremblay victim had been sexually assaulted. The autopsy found evidence consistent with consensual sexual activity in the week preceding death, though from the sperm samples it was impossible to determine whether she had been intimate with her killer.

The Tremblay victim had been hit using a whip, something that in principle might connect the two crimes, but the autopsy report described the blows as "slight," of the sort indulged in by couples into S&M.

A common link: the girl in Tremblay had been killed in a manner that several of the reports described as "brutal" (both legs had been broken with a blunt weapon like a baseball bat, she had been tortured for something like forty-eight hours before death, and the corpse had been dismembered using a butcher's knife); but the care with which the killer had drained the body of blood, washed it thoroughly, and returned it to society as clean as a new pin was inconsistent with the gruesome glee with which the killer in Courbevoie had spattered walls and ceilings, taking obvious delight in seeing blood flow.

Camille picked up the photographs again. It was impossible to become inured to this ghastly smile, which somehow called to mind the severed head nailed to the wall. Camille was overcome by a wave of tiredness. He closed the file, turned out the light, and went to join Irène.

At about 2:30 a.m., he was still wide awake. Pensively he stroked Irène's belly with his small, chubby hand. Irène's belly was a miracle. He watched her sleep, this woman whose scent filled him just as she seemed to fill this room, to fill his whole life. Sometimes love really was that simple.

Sometimes, as tonight, he would gaze at her, seized by the terrible feeling of this miracle. Camille found Irène incredibly beautiful. But was she really beautiful? It was a question he had asked himself twice. The first time when they had had dinner together three years earlier. Irène had been wearing a midnight-blue dress buttoned from throat to hem, the sort of dress that men cannot help but imagine unbuttoning, which is precisely why women wear them. Pinned to the breast was a simple gold brooch.

At the time he remembered something he had read long ago, something about "the ridiculous penchant of men for demure blondes." Irène had a sensual beauty that gave the lie to such a thought. Was Irène beautiful? Yes.

The second time he had asked himself this question was seven months ago: Irène had been wearing the same dress, only the jewelry was different; she now wore the brooch Camille had given her on their wedding day. She was wearing makeup.

"Are you going out?" Camille had asked when he got home.

In fact, it was not so much a question as a probing statement, something particular to him that dated from the time he had believed his relationship with Irène was one of those interludes that life has the good grace to offer a man once in a while, and the good sense to take away again.

"No," Irène had said, "I'm not going out."

Her work at the editing studio left little time to make dinner. As for Camille, his working day was dictated by the sorrows of the world; he arrived home late and left early.

"You are extremely beautiful, Madame Verhœven," Camille said, placing a hand on her breast.

"A little aperitif first," said Irène, slipping from his embrace.

"Of course. So what are we celebrating?" asked Camille.

"I have news."

"What sort of news?"

"Just news."

Irène sat next to him and took his hand.

"Looks as though it's good news."

"I hope so."

"You're not sure?"

"I'm not completely sure. I'd rather the news had come on a day when you didn't seem so preoccupied."

"No, no, I'm just tired," Camille protested, stroking her hand by way of apology. "I just need a good night's sleep."

"The good news is that I'm not tired, but I'd happily go to bed early, too."

Camille smiled. The day had been measured out in stab wounds, difficult arrests, screaming and shouting in the offices of the *brigade criminelle* . . . one vast gaping wound.

But Irène was expert at making things right. She knew how to boost his confidence, how to take his mind off things. She talked about the studio, about the film she was editing ("complete nonsense . . . you wouldn't believe how bad it is"). The conversation, the warmth of the apartment, the tiredness of the day slipping away. Camille felt a drowsy contentment welling up inside him. He was no longer listening to her words; the sound of her voice was enough. Irène's voice.

"Okay," she said. "Let's eat."

She was about to get up, then suddenly seemed to remember something.

"Two things, before I forget. Three things, actually."

"Shoot," Camille said, draining his glass.

"Françoise has invited us to dinner on the thirteenth. Does that work?"

"Works for me," Camille said after a moment's thought.

"Good. Second thing: I need to do the accounts, so go and get me your credit card statements."

Camille clambered down off the sofa, took his wallet out of his knapsack, fished inside, and pulled out a wad of crumpled receipts.

"You're not going to do the accounts tonight, are you?" he said, setting the receipts on the coffee table. "Today has been tough enough already."

"Of course I'm not," said Irène, heading into the kitchen. "Come on, let's have dinner."

"You said there were three things?"

Irène stopped and turned, pretending to rack her brains.

"Oh, yes—one last thing: how do you feel about being a father?"

She was standing in the doorway to the kitchen. Camille stared at her stupidly, his eyes automatically resting on her belly which was still completely flat. He looked at her face, saw the laughter in her eyes. A baby had been the subject of long discussions. They could not seem to agree. Camille's opening gambit was to play for time, while Irène opted for intransigence. Next Camille resorted to the question of genetics, but Irène thwarted this by providing detailed research. At this point, Camille played his trump card: he refused. Irène trumped his trump card: I'm already the wrong side of thirty . . . The die was cast. And now the game was won. And so for the second time he asked himself if Irène was beautiful. The answer? Yes. He had the feeling that he would never again ask himself this question. And for the first time since he could remember, he felt his eyes well with tears, tears of sheer joy, like life itself exploding in his face.

21

Now here he was, lying in bed, one hand resting heavily on her belly. And beneath his hand, he could feel a forceful, muffled kick. Wide awake, he lay without moving a muscle and waited. In her sleep, Irène let out a soft moan. A minute passed, and another. Patient as a cat, Camille waited intently and there came a second kick, right under his hand, different this time, a sort of twisting motion like a caress. He felt as he always felt, his every thought blotted out by the absurd happiness of feeling it move, as though everything in his life had begun to move. All human life was here. It lasted only a fleeting moment before his thoughts were again interrupted by the image of a girl's head nailed to a wall. He tried to dismiss the image, to focus on Irène's warm belly, on all the happiness in the world, but the damage was already done.

Reality had triumphed over imagination, and images began to flash through his mind, slowly at first. A baby, Irène's swollen belly, the cry of a newborn child he could almost hear. The film began to speed up: Irène's beautiful face when they made love, her perfect hands, severed fingers, Irène's eyes, the ghastly rictus grin of another woman, a smile slashed open from ear to ear . . .

Camille woke feeling amazingly lucid. He and life had long been engaged in a battle of wills. Now, suddenly, he felt that the discovery of the bodies of these two mutilated women was about to turn a battle of wills into open warfare. The murdered women were no different from the woman he was caressing; like her, they had pale, rounded buttocks; firm, youthful flesh; in sleep their faces were probably like hers, with that curious expression like a swimmer underwater; the same deep, regular breathing; the soft snore; the moments of apnea that could panic a man who loved them as he watched them sleep; women with hair like Irène's, which curled about her heartbreakingly slender neck. Those murdered girls were no different from this woman he so loved. And yet, one day they had been—what?—invited, recruited, coerced, kidnapped, paid? However it had come about, they had been mutilated by men whose only desire was to dismember young women with smooth, pale buttocks, who had been unmoved by the pleading looks of these women when they realized they were going to die; they may simply have excited them, and so these young women who had been born to live had somehow come to die in this apartment, in this city, in this century where he, Camille Verhœven—an utterly unremarkable policeman, the runt of the *brigade criminelle*, a pretentious, love-struck troll—was stroking the beautiful belly of this woman who was constantly new, a miracle. Something was awry. In one last, weary flicker he saw himself devoting every ounce of his strength to two goals: first, to cherish this body he was stroking, from which, in time, would emerge the most astonishing gift; second, to hunt down the men who had mutilated those women, who had fucked them, raped them, killed them, dismembered them, splattering the walls with their blood.

Just before he drifted off, Camille had time to voice one last doubt:

"I'm so tired."

Tuesday, April 8

1

On the *métro* he read the papers, and his fears—or, as with any hypochondriac, his diagnosis—were confirmed. The media had already made the link with the Tremblay murder. The speed with which the story had reached the papers was as astounding as perhaps it was inevitable. Stringers were hired to coax information from local police stations, and it was common knowledge that many officers leaked stories to particular papers. Even so, Camille took a moment to try and work out the route the story would have taken since midafternoon the day before, but soon realized it was hopeless. The facts were as they were. The papers had revealed that the police had linked the Courbevoie killings, about which they had few details, with the Tremblay murder, on which, by contrast, they all had thick files. The headlines crackled with lurid sensationalism; the editors had clearly had fun: THE WREATH OF SEVERED FINGERS; THE TREMBLAY BUTCHER STRIKES IN COURBEVOIE; or TREMBLAY TERROR LINKED TO COURBEVOIE CARNAGE.

He stepped into the mortuary and headed for the viewing suite.

Maleval, with his occasionally inventive bluntness, considered that the world was divided into two categories: cowboys and Indians, a somewhat simplistic version of the distinction people made between introverts and extroverts. Camille and Doctor Nguyên were both Indians: silent, patient, sharp-eyed and attentive. They were men of few words, and could make themselves understood with a simple glance.

Perhaps the Vietnamese refugee and the pocket-sized policeman shared a solidarity born of adversity.

Évelyne Rouvray's mother looked like a yokel just up from the country. She was wearing a curious getup that was not quite her size. To Camille, she seemed smaller now, and older. Grief, probably. She stank of alcohol.

"This won't take long," Camille said.

They stepped into the viewing room. On the table, covered by a white sheet, lay something that now vaguely resembled a human body. Camille helped the woman shuffle toward the table and nodded to the man in the white coat to carefully pull back the sheet to expose the face, but not the neck, beyond which there was nothing to see.

The woman stared blankly, her face expressionless. The head lying on the table looked like a theater prop with death coiled inside it. The head did not look like anything or anyone, but the woman said "yes," a simple, bewildered "yes." And she had to be caught before she collapsed.

2

There was a man waiting in the corridor.

Like everybody else, Camille tended to judge men against his own height. To him, the man did not seem particularly tall—five foot six, perhaps. What immediately struck him were his eyes. He was about fifty, the sort of person who looks after himself, keeps himself in shape and runs fifteen miles on Sundays, rain or shine. A perceptive man. Well dressed, but not ostentatious. In his hands he held a pale leather folder; he was waiting patiently.

"Dr. Édouard Crest," he announced, proffering his hand. "I've been appointed by Juge Deschamps."

"Thanks for coming so quickly," Camille said, shaking the man's hand. "I requested you because we need someone to draw up a psychological profile of these guys, of what motivates them . . . I've run off copies of the preliminary reports." Camille handed the doctor a folder and watched closely as he leafed through the first pages. "Handsome man," Camille thought, and immediately, inexplicably, he thought of Irène. He felt a fleeting wave of jealousy that he quickly dismissed.

"Time line?" he asked.

"I'll let you know after the autopsy," Crest said. "It will depend on the evidence I can pull together."

3

At a glance, Camille knew that what was to come would be grotesque. Having to confront the horror of what had been done to Évelyne Rouvray's head was one thing, but performing an autopsy that resembled a ghoulish jigsaw puzzle would be something else entirely.

Usually, the corpses taken from the drawers of a mortuary fridge stirred a terrible feeling of pain, but that very pain was somehow alive. To suffer, one had to be alive. This time, the body appeared to have dissolved. It arrived as a series of packages, like slabs of tuna weighed out at a fish market.

On the stainless steel tables of the autopsy room lay shapeless masses of different sizes. Not all the parts had been removed from the drawers, but already it was difficult to imagine how these pieces had ever been one body, let alone two. It would never occur to someone at a butcher's stall to mentally reconstruct the slaughtered animal.

Dr. Crest and Dr. Nguyên shook hands as if they were at a conference. The delegate for lunacy greeting the delegate for atrocity. Then Dr. Nguyên put on his glasses, checked that the tape recorder was working, and decided to begin with the stomach.

"The deceased is a Caucasian woman age approximately . . ."

4

Philippe Buisson de Chevesne was not the best in the business, but he was certainly one of the most tenacious. The message "Commandant Verhœven does not intend to speak to the press at this stage of the investigation" did not faze him.

"I'm not asking for a press statement. I just want a couple of minutes of his time."

He had begun calling late the night before. He began again first thing in the morning. At 11 a.m., the switchboard informed Camille of his thirteenth call. The switchboard sounded tetchy.

Buisson—who in his by-line dispensed with the aristocratic "de Chevesne"—was not exactly a star reporter. He did not have what it took to be a great journalist, but he was nonetheless a *successful* journalist because he focused his formidable instincts on the story in hand. Perhaps because he was aware of both his strengths and limitations, Buisson chose to cover lurid crime stories, a choice that proved astute. He was no stylist, but he was an effective writer. He had made a name for himself covering a number of high-profile cases where he had succeeded in digging up a few minor details. A little news and a lot of showmanship. Buisson was no genius, so he milked this formula assiduously. The rest had been down to luck, which clearly favored heroes and scumbag journalists equally. Buisson had stumbled upon the Tremblay murder and had been among the first to realize its true implication: a vast readership. He had covered the case from beginning to end, so it had been no surprise to see him show up in Courbevoie now that the two cases had been linked.

Camille spotted him as soon as he came out of the *métro*. A tall guy, trendy, in his thirties. A nice voice he had a tendency to overuse. A little too much charm. Cunning. Intelligent.

Camille immediately shut down and quickened his pace.

"I just need a couple of minutes . . . ," Buisson said, buttonholing Camille.

"If I had two minutes, I'd be happy to give them to you . . ."

Camille was walking briskly, but given his height, walking briskly meant walking at the unhurried pace of a man like Buisson.

"You'd be wise to make a statement, *inspecteur*. Otherwise the hacks are likely to write up any old shit . . ."

Camille stopped.

"You're behind the times, Buisson. No one's called me '*inspecteur*' for years. As for reporters writing any old shit, is that a promise or a threat?"

"Neither—obviously it's neither." Buisson smiled.

Camille had stopped, and this was his mistake. One point to Buisson. Camille realized this. The two men eyeballed each other.

"You know how it is," Buisson went on. "If they've got nothing to go on, journalists tend to invent things . . ."

Buisson had been known to divorce himself from the sins he ascribed to others. From the look in his eyes, Camille suspected he was capable of anything, of the worst excesses and possibly more. The difference between a good predator and a great predator is instinct. Buisson clearly had the perfect genetic makeup for the job.

"Now that the Tremblay case has come up–"

"News travels fast . . ." Camille cut him short.

"Well, I covered the Tremblay case, so obviously I'm interested."

Camille looked up. "I don't like this man," he thought. And immediately he sensed that the antipathy was mutual, that unwittingly they had developed a low-grade repugnance for each other that neither would ever shake.

"You'll get nothing out of me I haven't told the rest of the press," Camille snapped. "You want a comment? Ask someone else . . ."

"Don't you mean someone higher up?" Buisson peered down at the *commandant*.

The two men stared at each other for a moment, astounded by the rift that had suddenly opened up between them.

"I'm sorry," Buisson muttered.

Camille, for his part, felt strangely relieved. Sometimes contempt is a consolation.

"Listen," Buisson went on, "I'm really sorry . . . a slip of the tongue . . ."

"I didn't notice," Camille interrupted.

Then he walked off, the journalist trotting after him. The atmosphere between the two men had shifted considerably.

"You could at least tell me something. What have you come up with so far?"

"No comment. We're proceeding with our investigation. For further information, contact Commissaire Le Guen. Or the *procureur*."

"Monsieur Verhœven, these cases are getting a lot of press. Editors are itching for a story. I'll bet you that by the end of the week the tabloids will have come up with plausible suspects and published E-FIT pictures that half the population of France will swear blind is the other half. If you don't give the papers something to work with, they'll whip up mass hysteria."

"If it were up to me," said Camille curtly, "the press wouldn't be informed until we make an arrest."

"You'd be prepared to gag the press?"

Camille stopped again. Things had gone beyond point scoring or strategy.

"I would stop them from creating 'mass hysteria,' or in layman's terms, publishing bullshit."

"So we can expect nothing from the *brigade criminelle*?"

"On the contrary, you expect us to catch the killer."

"So you think you don't need the press?"

"For the time being, it means precisely that."

"For the time being? That's pretty jaundiced!"

"I live in the moment."

Buisson seemed to think for a minute.

"Listen, I think there's something I can do for you if you want. Off the record, strictly personal."

"I'd be surprised."

"It's true. I can get you some PR. I've just taken over writing the weekly Personal Profile, you know, full-page article, big photo, all that crap. I've been working on a profile of this other guy . . . but that can wait. So, if you're interested . . ."

"Give it a rest, Buisson."

"I'm serious! You can't buy this kind of publicity. All I'd need from you is a couple of personal anecdotes. I'd make it a glowing write-up, I swear . . . and in return, you keep me up to speed on the investigation—you wouldn't have to get your hands dirty."

"Like I said, Buisson, give it a rest."

"You're a hard man to do business with, Verhœven . . ."

"*Monsieur* Verhœven!"

"If I might give you a little advice: Don't take that kind of tone, *Monsieur* Verhœven."

"*Commandant* Verhœven!"

"Fine," said Buisson in a chilly tone that gave Camille pause. "Have it your way."

Buisson turned on his heel and strode off. If Camille sometimes came across as media friendly, it was patently not down to his tact as a negotiator.

5

Given his height, Camille preferred to remain standing. And since he didn't sit down, no one else felt they were allowed to sit, and every new recruit adopted this implicit code: at the *brigade*, meetings were held standing up.

The previous evening, Maleval and Armand had spent quite a lot of time trying talking to neighbors to get witness statements. They hadn't held out much hope, given that there were no neighbors. Especially at night, when the area was about as busy as a whorehouse in heaven. While he'd been waiting for a signal from the girls, José Riveiro had noticed no one in the area, but it was possible that someone had passed by later. They had had to tramp over a mile before they found any sign of life—a couple of shopkeepers in a residential suburb who, needless to say, could tell them nothing whatsoever about any hypothetical comings and goings. No one had seen anything out of the ordinary, no trucks, no vans, no delivery men. No inhabitants. To listen to them, you would think the murdered girls could only have got there by the intercession of the Holy Spirit.

"Our killer was obviously careful when he picked his location," said Maleval.

Camille studied Maleval more closely. A little comparison test: what was the difference between Maleval, leaning in the doorway fishing a well-thumbed notebook out of his pocket, and Louis, standing next to the desk, arms folded, a notebook in his hand?

Both men were well dressed; each, in his own way, was charming. The difference was sexual. Camille reflected for a moment on this curious notion. Maleval loved women. He bedded women. He never seemed to have enough. He was driven by his sexual urges. Everything about him exuded a need to seduce, to conquer. It's not that he always wants more, Camille thought, it's the fact that there is always some other woman to be charmed. Maleval did not truly love women, he was a skirt chaser. He had only to sense new prey and he was on the prowl; his suits were his battle fatigues. He was an off-the-rack man. The loves of Louis, on the other hand, like his elegant suits, were exquisitely tailored. Today, to greet the first rays of sunshine of the season, Louis was wearing a pale suit, a striking light-blue shirt, a club tie, and as for his shoes . . . "The upper crust," Camille thought. On the subject of Louis's sexuality, however, Camille knew very little. Which is to say nothing at all.

Camille pondered the relationship between the two men. It seemed cordial. Maleval had joined the *brigade* a few weeks after Louis. They got along well. They had even socialized occasionally in the early days; Maleval had said, "Oh, Louis might look like an altar boy, but take him out and he's a sleazy little devil. I tell you, when rich boys slum it, they go all the way." Louis had made no comment. He simply pushed back his bangs. Camille couldn't remember which hand he had used.

Maleval's voice shook Camille from his thoughts.

"The image of the human genome has appeared in newspapers and magazines," said Maleval. "It's been all over the media. And we might as well forget about the faux cowhide. They're not exactly fashionable at the moment, but back in the day people snapped them up. It would be impossible to find out where that particular one came from. The wallpaper in the bathroom looks new, but there's no easy way to tell where it came from. We'd have to contact wallpaper manufacturers . . ."

"Sounds like a thankless task for somebody," Louis said.

"Tell me about it! As for the stereo, millions of that model have been sold. The serial numbers have been removed. I sent it down to the lab, but they reckon the numbers were burned off using acid. Frankly, I wouldn't hold out much hope."

Maleval looked over for Armand to take over.

"I haven't got much either–"

"Thanks, Armand," Camille cut him off. "We're grateful for your input. Most constructive. It's been very helpful."

"But Camille . . . ," Armand said blushing.

"I'm joking, Armand. I'm joking."

The two men had known each other for fifteen years and, having started out in the force together, had always been on first-name terms. Camille thought of Armand as a friend, of Maleval as a prodigal son, and of Louis as a kind of heir apparent.

Armand was still flushed; his hands trembled at the slightest little thing. Sometimes Camille felt a surge of pained sympathy for the man.

"So . . ." He gave Armand an encouraging look. "You've got nothing for us . . . ?"

"Actually, I do have something," said Armand, somewhat reassured, "but it's a bit thin. The bed linen in the apartment was standard issue; you can buy it anywhere. Same goes for the suspenders. The Japanese bed, on the other hand . . ."

"Yes?" Camille said.

"It's what they call a photon . . ."

"I think you mean a futon?" suggested Louis. Armand checked his notes, an operation that took quite some time but was revealing about his character. Nothing could be taken as true until it had been thoroughly verified. He was a rationalist.

"Yes," he said, looking up at Louis with vague admiration, "you're right, a futon."

"So, what about this futon?" Camille said.

"That's the thing—it was imported directly from Japan."

"From Japan? It's not uncommon for Japanese things to be imported from Japan, you know?"

"Well, yeah . . . ," Armand said. "I suppose it is common . . ."

A silence settled over the office. Everyone there knew Armand. They knew how dogged he could be. An ellipsis in Armand's speech could be the result of two hundred hours of investigation.

"Why don't you explain, Armand?"

"So, okay, it is pretty common, but this particular model comes from a factory in Kyoto. They make furniture mostly, chairs and beds and stuff . . ."

"Okay . . . ," said Camille.

"So, anyway, this"—Armand consulted his notes—"futon was made there. But what's interesting is that the large sofa was made there, too."

The room was silent again.

"It's huge. They don't sell many of them. This particular model went on the market in January. They've sold thirty-seven. The sofa in Courbevoie has to be one of those thirty-seven. I got a list of their customers."

"Fucking hell, Armand, couldn't you have just said that straight off?"

"I'm not done, Camille, I'm not done. Of the thirty-seven, twenty-six are still with furniture dealers. Eleven were exported from Japan, six of those for Japanese buyers. The rest were bought by mail order. Three of these were shipped to France. The first was ordered by a Parisian dealer for one of his customers, Sylvain Siegel. That's this one here . . ."

From his pocket Armand took a photograph of a sofa that looked exactly like the one in Courbevoie.

"Monsieur Siegel sent me the photo. I'm going to visit his place to check, but I think we can assume it's kosher . . ."

"And the other two?" Camille said.

"That's where it gets interesting. The other two were bought online direct from the factory. Sales to private individuals take longer to trace. The whole thing is done by computer—you have to find the right people to contact, you have to hope the guy knows his stuff, you need to track down the relevant files . . . The first was ordered by someone called Crespy, the second by someone called Dunford. Both are based in Paris. I haven't managed to contact Crespy; I've left a couple of messages, but he hasn't called back. If I don't hear anything by tomorrow, I'll drop in there. But we're not likely to turn up much, in my opinion . . ."

"In your 'humble' opinion?" Maleval sniggered.

Engrossed in his notes or his thoughts, Armand did not rise to the bait. Camille glanced wearily at Maleval. This was no time for jokes.

"I managed to talk to his cleaning lady. She said the sofa is there. That leaves only Dunford. Now he"—Armand looked up—"might well be our man. There's no trace of him. He paid by international money transfer, he had the sofa delivered to a self-storage company in Gennevilliers. According to the manager there, some guy with a van picked it up the day after it arrived. He doesn't remember anything much about him, but I'm going round to take a statement tomorrow morning so we'll see if anything else comes back to him."

"There's nothing to say he's our man," Maleval said.

"You're right," Camille said, "but at least it's a lead. Maleval, I want you to go to Gennevilliers tomorrow, with Armand."

The four men stood for a moment in silence, but they were all thinking the same thing: it was all a bit sketchy. The leads they had went precisely nowhere. The murder was not simply premeditated . . . it had been planned with great care; nothing had been left to chance.

"We're going to be run ragged chasing down the details. Because that's all we can do, because that's the game. But we can't let this grunt work distract us from the most important thing. The most important thing is not *how,* it's *why.*" Camille thought for a moment. "Anything else?"

"The second victim, Josiane Debeuf, lived in Pantin," Louis said, leafing through his notes. "We checked it out, but the apartment's empty. She worked the streets around the Porte de la Chapelle and sometimes around Porte de Vincennes. No one knows anything about her. She doesn't seem to have had a boyfriend. We've got nothing much on her."

Louis handed Camille a sheet of paper.

"Ah, yes, I'd forgotten about that," said Camille thoughtfully, putting on his glasses and skimming the list detailing the contents of the suitcase the killer had left behind. "Everything a well-traveled businessman could possibly need."

"And it's pretty classy stuff," Louis said.

"Really?" Camille said hesitantly.

"Well, I think so . . . ," Louis said. "But it bears out what Armand was telling us just now. Ordering a huge sofa from Japan just to hack women to pieces is pretty weird to say the least. But so is leaving behind a Ralph Lauren suitcase worth at least three hundred euros. Not to mention the contents—the Brooks Brothers suit, the shoehorn from Barneys New York, the Sharp portable photocopier . . . it all adds up. A rechargeable electric razor, a sports watch, a leather wallet, a top-of-the-line hair dryer . . . All this stuff would have cost a bundle . . ."

"Okay," Camille said after a long silence. "That just leaves the fingerprint. Even if it was made using a rubber stamp, it's still a very distinctive clue. Louis, can you make sure it's checked against the European database?"

"That's already been done." Louis flicked through his notes. "On December 4, 2001, during the Tremblay investigation. Nothing came up."

"Okay. We should probably rerun the search. Can you have all the necessary info resent to Europol?"

"It's just . . . ," Louis began.

"Yes?"

"That's a decision for the investigating magistrate."

"I know. Submit the new request for the moment. I'll sort out the paperwork later."

Camille handed out a brief memo he had written the night before that summed up the main points in the Tremblay case. Louis was tasked with going over all the witness statements in the hope of piecing together the young prostitute's last days and following up any leads on regular customers. Camille always found it entertaining to send Louis into seedy dives. He could just picture him climbing the sticky carpeted stairs in his perfectly polished shoes, stepping into sultry flophouse rooms in his dashing Armani suit. A sight for sore eyes.

"We don't really have the manpower."

"Louis, I am awed by your command of understatement."

As Louis pushed back his bangs with his right hand, Camille continued reflectively, "Though obviously you're not wrong."

He checked his watch.

"Okay. Nguyên promised me his preliminary findings by the end of the day. Which is very convenient. Ever since my thick skull showed up on the nine o'clock news, and especially since this morning's stories in the newspaper, the *juge d'instruction* has been getting a little impatient."

"In simple terms?" Maleval said.

"In simple terms, she's summoned us to her office at 5 p.m. for an update."

"Ah . . . ," said Armand. "An update . . . So what do we say?"

"That's rather the problem. There's not much to say, and what we *can* say is not exactly dazzling. This time we'll have the benefit of a little diversion. Dr. Crest will be giving a psychological profile, and Nguyên will be delivering his preliminary findings. But we're going to have to find something to go on."

"Any ideas?" asked Armand.

The brief silence that followed was very different from those that had preceded it. Camille seemed suddenly disoriented, like a hiker who has lost his way.

"I haven't the faintest idea, Armand. Not a clue. But there's one point we can all agree on. We're in deep shit."

6

Camille traveled in the car with Armand for the meeting with the investigating magistrate. Louis and Maleval said they would see them there.

"So, Juge Deschamps," Camille said. "Have you met her?"

"I can't remember."

"In that case, you've definitely never met her."

The car weaved through the traffic, using the bus lanes wherever possible.

"What about you?" Armand asked.

"Oh, I remember her!"

Juge Deschamps enjoyed an uncontentious reputation, which was quite a good sign. Camille remembered a woman of about his age, slim to the point of gauntness, with an asymmetrical face whose features—eyes, nose, mouth, cheekbones—could, considered separately, have seemed normal, even harmonious, but they looked as though they had been randomly thrown together, giving her an expression at once intelligent and—quite literally—chaotic. She wore expensive clothes.

Le Guen was already there in her office when Camille showed up with Armand and the pathologist. Maleval and Louis arrived immediately afterward. Firmly ensconced behind her desk at the controls, the investigating magistrate was a little younger and much slimmer than Camille remembered her, though otherwise unchanged. Her face radiated refinement rather than intelligence, and her clothes were not simply expensive: they were exclusive.

Dr. Crest arrived some minutes later. He brusquely shook Camille's hand, gave him a vague smile, and took a seat by the door as though not intending to stay any longer than necessary.

"We're going to need everyone's skill on this one," the judge said. "You've watched the television, you've seen the papers; this case is all over the news. So we need to move quickly. I'm under no illusions, and I'm not going to ask the impossible, but I want to be kept updated on a daily basis, and I would ask you all to be exceptionally discreet in matters relating to this investigation. Journalists are bound to buttonhole you, but I plan to take a hard line on any breach of judicial confidentiality. I hope I make myself clear . . . In all likelihood, the media will be waiting for me when I leave this meeting, and I will have to give them some details. I need to hear what you have to say before deciding what and how much can be released to the press. In the hope that it might calm things down a little . . ."

Le Guen was nodding vigorously as though he were spokesperson for the group.

"Very well," the *juge* said. "Dr. Nguyên, we're all ears."

The young pathologist cleared his throat.

"We won't have the full results back for several days. However, the autopsy has given us sufficient information to put forward some conclusions. Contrary to appearances and to the extent of the damage inflicted, it seems we are dealing with a single killer."

The silence that followed this initial remark positively quivered.

"A man, in all probability," Nguyên continued. "He used a range of tools—an electric drill fitted with a wide masonry bit, hydrochloric acid, an electric chain saw, a nail gun, several knives, a lighter.

Obviously it is difficult to produce an exact time line of the events; some elements seem, shall we say . . . confused. Generally speaking, traces were found on both victims to indicate sexual activity—oral, anal, and vaginal—both with each other and with an unknown male partner, whom we can presume is our killer. Given the rather . . . uninhibited nature of these activities, we were surprised to find evidence of condom use. A rubber dildo was also used. From the information we have so far on the actual killings, it is not yet possible to determine the sequence of events. There are some conclusions we can draw, however. For example, it would be impossible for the killer to ejaculate into the skull before severing the head of the victim."

The silence was beginning to weigh heavily on the group. Nguyên looked up, adjusted his reading glasses, and continued.

"It is likely that both victims were sprayed repeatedly with some form of poison gas. They were stunned—possibly using the handle of the electric drill or nail gun, though that is only speculation, but we do know the same weapon was used. The blows in each case were of the same force, which was not sufficient to render the victims unconscious for any length of time. In other words, we can hypothesize that while the victims were numbed, suffocated, and dazed, they were aware of what was happening to them up until the moment of death."

Nguyên looked down at his notes, hesitated for a moment, and then carried on.

"You'll find the details in my report. The injuries to the first victim were bite marks. She would have bled profusely. As for the head, Évelyne Rouvray's lips were cut away, probably using nail scissors. She had deep lacerations to her abdomen and legs, and her stomach and genitals were burned using undiluted hydrochloric acid. The victim's head was discovered on a dresser in the bedroom. Traces of sperm were found in her mouth, and analysis will almost certainly prove they were *post mortem*. A few more details before we move on to Josiane Debeuf–"

"Is there much more of this?" Camille said.

"A little, yes," the pathologist said. "Josiane Debeuf was tied to the side of the bed using the six pairs of suspenders found at the scene. The killer first burned off her eyebrows and lashes using matches. I will spare you some of the more painful details . . . Let's just say that the killer forced his hand into her throat, grabbed what he could and pulled everything out through her mouth . . . It was Josiane Debeuf's blood that was used to scrawl I AM BACK in capitals on the wall of the apartment."

Silence.

"Any questions?" asked Le Guen.

"The connection with the Tremblay case?" Juge Deschamps looked to Camille.

"I read the case file last night. There's a lot of cross-checking still to be done, but the fingerprint made using a rubber stamp is the same. In each case it appears to have been used as a signature."

"That's not a good sign," Deschamps said. "It means the guy wants to be famous."

"Up to a point, he is a classic sociopath," Dr. Crest said suddenly. It was his first contribution to the conversation, and everyone turned to look at him.

"Forgive me for interrupting . . . ," he said, though from the tone of his voice and the poise with which he delivered the apology, this had been carefully calculated, and he was seeking no one's forgiveness.

"Please, carry on," Deschamps said, as if, even though Crest had already taken the floor, he still sought her official permission.

Crest was wearing a gray three-piece suit. Elegant. His first name, Édouard, fitted him like a calfskin glove, Camille thought as he watched Crest step into the center of the room. The man's parents had chosen the name wisely.

The doctor cleared his throat and scanned his notes.

"From a psychological viewpoint, we are dealing with a classic case that is archetypal in construction, if a little banal in implementation. Constitutionally, he is an obsessive. Contrary to appearances, he probably does not have murderous fantasies. His fantasies are more likely to be possessive, culminating in destruction. He seeks to possess women, but possessing them does not calm his anxieties. So he tortures them. But the torture does not help, so he kills them. But even murder does not alleviate his desires. He can possess these women, violate them, torture and dismember them, but it does not bring him peace. He feels charged with a mission. Swept along by something greater than himself, he dimly senses that he will never find peace. He will never stop, because his mission has no end. Over the years, he has nurtured an absolute hatred of women. Not because of what they are, but because they cannot bring him peace. Deep down, this man's tragedy is that he is lonely. He is capable of orgasm, in the everyday sense of the term, meaning he is not impotent, he can achieve erection, and can ejaculate; but everyone knows that such things have little to do with sexual gratification, in which the participant reaches another level. This man has never known gratification. Or if he ever did, it is now a door forever closed and whose key is lost. And ever since, he has been searching for that key. This is not some cold, unfeeling monster numb to human suffering, a sadist, if you will. He is an unhappy man who tortures women because he himself is tortured."

Dr. Crest spoke with slow, measured care and was clearly confident in his abilities as a pedagogue. Camille studied his hair, the widow's peaks on either side that receded almost to the crown of his head, and he had the sudden feeling that this man had never been more attractive to women than in his forties.

"My initial analysis—and I assume it was yours, too—was the meticulousness with which the crime scene was staged. Usually, with this type of criminal, one finds a number of symbols intended, in the strict sense of the word—if I may put it this way—to 'mark' their work. These signs are intricately linked with their fantasies, most often to their initial fantasy. Indeed, this is what I believed was the intention of the fingerprint stamped on the wall and, even more so, the words I AM BACK, which are clearly intended as a signature. But working from the preliminary reports you provided," he said, turning to Camille, "I was struck by the fact that there are too many markers. Far too many. The props, the locations, the staging all lead one to expect a *single* mark intended as a signature to the crime. Given this fact, I think we have to change the paradigm. What is clear is that he painstakingly prepares everything. He clearly has a carefully thought-out plan. In his eyes, every single detail is important, crucially important, but it would be pointless to try to work out what the presence of individual objects might mean. It is not a case, as with similar crimes, of exploring what place these objects have in his private life. It is the ensemble that matters. Because the individual objects have, in a sense, no intrinsic importance. Trying to decipher the meaning of each sign would be a waste of time. It would be like trying to interpret each line of a Shakespeare play. Such an approach would make it impossible to understand *King Lear*. We need to focus on the *universal*. But . . ." He paused and turned again to Camille. "That goes beyond the scope of my skills, my science."

"Sociologically, what sort of man are we looking at?" Camille asked.

"White, European, educated. Not necessarily intellectual, but cerebral nonetheless. Age between thirty and fifty. Lives alone. He may be widowed or divorced . . . but I suspect he's a bachelor."

"What sort of repetitive patterns should we be focusing on?" asked Louis.

"That's a tough call. In my opinion, this is not his first crime. I would say it is like a capillary wave; he works in concentric circles moving outward from the center. He may have started out raping women, then later torturing them before moving on to murder. That would be the obvious trajectory. The constants in this case are few. The only things we can pinpoint with any certainty are the victims are prostitutes; they are young; he tortures them; he kills them. Beyond that . . ."

"Is he likely to have a history of mental illness?"

"It's possible. For minor behavioral problems. But we're dealing with an intelligent man, someone so used to deluding himself that it is easy for him to dupe others. No one has been able to give him peace. Women are his last hope. He desperately demands some-thing that they cannot give, and in doing so his violence will con-tinue to escalate until and unless you arrest him. He has devised a logic schema for his urges. This logic, which I mentioned a moment ago, this intricate staging . . . It is because of this that he can move from desire to deed. But the pattern is not the goal, in my opinion. You might argue that this is the case with most serial killers, but he is different. The evident perfectionism indicates that he has an exaggerated opinion of his work. I'm not talking about some noble mission . . . but it's not far off. For as long as this mission persists, two things are certain: the first is that he will go on killing; the sec-ond is that the barbarity of his crimes can only increase."

Crest looked from the *juge* to Camille and then to Le Guen; then he stared uneasily at the assembled company.

"This man is capable of committing barely imaginable acts of violence . . . if he has not already done so."

Silence.

"Anything else?" Juge Deschamps asked, laying her hands on her desk.

7

"Maniac!"

Irène, that evening. Dinner at a restaurant.

Time had passed at an alarming rate since the announcement of her pregnancy. Her belly and face had filled out; her movements were slower, heavier. And to Camille's eyes these changes had not been as gradual as he expected; they came in sudden waves, in stages. Arriving home one evening, he noticed that her freckles had suddenly multiplied. He said something about it, in a nice way, because he found it pretty but a little startling. Irène had smiled and patted his cheek.

"Darling . . . it really hasn't been all that sudden. It's just that we haven't had dinner together for more than a fortnight."

This rankled. The image Irène had conjured was a cliché—the man at work, the woman waiting patiently at home—and he didn't know what pained him more, the situation itself or the sheer banality of it. Irène was never out of his mind—she filled his whole life: a hundred times a day he thought about her, a hundred times a day the fact that they were about to have a baby suddenly overwhelmed him, disrupting his work, and he saw the world anew as though he had just had cataracts removed. So, no, he could hardly be accused of abandoning Irène . . . But in his heart, he could not deny the fact that he had missed a turning. During the first months there had not been a problem. Irène had still been working hard, sometimes late into the night, and they had always lived their life making a virtue of necessity. Some evenings they would meet up on the spur of the moment in some restaurant midway between his office and hers, or they could call each other, shocked to realize it was almost 10 p.m., and rush to catch a late-night showing at a nearby movie theater. It had been a simpler time, filled with simple pleasures. Things had changed after Irène had had to stop work and began spending whole days at home. "He keeps me company," she would say, stroking her belly, "but he's not much of a talker yet." And this was the turning that Camille had missed. He had gone on working as before, not realizing that their lives were no longer in sync. So tonight, there could be no question of failure. At the end of the day, and after much hesitation, he decided to ask Louis, who knew everything there was to know about propriety.

"Look, I need some advice about a restaurant. Something first rate. It's our wedding anniversary."

"I'd recommend Chez Michel," Louis said. "It's impeccable."

Camille was about to ask how much it would set him back, but his self-respect flashed a warning light and he said nothing.

"Otherwise there's L'Assiette." Louis said.

"Thanks, Louis, I'm sure Chez Michel will be perfect. Thanks again."

8

Irène was ready and clearly had been for quite some time. Camille restrained an urge to check his watch.

"Don't worry." Irène smiled. "It's okay. You're late, but within the bounds of acceptability."

As they headed to the car, Camille worried that Irène's tread seemed heavier: she was waddling like a duck; her back was arched, her belly lower; everything about her seemed weary.

"Are you all right?"

She stopped for a moment, laid a hand on his arm, and, suppressing a smile, she said, "I'm fine, Camille."

He thought he could sense exasperation in her tone and in that guarded smile, as though he had already asked the question and ignored the answer. He cursed himself for not taking enough interest in her. Irritation gnawed at him. Even though he loved this woman, perhaps he was not a good husband. They walked for a while, neither of them speaking, the silence between them like some inexplicable abandonment. Words failed. As they passed a movie theater, Camille fleetingly noticed the name of an actress,

Gwendolyn Playne. As he opened the car door, he wondered why the name seemed familiar, but nothing came to him.

Irène got into the car without a word, and Camille asked himself how they had got into this mess. Irène must have been asking herself the same question, but she was the wiser of the two. Just as he was about to drive off, she took his hand and placed it on her thigh, high up next to her swollen belly, then laying a hand on his neck she pulled him close and kissed him long and hard. They stared at each other, surprised to have burst the bubble of silence in which they had seemed trapped.

"I love you, Monsieur Verhœven," Irène said.

"And I love you, Madame Verhœven," said Camille, studying her closely. He ran his fingers across her forehead, around her eyes, over her lips. "I love you, too."

Chez Michel. It was, as Louis had promised, impeccable. Utterly Parisian, with mirrors everywhere, waiters in starched black pants and white coats, raucous as a railway station, the Muscadet ice cold. Irène was wearing a dress printed with red and yellow flowers. But although she had been careful to buy the largest size, the dress had failed to keep pace with her burgeoning pregnancy and the buttons now yawned slightly as she sat down.

The restaurant was crowded, but the noise afforded them perfect privacy. They talked about the film Irène had had to give up editing when she took maternity, and Irène asked Camille about his father.

The first time Irène had come to dinner, Camille's father had taken to her as though they had known each other all their lives. At the end of the meal he gave her a present—a painting by Basquiat. Camille's father had money. He had taken early retirement, sold his practice for an exorbitant sum—Camille did not know how much exactly, but more than enough to buy a lavish, impossibly large apartment, pay a cleaning lady he did not really need, buy more books than he had time to read, more music than he could listen to, and, over the past two years, travel widely. One day he had asked Camille's permission to sell a number of his mother's paintings, having been pestered by gallery owners since she closed her studio.

"She painted them for people to see," Camille said.

He himself had none of his mother's paintings. The only ones he might have wished to own were the first and last.

"Obviously, the money will all come to you eventually," his father had said.

"Spend it on yourself," Camille had said, vaguely unsettled by the conversation. The subject never came up again, and the paintings were still in his mother's old studio.

"I called him the other day," Camille said to Irène. "He seems fine."

Irène devoured her food as Camille gazed at her.

"Remember to thank Louis for the recommendation," she said, pushing her plate away.

"I'll give him the bill while I'm about it."

"Cheapskate."

"I love you."

"I should hope so."

"So, how's your case coming along?" Irène asked as dessert was being served. "I heard the investigating magistrate on the radio today . . . what's her name? Deschamps, is it?"

"Yeah. What did she have to say for herself?"

"Not much, but the case seems pretty grim."

Seeing Camille look at her questioningly, she continued. "She said that two young women had been murdered in Courbevoie. She didn't go into details, but it sounded horrific . . ."

"It is."

"She mentioned some connection to a cold case in Tremblay. Did you work on that?"

"No, it wasn't one of mine then, but it is now."

He did not really feel like discussing the case. To talk about the death of two young women with his pregnant wife on their wedding anniversary felt somehow obscene. But Irène had surely noticed that the dead girls had occupied his every waking thought in the last days, and that each time he managed to put them out of his mind, something or someone reminded him of them. He gave her a general outline of the case, at pains to avoid certain words, certain images, only to trail off into awkward silences, his eyes darting around the restaurant as though searching for some way to explain. His clear, measured account suddenly stopped in midstream as words failed him, and he raised his hands in a helpless gesture. Irène realized that he could not describe the unspeakable.

"The guy's clearly a psycho . . ." was Irène's verdict.

Camille tried to explain that during a lifetime spent on the force, not one in a hundred officers would ever have to deal with a case like this, and not one in a thousand would want to be in his shoes right now. Like most people, Irène's notion of what his work entailed seemed to come from the detective novels. He foolishly suggested this to her, and Irène snapped:

"When have you ever seen me read a crime novel? I can't stand them."

"You've read some in your time!"

"I read *And Then There Were None* as a teenager. When I went to Wyoming as an exchange student my father thought it would be the best way to prepare me for the American mind-set. He never was much good at geography."

"I'm not a great fan myself," Camille said.

"I've always preferred movies," she said with a smile.

"I know . . ." He smiled, too. They knew each other too well. With the point of his knife, Camille traced the outline of a tree on his napkin. He looked up at her and took a small box from his pocket.

"Happy anniversary."

Irène had long since accepted that her husband had no imagination. He had given her jewelry on their wedding day, he had given her jewelry when she told him she was pregnant, and now, a few months later, here he was again. But she was not disappointed. She knew she was fortunate compared with those women whose only attentions from their husbands were a Friday night fumble. Irène, on the other hand, had more imagination. She held out the large, gift-wrapped package Camille had seen her putting under her chair as they sat down.

"Happy anniversary to you, too."

Remembering every one of Irène's gifts, each different from the last, Camille felt a little embarrassed. He tore off the wrapping paper, the diners at the next table glancing over curiously, and took out a book: *The Caravaggio Mystery*. On the cover was a detail from *The Fortune Teller* : three hands, one palm up, proffered in surrender. Camille, who was familiar with the painting, mentally conjured it now in its entirety: a woman in a white turban whose eyes seem to promise something more than fortune telling, a young man with his gloved hand resting on the pommel of his sword, that youthful, ineffectual arrogance. It was just like Irène to offer her policeman husband the collected works of a murderous painter.

"Do you like it?"

"I love it!"

His mother had loved Caravaggio. He still remembered her talking about *David with the Head of Goliath*. Leafing through the book now, he came across the painting. He stared into the face of Goliath. This was clearly a day for severed heads.

"You would swear that it's a depiction of Good versus Evil," his mother used to say. "Look at the fury in David's eyes, while Goliath's expression is calm and sorrowful. Where is Good, where is Evil? Now there's a question . . ."

9

After dinner they took a little stroll, wandering hand in hand as far as the *grands boulevards*. In public, Camille had only ever been able to hold Irène's hand. He would have liked to put his arm around her shoulder, to slip his arm around her waist, to be like other men, and felt saddened not to be able to make this proprietorial gesture. Over time, this sadness had faded. Holding her hand was a more subtle sign of possession, and one that suited him now. Almost imperceptibly, Irène's pace slowed.

"Tired?"

"A bit, maybe." She smiled, breathing hard.

She ran a hand over her belly as though smoothing an invisible crease.

"I'll go and get the car," Camille said.

"No, you don't have to do that."

But he did have to.

It was late. The boulevards were still thronged with people. They agreed that Irène would sit at a table outside one of the cafés while he went to get the car.

At the corner Camille turned back to look at her. Her face had changed, and Camille felt a pang of dread because suddenly the distance between them seemed unbridgeable. Even as she watched the passers-by, her hands clasped over her stomach, Irène had retreated into her own little world, into the mystery of the life growing within her, and Camille felt excluded. But his fears subsided because he knew that this distance that separated them was not about the love they shared. It was much simpler: she was a woman; he was a man. This was the chasm between them, but it was no wider today than yesterday. And it was this distance that had drawn them together. He smiled.

This was what he was thinking when he lost sight of her, his view blocked by a young man who now stood next to him, waiting, like Camille, for the traffic lights to change. "Young people are so tall these days," Camille thought, realizing that he barely came up to the boy's elbow. He had read something recently about the fact that the whole world was growing taller. Even the Japanese. As he reached the other side of the street, already fumbling in his pocket for the car keys, the missing link in his earlier train of thought suddenly came to him: Gwendolyn Playne reminded him of Gwynplaine, the hero of Victor Hugo's *The Man Who Laughs*, and of a quote he thought he had forgotten: "The tall are what they choose to be. The short are what they can be."

10

"The palette knife is used to work on the depth of a painting. Watch . . ."

Mama does not often take the time to offer advice. The studio smells of turps. Mama is working with reds. She applies liberal quantities—blood reds, carmines, reds dark as night. The palette knife bends under her pressure, leaving thick layers that she then spreads using lighter touches. Mama likes reds. I have a Mama who likes reds. She looks at me affectionately. "You like reds, too, don't you, Camille?" Instinctively, Camille recoils, suddenly gripped by fear.

Camille woke with a start shortly after 4 a.m. He leaned over Irène's distended body, holding his own breath for a moment the better to listen to her slow, regular breathing, the faint snore of a woman grown heavy. He gently laid a hand on her belly. Only when he feels her warm skin, the smooth tautness of her belly, does he slowly begin to breathe again. Still dazed with sleep, he glances around him at the darkness, their bedroom, the window glowing faintly from the streetlights. He tries to calm his pounding heart. *Something is seriously wrong*, he thinks, noticing the beads of sweat trickling between his eyebrows and blurring his vision.

Cautiously, he gets up and goes to the bathroom, where he splashes cold water on his face.

As a rule, Camille does not dream much. "My subconscious leaves me in peace" is how he puts it.

He goes to pour himself a glass of cold milk and sits on the sofa. Everything about him feels weary, his legs are heavy, his back and neck are stiff. To relax, he rolls his head first up and down and then from side to side. He tries to dispel the image of the two mutilated girls in the warehouse apartment at Courbevoie. His thoughts circle some nameless fear.

"What the hell is wrong with you?" he wonders. "Get a grip!" But still his thoughts are muddled. "Take a deep breath. Think of all the horrors you have seen, all the mangled bodies you have encountered in your career—these two may be more horrifying, but they are not the first and will not be the last. Just do your job. It's a job, Camille, not a mission. You do what you can. You do your best, you find these guys, this guy, but don't let this case take over your life."

But all of a sudden the final image from his dream surfaces. On the wall, his mother has painted the face of a young girl, the face of the dead girl in Courbevoie. And the dead face comes alive; it seems to unfurl, to blossom like a flower. A dark red bloom with many petals like a chrysanthemum. Like a peony.

Camille stops dead. He is standing in the middle of the living room. He knows that something, something he cannot yet name, is happening inside him. He stands stock still. He waits, his muscles tensed, his breathing shallow, careful not to break the thread, this slender delicate thread inside him . . . Eyes closed, motionless, Camille probes this image of the girl's head nailed to the wall. But in his dream the key is not her head, it is this flower . . . There is something else . . . Camille can feel it welling within him. Still he does not move, his thoughts coming in waves and ebbing into the distance.

With each new swell, some fact moves closer.

"Shit . . . !"

The girl is a flower. But which fucking flower? Camille is wide awake now. His brain seems to be working at the speed of light. Lots of petals, like a chrysanthemum. Or a peony.

And then suddenly a word comes on this tide of thoughts, obvious, intelligible, utterly unbelievable. And Camille realizes his mistake. His dream was not about the Courbevoie murder, but the girl in Tremblay.

It's not possible, Camille thinks, but he knows that it is.

He races into his study and, cursing his clumsiness, extracts the crime scene photos from the Tremblay file. He flicks through them, looks around for his glasses but cannot find them. So he takes each photograph and holds it up to the blue light from the window. Eventually he comes to one he has been searching for. The girl's face, her smile extended from ear to ear with a razor. He thumbs through the file again and finds the photograph of the body sliced in two . . .

I don't believe it . . . , Camille thinks, glancing toward the living room.

He leaves the study and stands in front of his bookcase. As he shifts the pile of books and newspapers that have accumulated on the library stool in recent weeks, his thoughts check off each link in the chain: Gwynplaine, *The Man Who Laughs*. A woman's head, a razor smile, the woman who laughs.

And the flower is not a peony . . .

Camille clambers up the library steps, his fingers running along the spines of the books. A handful of titles by Simenon, some English writers, a few Americans: Horace McCoy and, next to him, James Hadley Chase's *The Flesh of the Orchid*.

"Not an orchid . . . ," he mutters, placing a finger on a book and tipping it toward him. "A dahlia. And certainly not red."

He slumps onto the sofa and stares at the book in his hand. On the cover is a young woman with dark hair; from her hairstyle it looks like a portrait from the 1950s. Automatically, he checks the copyright page: 1987.

On the back cover, he reads:

June 15, 1947: A naked, mutilated corpse is discovered on a patch of
waste ground in Los Angeles; the body is that of a young woman of
twenty-two: Betty Short, nicknamed "The Black Dahlia" . . .

He remembers the story fairly well. He flicks through the pages, here
and there registering a word, a sentence, and pauses on page 87:

It was the nude, mutilated body of a young woman, cut in half at the
waist. The bottom half lay in the weeds a few feet away from the top,
legs wide open. A large triangle had been gouged out of the left thigh,
and there was a long, wide cut running from the bisection point down
to the top of the pubic hair. The flaps of skin beside the gash were
pulled back; there were no organs inside. The top half was worse: the
breasts were dotted with cigarette burns, the right one hanging loose,
attached to the torso only by shreds of skin; the left one slashed around
the nipple. The cuts went all the way down to the bone, but the worst
of the worst was the girl's face.

"What are you doing . . . couldn't you sleep?"

Camille looks up; Irène is standing in the doorway in her nightdress. He puts the book down and goes to her, lays a hand on her
belly.

"Go back to bed, I'll be there in a minute."

Irène looks like a little girl woken by a nightmare.

"I'll be right there," Camille says again. "Go on, back to bed."

He watches Irène shuffle unsteadily back into the bedroom,
still thick with sleep. On the sofa, the book lies open at the page he
was reading. *It's a ridiculous idea*, he thinks. Even so, he sits down
and picks up the book again. He skims to find the passage he was
reading:

It was one huge purpled bruise, the nose crushed deep into the facial
cavity, the mouth cut ear to ear into a smile that leered up at you, somehow mocking the rest of the brutality inflicted. I knew I would carry
that smile with me to my grave.

"Jesus Christ . . ."

Camille flicks through the book, then sets it down. Closing his eyes, he sees the photograph of Manuela Constanza, the rope marks around her ankles . . .

He goes back to his reading:

. . . her jet-black hair was free of matted blood, like the killer had given her a shampoo before he dumped her.

He put the book down again. He felt the urge to go back to his study, to look more closely at the photographs. No. It was a dream . . . It was bullshit.

Wednesday, April 9

1

"Come off it, Camille, you don't really believe this nonsense?"

9 a.m. Commissaire Le Guen's office.

Camille stared for a moment at his boss's pendulous jowls, wondering what was in them that could be so heavy.

"The thing that surprises me is that no one thought of it before now. You have to admit it's unsettling."

Le Guen listened to Camille as he read on, moving from one bookmark to the next. Then he took off his glasses and set them down in front of him. When he was in Le Guen's office, Camille preferred to stand. Once, he had tried sitting on one of the armchairs facing the desk, but he felt like he was at the bottom of a well lined with pillows and had to struggle to get out again.

Le Guen turned the book over, looked at the cover, and frowned.

"Never heard of the guy."

"It's a classic, if you don't mind my saying."

"If you say so."

"Have it your own way . . . ," said Camille.

"Look, Camille, we've got enough shit on our plate as it is. Now obviously what you've just shown me is—how can I put it?—unsettling, if you like, but what is it supposed to mean?"

"It means our guy copied this book. Don't ask me why, I don't know. But it all fits. I've reread the reports. All the details that didn't make sense during the first investigation are right here. The victim's body sliced in two at the waist. Not to mention the cigarette burns and the rope marks around the ankles. At the time no one could understand why the murderer washed the victim's hair, but now it makes sense. Reread the autopsy report. People didn't understand why some of the intestines were missing—the liver, the stomach, the gall bladder . . . Well, I'll tell you why—because it's all here in this book. No one could work out why there were marks"—Camille racked his brain for the precise phrase—"'benign marks' on the body, probably made by a whip. It's his personal addition, Jean, no one knows what it means"—Camille gestured to the book on which Le Guen had firmly planted his elbow—"but it's an addition. Everything else, the shampooed hair, the missing viscera, the cigarette burns . . . it's all here in this book, every detail, in black and white."

At times Le Guen had an odd way of looking at Camille. He admired the man's intelligence, even when it went off the rails. "Can you see yourself explaining all this to Juge Deschamps?"

"Me? No . . . You, on the other hand . . ."

Le Guen gave Camille a wounded look.

"You really think so?" Le Guen leaned over and took something from the briefcase next to his desk. "After this farrago?" He held out that morning's newspaper.

Camille fished his glasses out of the breast pocket of his jacket, although he did not need them to see the photograph and read the headline. He put them on nonetheless. His heart had begun to beat faster; his hands were clammy.

2

Le Matin. The whole back page.

The photograph: a shot of Camille taken from above. He is looking up; he seems uncomfortable. The shot was probably taken during the press conference. The image has been photoshopped. Camille's face looks larger than it is, his expression seems harsher.

Beneath the section header "Profile," a headline:

PLAYING WITH THE BIG BOYS

The horrific carnage in Courbevoie recently reported in these pages has just taken a bizarre new twist. According to Juge Deschamps, the investigating magistrate, a key piece of evidence—a fake fingerprint made using a rubber stamp—links the case to another no less gruesome case from November 21, 2001, when a grim discovery was made on a landfill in Tremblay: the body of a young woman who had been tortured and then literally cut in half. The killer was never found.

For Commandant Verhœven, this is good news. As lead detective on the case, he will once again have an opportunity to prove himself an exceptional police officer. One can hardly blame him for seizing every opportunity to further gild his name.

Adopting the maxim that the less one says, the wiser one appears, Camille Verhœven has perfected the art of being tight lipped and enigmatic. Even risking leaving journalists unsatisfied. But such things matter little to Camille Verhœven, whose sole concern is his reputation as a first-rate officer. A man of action, a man who gets results.

Camille Verhœven has his principles, and he has his role models, though the latter are not to be found among his colleagues on the Quai des Orfèvres. Oh no, that would be too ordinary for a man who sees himself as extraordinary. His role models are more likely to be Sherlock Holmes, Jules Maigret, and Sam Spade. Or even Rouletabille. He enthusiastically cultivates the logic of the first, the tenacity of the second, the world-weary manner of the third and any and all of the virtues of Gaston Leroux's hero. His discretion is legendary, but those who have been able to get close to him soon realize that he aspires to mythical status.

His ambition may be overweening, but it is based on solid foundations: Camille Verhœven is a skilled professional. And a police officer whose career has been unusual.

The son of the artist Maud Verhœven, Camille once dabbled in painting himself. His father, a retired pharmacist, comments simply: "He wasn't inept . . ." What remains of his earlier vocation (a few Japanese-inspired landscapes, some painstaking, rather heavy-handed portraits) are safely filed away by his devoted father. Aware perhaps of his limitations, or finding it difficult to make a name in his own right, Camille chose instead to study law.

At the time his father hoped he might become a doctor, but young Camille did not feel it necessary to please his parents.

He studied neither art nor medicine, instead opting for a master's degree in law and graduating magna cum laude. There can be no doubt he was a brilliant scholar: he had the choice of a career in academe or being called to the bar. Instead, he decided to enroll in the *École nationale supérieure de la police*. His family are perplexed:

"It was a curious choice," his father said thoughtfully. "But Camille always was a curious boy."

Curious indeed: the young Camille confounded all expectations and succeeded against all odds. He clearly enjoys turning up where he is least expected. One imagines that the recruiting board must have needed some persuading to accept a candidate who is barely four foot eleven, requires a specially adapted vehicle, and must depend on those around him to accomplish many everyday tasks. But Camille, who knows what he wants, achieved first place in the entrance exam, and, as though this were not enough, he went on to be top of his class. It was the start of a glittering career. Already circumspect about his reputation, Camille Verhœven sought no preferential treatment; indeed he has volunteered for some of the most grueling postings in the Paris suburbs, knowing that sooner or later they would lead him to the *brigade criminelle*.

It so happened that Commissaire Le Guen, a friend with whom he worked previously, wielded considerable influence within the *brigade*. And so, after only a few years working in suburban low-end housing projects, where he is remembered as being affable, if not particularly outstanding, our hero found himself leading a team within the *brigade criminelle*, where he finally showed what he is capable of. I say "hero," because already the word was being bandied about. Who first suggested it? No one knows. But it is true that Camille Verhœven proved himself equal to the depiction. He continued to be a diligent and conscientious officer and managed to solve a number of high-profile cases. He would say little, allowing his actions to speak for him.

If Camille Verhœven tends to keep the world at arm's length, he is also content to think of himself as indispensable and enjoys cultivating an air of mystery. Both within the *brigade criminelle* and without, all that is known about him is what he is prepared to tell. Behind this facade of modesty is a shrewd man: he is only too happy to show his reticence and his discretion on national television.

Currently, he is leading the investigation into a bizarre and shocking crime that he has described as particularly "feral." No further details are forthcoming. But the word—as short, powerful, and effective as the hero himself—makes it clear that we are dealing not with routine misdemeanors but with heinous crimes. Commandant Verhœven, who understands the power of words, is a past master in the art of understatement and feigns surprise when the media time bombs he leaves in his wake explode. A month from now our hero will become a father, but his child will not be his only gift to posterity: already he is what they call "a consummate professional," the sort of man who, with infinite patience, fashions his own legend.

3

Camille folded the newspaper carefully. Le Guen was unsettled by his friend's sudden calm.

"Just let them get on with it, Camille, do you hear me?"

And, since Camille said nothing:

"You know this hack?"

"He ambushed me yesterday. I don't know anything about the guy, but he seems to know a lot about me . . ."

"He certainly doesn't seem to like you very much."

"I don't give a shit about that. What bothers me is the snow-ball effect—now every other reporter will jump on the bandwagon and-"

"And the *juge* wasn't exactly ecstatic about the TV coverage last night . . . The case is barely underway, and you're already all over the media. I know it's not your fault, but this article . . ."

Le Guen gingerly picked up the newspaper and held it at arm's length, like a sacred icon. Or a lump of dog shit.

"A full page! With your photo and everything . . ."

Camille stared at Le Guen.

"There's only one thing to be done, Camille, and you know it as well as I do—we have to solve this case, and fast. Very fast. The connection to the Tremblay case should help matters and-"

"Have you read it, the Tremblay case file?"

Le Guen scratched his cheek. "Yeah, I know, there's not much to go on."

"*Not much?* That's a euphemism. We've got fuck all. And what little we do have only complicates things. We know we're dealing with the same guy, if it is just one person, and that is far from certain. In Courbevoie, he rapes his victims every which way; in Tremblay, no signs of sexual assault—can you see the connection? In Courbevoie he dismembers the victims using a butcher's knife and an electric drill; in the earlier case he takes the trouble to wash the intestines—or at least those he left behind. Please feel free to stop me when you see a connection. In Courbevoie . . ."

"Okay, okay . . ." Le Guen sighed. "The connection between the cases may not be directly useful."

"Not directly, no."

"But that doesn't mean that this theory of yours about some book . . ." Le Guen flipped the book over again, clearly unable to remember the title. "*The Black Dahlia-*"

"No doubt you've got a more persuasive theory," Camille interrupted. "I'm all ears." He fumbled in his inside jacket pocket. "I'll take some notes if you don't mind."

"Don't mock me, Camille," Le Guen said.

The two men were silent for a moment, Le Guen staring at the cover of the book, Camille staring at his friend's furrowed brow.

Le Guen had many faults—this was something on which all his ex-wives agreed—but no one could accuse him of being stupid. In fact, in his day he had been a talented and exceptionally intelligent officer, one who—following the Peter Principle—had been promoted into an administrative role until, in due course, he rose to the level of his incompetence. The two were old friends, and it pained Camille to see him in a position in which his real talents languished. For his part, Le Guen did his best not to mourn a past when he had been so obsessed with his work that it had cost him three marriages. Camille considered the weight his friend had piled on in recent years to be a form of self-defense. He believed Le Guen was arming himself against future marriages, content merely to manage those that lay behind him, and this meant watching his salary slip through the cracks of his life.

The rules by which their arguments were conducted were well established. Le Guen, faithful to his place in the pecking order, would stonewall relentlessly until he was eventually won over by Camille's arguments. At that point, he would switch from pain in the ass to partner in crime. In either role, he was capable of anything.

This time he was hesitating. Which was not good news as far as Camille was concerned.

"Listen." Le Guen looked Camille in the eye. "I don't have a better theory. But that doesn't mean your theory is right. So you've found some book that describes a similar crime? So what? Men have been murdering women since the dawn of time, and they've run through every possible scenario. They rape them, they rip them limb from limb; I defy you to find a guy who hasn't at least thought about it. Even me, but let's not go there . . . So it's obvious that after a while you're bound to find similarities between cases. And you don't need to go ferreting about in your library, Camille; you've got the whole sad circus of humanity right in front of you."

He looked at his friend sadly.

"It's not enough, Camille. I'll do everything I can to support you, but I'm warning you now that for Juge Deschamps it won't be enough."

4

"James Ellroy. Well, obviously it's a little unexpected . . ."

"That's all you've got to say?"

"No, no," Louis protested, "I agree, it is a little . . ."

". . . unsettling? Yes, I know, that's what Le Guen said. He even elaborated a brilliant theory about men killing women since the dawn of time . . . you get the picture. I don't give a damn about that."

Leaning in the doorway to the office, hands stuffed in his pockets, Maleval was sporting a wearier-than-usual version of his morning face, though it was not yet ten o'clock. Armand, scarcely visible against the coat rack, was staring thoughtfully at his shoes. Louis, sitting behind the desk since Camille had asked him to read the relevant passages, was wearing a lightweight green linen jacket, a pale cream shirt, and a club tie.

Louis's approach to reading was rather different from the *commissaire's*. When Camille gestured to his chair, Louis settled himself comfortably and read fluently, his hand resting on the facing page. The pose reminded Camille of a painting, but he could not remember which.

"What made you think of *The Black Dahlia*?"

"Difficult to say."

"So you think that the Tremblay murder was a homage to the book?"

"A *homage*? The words you come out with . . . He cuts the girl in two, he guts her, he washes both halves of the body, shampoos her hair, and then dumps the corpse on a landfill! If this is his idea of homage, I'd hate to see what happens when this guy starts writing his own parts."

"No, what I meant was . . ." Louis blushed furiously. Camille looked at the other members of the team. Louis had begun reading in a calm voice gradually distorted by the nature of the text. By the final pages, his voice had dropped so low they had to strain to hear him. No one seemed particularly voluble, and Camille wondered if this was because of the text itself or because of his theory. An awkward silence lingered in the office.

Verhœven suddenly realized that the atmosphere might have less to do with his theory than with the fact that, like him, everyone on the team had read the article in *Le Matin*. Copies had probably already done the rounds of the *brigade* and the *police judiciaire*, infiltrated the office of Juge Deschamps and even the ministry itself. Gossip spread of its own accord, like a cancerous cell. What were his team thinking? What had they inferred or deduced? Their silence was not a good sign. If they were sympathetic, they would have mentioned it. If they were indifferent, they would have forgotten it. Saying nothing meant they did not know what to think. That it had been a full-page profile, while certainly not flattering, was good publicity. Did they believe he had been aware of the piece, had actively contributed to it? There had been no mention of his team. Complimentary or otherwise, the article had talked only about Camille Verhœven, the man of the moment, and now here he was with his crackpot theories. The world around him seemed to have disappeared, and that disappearance was met with a silence that was neither censorious nor indifferent. It was merely disappointed.

"It's possible," Maleval ventured cautiously.

"But what could it mean?" Armand said. "I mean, what does any of this have to do with what we found in Courbevoie?"

"I've no idea, Armand! We've got an eighteen-month-old murder case in which every detail seems to come out of a book, that's all I know."

When this was greeted with a resounding silence, Camille added, "You're right, it's a stupid idea."

"So," Maleval said. "What do we do now?"

"We go and get a woman's point of view."

5

"I have to agree, it is curious . . ."

Bizarrely, on the phone Juge Deschamps's voice did not have the skeptical tone Camille had been expecting. She said the words as though she were thinking aloud.

"If you're right," the *juge* went on, "the Courbevoie murder should also show up in Ellroy's book, or in some other novel. It's worth checking . . ."

"Not necessarily," Camille said. "Ellroy's book is inspired by a real murder case. A young woman called Betty Short was murdered in precisely this way in 1947, and the novel is a fictionalized account of a case that would have been notorious in America. He dedicated the book to his mother, who was murdered in 1958 . . . There are a number of possibilities . . ."

"Yes, that does throw a different light on things."

The *juge* took a moment to think.

"Listen," she said at last, "there's a risk that the *procureur's* office won't take this lead seriously. I agree that several details in the two cases tally, but I can hardly suggest a bunch of hard-nosed detectives read the collected works of James Ellroy and turn the *brigade criminelle* into a reading room ..."

"No, indeed," Camille agreed, realizing that he had had no illusions as to her response.

Juge Deschamps was fundamentally a good person. From her tone of voice Camille could tell she was disappointed not to be able to suggest something further.

"Look, if this theory is backed up later by other evidence, then we'll see, but right now I'd be grateful if you could pursue ... more traditional lines of inquiry, do you understand?"

"I understand."

"You have to admit that these are ... exceptional circumstances. If it were just you and me, we might use this theory as the possible basis for the investigation, but we're no longer alone ..."

"Here it comes," Camille thought. His stomach was in knots. Not because he was scared, but because he was afraid of being hurt. Twice now he had been blindsided. First when the boys from *identité* had had the dumb idea of carrying out body bags right in front of a mob of journalists, and the second time by one of those journalists who had wormed his way into Camille's private life at just the wrong moment. Camille didn't much like being a victim; he didn't much like denying blatant fuck-ups when he made them, which meant right now he didn't much like what was happening, as though suddenly he'd been sidelined. No one—not Le Guen, not the *juge*, not even his team—gave his theory any credence. But Camille felt strangely relieved at not having to follow up a lead that was so far beyond the scope of his usual procedure. No, what hurt were those things he could not talk about. The words from Buisson's article for *Le Matin* still rang in his head. Someone had been poking their nose into his private life, someone who had talked to his wife, to his relatives; someone had mentioned Maud Verhœven, had talked about his childhood, his studies, his sketches, had told the world that he was about to be a father ... This, he felt, was grossly unfair.

At around 11:30 a.m., Camille took a call from Louis.

"Where are you?" Camille asked, irritably.

"Porte de la Chapelle."

"What the hell are you doing there?"

"Paying a little visit to Séfarini."

Camille knew Gustave Séfarini—he ran a "multi-client advisory service." He advised gangsters about easy targets in exchange for a small consideration. In the planning stages of major crimes, Séfarini did location scouting and his talents had earned him a reputation; he was the archetypal gentleman thug. After twenty years in the game, his police record was almost as pure as his love for his disabled daughter Adèle. He doted on the girl, and his selfless devotion to her was touching—if such a word could apply to a man who had spent twenty years organizing armed robberies that had left four people dead.

"If you've got a minute, it would be useful if you could stop by."

"Is it urgent?" Camille checked his watch.

"Yes, it's urgent, and I don't think it will take too long."

6

Séfarini lived in a little house overlooking the Périphérique; its filthy front garden vibrated constantly under the twin assaults of the eight-lane superhighway and the *métro* line that ran directly beneath its foundations. From the state of the house, and the beat-up Peugeot 306 parked outside, you had to wonder where Séfarini's money went.

Camille walked right in as though he owned the place.

He found Louis and his host in the 1960s Formica kitchen, sitting at a table covered with a wipe-clean tablecloth whose pattern had long since been worn away, sipping coffee from Duralex mugs. Séfarini did not seem particularly happy to see Camille. Louis, for his part, did not react, but went on toying with a mug whose contents he clearly had no desire to drink.

"So what's going on?" Camille said, pulling up the only empty chair.

"Well, as I was just saying to our friend Gustave here," Louis said, staring hard at Séfarini, "it's about his daughter, Adèle."

"Oh, yes," said Camille. "Where is Adèle, by the way?"

Séfarini gestured to the first floor with a mournful glance, then looked down at the tablecloth.

"I was just telling him," Louis went on, "that there have been rumors."

"Uh-huh," Camille ventured warily.

"I'm afraid so . . . Gossip is a terrible thing. I was just telling our friend that we're worried about Adèle. Very worried." Louis shot Camille a look. "There's been talk of inappropriate behavior, of abuse, of incest . . . Though I hasten to add that we lend no credence to these persistent rumors."

"Of course not . . ." Camille was beginning to see where Louis was going with this.

"But even if we don't believe them," Louis said, "Social Services may take a different view. After all, we know Gustave, we know he's a good father, but what can they do? They've had letters."

"Letters like that can screw up a man's whole life."

"You're the ones trying to screw me!" Séfarini shouted.

"Now, now, Gustave!" Camille said. "When you've got children, you need to learn to mind your language, for fuck's sake!"

"So, anyway"—Louis's voice was sorrowful—"I was in the area and I thought, why don't I pop in and have a quiet word with Gustave, who, by the way, is friends with Lard-Ass Lambert . . . And, I was just explaining to Gustave, Adèle would have to be taken into care. Until his name was cleared. I mean, it's no big deal; it shouldn't take more than a couple of months. I'm not sure they'd get to spend Christmas together, but maybe if we put in a good word . . ."

Camille's antennae began to quiver.

"Come on, Gustave, why don't you tell Commandant Verhœven everything. I'm sure there must be something he can do for Adèle—right, boss?"

Camille nodded, "I'm sure we can work something out."

During this exchange Séfarini's dim intellect had been working overtime. He kept his head down, but his brow creased and his eyes darted about as he racked his brain.

"Go on, Gustave, tell us about Lard-Ass Lambert . . ."

So Séfarini told him all about the holdup in the Toulouse shopping center that had taken place on the same day Manuela Constanza was murdered in Tremblay-en-France. Hardly surprising . . . after all, he was the one who had spotted the loopholes in the security system, drawn up the plans, and managed the operation.

"Why should I care about any of this?" Camille said.

"Because Lambert wasn't there. I know that for a fact."

"Lambert must have had a motive for confessing to a crime he had nothing to do with. A pretty powerful motive."

Standing on the footpath beside their cars, the two men stared out at the bleak landscape. Louis's cell rang.

"That was Maleval," said Louis when he had hung up. "Lambert's been out on parole for the past two weeks."

"We have to move fast. We have to move now."

"I'm on it," Louis said, keying a number into his phone.

7

Rue Delage, number 16, fifth floor, no elevator. How would his father manage a few years from now, when Death began to prowl? It was a question that often occurred to Camille, and he always shrugged it off, clinging to the hope—the fantasy—that it would never come to pass.

The stairwell smelled of polish. Camille's father had spent his whole life in a dispensary that smelled of drugs and medicines; his mother smelled of turpentine and linseed oil. Camille distinguished his parents by their smell.

He felt sad and weary. What did he have to say to his father? Was there anything to be said, or was it enough to watch him live his life, keep him close like some talisman whose true purpose will forever remain mysterious?

After his wife's death, Camille's father sold their apartment and moved to the twelfth arrondissement, near Bastille, where he discreetly and conscientiously cultivated the manner of a modern widower, a subtle combination of structure and solitude. His father opened the door, and, as usual, the two men embraced awkwardly.

Their awkwardness was due to the fact that, contrary to the norm, this father was still taller than his son.

A peck on the cheek. The smell of *boeuf bourguignon.*

"I bought a *bourguignon* . . ."

His father was a master at stating the obvious. They sat opposite each other, sipping an aperitif. Camille invariably sat in the same spot, set his glass of fruit juice down on the coffee table, folded his arms, and asked, "So, how have you been?"

"So," said Camille, "how have you been?"

The moment he stepped into the room, Camille had noticed a copy of *Le Matin* lying on the floor next to his father's armchair.

"About the article, Camille"—his father nodded to the newspaper—"I can't tell you how sorry I am . . ."

"Don't worry about it"

"The reporter just showed up. I tried to call you."

"I'm sure you did, Papa; don't worry, it doesn't matter."

". . . but your phone was engaged. And we got talking and he really seemed to like you, so I wasn't suspicious. I'm going to write a letter to his editor! I'm going to demand a right of reply!"

"Don't be silly, Papa, there's nothing in the article that isn't true. The most he could be accused of is a skewed point of view. Legally speaking, a right of reply is very different. Honestly, let it go."

He almost added "You've done enough damage already" but bit his tongue. His father seemed to sense the reproach.

"I'm sorry . . . This whole thing is bound to cause trouble for you . . . ," he muttered and fell silent.

Unsure whether his father was apologizing for the trouble his thoughtlessness had caused or for being gullible enough to be taken in by the reporter, Camille simply smiled and changed the subject.

"So, I hope you're planning to stick around to meet your grandson?"

"You really seem determined to wind me up . . ."

"It's not me, it's the ultrasound . . . And if you're going to be angry just because we're having a boy, you're not much of a father."

"No," his father protested, "I'm happy. I'm happy for you both. It's just that—I don't know why—but I got it into my head that I was going to have a granddaughter. Maybe it's because it's been so long since there's been a woman in my life."

Camille had a sneaking suspicion that there *was* a woman in his father's life. For some years now, he had been going out more often; he would go away for several days and was always evasive about the reasons for these trips. Camille had long since assumed his father was seeing someone.

"What are you going to call him?" his father asked.

"We're not sure. We talk about it, argue about it; we make up our minds and then change them . . ."

"Your mother named you after Pissarro. And she loved the name long after she stopped loving the artist."

"I know," Camille said.

"We'll talk about you later; first tell me how Irène is."

"I think she's getting bored, being stuck at home."

"It'll be over soon . . . I thought she looked tired."

"When?"

"She dropped by last week. I felt ashamed. Given her condition, I should have been the one to make the effort, but you know me, I never seem to get out of here. Anyway, she just popped round unannounced."

Camille pictured Irène struggling up the four flights of stairs, stopping at every landing to catch her breath, hands clasped over her swollen belly. Her impromptu visit was more than it seemed; it was a message to him, a reproach. By visiting his father, she was supporting Camille, while he had not been supporting her. He wanted to call her right away but realized that he didn't want to apologize; he simply wanted to share his pain, to tell her how he felt. He loved Irène more than life itself, and the more he blundered and failed to show that love, the more it pained him.

The polite ritual followed its usual course until Camille's father, with feigned casualness, said:

"Kaufman . . . do you remember Kaufman?"

"Pretty well, yes."

"He came to see me a couple of weeks ago."

"Must have been quite some time since you saw him last."

"Yes, I only saw him once or twice after your mother's death."

A vague, almost imperceptible shudder ran through Camille. The sudden panic he felt was caused not by the mention of one of his mother's artist friends—a man whose work he had always admired—but by the tone of his father's voice. There was something embarrassed, something forced about his studied indifference.

"So what did he want?" Camille said encouragingly, seeing his father dither.

"Listen, Camille, if it were up to me, I wouldn't even mention it. But he insisted I talk to you." His father's voice rose as though defending himself against an accusation.

"Go on."

"I'd say no, but it's not entirely my decision to make . . . Kaufman is giving up his studio. His lease isn't up for renewal, but the place is too small for him—he's working on large canvases these days."

"And . . ."

"And he asked if we were planning to sell your mother's."

Camille had always feared this moment would come, but perhaps because he so dreaded the idea, he had grown used to it.

"I know what you're going to say, and–"

"No," Camille interrupted him, "you don't know."

"All right, then, I don't. But I can guess. In fact I told Kaufman you would never agree to the idea."

"But you brought up the subject anyway . . ."

"I'm talking to you about it because I promised him I would! And, anyway, I thought, given the circumstances . . ."

"What circumstances?"

"Kaufman is offering a fair price. With a baby on the way you might be thinking of moving, getting a bigger place, I don't know . . ."

Camille was surprised by his own reaction.

Monfort was a hamlet, the last vestige of a village that had once stood on the edge of Clamart forest. These days, the area was ringed by housing developments and grandiose mansions, and the forest no longer felt like the untamed wilderness Camille had known when he had gone there with his mother as a child. The studio was the old gatehouse of an estate that, through the mismanagement of a succession of heirs, had gradually disappeared until all that remained was this lodge. His mother had knocked through all the partition walls to create one big space, and Camille had spent long afternoons there watching her work, in the swirling fumes of paint and white spirit, sometimes sketching on a little table she had set up for him next to the wood stove, which, in winter, radiated a heavy, sweet-smelling heat.

The studio itself had little charm. The walls were whitewashed, the terracotta tiles on the floor wobbled underfoot, and the glass roof through which light streamed was covered in grime for much of the time. Now, once a year, Camille's father would air the place; he would try to dust, but he would quickly lose heart and sit in the middle of the studio like a castaway, gazing around him at these few relics of a wife he had loved dearly.

Camille remembered the last time he had been there. Irène had always wanted to see Maud's studio but, sensing his reluctance, had not insisted. Then one day, passing near Monfort as they drove back from a weekend away, Camille had suddenly asked: "Do you want to see the studio?"

In fact, as they both knew, it was Camille who wanted to go there, so they made the detour. To ensure the place was secure and the garden kept tidy, Camille's father paid a small stipend to a neighbor, who nevertheless evidently did not do much. Camille and Irène stepped around the clumps of nettles and, with the key that had been kept under the flower pot for years, opened the door, which creaked dully.

Stripped of its furniture, the studio seemed bigger than ever. Irène poked around casually, merely glancing at Camille if she wanted to turn over a canvas or take a painting to the large picture window to see it in the light. Camille simply sat, unwittingly, in the very spot where his father sat when he came here alone. Irène commented on the paintings with a precision that surprised Camille and stared for a long time at one of Maud's later works, a composition of dark reds hurled onto the canvas with a sort of fury. She was holding it at arm's length, and Camille could only see the back of it. In her large, open hand, Maud had written in chalk "Savage Pain."

One of the few paintings to which she had ever given a title.

As she set the canvas down, Irène saw that Camille was crying. She wrapped her arms around him and held him for a long time.

He had not been back to the studio since.

"I'll think about it," Camille said at last.

"Whatever you like," his father said draining his cup. "The money will go to you in any case. For your son."

Camille's cell phone chirruped—a text message from Louis: *Lambert not in his lair. Stake out? Louis.*

"I have to go," Camille said, getting to his feet.

His father gave him the same surprised look he always did, apparently astonished that time had passed so quickly. But for Camille it was always the same: at some point a signal would go off in his head. Once it did, he found he could not sit still; he had to leave, had to get out of there.

"That thing with the reporter . . . ," his father said, getting up.

"Don't worry about it."

The two men embraced, and moments later Camille was in the street. Looking up, he was not surprised to see his father leaning over the balcony and giving that little wave. Sometimes Camille reflected that one day he would see it for the last time.

8

Camille called Louis.

"We've found out a bit more about Lambert," Louis said. "He went straight home as soon as he was released on parole. That was on the second. From talking to his associates, he seemed in good spirits. One of his cronies, Mourad, a snot-nosed kid who deals drugs for him in Clichy, said that Lambert was planning a trip; he was due to leave on Tuesday. One of his henchmen, Daniel Royet, was supposed to be going with him. We haven't been able to track him down either. Since then, there's been no news. I've arranged for a twenty-four-hour watch on Lambert's place."

"Gustave had better keep his head down. We've got two days to figure this out. After that, Lambert is likely to disappear for a long time . . ."

They discussed the teams who would stake out places where Lambert was likely to show up. Two key locations had been identified. By some miracle—or by dint of being nagged—Le Guen, who knew Camille did not have the resources to cover the operation, provisionally assigned two teams, which Louis was tasked with coordinating.

9

He set the pile of books on his desk: *Brown's Requiem, Clandestine, Killer on the Road,* then *Suicide Hill, Dick Contino's Blues*; then the L.A. Quartet: *The Black Dahlia, The Big Nowhere, L.A. Confidential,* and *White Jazz*; lastly, *American Tabloid.*

He picked one up at random. *White Jazz.* It was not an entirely random choice. On the cover was the portrait of a woman resembling the one on *The Black Dahlia.* Her style and general appearance were similar, though on *White Jazz* the face was rounder, the hair fuller, the makeup heavier, and the model was wearing earrings. Abandoning the more spontaneous style he had adopted on *The Black Dahlia,* the illustrator had opted for a slightly sleazy Hollywood vamp. Camille had not previously considered whether his three victims looked alike. Though it was not too hard to draw comparisons between Évelyne Rouvray and Josiane Debeuf in Courbevoie, what could they possibly have in common with little Manuela Constanza in Tremblay?

On his desk blotter he scrawled three words, added "Louis," and underlined them twice.

"It seems rather an arduous task . . ."

Arduous? . . . Louis's use of vocabulary was a mystery to Camille.

"That's your pile," he said. "This one here is mine."

"Ah."

"We're looking for a scene with a large apartment, two women who have been raped and dismembered. We should be able to skim-read."

The early books had a somewhat "classic" feel. Private detectives, their desks piled high with unpaid bills, moldered in grubby offices sipping coffee and munching doughnuts. Out of the blue, crazed killers unleashed their psychopathic tendencies. But gradually the style evolved; it became more savage, more visceral as Ellroy began to trade in inhumanity at its most elemental. The seediest districts of the city became a metaphor for a desperate, disillusioned humanity. Love took on the acrid taste of urban tragedy. Sadism, violence, cruelty, the dregs of our wildest fantasies were made flesh, and with them came injustice, revenge, women battered, and bloody murders.

The afternoon flew past.

As he grew tired, Camille was tempted to skim the few hundred pages remaining, hunting only for certain key words and phrases . . . but which words, which phrases? He quickly abandoned this idea. How many times had he seen an investigation drag on or founder because procedures had been hurried or were insufficiently systematic? How many anonymous killers owed their freedom to the carelessness of weary officers?

Every hour, Camille stepped out of his office and, on the way to the coffee machine, paused in the doorway of Louis's office and watched him poring over the books with the diligence of a theology student. Neither of them said a word; a look was enough for each to confirm that what had seemed such a promising lead was now a dead end, that what few notes they had would likely prove irrelevant when the passages were reread, that in all likelihood this would still be the case when the books and the men were exhausted.

Camille made notes on slips of blank paper. The tally was profoundly depressing. A teenage girl asphyxiated with a pair of panties
soaked in acetone; a naked woman hung by her feet above her bed;
another dismembered with a hacksaw after being shot through the
heart; a third who was raped and then stabbed to death . . . A universe of carnage, peopled by impulsive psychopaths, shady deals,
and old scores settled in ways that seemed utterly different from
the methodical work of whoever had committed the murders in
Courbevoie and Tremblay. The only unsettling parallel was the one
Camille had first noticed, but there was a yawning gap between the
way the Tremblay murder precisely mirrored the scene in *The Black
Dahlia* and the vague similarities he had found in certain passages
to elements of the Courbevoie killings.

Louis had drawn up his own list. When he appeared in Camille's
office to go through their findings, Camille shot him a questioning
look and immediately realized Louis had fared no better than he.
He glanced at the notepad on which Louis, in his ornate handwriting, had jotted down his thoughts: gunshot wounds, stab wounds,
knuckledusters, rapes, another hanging . . .

"Okay," Camille said. "I think we're done here."

10

At six o'clock, the team reassembled in Camille's office for the final briefing of the day.

"Who wants to start?" Camille said.

The three men looked at each other. Camille heaved a sigh.

"Louis, you go first."

"We've had a quick look through a number of other novels by James Ellroy, because the *patron* here thinks . . ." He bit his tongue. "Sorry."

"Two things, Louis," said Camille with a smile. "First, since I am your *'patron,'* thanks for correcting yourself—you know how I feel about that word. Second, as far as the books are concerned, try and make it sound positive."

"Fine," Louis said, returning the smile. "To put it simply, we've been through pretty much the complete works of James Ellroy and have found nothing to substantiate the theory that the murders are being copied from his books. Is that okay?"

"Perfect. Louis, you're a gentleman. I would add that we both wasted half a day on that theory. And it's bullshit. I think that covers it . . ."

The three men smiled.

"Come on then, Maleval, what have you got for us?"

"What have you got if you haven't even got 'nothing'?"

"Nothingness?" Louis said.

"Nada?" chimed in Armand.

"Okay," said Maleval, "in that case, I have a nothingness of nada. The faux cowhide has no label that would allow us to trace where it was bought or made. The black-and-white wallpaper in the bathroom did not come from a French factory. I'm expecting a list of the main foreign manufacturers tomorrow morning. There'll be five hundred at the very least. I'll try an international search, but I'm guessing our guy didn't buy the wallpaper in person and hand over a copy of his I.D."

"You're right, it's not very likely," said Camille. "Next?"

"At the Mercure hotel where Évelyne Rouvray first met her client—the man who would kill her—the room was paid for in cash. No one remembers anything. As for forensics, the lab hasn't managed to decipher the serial numbers on the stereo, the TV, the CD player, and so forth. The makes and models are commonplace; hundreds of thousands of these things have been sold. The trail stops there."

"Right. Anything else?"

"One more dead end, just for a change . . ."

"Go on . . ."

"The video is a clip from an American weekly TV show that's been running on U.S. 9GAG for the past ten years. It's a popular program. The clip on the tape was broadcast four years ago."

"How did you find out?"

"I called TF1, they bought French rights. The show is so shit they stopped running it, but they sometimes use the best clips to plug gaps in programming. The one of the dog peeling an orange was broadcast last on February 7. Our man might have recorded it then. As for the matchbook, it's obviously a mock-up. The blank matchbook itself is standard issue; you can get them at any tobacconist. *Le Palio*'s logo was added using a generic color printer, four hundred thousand of which have been sold in France. The paper used is widely available, as is the glue."

"Sounds like the name of a club . . ."

"Probably, or a bar. Anyway, it's irrelevant."

"You're right. It'll get us nowhere."

"That's about the size of it."

"That's not quite true," Louis said without looking up from his notepad.

Maleval and Armand turned to look at him. Camille stared at his feet and said:

"Louis is right. It is relevant. In the staging of the crime scene, it falls into a different category. There are two types of clue: those commercially produced objects whose source we are unable to trace, and those that were carefully and deliberately created as set dressing. It's a bit like your Japanese sofa," he said, glancing at Armand.

Caught unawares, Armand fumbled for his notepad.

"Yes, I suppose, except that we haven't managed to identify this Dunford guy. Bogus name, payment by money order, delivery to a self-storage warehouse in Gennevilliers in the name of . . ." He flicked through the pages. "Peace. And then the trail goes cold."

"Peace?" Maleval muttered. "As in 'world peace'? Our guy must think he's a comedian."

"Hilarious," Camille said.

"But why does our man use foreign names?" Louis said. "It is a little strange . . ."

"My guess is that our man's a snob," Maleval said.

"So, what else?" Camille said.

"What we found out about the magazine is a little more interesting. Though only a little . . . It's the March issue of *GQ*, a British men's magazine . . ."

"American," Louis corrected.

Armand checked his pad.

"You're right, it is American."

"And in what sense is that interesting?" Camille said irritably.

"The American edition is sold by a very few English bookshops in Paris. I phoned three of them and got lucky. About three weeks ago a man ordered a back issue from Brentano's on the avenue de l'Opéra, specifically the March issue."

Armand went back over his notes, clearly determined to give a blow-by-blow account of his investigation.

"Keep it short, Armand," Camille said, "keep it short."

"Hang on. Right, the woman at the bookshop is certain that it was ordered by a man. He came in on a Saturday afternoon, their busiest time. He ordered the magazine and paid cash in advance. The girl doesn't remember any identifying features; 'a man' is all she would say. A week later—same day, same time—he came back to pick it up. The girl working that weekend doesn't remember him at all."

"Well, that's handy," Maleval said.

"The contents of the suitcase haven't turned up much either," Armand said, "though we're still making inquiries. Although they're all designer brands, and expensive, they're pretty common, so unless we have a stroke of luck . . ."

Camille suddenly remembered something.

"Louis . . . what's his name, you know, the guy . . . ?"

Louis, who seemed to be able to follow Camille's line of thought the way a hound follows a scent, said, "Haynal, Jean Haynal. There's no record of him in our files. I did a search, but I'll spare you the details. All the Jean Haynals we've been able to trace are either the wrong age, or they're dead, or they left Paris a long time ago. We're still working on it, but I don't hold out much hope."

"Okay," Camille said.

The results of their inquiries were pretty threadbare, but they had one lead: the absence of clues and the meticulousness with which the scene had been staged were themselves clues. Camille was persuaded that sooner or later, these various leads would converge and that unlike most cases, in which the picture becomes clearer, like a photograph in a developing bath, this one would be different. Everything would suddenly fall into place. It was simply a matter of perseverance.

"Louis," he said, "I want you to try and find a connection between the two women in Courbevoie and the girl in Tremblay, places where they might have hung out, perhaps without actually having met, any relationships they had in case they had a mutual acquaintance . . . you know the kind of thing . . ."

"Okay." Louis jotted it down.

All three notepads were snapped shut simultaneously.

"See you all tomorrow," Camille said.

The three men filed out of the office.

Louis reappeared a few moments later. He carried in the pile of books he had been working on and set them on his boss's desk.

"Pity, isn't it?" Camille said, grinning.

"Yes, a real shame. It was such an elegant theory . . ."

Then, just as he was leaving again, he turned back to Camille.

"But then, maybe the cases we deal with are not as elegantly plotted as fiction . . ."

"Maybe not," Camille thought.

Thursday, April 10

1

"I don't think the *juge* is going to like it, Camille."

CRIME IMITATES ART

Courbevoie–Tremblay

Juge Deschamps, investigating magistrate in the double murder committed in Courbevoie, has revealed that a fake fingerprint found at the crime scene links the killing to the murder of Manuela Constanza, a 24-year-old prostitute whose mutilated body, hacked in two, was discovered on a landfill. It would appear that Commandant Verhœven, the officer in charge of the case, is dealing with a serial killer. However, this new information, which should theoretically have made solving the cases easier, seems to have made it more complex. The first surprise is the killer's modus operandi. Usually, serial killers dispatch their victims in the same way, but the details of the two cases show no similarity. In fact, the manner in which the women have been killed is so dissimilar that one cannot but wonder whether the fake fingerprint found in Courbevoie is a red herring.

Unless there is some other explanation, one in which the disparities between the killings are precisely what connects them. That at least seems to be the theory of Commandant Verhœven, who has suggested a startling link between the Tremblay murder and an American crime novel by James Ellroy. In the novel . . .

Camille threw the paper down.

"Fucking hell!"

He reopened it and turned to the last paragraph of the article.

It is probably safe to assume that, despite these unsettling similarities, Verhœven's somewhat cerebral theory is unlikely to find favor with famously pragmatic Juge Deschamps. Right now, and in the absence of hard evidence, Commandant Verhœven should perhaps be focusing on leads that are less fictitious.

2

"The guy's an asshole."

"Maybe, but he's a well-informed asshole."

Le Guen, lolling in his vast armchair like a beached sperm whale, stared hard at Camille.

"What do you think?"

"I'm not sure. But I don't like it."

"Deschamps isn't exactly thrilled either," Le Guen said. "She called first thing this morning."

Camille shot his friend a questioning look.

"She's reasonably calm. She's seen it all before. She knows it's not your fault. But you know how it is, shit like this will get to everyone eventually."

Camille knew only too well. Before coming to see Le Guen, he had gone to his office. Half a dozen newspapers, several radio stations, and three TV channels had already requested confirmation of the details published in *Le Matin*. While waiting for his boss to arrive, Louis—in a smart gray suit, matching shirt, and pale yellow socks—had been forced to play receptionist, fielding inquiries with

a very British stiff upper lip and pushing his hair back—left hand—
every twenty seconds.

"Get in here!" Camille said in a low growl.

Ten seconds later, Maleval and Armand trotted into his office.
Sticking out of Maleval's jacket pocket was a copy of *Paris-Turf*, odds
already scrawled in the margins in green ballpoint pen. Armand
was clutching a carefully folded sheet of paper and an IKEA pencil.
Camille did not look up. The atmosphere was explosive.

Camille opened the newspaper at page four.

"We are dealing with a reporter who seems to be *very* well
informed," he snarled. "This is going to make our work a little more
complicated."

Maleval had not yet read the article. But Camille was pretty sure
Armand would have seen it. He knew Armand's routine: he left
home every morning with half an hour to spare, then sat on the
station platform keeping an eye on three wastepaper baskets. Every
time a passenger threw away a newspaper, Armand would get up,
check which paper it was, then sit down again. Armand was very
particular about his reading matter: he only read *Le Matin*. For the
crossword.

Maleval gave a low whistle as he tossed the paper onto the desk.

"That's one way of putting it," Camille said. "Now, I know there
are a lot of people working on this case: the forensics team, the
lab technicians, the *juge*'s assistants . . . the leak could have come
from anywhere. But I need you all to be extra careful. Am I making
myself clear?"

He immediately regretted the question, which hung in the air
like an accusation.

"All I'm asking is that you do what I do: keep your mouths shut."

The team mumbled their agreement.

"No news on Lambert?" Camille asked in what he hoped was a
conciliatory tone.

"We haven't got very far," Louis said. "We've been asking around,
but discreetly so as not to alert his friends. We've managed to

confirm that he left town, but so far we have no idea where he might have been heading."

Camille thought for a moment.

"If we don't turn up something in the next couple of days, we'll round up his known associates, see if we can't get to the bottom of this. Maleval, I need you to draw up a list in case we need it."

3

Camille glanced at the pile of Ellroy novels and heaved a sigh. On his desk blotter, in a blank space between the countless sketches he'd made—because drawing helped him to think—he wrote: *Tremblay—Black Dahlia—Ellroy.*

As he tried to concentrate on what he had just written, his eyes fell on another book, one he had bought from the Librairie de Paris and promptly forgotten: *Themes and Tropes in Crime Fiction.* He turned it over and read the back cover:

The detective novel was long considered a minor genre. More than a century passed before critics were prepared to mention it alongside "real" literature. Its relegation to the ranks of marginal writing owed much to what readers, authors, and editors thought literature was supposed to be and therefore to normative cultural values, but it is widely believed that the genre was also dismissed because of its subject matter: crime. This popular fallacy—as old as the genre itself—seems to ignore the privileged position accorded to murder and detection in literary works by Dostoevsky and Faulkner, in medieval literature and in François Mauriac. In fiction, crime is as old as love.

"It's excellent," the bookseller had said when he noticed Camille leafing through the book. "Ballanger is a real connoisseur, an expert. It's a pity he never wrote anything else."

Camille stared out of the window for a long minute. What did he have to lose? He glanced at his watch and picked up his telephone.

4

From the outside, the university looked a little like a hospital where no one would want to be treated. From floor to floor the signage gradually petered out, and the Department of Modern Literature was apparently lost in a labyrinth of corridors plastered with lecture schedules and posters soliciting support for various marginalized communities.

Luckily, information on "The Detective Novel: Noir Fiction," the course offered by Fabien Ballanger, occupied a niche at the bottom of the notice board, the perfect height for Camille.

He spent half an hour looking for the room where the class was taught to some thirty students he chose not to disturb, and a further half hour finding the vast student canteen, ripe with the smell of weed. He returned to the lecture room in time to take his place in the line of students waiting to talk to a tall, thin man who answered them laconically while constantly rummaging in a black briefcase stuffed with papers. A few students were chatting in small groups, talking so loudly that Camille had to raise his voice to be heard.

"Commandant Verhœven. I phoned earlier . . ."

Ballanger glanced down at Camille and stopped rummaging in his briefcase. He was wearing a baggy gray cardigan. Even when he was still, he seemed harried and anxious, the kind of man who is constantly engrossed in his own thoughts. He frowned to indicate that he remembered no such call.

"Commandant Verhœven. Of the *brigade criminelle*?"

Ballanger glanced around the room as though looking for someone.

"I don't have much time," he mumbled.

"I'm investigating the deaths of three young women, all of whom were dismembered, so I'm a little pushed for time myself."

Ballanger looked at him again.

"I don't see what I can possibly-"

"If you could give me a few minutes of your time," Camille interrupted, "I'll explain."

Ballanger pushed up the sleeves of his cardigan the way someone else might adjust their glasses. At length he smiled begrudgingly; it was a facial expression that clearly did not seem to come easy to him.

"Very well. Give me ten minutes."

Ballanger reemerged only three minutes later to find Camille still waiting in the corridor.

"I can spare a quarter of an hour," he said, shaking Camille's hand as though they had only just met. He strode down the hall, and Camille had to jog to keep up. Ballanger stopped at his office door, extracted a bunch of keys from his pocket, and methodically opened the three locks.

"We've had our computers stolen," he said. "Twice last year."

He ushered Camille inside. Three desks, computer monitors, a few bookshelves, and a deathlike hush. Ballanger gestured to a chair, then took a seat facing Camille and studied him in silence.

"A few days ago, the bodies of two young women were discovered in an apartment in Courbevoie. We have very little to go on. We know that the victims were tortured, sexually abused, and dismembered..."

"Yes, I heard something about the case," Ballanger said.

His chair pushed away from his desk, his elbows resting on his splayed knees, Ballanger's gaze was solicitous, supportive, as though he were trying to encourage Camille to make some particularly painful confession.

"We've linked the crime to an earlier case. The murder of a young woman whose body was found on a landfill, sliced in two at the waist. Does that ring any bells?"

Ballanger suddenly sat bolt upright, the color draining from his face.

"Should it?" he blustered.

"No, don't worry," said Camille, "I'm here to talk to you as a *professeur*, not as a suspect."

Human relationships can be like train tracks: when they diverge, it takes a switch point before the two can once again run parallel. Ballanger felt threatened; Camille offered a change of course.

"You may have heard something about the murder. November 2001, in Tremblay-en-France."

"I rarely read newspapers," Ballanger said.

Camille could feel the man's tension.

"I don't see what I could possibly have to do with two-"

"Nothing at all, Professeur Ballanger; don't worry. I came to see you because I believe the two crimes could be connected—though this is only a theory, you understand—with crimes from detective novels."

"How, exactly?"

"We don't know *exactly*. The Tremblay murder is eerily similar to one described by James Ellroy in *The Black Dahlia*."

"That's original!"

Camille could not tell whether Ballanger's reaction was one of relief or astonishment.

"You're familiar with the novel?"

"Of course. But what makes you think that-"

"I cannot go into detail about the investigation. Our theory is that the two crimes are linked. Since the first murder seems to have been directly inspired by Ellroy's book, we were wondering whether the others . . ."

"... might have been drawn from some other book by Ellroy!"

"No—we've checked, and that doesn't seem to be the case. I think the crimes might have been taken from some other novel. Not necessarily anything by Ellroy."

Ballanger's elbows once more rested on his knees. He cradled his chin in his hands and stared at the floor.

"And you're asking me ..."

"To be blunt, Professeur Ballanger, I'm not much of a fan of crime fiction. My knowledge of the genre is . . . well, rudimentary. I'm looking for someone who might be able to help me, and I thought of you."

"Why me?"

"Your book on noir fiction."

"Oh, that," said Ballanger. "It's something I wrote ages ago. It really needs updating. The genre has evolved considerably since then."

"So, can you help us?"

Ballanger scratched his chin. He had the embarrassed air of a doctor bearing bad news.

"I don't know whether you've been to a university, *monsieur* ..."

"Verhœven. Yes, I did my law degree at the Sorbonne. Though that was a while ago."

"Oh, I'm sure nothing has changed much. These days, we're all specialists."

"Which is precisely why I'm here."

"That's not exactly what I meant . . . I did my dissertation on crime fiction. It's a vast field. I focused my research exclusively on novels published in Gallimard's *Série Noire*. I limited the scope of my analysis to the first thousand titles. These I do know intimately, but they are only a thousand in a genre that encompasses untold numbers of titles. My study of the hermeneutics of the detective novel unavoidably led to some forays beyond the limits of my subject matter. Ellroy, for example, was not published in the *Série Noire*; he is not—or at least not yet—considered part of the core canon of noir fiction. I know the man's work, I've read his books, but I could hardly claim to be an expert."

Camille was beginning to get irritated. Ballanger seemed to be talking like a book just to say that he had not read enough of them.

"Your point being?"

Ballanger shot him a look of exasperation mixed with astonishment, a look he clearly reserved for his most recalcitrant students.

"My point is that if the cases you mention fall within the scope of my corpus, then perhaps I can help you. Though, as I said, it is but a fraction of the canon."

Camille fumbled in his pocket, extracted two folded sheets of paper, and handed them to Ballanger.

"Here's a brief description of the case I mentioned earlier. If you could just take a look. You never know."

Ballanger unfolded the sheets, decided to postpone his reading until later, and tucked them into his pocket.

Just then the phone in Camille's pocket vibrated.

"Could you excuse me for a moment?" Without waiting for a response, he took the call.

It was Louis. Camille whipped out his notepad and scribbled something intelligible only to himself.

"Okay, meet me down there," he said.

Camille stood up, and Ballanger, startled, jumped to his feet as though he had received an electric shock.

"I'm sorry, Professeur Ballanger," Camille said on his way out of the door. "I'm afraid I may have wasted your time . . ."

"Oh?" Ballanger said, curiously disappointed. "So your theory was wrong?"

Camille turned back. Something had just occurred to him.

"On second thought," he said, as though overcome by a sudden flash of inspiration, "I believe I may need to call on you again very soon."

In the taxi back to Paris, Camille wondered whether in his whole life he had read a thousand books, worked out a rough figure based on having read twenty books a year (and that only in a particularly good year), which, rounded up, came to four hundred; he brooded bitterly on the inadequacy of his education.

5

Rue du Cardinal-Lemoine. An old-fashioned bookshop utterly unlike the sterile, sprawling shops lit by fluorescent tubes. Everything here spoke of craftsmanship: the polished parquet floor, the wooden bookshelves, the brushed-aluminum ladders, the soft lighting. The atmosphere, at once calm and stately, prompted voices to drop to a whisper. It was a foretaste of eternity. Next to the door was a magazine rack, in the center a table groaning under the weight of books of all sizes. At first glance, the place looked dusty and disordered, but on closer inspection it was clear that it was spick and span and organized according to a logic of its own. On the right-hand side were ranks of books with yellow spines, and on the facing wall was the *Série Noire* collection, possibly in its entirety. It felt less like walking into a bookshop than stepping into another universe. Crossing the threshold was like entering the refuge of the specialist, part monastery, part cult.

When they arrived, the shop seemed deserted, but at the tinkle of the bell above the door a tall man appeared as if from nowhere. Dressed in drab blue pants and a matching cardigan, he was about forty and had a serious, almost anxious face on which was perched a pair of half-moon glasses. He exuded a smug self-confidence. "This is my demesne," his tall, thin frame seemed to say, "I am lord of all I survey. I am a specialist."

"How may I be of service?" he asked.

He approached Camille, but maintained a certain distance as though unwilling to come too close, so he wouldn't have to look down.

"Commandant Verhœven."

"Ah, yes . . ."

He turned to fetch something, and handed Camille a book.

"I read the article in the newspaper. In my humble opinion, there can be no doubt in the matter . . ."

A paperback. The bookseller has marked a passage in the middle of the book with a yellow bookmark. Camille studies the cover. The illustration is a low-angle shot of a man with a bright red tie, wearing a hat and a pair of leather gloves and holding a knife. He seems to be in a stairwell.

Camille takes out his glasses and reads the title page:

BRET EASTON ELLIS

AMERICAN PSYCHO

He turns the page.

COPYRIGHT © 1991

TRANSLATION © 1992

There is a preface by Michel Braudeau:

Bret Easton Ellis was born in 1964 in Los Angeles [. . .] His literary agent managed to secure an advance of $300,000 for him to write a novel about a New York serial killer. When the manuscript was delivered, the publisher wrote off the advance and refused to publish the book. Horrified. Vintage Books, however, did not hesitate. Despite (or perhaps because of) the scandal triggered by the release of a few excerpts in galley proof, it defied public opinion and feminist activists [. . .] Ellis was obliged to hire a bodyguard; he received truckloads of hate mail and death threats. He also sold thousands of copies of *American Psycho* in the United States.

Louis does not read over his boss's shoulder. He wanders around the bookshop while the owner, feet slightly apart, hands clasped behind his back, stares out at the street. Camille feels something akin to excitement welling inside him.

At the passage indicated by the bookmark, there are horrors indeed. Camille begins to read, silent, focused. From time to time he shakes his head and murmurs, "It's not possible . . ."

In the end Louis succumbs to temptation. Camille holds the book slightly to one side so that his assistant can read along with him:

Midnight. The conversation I have with the two girls, both very young, blond hardbodies with big tits, is brief, since I'm having a difficult time containing my disordered self.

"I marked them with a cross," the bookseller says, "the passages I thought were significant."

Camille is not listening, or he does not hear. He reads on:

. . . it starts failing to turn me on [. . .]

Torri awakens to find herself tied up, bent over the side of the bed, on her back, her face covered with blood because I've cut her lips off with a pair of nail scissors. Tiffany is tied up with six pairs of Paul's suspenders on the other side of the bed, moaning with fear, totally immobilized by the monster of reality. I want her to watch what I'm going to do to Torri, and she's propped up in a way that makes this unavoidable. As usual, in an attempt to understand these girls I'm filming their deaths. With Torri and Tiffany I use a Minox L.X. ultra-miniature camera that takes 9.5 mm film, has a 15 mm f/3.5 lens, an exposure meter and a built-in neutral density filter, and sits on a tripod. I've put a CD of the Traveling Wilburys into a portable CD player that sits on the headboard above the bed, to mute any screams.

"Shit . . . ," Camille says to himself. His eyes move from one word to the next. He is reading more slowly now. He tries to think. But he cannot. He feels sucked in by the letters dancing before his eyes. He needs to concentrate; a thousand ideas suddenly crowd into his brain.

Then, turning her over again, her body weak with fear, I cut all the flesh off around her mouth and . . .

Camille looks up at Louis and sees the reflection of his own expression.

"What on God's earth is this book . . . ?" Louis says, struggling to understand.

"Who on God's earth is this guy?" Camille says, and goes back to reading.

With the blood from one of the corpses' stomachs that I dip my hand into, I scrawl, in dripping red letters above the faux-cowhide paneling in the living room, the words I AM BACK . . .

6

"I've got just one word for you: Bravo."

"There's no need to mock . . ."

"I'm not, Camille," Le Guen reassured him. "To be honest I didn't have much faith in your theory. Look, I hold my hands up . . . But just tell me one thing."

"Go on," Camille said, clicking his mouse to download his e-mail.

"Tell me you didn't send a request to the European database without getting authorization from Juge Deschamps?"

Camille pursed his lips. "I'll work it out . . ."

"Camille," Le Guen groaned wearily, "don't you think we've got enough shit on our plate? I've just had her on the phone. She's furious. On day one, there you were on television, there was that profile of you in the paper on day two, and now this. It's as if you're doing it deliberately. I'm sorry, Camille, but I've done all I can for you."

"I'll work things out with her. I'll explain . . ."

"From her tone of voice, you'll have your work cut out. Besides, I'm the one she holds responsible for your fuck-ups. There's a crisis meeting at her office tomorrow morning first thing."

When Camille did not reply, he added:

"Did you hear me, Camille? First thing tomorrow. Camille, are you there?"

"I received your fax, Commandant Verhœven."

Camille immediately registered Juge Deschamps's curt, brittle tone. There was a time when he would have been prepared to bow and scrape. On this occasion, he simply walked around his office since the printer was too far away for him to reach the page he had just printed out.

"I've just read the extract of the novel you sent. It would appear that your theory is correct. As you can imagine, I will have to meet up with the *procureur*. And, to be blunt, that is not the only thing I intend to discuss with him."

"Yes, I can imagine; the *divisionnaire* just phoned me. Listen, *madame le juge–*"

"*Madame* la *juge*, if you don't mind," Deschamps interrupted.

"My apologies."

"You have little flair for procedure, certainly. I've just had confirmation that you used my authorization to submit an inquiry to the European database. As you are no doubt aware, this was–"

"A gross error of judgment?"

"It was egregious misconduct, *commandant*! And I will not stand for it."

"I'll work things out, *madame la juge* . . ."

"You don't seem to realize, *commandant*, that I am the one to 'work things out'! You seem to forget that I have the power to grant you authorization."

"I haven't forgotten. But the thing is, *madame la juge*, though procedurally I may have been in the wrong, technically I was right. In fact, I think you would be wise to sanction the request as quickly as possible."

There was an ominous silence on the other end of the line.

"Commandant Verhœven," Deschamps said ultimately, "I think I may have to ask the *procureur* to remove you from this case."

"That is within your power. But when you do ask him to replace me," Camille said, rereading the slip of paper he was holding, "could you mention that we have a third crime on our hands?"

"Excuse me?"

"In response to the European inquiry authorized by you, I've received a response from Detective . . ." Camille took a moment to find the name at the top of the e-mail. ". . . Timothy Gallagher, Glasgow CID. They have an unsolved murder case dating from July 2001, the victim was a young woman. On her body they found a fake fingerprint identical to the one we submitted in our inquiry. Whoever takes over the case from me should really call him as soon as possible . . ."

After he had hung up, Camille went back to his list: *Tremblay = Black Dahlia = Ellroy*; *Courbevoie = American Psycho = Ellis*. To this, he now added: *Glasgow = ? = ??*

7

Since the detective inspector was not there, Louis's call was put through to his superior, Superintendent Smollett, a pure-blood Scotsman, to judge by his accent. The superintendent told Louis that Scotland had only recently joined the PJC—the Police and Judicial Co-operation in Criminal Matters program—and that explained why they never received the earlier request concerning the finger-print left at the Tremblay crime scene.

"Ask him which other countries have only recently joined the program."

"Greece," Louis repeated, listening to the superintendent, "and Portugal."

Camille made a note to send a request to the police forces of both countries. Following his instructions, Louis asked if they could have a copy of the case file and requested that Detective Inspector Gallagher call him as soon as possible.

"Ask him if Gallagher speaks any French."

Covering the receiver, Louis translated the reply with a respect-ful, slightly sardonic smile: "You're in luck . . . his mother is French."

Before hanging up, Louis chatted for a moment with the super-intendent and then burst out laughing. Camille looked at him quizzically.

"I was asking whether Redpath had recovered from his injury," Louis explained.

"Redpath?"

"The Scottish rugby player. He was injured in the match against Ireland a couple of weeks ago. If he's not fit to play on Saturday, Scotland has no chance of beating Wales."

"And?"

"He's fit to play," Louis said with a satisfied smile.

"You're a rugby fan?"

"Not particularly," Louis said, "but since we need the Scots, it's not a bad idea to speak their language."

8

Camille headed home at about 7:30 p.m. Worried. He lived on a quiet street in a lively neighborhood. He thought again about what his father had suggested. Perhaps moving on would not be such a bad idea. His cell rang. He checked the screen: Louis.

"Don't forget flowers . . . ," Louis said simply.

"Thanks, Louis, you're one of a kind."

This was what Camille's life had come to: expecting his assistant to remind him to think about his wife. Having walked straight past the florist without even noticing, Camille now angrily turned on his heel and in doing so headbutted a man in the chest.

"I'm sorry . . ."

"Don't worry, *commandant*, no harm done."

He recognized the voice even before looking up.

"So you've taken to stalking me now?" Camille snapped.

"I was trying to catch you up."

Camille kept going without a word. Buisson had little difficulty keeping pace.

"Aren't you beginning to find this farce a little repetitive?" Camille said, stopping suddenly.

"Got time for a quick drink?" Buisson said, nodding to a nearby café with a winning smile as though they were old friends delighted by this chance meeting.

"You might, but I don't."

"There's another thing that's getting a little repetitive. Listen, *commandant*, I apologize for the article. I saw red, as they say."

"Which article would that be, the first or the second?"

The two men had stopped in the middle of the rather narrow pavement, making it difficult for pedestrians to pass as they hurried to buy groceries before the shops closed.

"The first . . . the second was purely informative."

"Exactly, Monsieur Buisson; you seem to be a bit too well informed."

"What sort of journalist would I be if I weren't? You can hardly criticize me for that. No, the person I feel badly about is your father."

"I doubt you lost any sleep over it. You obviously go for easy prey. I hope you managed to sell him a subscription while you were at it."

"Come on, *commandant*, let me buy you a coffee. Five minutes."

Camille had already turned to go. But since the journalist continued to dog his step, he said:

"What exactly is it that you want, Monsieur Buisson?"

By now his tone was more weary than angry. This was probably how the reporter usually got his way: by wearing his victims down.

"Do you really believe this hypothesis of yours about the novel?"

"Honestly, no." Camille did not take the time to think. "It's an unsettling coincidence, nothing more. One possible lead, that's all."

"You *do* believe it!"

Buisson was more perceptive than Camille had given him credit for. He made a mental note not to underestimate this man. They had now arrived at the doorway to his building.

"I don't believe it any more than you do."

"Have you found any more evidence?"

"If we had found anything new," Camille said, punching in the keycode, "do you really think I would confide in you?"

"So Courbevoie being a scene right out of *American Psycho*, is that just another 'unsettling coincidence'?"

Camille stopped dead and turned to face the reporter.

"I'll make a deal with you," Buisson said.

"I'm not a hostage."

"I'll keep that nugget of information to myself for a couple of days so you can get on with the investigation."

"And in exchange?"

"When anything else happens, you give me a heads-up. A couple of hours, that's all. It's a fair deal."

"And if I don't?"

"Oh, *commandant*." Buisson feigned a heavy sigh of regret. "Surely we can come to some arrangement?"

Camille stared into the man's eyes and smiled.

"Goodbye, Monsieur Buisson."

Tomorrow morning was already off to a bad start. A very bad start.

"Shit!" he muttered as he opened the door to his apartment.

"What's the matter, darling?" Irène called from the living room.

"Nothing," Camille called back, remembering the flowers.

Friday, April 11

1

"Did she like them?" Louis said.

"Did she like what?"

"The flowers."

"You have no idea . . ."

From Camille's tone, Louis knew something had gone awry but did not ask.

"Have you got the papers, Louis?"

"They're in my office."

"Have you read them?"

Louis simply pushed his hair back with his right hand.

"I have to be in Deschamps's office in twenty minutes, so just give me a quick summary."

"The Courbevoie-*American Psycho* connection is all over the papers."

"Bastard!"

"Who's a bastard?"

"Oh, the world is full of bastards, Louis, but that hack from *Le Matin*, Buisson, is leagues ahead of the rest." Camille told Louis about his encounter the previous evening.

"So, not content just to publish the information, he's passed it on to his fellow hacks," Louis said.

"What do you expect? The guy's all heart. Could you order a car for me? No point in me being late on top of everything else."

It was only on the way back, in Le Guen's car, that Camille finally flicked through the papers. The *juge* had only briefly referred to the matter. Now that he saw the headlines, he could understand why she had been incandescent.

"Jesus, I've screwed this whole investigation," he said, scanning the front pages.

"I'm not sure how else you could have gone about it," Le Guen muttered.

"Thanks for the support, boss. I'll bring you back a kilt."

The papers had already given the killer a name: The "Novelist." The first glimpse of glory.

"As I see it, the killer will probably be thrilled," Camille said, putting on his glasses.

Le Guen turned to look at him in surprise.

"You seem to be taking this pretty calmly, all things considered. You're threatened with suspension for failing to follow police protocol, you've been warned that you could be taken off the case for breach of judicial confidentiality, and you seem to be able to laugh it off."

Camille let his hands fall onto the crumpled newspapers. He took off his glasses and looked at his friend.

"It's killing me, Jean," he said, suddenly overwhelmed. "It's really killing me."

2

At the end of the shift, Camille stepped into Armand's office just as he was coming off the telephone. Before looking up at Camille, Armand took his IKEA pencil—now worn down to a stub—and painstakingly crossed out a line on a vast computer printout that spilled over the sides of his desk and onto the floor.

"What's that?"

"A list of wallpaper shops. Specifically those that stock the Dalmatian print."

"How far have you got?"

"Number thirty-seven."

"And?"

"And, I'm about to call number thirty-eight."

"Obviously."

Camille glanced over at Maleval's desk.

"Where's he got to?"

"Some shop on the rue de Rivoli. A salesgirl there says she remembers selling a Ralph Lauren suitcase to a man three weeks ago."

Maleval's desk was always a mess: folders, reports, photographs spilling out of case files, old notebooks, and among these, decks of cards, racing magazines, betting slips. It resembled a teenager's bedroom during the summer breaks. There was something of the obstreperous teenager about Maleval. When he had first come to the department, Camille had remarked that he might do well to keep his desk tidier.

"Say you were sick and someone had to replace you at the drop of a hat . . ."

"Always fit as a fiddle, boss."

"Not first thing in the morning, from what I've seen."

Maleval had smiled.

"Some guy once said there are two types of order, vital order and geometric order. I go for vital order."

"That would be Bergson," Louis said.

"Mathieu Berson, who plays for Aston Villa?"

"No, Henri Bergson, the philosopher."

"If you say so," muttered Maleval.

Camille had smiled.

"Not everyone at the *brigade* has a partner who can quote Bergson."

Despite his quip, that evening Camille had consulted an encyclopedia to see what there was about the Nobel prize–winning writer of whose work he had never read a word.

"So where's Louis?"

"Some brothel," Armand said.

"Doesn't sound like Louis."

"I mean he's interviewing Manuela Constanza's former colleagues."

"I suppose you'd prefer to be down at the brothel instead of stuck here tracking down wallpaper suppliers?"

"Not really. When you've seen one brothel . . ."

"Okay. I'm going to Glasgow on Monday so there's no way I can be home late tonight. I'll leave you to it. If you need anything . . ."

"Camille!" Armand called as he reached the doorway. "How's Irène doing?"

"She's exhausted."

"You should head home. I mean, we're not making much progress here."

"You're right, Armand. I think I'll knock off now."

"Give her my love."

Before he left, Camille stopped by Louis's office. Everything was filed, neatly ordered. He stepped into the room. The Lancel desk organizer, the Mont Blanc fountain pen . . . And, classified by subject, his files, his notes, his memos. Even the photographs of the victims from Courbevoie and Tremblay were pinned to a corkboard, precisely aligned like pictures at an exhibition. Louis's desk did not have the meticulous neatness of Armand's; it was logical and orderly, but not obsessive.

As he turned to leave, something caught Camille's eye. He scanned the room again and, unable to put his finger on whatever it was, left the office. But like a word in an advertisement or a name in a newspaper that rings a faint bell, the feeling continued to nag at him. He strode down the corridor, but still he could not shake the notion that he had missed something, and the thought of leaving the station without knowing what was intolerable. It was infuriating. He retraced his steps, and this time he saw it. He walked over to the desk. On the left-hand side lay Louis's list of men with the name Jean Haynal. He ran his finger down it, looking for the one he had fleetingly noticed earlier.

"Jesus Christ!" he shouted. "Armand! Get in here now!"

3

With lights and sirens blaring, it took them less than ten minutes to reach the quai de Valmy. The two men arrived at the offices of SOGEFI a few minutes before it closed at 7 p.m.

The receptionist did her best to stop them, first waving, then calling out, but they strode on resolutely, and she was forced to trot after them.

They burst into Cottet's office. It was empty. His secretary was hard on their heels.

"Messieurs . . . ," she began.

"Wait here." Camille raised a hand to stop her.

He walked over to Cottet's desk and sat in the absurdly expensive leather desk chair.

"Must be good to be the boss," he mused aloud, leaning back against the headrest and staring straight ahead. His feet did not touch the ground.

Angrily, he jumped down from the chair, clambered up, and knelt on it, then, dissatisfied with this position, he stood on the chair and a sardonic smile lit up his face.

"Your turn," he said to Armand, getting down. Not knowing what was going on, Armand circled the desk and settled into the director's chair.

"No doubt about it," he said with sudden satisfaction, staring out of the window that faced the desk: there, beyond the line of the rooftops, was a large neon sign—one of the letter "A"s had given up the ghost—that would have read: Transports Haynal.

"So, where exactly might we find Monsieur François Cottet?" Camille articulated each syllable.

"Well, that's the thing, actually. No one knows where he is. He hasn't been seen since Monday night."

4

The first two cars screeched to a halt in front of Cottet's house, in the process Armand accidentally knocking over a garbage can that had been left out on the pavement.

The man's definitely loaded. This was Camille's first thought as he looked up at the imposing three-story mansion, the grand flight of steps leading from the front door into extensive grounds separated from the road by an ornate wrought-iron fence. One of the officers in a third car got out and opened the gate. The cars roared up the driveway to the steps and even before they had come to a stop, four men, including Camille, had jumped out. The door was opened by a woman who, despite the fact that it was early evening, looked as though she had been woken by the sirens.

"Madame Cottet?" Verhœven said, climbing the steps.

"Yes . . ."

"We're looking for your husband. Is he at home?"

The woman's face suddenly brightened in a vague smile as though she had only just noticed the horde of police officers descending on her house.

"No," she said, stepping back from the door, "but you're welcome to come in."

Camille remembered Cottet well, his appearance, his age. His wife, a tall, slender woman who had clearly been a beauty once, was at least ten years older than her husband and not at all as Camille had imagined her. Though her looks had faded somewhat, her manner and poise marked her out as a woman of taste—in fact, she was almost chic, which could not be said of her husband, who had the charm and charisma of a pushy salesman. Though dressed in a pair of slacks that had seen better days and a very ordinary blouse, her languorous manner and a certain slowness in her movements made her the embodiment of what people call "noble bearing."

While Armand and two other officers dashed about the house, throwing open doors and wardrobes, searching every room, Madame Cottet poured herself a glass of whiskey. An oft-repeated gesture, perhaps, and one that had hastened her decline . . . that much was etched into her face.

"Could you tell us where your husband is, Madame Cottet?"

She stared at Camille in amazement. Then, finding it awkward to be looking down from such rarefied heights at such a short man, she settled herself comfortably on the sofa.

"With his whores, I presume. Why?"

"When was he last at home?"

"Truth be told, I have no idea, Monsieur . . . ?"

"Commandant Verhœven. Let me put the question another way: when did you last see him?"

"Let's see . . . what day is today?"

"Friday."

"Already? In that case Monday, at a guess. Yes, I believe it was Monday."

"But you're not sure?"

"I'm certain it was Monday."

"Four days ago. You don't seem worried."

"Oh, I'm afraid if I were to worry every time my husband 'went for a wander' . . . That's what he calls it."

"And do you know where he usually does his 'wandering'?"

"Not being in the habit of frequenting brothels with him, I have no idea."

Camille looked about him, taking in the cavernous drawing room, the colossal fireplace, the carved wood tables, the paintings, the rugs.

"And you're alone here?"

Madame Cottet gestured about her vaguely.

"What do you think?"

"Madame Cottet, your husband is wanted for questioning in connection with an ongoing criminal investigation."

She looked at him more attentively, and Camille thought he saw the hint of a Mona Lisa smile.

"And while I appreciate your irony and your detachment," Camille said, "we are investigating the deaths of two young women who were hacked to pieces in an apartment rented out by your husband, so you'll understand why I need to talk to him urgently."

"Young women, you say? Whores?"

"Two prostitutes, yes."

"As far as I know, my husband prefers to visit them," she said, getting up and pouring another Scotch. "He doesn't entertain them at home. At least, not as far as I know . . ."

"You don't seem to know very much about your husband's movements."

"True," she said curtly. "If he does dismember young women when he goes wandering, he has not confided as much to me. It's rather a pity, mind you. I might have found it amusing."

Quite how drunk she was Camille would have been hard pressed to say. She spoke clearly, articulating each syllable, which might mean that she was attempting to allay his suspicions.

Armand came downstairs with the other officers. He waved for Camille to join them.

"If you'll excuse me for a moment . . ."

Armand led Camille to a small study on the first floor: a handsome cherrywood desk, a state-of-the-art computer, a few files and folders, some bookcases lined with law books, real estate brochures, and four whole shelves of crime novels.

"Telephone forensics; get in touch with the lab," Camille said, as he made for the stairs. "And call Maleval and tell him he's to be on the scene while they're here. And tell him I'll need him to stay here overnight. Just in case . . ."

He went back to the drawing room.

"I think, Madame Cottet, that we need to have a little chat about your husband."

5

"I'll be gone two days at the most."

Camille looked at Irène, beached rather than seated on the living room sofa, her belly heavy, her knees splayed.

"So you brought me the flowers to celebrate your little trip?"

"No, I meant to bring them yesterday."

"By the time you get back, you might well have a son."

"I'm not going away for three weeks, Irène, I'll be gone a couple of days."

Irène went to look for a vase.

"What's really frustrating," she said, smiling, "is that I want to get angry, but I can't. They're really pretty, your flowers."

"They're *your* flowers."

She walked as far as the kitchen door and turned back to Camille.

"The reason I want to be angry is that we've talked about going to Scotland twice, you've spent two years thinking about it, and now you've decided to go without me."

"I'm not going on vacation, you know that."

"I wish it *were* a vacation," Irène called from the kitchen.

Camille went to join her. He tried to hug her, but Irène refused. Gently, but she refused.

At that moment, Louis telephoned.

"I just wanted to say . . . don't worry about Irène. Tell her she can call me anytime while you're away."

"Thanks, Louis, you're a good guy."

"Who was that?" Irène asked as he hung up.

"My guardian angel."

"I thought I was your guardian angel," Irène said, pressing herself against him.

"No, you're my matryoshka doll," he said, laying a hand on her belly.

"Oh, Camille," she said, and began to cry quietly.

Saturday, April 12, and Sunday, April 13

1

The team met up at 8:30 a.m. on Saturday morning. Even Le Guen.

"Have you been in touch with the *brigade financière*?"

"You'll have the information within the hour."

Camille began to allocate the workload. Maleval, who had spent all night in Saint-Germain, wore his usual shop-soiled expression. Armand was tasked with combing through Cottet's contacts, his address book, his e-mails—business and personal—and with ensuring that Cottet's description had been circulated to local squads the night before. Louis was to look into his bank accounts—business and personal—his cash inflow and outflow, and his calendar.

"Our killer needs three things. Time—something that Cottet, being his own boss, has lots of. He needs money, which Cottet clearly has. You only have to look at his company, his house. Even if not all of his property developments have made a profit. Thirdly, he needs organizational skills. Something else our man must have."

"Aren't you forgetting motive?" Le Guen said.

"Motive is something we can ask him about when we've tracked him down. Louis—any news on Lambert?"

"Nothing. We've still got teams watching the three locations he visits most regularly. No sightings so far."

"We're not going to get anything from the surveillance, are we?"

"I don't think so, no. We've kept things low key, but word is bound to have got about by now. . . ."

"Lambert, Cottet . . . I'm finding it difficult to see a connection between the two. That's something we need to look into. Louis, you deal with that."

"That's likely to be a lot of work."

Camille turned to Le Guen.

"Louis says it's a lot of work."

"If I had a bunch of officers standing idle, you'd know about it."

"Okay, Jean. Thanks for your support. I suggest we organize raids on Lambert's known associates. Maleval, you've got the up-to-date list?"

"I've counted eleven close contacts. If we're going for simultaneous busts, we're looking at four teams at least to make sure no one slips through the net."

"Jean?"

"I can allocate four teams for tonight, but only to conduct the raids."

"I'd suggest a coordinated action at 22:00 hours. That way we'll have space in the holding cells for everyone. Maleval, I'll need you to sort out the logistics. Armand, you liaise with him so we can set up the interviews." Camille glanced around the team. "In the meantime, I'll stay here and sort through whatever information came through last night."

By midmorning, Camille had managed to piece together most of François Cottet's career.

At twenty-four, having graduated without distinction from a second-rate business school, he joined SODRAGIM, a real estate

development company founded by its current CEO, Edmond For-
estier. Cottet managed a small department dealing in private housing. Three years later, he got his first big break when he married the
boss's daughter.

"I was . . . we were forced to get married," was how his wife had
put it, "but that proved to be a false alarm. As things turned out,
marrying my husband was a faux pas twice over."

Two years later, Cottet had his second stroke of luck: his father-
in-law was killed in a car accident in the Ardennes. Before he
turned thirty, Cottet was CEO of the company, which he immediately restructured to become SOGEFI, creating a number of satellite
companies to deal with various other market sectors. By the time he
was forty, he had managed the extraordinary feat of taking a peren-
nially profitable company and plunging it into the red, something
that spoke volumes about his gifts as an entrepreneur. There were
several bailouts from his wife, who had inherited a fortune sufficient to compensate for her husband's incompetence, an inheritance
that—given his propensity for financial blunders—would sooner or
later be exhausted.

To say his wife despised him would be an understatement.

"You met the man, *commandant*, so I hardly need to tell you: my
husband is a man of appalling vulgarity. Though I suppose in the
circles he frequents, that may well be seen as a virtue."

Madame Cottet had initiated divorce proceedings eighteen
months previously, but interminable financial complications and
applications by lawyers meant that the divorce had not yet been
granted. One interesting fact: Cottet had had a brush with the law
in 2001. He had been arrested on October 4 at 2:30 a.m. in the Bois
de Boulogne. Having beaten up a prostitute, punching her in the
face and the stomach, Cottet had been set upon by a gang of bruis-
ers working for her pimp. He had escaped with his life thanks only
to the intervention of a passing patrol car. He spent two days in
the hospital and then was tried and given a two-month suspended
sentence for indecent assault and actual bodily harm. Camille
leafed through the files and checked the dates. The Edinburgh

killing—the earliest of the murders—had taken place on July 10, 2001. Had Cottet's arrest taught him to plan his crimes more carefully? Or did his wife's constant references to "his whores" stem from the fact that she loathed him and would be only too happy to get him into trouble?

Camille reread Dr. Crest's provisional report and decided that, so far, Cottet's character was consistent with the profile he had been given.

2

The preliminary case conference took place at 12:45 p.m.

"The forensics team finished their work at the Cottet house this morning," Camille announced. "It will take two or three days to get results back on the fibers from Cottet's clothes and shoes, hair samples, and so forth. But even if the results are positive, they're not worth much until we manage to locate the man himself."

"I've no idea what goes on inside Cottet's head," Armand said when Camille nodded for him to speak, "but his wife was right, he's definitely into prostitutes. There's shitloads of porn on the guy's computer; his browser history is full of links to escort sites . . . Given the number of girls he tagged, it would have taken up a lot of his time. And," Armand could not resist adding, "I'm telling you, it must have cost a bundle."

Everyone smiled.

"There are no prostitutes in his address book. He obviously arranges his hookups online. On the other hand, there's a ton of business contacts, so it'll take a while to sort through them for anyone who might be of interest. But there's certainly nothing to connect him with anything we already have on the cases."

"The same can be said for his bank accounts," Louis continued. "There is no record of purchases of anything that might link him to the investigation: no nail gun, no Ralph Lauren suitcase, no bespoke Japanese sofa. On the other hand, for the past three years he has made large cash withdrawals. There's no obvious pattern, but I've cross-referenced the data, and there were sizable withdrawals in the periods leading up to the crimes we know about, but there are others, too. We'd have to be able to question him to get to the bottom of all this. The same is true of the diary. On the day of the Glasgow murder, Cottet was in Spain."

"Whether he actually went to Spain remains to be seen," Camille said.

"We're looking into that, but we don't expect to have an answer until early next week. He was in Paris in November 2001. Tremblay is in the suburbs, so there's no way to prove whether he was there or not. The same goes for Courbevoie. Until we track him down."

Since a description of Cottet had been circulated to all local and national police stations the night before, they agreed to leave it at that until Monday. Louis volunteered to be on call over the weekend, to telephone Camille at any hour of the day or night if there were any developments.

3

When he got home that afternoon, Camille put his parcels in the small room that Irène had been redecorating for the arrival of the baby. At first Camille helped out, but gradually he became swamped by work. They had been using the space as a box room, but since she stopped working, Irène had cleared out all junk and had the walls papered in cheery, pastel colors so that now the room, which had a connecting door to their bedroom, looked like a doll's house. "Just the right size for me," Camille thought. For a month now, Irène had been buying baby furniture, all of which was still in boxes. Looking at them, Camille broke into a sort of cold sweat. Irène could go into labor at any moment . . .

His cell phone rang, making him start. It was Louis.

"No, there's nothing new. It's just that you left the Tremblay file on your desk yesterday. I thought you were taking it to Glasgow."

"I forgot it."

"That's all right. I have it here. Do you want me to bring it round?"

Camille hesitated for a split second, surveyed the unpacked boxes, heard Irène humming to herself in the shower.

"No, that's fine. Do you mind if I come over?"

"No problem. I'm on call all weekend, so I'll be here."

Camille and Irène began to unpack the boxes, and in a moment of madness Camille even found himself assembling the crib and a chest of drawers. (Insert screws "A" into the upper holes "1C" position stabilizer bar "F" between crosspieces "2C" . . . Jesus Christ, which ones are the crosspieces . . . there are 8 × screw "A" and 4 × "B" . . . do not fully tighten the screws until dowels "B" have been inserted into the apertures "E" indicated in . . . "Irène, can you come take a look. Oh, darling, I think you've put it together upside down," etc.)

A good day.

That night they went out for dinner, and Irène, not wanting to be alone while Camille was in Scotland, decided she would go and spend a few days with her parents, who had retired to Bourgogne.

"I'll get Louis to drive you to the station," Camille suggested. "Or maybe Maleval."

"I'll take a taxi. Louis has more important things to do. Besides, if you're going to ask someone, I'd rather it was Armand."

Camille smiled. Irène was very fond of Armand. A sort of maternal affection. She loved his awkwardness and found his neuroses touching.

"How is he these days?"

"Oh, you know. If they gave out medals for being tightfisted, Armand would pawn his."

"It can't be any worse than it was."

"Oh, when it comes to Armand, it can. It's pitiful."

Maleval called in at 10:30 p.m.

"We've managed to pick up all of Lambert's cronies. There's only one missing."

"That's a pain."

"Not really. It's the kid, Mourad. He was stabbed last night; his body was found around noon today in a cellar in Clichy. With thugs like these, you can never be sure your list is up to date."

"Do you need anything from me?"

Thinking about Irène, Camille sent a brief prayer to heaven that he would not need to leave the apartment until he left for Glasgow.

"No, I don't think so. We've got them all in separate cells. Louis decided to stay here with us. And Armand's here, so there's three of us. We'll call if there's any news."

The "news," such as it was, arrived shortly after midnight.

"No one knows anything," Maleval told Camille, who was getting ready for bed. "We've cross-checked all the statements and they have only one thing in common: Lambert told them all the same thing at the same time."

"Which is?"

"Fuck all. Almost all of them are convinced he left town with Daniel Royet. He said he needed to get away for a while. Some of them were told it would only be a short trip, and he told one of his daughters he would be gone 'two days at the most.' He said nothing about where he was going."

"Okay. Send everyone home. You can deal with the paperwork on Monday. Go and get some sleep."

4

While Irène was dressing to go out to dinner, Camille stopped by to see Louis. The apartment building in which he lived reminded him of Cottet's opulent mansion. The majestic wooden staircase was beautifully polished, and on each landing high double doors afforded access to the apartments. As he came to Louis's door, he heard voices and hesitated.

Camille checked his watch and was about to ring the doorbell when he heard the voices again. Men's voices. They were shouting. He had no trouble recognizing Louis's voice, though he could not make out what he was saying. He was involved in a heated argument. The best thing to do, he thought, was to call Louis and tell him he was on his way. He thought about going back downstairs, but it was four flights. In the end, he went up to the next floor, and was just fumbling for his cell when the apartment door was flung open.

"And I don't need you saddling your fucking high horse and lecturing me!" roared a voice.

Maleval, thought Camille.

He peered over the banister. The man tearing down the stairs four at a time was wearing a jacket Camille immediately recognized.

Camille forced himself to wait for a long time. Wrapped up in his thoughts, he counted off the eight times he had to press the time switch on the light. He knew nothing about the relationship between the two men. Perhaps they were closer than he supposed. He had the unpleasant feeling he was prying into something that was none of his business. Finally he went back down the stairs and rang Louis's doorbell.

Monday, April 14

1

On Monday morning, Cottet was still on the run. The team watching his house had seen Madame Cottet go out on Saturday afternoon and return the same evening. Everything seemed normal.

Camille's flight took off at 11:30 a.m.

He had spent the weekend toying with an idea, and at 7:30 on Monday morning, he realized it had been a waste of time since he had already made his decision.

He left a message for Ballanger at the university; then he dialed the number of the bookshop.

"Jérôme Lesage." The bookseller's deep voice interrupted the greeting on the answering machine.

"Aren't you closed on Mondays?"

"Indeed we are, but I generally come in to catch up on paperwork."

Camille checked his watch.

"Could I possibly come over for a few minutes?"

"Today is Monday; the shop is closed."

The bookseller's tone was not quite brusque, but it was business-like, direct. To him, the police were no more important than any other customer. In simple terms, in the Librairie Lesage, the police were not going to lay down the law.

"But you're there," Camille said hesitantly.

"Indeed I am, and I'm listening."

"It would be better if we could meet."

"If it won't take too long . . ." Lesage relented.

Camille had only to tap lightly on the metal shutter, and the book-seller appeared at the next-door entrance. They shook hands quickly and went into the shop via a connecting door.

In the half-light, the bookshop looked sinister, almost menacing. The bookshelves, the cramped office tucked beneath the staircase, the piles of books, even the coat stand seemed shifting and dream-like. Lesage turned on some lights, but this did not seem to change things. Without daylight, the atmosphere of the place seemed gloomy and furtive. Like a lair.

"I'm going to Scotland," Camille began without thinking.

"And . . . that's why you came to see me, to tell me . . ."

"A young girl of about twenty was found strangled."

"Excuse me?"

"The body was discovered in a park."

"I'm afraid I don't see . . ."

"I was wondering whether, as in the previous case, this one might ring a bell." Camille was struggling to keep his temper.

"Listen, *commandant*," Lesage said, moving closer, "you have your job and I have mine. When I read about the Courbevoie case, it immediately reminded me of the scene in *American Psycho*. It seemed only right that I should let you know about it, but my 'col-laboration' ends there. I'm a bookseller, not a policeman. And I have no desire to switch careers."

"Meaning . . . ?"

"Meaning I don't want to be bothered every other day with an account of the cases you're working on. First, because I simply don't have the time. And secondly, because I have no taste for such things."

Lesage had stepped forward and now stood in front of Camille, making no attempt this time to keep his distance. Rarely had Camille—who was accustomed to such things—so keenly experienced being "looked down upon."

"If I were a police informer, you'd know about it, wouldn't you?"

"And yet you are a police informer. You have already provided vital information in a case without anyone having to ask." The man blushed. "Your principles seemed to be rather elastic, Monsieur Lesage," Camille said, turning toward the door.

In his fury, he had forgotten that the metal shutter was down. He turned back, walked around a table of books and headed for the side door by which he had come in.

"Where?" Lesage called after him.

Camille stopped and turned back.

"The murdered girl . . . where did it happen?"

"Glasgow."

Lesage immediately recovered his composure. He stared at his shoes for a moment, knitting his brow.

"Any details about the crime?"

"The girl was raped. Sodomized."

"How was she dressed?"

"A denim trouser suit, yellow platform shoes. From what I know all her clothes were recovered, except-"

"Her underwear?"

Camille's anger evaporated. He felt overwhelmed. He stared at Lesage, who now looked less like a professor than an oncologist about to deliver a diagnosis. He moved along the bookshelves, hesitated for a moment, then took down a book. On the cover, a man wearing a trilby hat leans on a pool table while, from the depths of the bar, the blurred silhouette of another man seems to be walking toward him. Camille read the cover: William McIlvanney. *Laidlaw*.

"Shit!" he muttered. "Are you sure about this?"

"No, but the details you just mentioned are in the book. I reread it recently, so I remember it pretty well. Then again, 'the worst is not the surest,' as they say. There may be significant discrepancies. It may not be–"

"Thank you," Camille said, flicking through the book.

Lesage made a curt gesture to indicate that, his duty now accomplished, he was eager to get back to work.

Camille paid for the book, tucked it under his arm, checked his watch, and walked out. The taxi was still double-parked.

As he left, Camille shuddered to think how many murders might be contained within the pages of the books in Lesage's shop.

2

On the way to the airport, Camille called Louis to tell him the news.

"*Laidlaw*, you said?"

"That's right. Have you heard of it?"

"No. Should I get a copy sent to Deschamps?"

"No, there's no need to panic her for the moment; first I need to read the book and have a chat with our English colleagues . . ."

"Scottish! For God's sake don't call them English while you're there . . ."

"Thank you, Louis. With our *Scottish* colleagues . . . to see whether the details in the book mirror those in the case. It shouldn't take more than a couple of hours. There'll be time enough to brief Deschamps when I get back."

Louis's silence was uncomfortable.

"You don't agree, Louis?"

"No, no, I agree. I was just thinking about something else. This bookseller of yours seems to be familiar with every last detail of these novels, doesn't he?"

"I thought the same thing. It troubled me a bit. To be honest, I don't believe in coincidence."

"He wouldn't be the first killer to worm his way into an investigation, to set the police on the trail of the murderer."

"It's classic behavior, I know. What are you suggesting?"

"Just that we take a closer look at him. Discreetly, of course."

"Go ahead, Louis. That way at least we'll know for sure."

In the departure lounge, Camille flicked through the McIlvanney book, glancing up every five minutes, unable to concentrate. Ten minutes passed, during which he nervously drummed his fingers on a glossy magazine.

Don't do it, he thought.

Then a flight attendant's voice announced that boarding would begin in ten minutes.

Unable to stand it any longer, he fumbled for his credit card and his cell phone.

3

Timothy Gallagher was a man of about fifty, thin and dark haired with a disarming smile. He was waiting for Camille in the arrivals hall holding a placard bearing his name. He registered no surprise at the *commandant*'s stature. In fact, it was difficult to imagine the man expressing surprise, or indeed any emotion beyond the cool authority of an officer of the law.

The two men had spoken twice on the phone. Camille had congratulated him on his excellent French and was sorry that the compliment sounded formulaic when in fact it was sincere.

"The lads here found your theory a little . . . startling," the Scot said.

"We were just as startled to be suggesting it."

"I can imagine."

Camille had pictured Glasgow as a city with only one season— buffeted by the wind and cold from one end of the year to the other. It is rare for one's sense of a place to be so quickly validated. Scotland seemed to be a country determined not to disagree with anyone.

To Camille, there was something ancient and aloof about Glasgow; it was a world unto itself. While the taxi drove them from the airport to Pitt Street, where Strathclyde Police Headquarters were located, Camille surrendered to the strange, exotic landscape of this pink-and-gray city that tended its parks and green spaces in the faint hope that one day summer might pay a visit.

Camille moved along the line, briskly shaking the hands of the officers in order of seniority. The meeting at police headquarters began at precisely the hour arranged.

Gallagher had taken the trouble to draft a report summing up the facts of the case and, given his colleague's rudimentary English, offered to read it to him in French. Camille shot the man a smile that was grateful but discreet, as though he had already adopted the Calvinist temperance of his hosts.

"Grace Hobson," Gallagher began, "was eighteen years old. A schoolgirl who lived with her parents near Glasgow Cross. She'd spent the evening with her friend Mary Barnes at the Metropolitan, a nightclub in the city center. The only unusual detail being that Grace's former boyfriend, William Kilmar, was at the club that night, and this made her nervous and irritable. According to witnesses, she kept looking at him out of the corner of her eye, and she was drinking pretty heavily. At about 11 p.m., Kilmar disappeared and Grace got up to leave. Her friend Mary Barnes saw her walking toward the exit. When she didn't come back, her friends assumed that the two of them had had an argument. They certainly weren't worried by her absence. At about 11:45 p.m., when they were heading home, they looked for her. No one had seen her since she left the club. Her naked body was found on the morning of July 10, 2001, in Kelvingrove Park. She had been sodomized and strangled. In his statement, Kilmar claimed he hadn't seen Grace. He confirmed that he left the club at about 11 p.m., met up with another girl outside the club, walked her home, and arrived back at his parents' house shortly before midnight. On his way home, he ran into two guys from school who lived in the area and were on their way home from a party. They chatted for a couple of minutes. His statement seemed genuine, and there was nothing to dispute the facts as he presented them. There were three surprising things about the case. First, the fact that the girl's panties were missing. The rest of her clothes were found at the scene. Next, there was the fake fingerprint made using a rubber stamp on one of the girl's toenails. Lastly, there was a beauty spot on her left temple. It was very realistic . . . in fact, we didn't realize it was fake until several hours later when her parents came to identify the body. Forensics determined that the mole had been placed there *post mortem*."

Camille asked a number of questions, and the officers were free and frank with their responses. Strathclyde police did not seem reluctant to share with him the details of the investigation. They showed Camille the crime scene photographs.

At this point, Camille took out the book he had bought from Lesage. Even this did not seem to surprise the officers. Camille offered to give them a brief account of the plot and a courier was dispatched to buy four copies of the original from the nearest book-shop. In the meantime they had a tea break, and the meeting began again at four o'clock.

Juggling French and English editions, they spent a long time comparing passages in McIlvanney's text with details from the investigation, focusing especially on the photographs.

> She was partly covered by foliage [. . .] Her head was skewed at a funny angle on her neck, as if she was listening for something. Gently, he moved the hair back from her forehead. The hair was stiff—surely not with lacquer, Laidlaw thought. It was probably frozen sweat and dust. On her left temple he saw a beauty spot, the one she had thought would spoil her chances.

In a spirit of reciprocity, Camille set out the details of the French investigations. The officers studied the elements in the case files with the same diligence as they would have had they been their own. Camille could almost see them thinking: "We're dealing with facts here, cold, hard facts, from which just one possible conclusion can be drawn: if this bizarre and extraordinary theory is correct, then we're dealing with one madman."

That evening, Gallagher drove Camille to the various locations of the investigation. It was much colder now, but people were strolling around in Kelvingrove Park in T-shirts in a touching attempt to convince themselves that the sultry suns of summer were already here. And perhaps, in Glasgow terms, this was summer weather. The two men visited the spot where Grace Hobson's body had been discovered. To Camille it looked exactly as described in McIlvanney's novel.

The area of Glasgow Cross where the victim lived was a quiet, city center neighborhood, with tall, imposing houses behind wrought-iron gates covered with many layers of black paint. Gallagher asked whether he wanted to meet the victim's parents, but Camille diplomatically declined. This was not his case, and he had no wish to give the impression that he had come to pass judgment on the earlier investigation. They moved on to the Metropolitan, a former movie theater converted into a nightclub. The exterior—this one a riot of neon light, its windows slathered with red paint—looked like the gateway to hell.

Camille was staying in a hotel in the city center. From there, he called Irène at her parents'.

"Did Louis drive you to the station?"

"Of course not, Camille, I took a taxi like a big girl. Well, like a very big girl, these days . . ."

"Tired?"

"A little. But it's my parents who really tire me out."

"I can imagine. How are they?"

"Same as ever . . . that's the problem."

Camille had only been to visit his in-laws three or four times. Irène's father, a retired math teacher, now village historian and president of almost every regional society, was a local celebrity. Smug to the point of tedium, he would regale Camille for several minutes with tales of his pitiful successes, his trivial victories, his society triumphs, after which he would challenge his son-in-law to a game of chess, lose three games in a row, and spend the rest of the day sulking and pretending he had a stomach upset.

"Papa wants us to call our son Hugo. God knows why."

"Did you ask?"

"He says it's a name for a conquering hero."

"Can't deny that. Ask him what he thinks of 'Caesar.'"

A brief silence.

"I miss you, Camille."

"I miss you, too."

"I miss you more. What's the weather like?"

"Here they call it 'changeable.' Which means it rained yesterday and it'll rain again tomorrow."

Tuesday, April 15

1

The Glasgow flight landed shortly after 2 p.m. In the arrivals area Camille found Maleval looking even grimmer than usual.

"No need to ask if there's bad news. The look on your face says it all."

Maleval took Camille's suitcase and handed him a copy of *Le Matin*.

"WITH *LAIDLAW*, THE 'NOVELIST' SIGNS HIS THIRD 'VOLUME.'"

There was only one possible source: the bookseller.

"Fucking hell!"

"My reaction exactly," Maleval said as he started the car. "Louis was a little more restrained."

Camille's cell indicated he had two missed calls, both from Le Guen. He didn't even bother to listen to his voice mail.

Had it been a mistake to give the journalist short shrift? Could he have bought himself more time?

But it was not this thought that made him feel weary. It was the thought of the inevitable response to the article and the dozens of similar articles that would probably appear the next day. He had seen no reason to inform Le Guen and Deschamps about the possible link between McIlvanney and the Glasgow murder before his trip; he had been wrong. The morning papers had just informed his superiors of a lead he had known about for two days. His removal from the case was no longer a possibility; it was a certainty. He had screwed up the investigation; from the very beginning of the case he had been slow to catch on. Even though four murders had now been linked, he could still not claim to have a definite lead. Even the media seemed to know more about the case than he did. Never in his career had Camille felt so helpless.

"Drop me off at my place." Camille's voice was jaded and almost inaudible. Then, almost to himself, he added, "We've had it."

"We'll track this guy down," Maleval declared in a burst of enthusiasm.

"Someone will track him down, but it won't be us. At least it won't be me. I reckon we'll be told to exit stage left, probably this afternoon."

"What are you talking about?"

Camille briefly summed up the situation and was surprised by Maleval's reaction. He seemed more upset than Camille. Over and over he muttered: "I don't fucking believe it."

But it did not matter what he believed; it was the truth.

As he read the article—written by Buisson, naturally—Camille's gloom turned to fury.

. . . After the murders lifted from the pages of James Ellroy in Tremblay and Bret Easton Ellis in Courbevoie, police have now discovered that the killer known as the "Novelist" may have struck outside France. Sources close to the investigation have confirmed that he is also suspected of the murder of a young girl in Glasgow on July 10, 2001, which would seem to be a faithful reenactment of a crime dreamed up by Scottish author William McIlvanney in his novel *Laidlaw*.

As he read, he looked up from the paper several times, brooding.

"That fucking shit," he muttered at one point.

"They're all the same."

"Who are you talking about?"

"Journalists."

"Actually, I was thinking about a different little shit."

Maleval fell silent. Camille looked at his watch.

"I've got a little shopping to do before I go home. Take the next right."

2

There was nothing to be said. The moment Camille strode into the bookshop brandishing the newspaper, Jérôme Lesage got to his feet and held out his hands, as though leaning against an invisible wall.

"I'm sorry, *commandant* . . . I swear, I-"

"The information you had was covered by judicial confidentiality, Monsieur Lesage. You have broken the law."

"So have you come here to arrest me, *commandant*? That seems a little ungrateful."

"What exactly is your game, Lesage?"

"The information you came looking for may be a secret as far as this investigation is concerned," the bookseller said, "but it's hardly a secret in literary circles, far from it. In fact, I'm rather surprised-"

"At what philistines we are, is that it?" Camille said scathingly.

"I wouldn't go as far as that. But, then again . . ." The ghost of a smile played on Lesage's lips. "So-" he began.

"So," Camille cut him off, "you had no qualms about prostituting your literary knowledge for a little publicity. You have the morals of a used-car dealer."

"Everyone loves publicity, *commandant*. But I would remind you that there was no mention of my name in the article. Unlike yours, if memory serves."

The retort stung. Camille realized it had been pointless to come here, and he regretted acting on this rash impulse. He tossed the paper onto Lesage's counter. He gave up trying to explain to this man the consequences that his actions—whose motive he did not really understand—would inevitably have on the investigation. Resignation won out. He left without a word.

"I'll just drop off my luggage and change," he said to Maleval as he got into the car. "Then we'll go down to headquarters and sound the retreat."

Maleval double-parked with his lights flashing. Camille collected his mail and trudged up the stairs. Without Irène, the apartment seemed terribly empty. In spite of himself, he smiled when he glimpsed the baby's nursery through the half-open door. Now he would have more than enough time to take care of his family.

What should have taken only a minute or two required more time than expected. Maleval considered calling the *patron* on his cell. He had been waiting for what felt like a long time and was sorry he had not checked his watch. He got out of the car and smoked a cigarette, and then another, staring up at the windows of Camille's apartment, which betrayed no sign of life. He had just made up his mind to call when Camille appeared.

"I was starting to get worried," Maleval said.

The wound Camille had suffered from the newspaper article was clearly beginning to fester. He seemed to Maleval even more haggard than before. Camille stood on the pavement for a moment, checking the voice mails from Le Guen. There were three now.

The first was incandescent:

"You're really starting to piss me off, Camille. This shit is all over the fucking papers, and I don't know a thing about it. Call me the second your flight lands, got it?"

The second, which had come a few minutes later, was more instructive:

"Camille... I've just had the *juge* on the phone... Best if we have a quick chat to discuss things because... well, this is going to be a shitstorm. Call me, okay?"

The last was almost sympathetic:

"We're due in the *juge's* offices at 3:30 p.m. If I don't hear from you before, I'll see you there."

Camille erased the messages. Maleval started the car. On the way, the two men did not say a word.

3

Le Guen was first to get to his feet; he shook Camille's hand, grasping his elbow. It was as though he were offering condolences. Deschamps did not move other than to nod toward the empty chair in front of her desk. She took a deep breath.

"Commandant Verhœven," she began coolly, staring down at her fingernails, "a disciplinary procedure is a rare occurrence, and one that I do not undertake lightly."

Deschamps's dressing-downs were never dramatic; they were calculated. That was the word: the calm, detached tone in the face of crisis, the terse delivery. Finally she looked up.

"There can no longer be any excuse or justification for your failings and your negligence. To be brutally honest, I did not even attempt to defend your actions. It was a lost cause. Given that I have already reprimanded you for breaches in procedure, to have given information to the press even before the *procureur*'s office–"

"That's not what happened," Camille interrupted.

"That does not make one whit of difference. Nor have I any interest in knowing what precisely did happen. I regret to inform you that you have been removed from this case."

"*Madame la juge . . . ,*" Le Guen began.

Camille raised a hand to interrupt him.

"Leave it, Jean. *Madame la juge,* I did not inform you of a connection between the Glasgow murder and the novel mentioned in the newspapers because the connection had not been substantiated. That confirmation only came today, which is why I am here now."

"I read all about it in the papers, *commandant,* and I'm delighted. But there has been no real progress on this case. All the media can talk about is you, but you still don't have a solid lead. You are precisely where you were on day one."

Camille sighed. He opened his briefcase and took out a small, glossy booklet that he showed to Deschamps.

"This is a magazine called *Nuits Blanches.* It's a weekly and specializes in detective fiction. They review new books, run profiles and interviews with writers."

Camille opened the magazine and turned to page five.

"And it has classified ads. Most of them looking for rarities, books that are out of print, that sort of thing."

He had to get up from his chair to hand the magazine to the *juge.*

"I've circled an ad on the bottom left. It's very short."

"'B.E.E.'? Is that what you're talking about? And underneath is . . . your home address?"

"Yes," said Camille, "B.E.E. stands for Bret Easton Ellis."

"What exactly is this about?"

"I tried to contact our killer. I ran a classified ad."

"On whose authority–"

"No, no, *madame la juge,* I think we've covered that subject already," Camille cut in. "The little speech about my shortcomings, my recklessness, my failure to follow accepted procedure . . . I agree with everything. But yet again I circumvented the chain of command. What can I say? I'm impulsive . . . it just sort of happened."

He handed her two printed sheets of paper.

"And this," he added, "arrived in the mail this morning."

Monsieur,

So good to finally make your acquaintance. Your advertisement came
as a relief to me. I almost said a deliverance, which perhaps gives some
sense of how much I have suffered over the years to see how blind, how
obtuse the world is. How unfeeling. It was a long, dark time, I assure you.
Over the years, I developed a lamentable opinion of the police force. For
I have seen my fair share of inspectors and detectives. Not a scrap of
ambition, not one iota of finesse. I came to think of these people as idi-
ocy incarnate. Gradually, I came to consider myself as a man with no illusions. In my moments of despair (and God knows I have known many),
I felt overwhelmed by the thought that no one would ever understand.

Before you, many passed me as though sightless, so many that
your appearance could not but kindle hope in me. You were not like
them; there was something different about you. Since you stepped onto
the stage which over time I have crafted with great patience, I have
watched you draw nearer to the heart of the mystery; I knew that you
would decipher it. And so you have. I knew it the moment I read the
newspaper article, that profile of you which I found so profoundly one-
sided. At the time, it was no more than a theory. But I knew you understood me. I knew that, before long, we would make contact.

"B.E.E.," you ask.

It is a long story. A long-cherished project that I could not bring
myself to embark upon until I was certain that I was equal to what, to
me, is the paragon. Bret Easton Ellis is a virtuoso, and it required great
modesty, great humility if I was to hope to serve his masterwork. And
it was a pleasure. Have you noticed (I know you have) how precisely I
recreated the scene? How faithfully I have served the master? It was a
difficult task. It required great preparation. I inspected a thousand locations, visited so many apartments. When I encountered François Cottet,
I—like you, no doubt—immediately had the measure of the man. What
a fool he is, don't you agree? But the location was perfect. It did not prove
difficult to snare such a dullard. His need for money was etched into
his face; his moral bankruptcy oozed from every pore. He imagined he

had clinched a brilliant deal. These words are like "open sesame" to such a man. In his defense, it should be said that he was conscientious and obliging. Indeed he unhesitatingly agreed to personally take delivery of the moving van I had leased. What more could one ask? (You will surely have noticed that I ordered the furniture in the name of Peace, an obvious homage to the author of the Red Riding Quartet . . .) Naturally, he did not know that there his role in my little drama would end. It did not prove difficult to lure him away on Monday night. By then you had scared him witless, and he was prepared to do anything to extricate himself from an imbroglio in which, truth be told, he played only a minor part. I took no pleasure in killing him. I abhor death. His demise was necessary, nothing more. You will find his body in the forêt de Hez near Clermont-de-l'Oise (three hundred yards north of the spot known as "La Cavalerie"; I erected a small cairn to mark the precise location). I do not doubt your ability to gravely convey the news to his family.

But to return to more important matters, if you don't mind. You will have noticed the painstaking care I have taken to recreate the scene as accurately as possible. Everything is in its place, each object precisely positioned. I am convinced that Ellis would be thrilled to see his scene so perfectly fashioned, so faithfully rendered: the suitcase and its contents, bought some months ago in England; the sofa, delivered care of our friend Monsieur Cottet. The most difficult task was in tracking down the hideous Dalmatian print wallpaper indicated by B.E.E. (a magnificent stroke of inspiration). In the end, I was compelled to order it from the United States.

The casting of the two young actresses for my drama was no easy task either.

In the rather vulgar slang of B.E.E.'s golden boy, Patrick Bateman, it was essential that they have "big tits" ("very young, blond hardbodies," as he describes them). I was most attentive to these details, and to their ages. As you must surely have observed, young women of that age with ample breasts are all too common, so this was not my primary concern. This is the real difference between a genuine director and humble stage manager. Young Évelyne was perfect. Making love with her the first time was not unduly taxing, though I did so only because it was necessary to the plan that I had conceived. The only way I could think to gain her trust was to present myself as a harmless, undemanding "john," a little dull but prepared to pay handsomely. She played her part with studied indifference and it was perhaps this apparent detachment tinged with contempt for the needs of the men who paid her that persuaded me to cast her. I was so proud of her when I saw her arrive in Courbevoie with little Josiane. She, too, was perfect. I nurture talent; it is essential to my craft.

That night, Camille, I experienced an attack of stage fright. By the time they arrived, everything was in readiness. The tragi-comedy could begin. Life would finally imitate art. Better yet, art and life would, thanks to me, finally become one. During the early part of the evening, my impatience was so keen that I feared my young companions would think me too nervous. The three of us indulged in foreplay, I served champagne, and I asked of them only what was strictly necessary for my plan.

After an hour of sexual congress during which I directed them to perform precisely those acts detailed by B.E.E., the moment finally came and I felt my chest tighten. I had to draw on all my skill and patience to coax their bodies into precisely the same pose as the characters on which I modeled them. From the moment I ripped out Évelyne's labia with my teeth, from the moment she let out her first howl of terror, everything happened precisely as it had in the book, Camille. That night, I experienced a triumphant success.

Yes, that is how I felt that night. A triumphant success. And I think I can say my success was shared by my two young costars. If you could have seen how Évelyne wept, the sincere, beautiful, lingering tears, when, much later that night, she saw me coming toward her with a steak knife! And I know that had B.E.E. deigned to leave her lips intact at this point of the tragedy, Évelyne would have smiled, I know that she would have felt what, after my long years of patience, was now our shared triumph. I offered her the opportunity of becoming a living part of a work of art and, beyond the pain, utterly sublimated at the acme of this drama, I know that some part of her, the deepest, most mysterious part of her, gloried in that moment. I dragged her from her pitiful existence and elevated her miserable fate to the rank of destiny.

Nothing is more intense, as any lover of art will attest, than the emotion conveyed to us by artists. The means by which I access such sublime emotions is by serving such artists. I know that you will understand. Everything was meticulously executed. Down to the last detail. The scene as you discovered it is an exact likeness of the original.

Imbued with every word, every comma of the book, I felt like an actor who when liberated from the text finally becomes himself. You will see it for yourself someday, since I filmed the scene using the "Minox L.X. ultra-miniature camera that takes 9.5 mm film" stipulated by Ellis. The screenplay made no provision for leaving it at the scene, hence you have been deprived of the film. It is a pity, but that is how the artist conceived it. When you finally see it, you too will be astounded by the truth, the "bitter truth" of the scene. You will hear the Traveling Wilburys play as I struggle to sever the fingers with a pair of nail scissors, you will feel the diabolical power of the scene where I, Patrick Bateman, cut off Évelyne's head with a saw and walk around the room carrying the head on my tumescent penis and the scene I never tire of, where, with my bare hands, I rip open the girl's belly. It is magnificent, Camille, I assure you, utterly magnificent.

Have I said all I need to say? Have I forgotten anything? Do not hesitate to ask if you require further information. Besides, I feel sure that we will have many other opportunities to correspond.

Your obedient servant

P.S.: In retrospect, and without wishing to offend, I hope you will agree that it is touchingly appropriate that you were chosen to investigate the case of the Black Dahlia, whose real name, as you know, was Betty "Short." A subject about which you know something. I append this post scriptum for your superior officers in case they should have the disagreeable idea of removing you from the case (we are TOGETHER in this, you and I, as you well know). Tell them in no uncertain terms that, without you, any hope that they might hear from me again is fruitless . . . but that my work will continue.

Judge Deschamps set down the letter, stared at it for a moment, then picked it up and handed it Le Guen.

"I confess I do not care for your behavior, *commandant* . . ."

"Really?" Camille said. "Compared with our killer, I'm . . ."

Seeing the look on Deschamps's face he trailed off.

"If you could excuse me for a few minutes, *monsieur le division-naire*," Deschamps said to Le Guen, as though Camille had suddenly ceased to exist, "I will need to discuss this with my superiors."

Le Guen finished reading the letter in the corridor. He smiled.

"I had a feeling you would bounce back. But I didn't think it would happen quite like that."

4

"Good trip?" Armand said, sucking in acrid smoke with the relish of a tramp.

"Difficult landing, Armand. It was touch and go."

Armand stared at the stubby cigarette butt between his fingers and was forced to accept he would not get another drag out of it. Regretfully, he extinguished it in an ashtray emblazoned with the logo *optique moderne de Châteauroux.*

"I've got news. And it's not good . . ."

"Oh . . ."

They heard Louis out in the corridor.

"This is absolutely the last time!" he was saying, his voice firm and quite loud.

Camille got up and stepped out of the office to find Louis glaring at Maleval.

Both men turned and smiled awkwardly. Whatever it was about, the argument had come at a bad time. Camille decided to remain neutral and behave as though he had heard nothing.

"Come on, Louis, action stations, I need you to get everyone together," he said, heading toward the photocopier.

When the team was assembled, he handed them copies of the letter sent by the killer. They read in reverential silence.

"Le Guen is prepared to provide us with operational backup," he announced. "They should get here tomorrow or the day after, he's not sure, but we're definitely going to need them."

"Uh-huh," Armand, Maleval, and Louis agreed as they finished reading.

Camille gave them a moment.

"This guy's a fucking nutcase," Maleval said.

"I've asked Dr. Crest to revise his psychological profile. But in principle I'd have to agree, he's a nutcase. That said, at least we have a lead."

"We can't be sure it's from him . . . ," Armand said. "I mean, all the stuff he comes out with has already appeared in the papers."

"I suspect that in a few hours' time, we'll have found Cottet's body. That should be enough to convince you."

"The letter confirms everything we already know, but he doesn't tell us much that's new," Louis said.

"I thought the same. The guy is careful. But let's go through the details anyway. The wallpaper is American. Armand, you know what you have to do. We also know he visited a lot of apartments. That'll be more difficult. We'll need to run a check in Paris and the suburbs of housing developments likely to have fitted his criteria. The letter confirms that Josiane Debeuf was introduced to him by Évelyne Rouvray. We're not likely to turn up anything on that front. We might be able to find something on the Minox camera he says he used . . ."

"I'm in no hurry to see the film," Maleval said.

"No one is, I'm sure, but we need to add it to our list. Maleval, can you go round to the furniture warehouse in Gennevilliers and see if the security guard can identify Cottet from a recent photograph? And . . . I think that's everything."

"It's not much, is it?"

"Oh yes, there's one more thing: the letter was posted in Courbevoie, right next to the crime scene. The man's got style."

5

A peaceful, melancholy expanse of woodland, the forêt de Hez is a lethal place for property developers.

The local *gendarmes* sealed off the area and a full forensics team from *l'identité judiciaire* was dispatched. The burial site was secluded, sheltered from passing ramblers, and easily accessible by road, which made it probable that Cottet had been killed elsewhere and his body dumped there. The forensics officers had already been working for more than an hour under the glare of spotlights powered by a generator; they conducted a painstaking fingertip search of the area before those tasked with exhuming the body were allowed to move in. Toward 9 p.m. it turned bitterly cold. The bright arc lamps and the police lights flashing blue beams through the budding leaves gave the dark forest an almost ghostly atmosphere.

By 10 p.m. the body had been exhumed without complications.

Cottet's corpse was dressed in a fawn suit and a pale-yellow shirt, and it was clear from the moment it was disinterred that he had received a shot to the head. Clean. It was agreed that Camille would call Madame Cottet and arrange for the body to be identified; Maleval would attend the autopsy.

Wednesday, April 16

1

"I'm going to ask one of my colleagues to take your statement, Madame Cottet. But in the meantime, I have a question."

They were standing in the corridor leading to the mortuary.

"I believe I'm right in thinking your husband was a fan of crime fiction."

Strange though the question must have sounded, Madame Cottet did not seem surprised.

"Yes, he read little else. That was about the limit of his intellectual ambition."

"Is there anything more you can tell me?"

"Not really. My husband and I have barely been on speaking terms for a long time, and when we do talk, it's not about his choice of reading matter."

"Forgive me for asking, but . . . was your husband a violent man? I mean, was he ever violent toward you?"

"My husband was not a brave man. He was ... physical, certainly, and he could be a little brutish, but not in the sense that you mean."

"Let me be more precise, then. What was he like ... sexually?" Camille was weary of euphemisms and decided to be blunt.

"Rapid." Madame Cottet seemed determined to needle him. "In fact, perfunctory, if I recall. He was not kinky; he had a limited imagination. He was utterly ordinary. He preferred oral, though was curious about anal; what more can I tell you?"

"I think you've told me enough."

"A premature ejaculator."

"Thank you, Madame Cottet. Thank you."

"Not at all, Monsieur Verhœven, not at all. It's always a pleasure to talk to a true gentleman."

Camille decided to let Louis conduct the interview.

2

Camille invited Louis and Le Guen to lunch. Louis was wearing a
teal-blue suit, a sober striped shirt, and a midnight-blue tie with
the crest of an English university. Le Guen invariably looked upon
Louis as an anthropological curiosity. He seemed astonished that
nature, having exhausted every possible combination, was still
capable of producing such a specimen.

"Right now," Camille said, digging into his leeks, "we're dealing
with five victims, three staged crime scenes, three novels, and two
missing persons."

"Not to mention the press, the investigating magistrate, the public prosecutor's office, and the minister," Le Guen added.

"If you want to be really pedantic, yes."

"*Le Matin* was ahead of the pack yesterday morning, but every
other rag has caught up by now, as I'm sure you've seen–"

"I prefer to avoid the tabloids."

"You're wrong to. If things carry on like this, this 'Novelist' of
yours is likely to win the Prix Goncourt. I was talking to Deschamps
earlier. You'll laugh."

"Try me."

"Apparently the minister is 'deeply troubled.'"

"Troubled? A minister? You jest!"

"Not at all, Camille. To me, a minister who is deeply troubled is deeply troubling in itself. But ministerial anxiety has practical benefits. Everything we were told was impossible yesterday is now top priority. By this afternoon you'll have a bigger squad room and a lot more officers."

"Do I get to choose?"

"Don't push your luck! Sentimentality does not equal magnanimity, Camille."

"I need to enlarge my vocabulary. What, then?"

"I'll let you have another three officers. By four o'clock."

"Meaning six o'clock?"

"Give or take."

The three men ate for a moment in silence.

"That said," Louis ventured, "With that last classified ad of yours, we've reclaimed the initiative to some extent."

"To some extent," Camille said.

"This guy's got us by the balls," said Le Guen.

"Jean, please! We're gentlemen! At least, that's how Madame Cottet referred to me this morning."

"What's she like?"

Camille glanced at Louis.

"Intelligent," Louis said, sipping his wine. "Good family. From what she said, she and her husband didn't so much live together as share a house. They've always been from completely different worlds, and over time they drifted even further apart. She claims to know very little about her husband's private life; they lived separate lives."

"It wouldn't have been hard to outsmart her husband," Camille said. "Thick as shit . . ."

"He was obviously an easy mark," Louis agreed. "Maleval showed his photograph to the foreman at the self-storage place in Gennevilliers. There's no doubt it was him."

"He was clearly being used, so we still don't have much to go on."

"All we know for certain," Louis said, "is that our killer is reenacting scenes from crime novels and-"

"From novels," Camille interrupted him. "They've been crime novels so far, but there's nothing in his letter to suggest that his 'masterwork' is finished. He could throw a woman under a train and claim he's recreating *Anna Karenina*, poison some woman in the ass-end of Normandy to restage *Madame Bovary* in period costume . . . or . . ."

". . . drop a thermonuclear device on Japan to play out *Hiroshima Mon Amour*," Le Guen said in an attempt to display his erudition.

What sort of logic drove this man? Why had he chosen these particular books over any others? How many murders had he reenacted before the Tremblay case? And then there was the elephant in the room: how many more murders might this maniac reenact before they arrested him?

"What do you think, Camille?"

"About what?"

"What Louis just said . . ."

"I'm going to need Cob."

"I don't see the connection . . ."

"Listen, Jean, I don't give a shit which other officers you assign to me, but I need Cob to run computer research."

Le Guen took a moment to think about it.

At forty, Cob was something of a legend in the force. With few academic qualifications, he had joined the newly created Technology Crime Division of the *brigade criminelle* as a lowly junior. Since he had little chance of passing the cut-throat *concours administratifs* and would have to rely on promotions based on length of service, Cob seemed perfectly content to remain a junior officer because his computing skills meant he was always assigned to sensitive cases. Every officer in the *brigade* knew about Cob's technical wizardry, especially his immediate superiors, who were suspicious initially, until they realized that he was not a threat to their positions. Having once been treated like a sort of idiot savant by the departments to which he was assigned, he was now considered a genius. He was constantly in demand. Camille did not really know the man, having run into him only in the canteen, but he liked Cob's style. Cob's face was as square and white as a computer monitor, and his somewhat sullen manner belied an ironic detachment and a deadpan sense of humor that appealed to Camille. But it was not for his sense of humor that Camille had requested him: the investigation needed a gifted computer expert, and everyone at the *brigade* knew that Cob was the best.

"Okay, fine . . ." Le Guen sighed. "But, to get back to what Louis was saying—what *do* you think?"

Camille, who hadn't been listening to a word of their conversation, looked at his partner and smiled: "I think Louis is always right. It's axiomatic."

3

"Obviously, anything we discuss here is protected by judicial confidentiality."

"Obviously," said Fabien Ballanger, who clearly had only the vaguest idea of how investigations were conducted in the real world.

Sitting behind his desk, his head resting pensively on one fist like Rodin's *Thinker*, Ballanger waited for Camille to get to the point, his imploring eyes trying to lighten the *commandant*'s burden by granting him general absolution.

"We currently have four murder cases on our hands."

"Two more than when we last spoke . . ."

"Exactly."

"Which, obviously, seems like a lot," Ballanger said, staring down at his hands.

Camille gave a brief outline of how each of the crimes had been committed.

"We have now determined that three of these murders were precise reenactments of scenes from *American Psycho*, *The Black Dahlia*, and *Laidlaw*. Are you familiar with the books?"

"Yes, I've read all three."

"Can you think of anything that might connect them?"

"Not really," Ballanger said, after giving the matter some thought. "One Scottish writer, two Americans. They work in very different genres. In literary terms, *Laidlaw* and *American Psycho* are a world apart. I can't remember precisely when they were published, but I'm pretty certain there's no correlation in the dates."

"If our theory is correct, there has to be some link."

Ballanger frowned for a moment, then said: "Maybe your killer just happens to like those books."

Camille couldn't suppress a smile, and Ballanger smiled, too.

"I hadn't thought of that," Camille said finally. "Stupid of me."

"When it comes to taste, readers can be very eclectic."

"Murderers less so. They tend to be more logical. Or at least, they have their own twisted 'logic.'"

"This might be in bad taste."

"Spit it out."

"I'd say that in each case he's chosen an exceptionally fine book!"

"Good," said Camille, smiling, "I'd much rather hunt down a man of taste. It's more fulfilling."

"Your . . . your killer . . . is obviously well read. He's something of an expert in the genre."

"He would seem to be. He's definitely one sick bastard. But we still have one crucial question: how far back does this thing go?"

"I'm not sure what you mean," Ballanger said.

"We know about all the murders that he 'signed.' If we're lucky, we can work out where this ends. But what we don't know is which novel started the whole thing off, and where. And when."

"I see . . . ," Ballanger said, though plainly he did not.

"There may be other murders dating years before the one in Glasgow," Camille said. "His scope is vast, his plan is grandiose. The novels we've already managed to identify, would you say they're classics?"

"Well, they're all pretty well known. I'm not sure I'd call them 'classics,' at least not in terms of the literary canon."

"If that's the case, I have to say I'm a little surprised." Camille appeared heartened by Ballanger's response. "Because if he wanted to pay homage to crime fiction, it would be logical to begin by reenacting what you might call a 'classic of the genre,' would it not?"

Ballanger's curiosity was piqued.

"You're right. That would make good sense."

"So, in your opinion, how many 'classics' could we be talking about?"

"Oh, I don't know. The list would be pretty long," Ballanger said, thinking, "Well, maybe not that long. In crime fiction, what constitutes a 'classic of the genre' is moot. Personally, I think the choices are sociological and historical rather than strictly literary."

Camille looked at him quizzically.

"Sociological in the sense that the reading public often consider certain books to be masterpieces in the teeth of critical opinion. Historical in the sense that a classic is not necessarily a masterpiece. Lieberman's *City of the Dead* is a masterpiece, but it's not considered a classic. The opposite is true of Christie's *And Then There Were None*. Now, *The Murder of Roger Ackroyd* is both a masterpiece *and* a classic."

"I need you to be categorical, Professeur Ballanger," Camille said. "If I were a *professeur* of literature I'd be happy to sit here quibbling about semantics, but I'm a detective investigating a series of cases in which young women have been horribly murdered. So, how many masterpieces, classics, call them what you will, how many are there, roughly?"

"I'd say about three hundred. Roughly."

"Three hundred? Could you draw up a list of titles and give me some idea where we could find synopses for them? That way we can try to cross-reference cold cases with plot elements from these novels."

"Why are you asking me?"

"Because I need someone who not only has the requisite knowledge but is capable of refining it, condensing it. It's not going to come as a surprise to you that we don't have too many literary experts down at the *brigade criminelle*. I had considered asking a specialist bookseller."

"Not a bad idea," Ballanger said.

"We know one, but he's not exactly . . . cooperative. I'd prefer to entrust the task to—how should I put it?—one of the eminent educationalists in the service of the Republic."

Ballanger seemed to think this was a nice touch. The grandiloquent term made it hard for him to refuse; it appealed to his sense of honor and decency.

"Yes, I suppose I could do it," he said. "The list wouldn't be too difficult to compile, though I warn you, the choices will inevitably be subjective."

Camille indicated that he accepted this.

"I'm bound to have a number of monographs and papers on the subject lying around. And I could ask some of my students to lend a hand . . . Two days?"

"Perfect."

4

The interest senior officers take in high-profile cases can be measured by the resources they allocate to investigating officers. That afternoon, Camille discovered that he had been allocated a large squad room in the basement. With no windows.

"Damn," he said to Le Guen. "One more murder, and they'd probably have given us a room with a view."

"Probably," Le Guen said, "but one fewer murder and you wouldn't have had those computers."

Technicians were setting up a bank of five computers while workmen installed corkboards, flip charts, a floor-standing water cooler that also dispensed hot water for instant coffee, office desks and chairs, and several phone lines. Juge Deschamps had called Camille on his cell to arrange the first briefing. They settled on 8:30 a.m. the following morning.

By 6:30 p.m, the whole team had assembled. Not all the chairs had been delivered, but this did not matter since, in keeping with tradition, the first team meeting was held standing up.

"Let's start off with the introductions," Camille began. "I'm Commandant Verhœven—call me Camille . . . it's simpler. This is Louis: he'll be coordinating the team. Any leads you come up with go straight to him. He'll also be assigning duties."

The four newcomers looked silently at Louis and nodded.

"This is Maleval. On paper, he's called Jean-Claude, but everyone calls him Maleval. He is in charge of resources. If you need computers, cars, equipment, whatever, talk to him."

Maleval gave the new recruits an awkward wave.

"Last but not least, Armand. He and I are the senior officers here. You'll never meet a more meticulous officer. If you've got any doubts about a line of inquiry, talk to him. He'll be happy to help out. He's an exceptionally generous man."

Armand stared at the floor and blushed.

"Right, now, the newcomers."

Camille fished a piece of paper from his pocket and unfolded it. "Élisabeth . . ."

A fifty-something woman of ample proportions with an honest face dressed in a trouser suit of indeterminate vintage.

"Hi," she said, raising a hand. "Good to be here."

Camille liked her right away, the way she spoke, her easy manner.

"Welcome, Élisabeth. Have you worked on any other major cases?"

"I worked on the Ange Versini case . . ."

Everyone at the *brigade* remembered the case of the Corsican man who had strangled two children and evaded capture for eight weeks before being gunned down at point-blank range on the boulevard Magenta after a high-speed chase that had created a lot of front-line damage—and a few front-page headlines.

"Good work. I hope we'll add to your list of credits."

"I hope so, too."

She seemed anxious to get to work. She glanced over at Louis and gave him a friendly smile and a nod.

"Fernand?" Camille asked, looking down at his list.

"That's me," said a man in his fifties.

Camille quickly sized him up: the solemn, slightly vacant expression, the rheumy eyes, the pasty complexion of an alcoholic. Ever the pragmatist, Le Guen had already tipped off Verhœven: "I suggest you use him in the mornings. After that, there's no one home . . ."

"You've been seconded from Vice, is that right?"

"Yeah, I don't know much about the *brigade criminelle*."

"I'm sure you'll prove your worth here," Camille said with a confidence he did not really feel. "You'll be working with Armand."

"By a process of elimination, I assume you must be Mehdi?" Camille turned to a young man of about twenty-five. Despite the jeans and the T-shirt, no doubt worn to show off his gym-toned body, despite the iPod headphones that dangled around his neck, Mehdi had a serious and alert expression that Camille found charming.

"That's me. I'm with the Eighth Brigade. Well, obviously I haven't been there long."

"This will be good experience for you, kid. You'll be working with Maleval."

Mehdi nodded at Maleval, while Camille instantly regretted referring to a fellow officer as "kid." He was clearly getting old.

"Finally, this is Cob," Camille said, stuffing the piece of paper back into his pocket. "We know each other, but we've never actually worked together . . ."

Cob looked over at Camille.

"Not until now."

"Cob will be our technical genius."

Cob greeted the ripple of recognition with nothing more than a raised eyebrow.

"If there's anything more you need, Cob, just tell Maleval and he'll arrange it."

Thursday, April 17

1

"For now, we've found nothing to contradict our initial assessment. We're dealing with a profoundly misogynistic sociopath."

Deschamps's first briefing had begun on time at 8:30 a.m. Dr. Crest, having set his briefcase on one of the desks, was addressing the assembled company from notes scrawled in his tall, sloping hand.

"The letter Commandant Verhœven received from the suspect has done much to round out the clinical profile I have been working up but in no way refutes my preliminary findings. The suspect is educated, cultured, and arrogant. Aside from his interest in crime fiction, he is extremely well read. He will most likely have a degree in the humanities—philosophy, history, something of that nature. Sociology, possibly. His pretentiousness is obvious from the fact that he feels the need to flaunt his knowledge. What is immediately apparent in the letter is the cordiality of his tone. He needs you to admire him, *commandant*. He clearly likes you, and he knows you."

"Personally?"

"Not necessarily, though anything is possible. I'm more inclined to think that he knows you in the sense that he's seen you on television, or read about you in the papers."

"That's a relief," Camille said, and for the first time, the two men exchanged a smile. And the first smile between two men is either a sign of respect or a sign of trouble brewing.

"That little advertisement of yours was cleverly worded," continued Dr. Crest.

"Really?"

"Oh, yes. Brief and to the point, careful not to address him personally. You invited him to talk about 'his work,' and I believe that this is why he responded. He feels a need to explain himself so was bound to seize on any opportunity. You gave him that opportunity. The worst thing you could have done would have been to ask what makes him tick, as though you didn't understand him. From the way you phrased your question, you implied that you already knew, that you understood him, making him feel—how shall I put this?—as though you shared a particular worldview."

"Actually, I didn't really think about what I was saying."

Crest allowed Camille's words to hang in the air for a moment.

"You must have been thinking about it subconsciously," he went on. "That said, I don't really believe that we have learned much about what motivates him. The letter indicates that he considers himself to be working on 'his masterpiece,' which, for all his false modesty, he feels he should rank alongside the great writers that he has chosen to emulate."

"But why?" Élisabeth asked.

"That's a very different question."

"A frustrated writer?" she suggested, voicing a possibility each of them were contemplating.

"It's one possibility, certainly. In fact, it may be the most plausible hypothesis."

"If he's a frustrated writer, he's probably written a couple of novels," Mehdi said. "We could talk to agents and publishers?"

No one was surprised by the young officer's naivety. Camille gave a little sigh and rubbed his eyes.

"Mehdi, half the population of France are frustrated writers. The others are frustrated artists. There are hundreds of editors in Paris, and every one of them is sent thousands of manuscripts each year. Even if we were only to cover the past five years . . ."

"Okay, okay, I get it." Mehdi held up his hands in surrender.

"Do we have any idea how old he might be?" Élisabeth said, coming to the young man's rescue.

"Between forty and fifty."

"Social class?"

"I'd say upper middle class. In his desperation to prove just how clever he is, he overplays his hand."

"Like posting the letter from Courbevoie?" Louis said.

"Precisely!" Crest answered, surprised at this observation. "That's exactly what I mean. It's melodramatic. He tries too hard. And that could be useful to us. This killer is careful, but he's so self-important that he runs the risk of making a mistake. He has a desperate need for approbation. And yet he is deeply solipsistic. This goes to the heart of, is the crux of his conflicted personality. Though it is not the only one."

"Meaning?" Camille said.

"Obviously, there are still a lot of things we do not know, but one in particular troubles me. I don't understand why he went to Glasgow to carry out the murder from McIlvanney's novel."

"Surely because that's where the murder is supposed to take place!" said Camille.

"I've thought about that. But in that case, why restage the crime from *American Psycho* in Courbevoie rather than New York? After all, that's where the novel takes place, is it not?"

Camille was forced to acknowledge that he had not considered this discrepancy.

"Similarly," Crest went on, "the Tremblay murder should have taken place in . . ."

"Los Angeles," Louis said.

"You're right. It doesn't makes sense," said Camille, shrugging. "But what we need to do now is think about the next ad I place."

"I agree. I've been giving it some thought. It's crucial that we gain his trust. If you question his motives, you'll only destroy your good work so far. You need to treat him as an equal; he needs to believe you understand him, admire him even. You'll have to flatter him."

"What do you suggest?"

"Don't address him personally. You might ask for details about one of the other murders. After that, we'll see."

"The magazine comes out on Mondays, which means leaving a week between ads. That's too long."

"There is a way we could speed things up." Cob spoke for the first time. "The magazine has a website. I checked it out. You can submit a classified ad online and it would appear by tomorrow."

Camille brought the meeting to a close, and he and Dr. Crest together discussed the wording of the second ad, which Verhœven then ran by Deschamps. It consisted of just three words: "Your *Black Dahlia*?" Like the first, it was signed simply "C.V." Cob was tasked with submitting it to the website.

2

The list supplied by Fabien Ballanger ran to a hundred and twenty titles. At the bottom Ballanger had scrawled "Synopses to follow. In five or six days . . ." One hundred and twenty titles set over two columns—enough reading matter for two years, maybe three. An authoritative introduction to crime fiction, perfect for someone curious to investigate the genre, but utterly useless in the context of a criminal investigation. Camille could not help but check to see how many he had read (there were eight) and how many he had heard of (which took his total to sixteen). He felt a brief pang of regret that the killer was not a connoisseur of art instead.

"How many of these have you heard of?" he asked Louis.

"I'm not sure," Louis said, scanning the list. "Thirty, maybe . . ."

Ballanger had brought all his expertise to bear, which was precisely what had been asked of him, but such an extensive list made investigation impossible. Camille realized that it had been a good idea only in theory.

On the telephone, Ballanger sounded pleased with himself.

"We're busy putting together the synopses. I've got three of my students working on it. They're completely obsessed."

"It's too much work, Professeur Ballanger."

"Don't worry about them; they don't have much on this term."

"No, I meant the list: a hundred and twenty titles is unworkable."

"How many can you handle?"

From the *professeur*'s tone it was apparent that they lived in different worlds, Camille in the murky, mundane lowlands where murder was commonplace, and Ballanger in the lofty towers of art and literature.

"To be honest, Professeur Ballanger, I have no idea."

"Then how the devil am I supposed to know?"

"Assuming that the murderer is picking titles based on his personal tastes," Camille said, ignoring Ballanger's touchy remark, "the list I asked you to draw up will be useless. Given what we already know, this man is not a rookie; he clearly knows everything there is to know about crime fiction. But it would be surprising if his personal list didn't include at least one or two classics. These are the books we need to identify. And that's how you can help."

"I'll draw up a new list myself."

Camille's thanks fell on deaf ears; Ballanger had already hung up.

Friday, April 18

1

Armand and Fernand were an ideal pairing. Within two hours of meeting, they were behaving like an old married couple: Armand had already "borrowed" his new colleague's newspaper, his pen and notepad, and shamelessly helped himself to cigarettes (even slipping a few into his pocket for later); in exchange, he pretended not to notice Fernand's frequent absences or the way he always came back from the toilets sucking a mint. At Louis's instruction, they had given up researching the long list of wallpaper manufacturers and were now focused on housing developments the killer might have visited while looking for an apartment in Courbevoie. Mehdi had headed off to the post office in Courbevoie on the outside chance of finding someone who remembered the killer. Maleval was making inquiries about recently bought chain saws and Minox cameras. Meanwhile, Louis, armed with a warrant, went to the offices of *Nuits Blanches* magazine to request their list of subscribers.

Sometime around midmorning, Camille was surprised to see Professeur Ballanger show up. The frustration he had apparently felt the night before was gone, and he sidled into the squad room with a strange reticence.

"You didn't need to put yourself to such trouble . . . ," Camille said.

No sooner had he said the words than he realized that it was prurient curiosity that had led Ballanger to personally deliver the fruits of his labor rather than simply sending an e-mail. Ballanger studied the squad room with the same incredulous amazement as a tourist visiting the catacombs. Camille showed him around and introduced him to Élisabeth, Louis, and Armand—the only officers present—pointedly emphasizing Professeur Ballanger's "invaluable assistance" in their investigation.

"I've reworked the list."

"That's very kind," Camille said, taking the stapled sheets that Ballanger held out to him. There were now fifty-one titles, each followed by a synopsis running from a couple of lines to a quarter of a page. He quickly scanned the pages, stopping at a title here and there: *The Purloined Letter*, *L'affaire Lerouge*, *The Hound of the Baskervilles*, *Le Mystère de la chambre jaune*. Without thinking, Camille glanced over at the bank of computers. Having been a dutiful host, he was now anxious to be rid of Ballanger.

"Thank you so much," Camille said, making to shake his hand.

"Perhaps I could expand a little on my notes?"

"Your synopses seem clear to me."

"If I may . . ."

"You've already done more than we could have hoped for. We're very grateful."

Mercifully, the *professeur* did not take offense.

"All right. I'll leave you to it," he said, regretfully.

"Thanks again."

The moment Ballanger had left, Camille raced over to Cob.

"This is a list of classic crime novels."

"I can guess . . ."

"We need to identify the salient elements of the crimes described in them and look for any cold cases that seem to correspond."

"When you say 'we' . . ."

"I mean 'you.'" Camille grinned.

He took a few hesitant steps, then came back, looking thoughtful.

"There's something else I need you to do."

"Camille, I'm going to be tied up for hours on this."

"I know that. But there's something else I need. Something I suspect might prove pretty complicated."

It was always best to appeal to Cob's finer feelings. These feelings—like everything else about him—were essentially computerlike. The only thing more likely to pique his interest than a difficult task was an impossible one.

"It's to do with the cold cases. I need all the information we have on the killer's modus operandi in each investigation."

"So what exactly are we looking for?"

"Logical inconsistencies, baffling details, pieces of evidence that seem unrelated to the case. One-time crimes in which something about the evidence seems improbable. We need to go through the list of classic crime novels, but it's probable that our killer is choosing books on the basis of his personal taste, and there's no guarantee that those novels will be on our list. The only way to identify them is to look for logical inconsistencies, details that don't fit with the MO because they've been lifted directly from a novel."

"I don't have the heuristic algorithms designed for that kind of search."

"I know that. If you did, I wouldn't be asking, I'd do it myself."

"Parameters?"

"Let's say metropolitan France over the last five years."

"Nothing too taxing, then!"

"How long will it take?"

"No idea," Cob said pensively. "First I'll have to write an algorithm."

2

"You've had your doubts about him from the beginning." Camille smiled.

"Not particularly, no," Louis protested. "But he wouldn't be the first murderer to deliberately contact the police."

"I know; you explained."

"Yes, but since then I've discovered a number of other disturbing facts."

"I'm listening."

Louis flipped opened his notebook.

"Jérôme Lesage, forty-two, single. He inherited the bookshop from his father, who died in 1984. Studied literature at the Sorbonne. His dissertation was on 'The Oral Tradition in Detective Fiction.' He graduated with distinction. Family: one sister, Christine; she's forty; they live together."

"You're kidding."

"Absolutely not, they live in the apartment above the bookshop. It's all part of their inheritance. On April 11, 1985, Christine Lesage marries one Alain Froissart."

"All this detail!"

"I mention it because it's relevant: her husband died in a car crash ten days later, on April 21, leaving her a sizable fortune he had inherited from his family: for generations they owned woolen mills in northern France before successfully moving into off-the-rack clothing. Froissart was the sole heir. In the years that followed, Christine spent a period in a psychiatric clinic and there were several stays in sanatoriums. In 1988, she came back to Paris and moved into her brother's apartment. She still lives there.

"Now, our killer is obviously well off, and Lesage has access to a lot of money: that's the first point. Point two: the time line. On July 10, 2001, Grace Hobson was murdered in Glasgow. Lesage's bookshop was closed for the month of July because brother and sister were on vacation in England—Lesage has a friend in London, and they stayed with him for two weeks. But London to Glasgow can only be—what?—an hour by plane."

"It all sounds a bit far fetched."

"Maybe, but it's possible. Manuela Constanza was murdered on November 21, 2001. Right here in Paris. Lesage could have done it; he's got no alibi. Nor does he have an alibi for the Courbevoie murders on April 6. Paris, Courbevoie, Tremblay, they're all within an hour's drive, meaning Lesage had opportunity."

"It's all circumstantial."

"He told us about two of the three books. He contacted us in the first instance. And we don't know what his motive was for leaking information to the press. He claims he was tricked into it, but if he's our killer, he could just as easily have done it because he wanted the publicity."

"It's possible."

"He subscribes to *Nuits Blanches*," Louis said, waving the list he had requisitioned from the publisher.

"Oh, Louis!" Camille said, snatching the list and thumbing through it. "He's a specialist bookseller—he probably subscribes to every magazine going. Look, there are dozens of bookshops on this list. There's all sorts in here: booksellers, journalists, libraries, newspapers. It's entirely possible my father is on this list . . . Bingo! There he is! And anyone with Internet access can read the classified ads; there's no paywall."

Louis held up his hands in surrender.

"Okay," Camille continued, "what do you suggest?"

"Check his finances. It's a bookshop, so there'll be a lot of cash transactions. We'd need to take a detailed look at his accounts, earnings, expenditure, look for any substantial unexplained withdrawals. After all, these murders have to be pretty expensive undertakings."

Camille thought for a moment.

"Get me Deschamps on the phone."

Saturday, April 19

1

10 p.m. at the Gare de Lyon.

Seeing her waddle toward him, Camille was surprised to note that Irène's face was rounder, her stomach more swollen even than when she left. He insisted on taking her suitcase, kissed her awkwardly. She looked utterly drained.

"Good break?"

"You've heard the highlights," she said, breathless.

They took a taxi, and the moment they arrived home, Irène collapsed onto the sofa with a sigh of relief.

"Can I get you something?" Camille said.

"Tea would be nice."

Irène talked about her time away.

"My father talked and talked and talked, he went on and on and on about himself. I don't know why I'm surprised; it's the only subject he knows anything about."

"Sounds exhausting."

"They're very sweet."

She asked about the investigation. He gave her a copy of the letter sent by the killer, which she read while he went downstairs to fetch the mail.

"Are you here for dinner?" she asked when he reappeared.

"I don't think so . . . ," Camille said, his face ashen. In his hand was an unopened letter. The postmark read: Tremblay-en-France.

Dear Commandant,

I am honored that you have taken such an interest in my work.

I know that you and your team have been busy and that my missives have generated a lot of activity and undoubtedly left you exhausted. For this I apologize. If I could lighten your load, I would do so in a heartbeat, believe me. But I have my own work to accomplish, and I know you understand that.

Here I am, rambling on, when doubtless you are anxious for me to get to the point.

So: *The Black Dahlia*.

The book is a masterpiece, don't you agree? And my homage to it was also a masterpiece, even if I do say so myself. "My" Dahlia, as you so fittingly refer to her, was a grubby little whore. Graceless and a little vulgar, perhaps. From the moment I saw her, I knew she was better suited to a role in Ellroy's novel than to standing on street corners. Her body was, shall we say, acceptable. Unfortunately, Ellroy's descriptions focus on the body in death rather than in life. During my long nocturnal perambulations, I repeated phrases from the novel over and over through the red-light districts of Paris, from rue Saint-Denis to Pigalle, from the Champs-Élysées to the Bois de Boulogne. I began to despair of ever finding such a rare pearl. Then, one night, I found her unexpectedly—or rather, all too predictably—standing on the corner of the rue Saint-Denis dressed garishly in thigh-high red boots, her tawdry undergarments visible thanks to a plunging neckline and a split skirt. It was her smile that won me over. Manuela had a wide mouth and naturally jet-black hair. I asked her price and went upstairs with her. It was an ordeal, Camille, I assure you. The place was squalid beyond belief; the room was pervaded by the stench of sweat, which the scented candle burning on the chest of drawers did little to dispel, and the bed—a mattress on a wooden pallet—was such that no healthy person would have agreed to lie on it. We did the deed standing up; it was the only way.

Thereafter, I waged a long tactical campaign. Prostitutes are by nature wary, and even if their pimps are not immediately visible, one senses their presence behind the half-open doors, glimpses shadowy figures in the hallways. I was obliged to return on several occasions, to convince her that I was harmless, gentle, undemanding, charming.

I was careful not to visit this brothel too frequently, nor to always visit at the same time lest my presence be remarked upon; her friends might have been able to identify me later.

At the close of one of our encounters, I suggested we meet else-where, "for the night." She could name her price. I had not imagined it might require quite so much negotiating. She said she needed to dis-cuss it with her pimp. At that point, I could have changed my mind, looked for some other partner, but I am, I confess, somewhat single minded, and during our trysts I had projected onto the girl all the images from the book. By now, she was the living embodiment of Betty Short; she seemed so perfect in the role that I could not bring myself to give her up. In hindsight, I was lucky, you might say. It was, after all, an unnecessary risk. And so I met with her gorilla, Lambert. What a character! I don't know whether you knew him in life—ah, yes, he's dead now, but I'll come back to that. He was . . . like a character from a novel. Beyond caricature. He treated me with contempt, and I allowed him to. That was the game. He needed to "know exactly who he was dealing with," he told me. The man clearly enjoyed his work. Like any other pimp, he doubtless beat the girls, but his tone was protective, almost paternal. To cut a long story short, I explained that I wanted "his girl" for one night. He fleeced me, Camille, fleeced me shamefully. But, as I have said, that was the game. He demanded to know where we would be spending the night, which complicated matters. With the embarrassed reluctance of a married man, I gave him a false address, and that seemed to satisfy him. Or at least, so I believed. Manuela and I met the following day. I feared she might stand me up, but, for them, this was a good deal.

In the area around the rue de Livy, a stone's throw from the landfill, there are a number of derelict houses that the government has long planned to demolish. Some are bricked or boarded up, but there are two standing empty. I chose 57B. As I drove Manuela there that night, I sensed she was apprehensive, but I was so sweet, so awkward, so insecure, that even the most insolent whore would have been convinced.

Everything had been prepared in advance. As soon as we stepped inside, I delivered a heavy blow to the back of her head, and she collapsed without so much as a groan. Then I brought her body down to the cellar.

Two hours later, she woke to find herself naked, tied to a chair, in the blinding glare of the spotlight. She was shivering and wide eyed with terror. I told her what was going to happen, and, for the first few hours, she writhed and twisted in an effort to break free; she tried to scream, but the duct tape covering her face made it impossible. I found all this upheaval exasperating. I decided to break her legs first. With a baseball bat. After that, things proceeded more smoothly. She could not stand; she could still crawl, though not for very long. Nor very far. This greatly facilitated my tasks, whether whipping her, according to the description in the novel, burning her breasts with cigarettes (though, as I'm sure you will have noticed, there is no other mention of cigarette burns in Ellroy's works). The torture was somewhat protracted, but never tedious. The most difficult task was to recreate the smile of the Black Dahlia. Since it had to be done at the first attempt, I could not afford the slightest mistake. In the event, Camille, it was my crowning achievement.

In my work, you know, every detail is important.

Like a jigsaw puzzle, which achieves formal perfection only when it has been assembled, each tiny piece has its precise place. Should a single piece be missing, the finished work would be different; neither more nor less beautiful, but different. My mission is to ensure that the fictional worlds of great writers are scrupulously brought to life just so. It is that scrupulousness that crowns my work with greatness, and as a result the smallest detail must be studied, its every consequence calculated. Hence the crucial importance of recreating that smile, and doing so perfectly. My art is imitation; I reproduce, I am a copyist, in the manner you might say of a medieval monk. My self-abnegation is total, my devotion boundless. I have dedicated my life to the service of others.

As I inserted the blade next to her ear, as close as possible to the scalp, gripping her hair to hold the head in place, as I carved a deep gash extending to the corner of her mouth in a single fluid arc, I knew from the animal howl that rose from the very depths of her to emerge from this new half mouth that shed blood like long, viscous tears, that I had achieved my aim. I was more careful still as I began the second part of our smile, though the gash was perhaps a little too wide. Nonetheless, recreating the Dahlia's smile was, as you can imagine, infinitely rewarding. In that magnificent smile I suddenly saw distilled all the beauty of the world. Once more I was reminded how much my masterwork depended on a scrupulous attention to detail.

Once Manuela was dead, I cut her up, as described in the book, using a butcher's knife. I am no specialist in anatomy, and more than once I had to consult the medical textbook I had been studying so that I might identify the organs I needed to excise from my Black Dahlia. The intestines were obvious, as were the liver and the stomach, but would *you* be able to locate the gall bladder?

To wash the twin halves of the body, I had to take them upstairs and, since the water supply had long since been cut off, I used water from a rain barrel the previous residents had left in the back garden. I was careful to wash the hair thoroughly.

By the early hours of morning, dawn had begun to break so I could not venture to the landfill there to put the finishing touches to my composition. Fearing I might encounter some passer-by, I preferred to return home. I was more exhausted than you can imagine, exhausted yet exultant. The following day, as soon as it grew dark, I went back to finish my work by disposing of the two sections of the body exactly as prescribed by the book.

My only error, if I might call it that, was to drive past the house again. Only as I arrived home did I realize that a motorcycle had been following me. I had glimpsed it behind me as I drove back to Paris, but as you can imagine, my customary vigilance was compromised by the exhilaration I felt at having completed my work, by the deep sense of satisfaction. I was opening my front door as the driver, his face obscured by his helmet, briefly turned to stare at me. In that moment I realized I had been caught in a trap. That Manuela had not reappeared that day would not have concerned her pimp since she worked only at night, but when she had not reappeared the following evening . . . I concluded that, unbeknownst to me, I had been followed the previous night. Manuela's pimp, having returned to the scene of my crime, had passed me near the house and followed me. That hulking brute Lambert now knew where I lived; I was at his mercy; my accustomed self-possession was shattered. I immediately left Paris. I was gone only one day, but it was a day of the purest terror, a dread only those who have experienced it can understand. The following day, I was reassured. I read in the papers that Lambert had been arrested for his part in an armed robbery. Unlike the police who arrested him and the *juge* who sentenced him, I knew that Lambert was playing a long game, that he had played no part in the crime for which he had been sent to prison. Eight months. The prospect of serving a third of his sentence was, in his eyes, well worth what he hoped to extort from me on his release. I waited calmly for him. For the first few weeks, I did nothing to elude the rigorous surveillance Lambert had organized from his prison cell. The most prudent course of action was to carry on as normal and give no hint of my concerns. My subterfuge paid off. Convinced that I believed myself safe, he was reassured. That was his undoing. When I learned that he was about to be released on parole, I took a few days' vacation. I went to stay in a house I own in the country, one that I seldom visit since I have never enjoyed my stays there. Though I enjoy the grounds, the house itself is too big, and too remote now that the surrounding villages have been abandoned. There I waited for him. He was obviously overconfident and impatient; he came almost immediately, accompanied by one of his goons. After dark, they crept into the house through the back door, intending to take me by surprise, and each got a blast from my shotgun full in the face for their pains. I buried them in the grounds. I hope you are in no hurry to find them . . .

There you have it. I am sure, now that you see how dedicated I am in my work, you will have a clearer understanding of me and will be better able to judge my other endeavors at their true worth.

I remain, Sir, your obedient servant.

Monday, April 21

1

Le Matin:

POLICE MAKE CONTACT WITH THE "NOVELIST" VIA CLASSIFIED ADS

The case of the "Novelist" is proving to be truly extraordinary. The very nature of the murders is unusual: police have already recovered the bodies of four young women (one of them in Scotland) murdered in the most appalling manner. Then there is the unusual nature of the killer's modus operandi: it has been established that he is staging murders modeled on fictional scenes from crime novels. Finally, there are the unorthodox methods the police have used in conducting their investigation.

Commandant Verhœven, who is leading the case with Juge Deschamps as investigating magistrate, has made contact with the serial killer via . . . a classified advertisement: "Talk to me about B.E.E." This is without doubt a reference to Bret Easton Ellis, author of *American Psycho*, the book on which the "Novelist" based the Courbevoie double murders. The advertisement appeared in last Monday's edition of the crime magazine *Nuits Blanches*. Although it is not known whether the killer read it, or responded to it, it is certainly a highly unusual investigational tool. Commandant Verhœven, clearly unembarrassed by the novelty of his approach, placed a second ad on the magazine's website. As concise as the first, the ad reads simply "Your Black Dahlia?," an explicit reference to another of the "Novelist's" crimes: the murder of a young prostitute in November 2001 whose body, hacked in two at the waist, was found on a landfill in Tremblay-en-France. A murder directly inspired by James Ellroy's masterpiece *The Black Dahlia*.

We contacted the Ministry of Justice as well as the Ministry of the Interior to ask whether this somewhat unorthodox approach was sanctioned by the authorities. Perhaps understandably, they declined to comment.

For now, at least . . .

Camille flung the newspaper across the room while his team pretended not to notice.

"Louis!" he shouted. "Go and get him and bring him to me!"

"Who?"

"That little shit Buisson! I want you to find him right now and drag him in here by the scruff of the neck!"

Louis simply bowed his head and pushed back his bangs. Armand was the first to speak.

"Camille, I'm sorry, but that would be really stupid."

"Stupid?" Camille roared, whipping around and stomping across the room, picking things up and slamming them down again as though determined to smash something, anything.

"Listen to me, Camille, you need to calm down."

"Armand, I'm sick to the back teeth of this guy. It's bad enough that we're up shit creek without him scuttling the boat. What about journalistic ethics? The guy is scum. He publishes, and we're the ones who are damned! Louis, go and find him!"

"First I just need to–"

"First you need to do nothing! Fetch him, and bring him here. If he refuses, I'll send in every officer in the *brigade criminelle* to drag him out in handcuffs and throw him in a cell!"

Louis decided it was pointless to refuse. Camille had obviously lost all touch with reality. Just as Louis was about to leave, Mehdi held out his cell to Camille: "*Patron*, it's some journalist from *Le Monde . . .*"

"Tell him to go fuck himself," Camille said, wheeling around, "and if you call me '*patron*' one more time, you can go fuck yourself as well."

2

Being a judicious young man, Louis decided to adopt the role of his boss's superego—it was a role he was called upon to perform quite often. He suggested that Buisson come to the *brigade*'s offices voluntarily "at the request of Commandant Verhœven," and the journalist accepted with good grace. There was time for Camille to calm down, but the moment Buisson stepped into the squad room, he lost it.

"You're a complete shit, Buisson," he said.

"I'm sure the word you were looking for is 'journalist'?"

The mutual hostility of their first encounter was swiftly rekindled. Camille had decided to talk to Buisson in his office, for fear the journalist might pick up some new piece of information he did not already possess. It was a vain precaution, however, since the journalist seemed very well informed. Louis, for his part, kept close to Camille, ready to intervene in case things came to a head.

"I need to know where you're getting your information from."

"Oh, *commandant*, we're both old enough and ugly enough not to play that particular game . . . You're asking me to compromise a source, and as you know perfectly well-"

"Some of the details you've published violate judicial confidentiality. I have the means–"

"You have no means," Buisson cut him short, "and, more importantly, you don't have the right."

"I have the right to remand you into police custody. That wouldn't cost me a thing."

"It would cost you another scandal. And on what grounds, if I might ask? Are you contesting my right to free speech?"

"Don't try to play the ethics card with me, Buisson, you'd be a laughing stock. Even my father–"

"So, what precisely do you intend to do, *commandant*? Arrest every journalist in Paris? You appear to have delusions of grandeur."

Camille studied the man for a moment, as though seeing him for the first time. His infuriating grin never fading, Buisson stared back at him as though they had known each other for decades.

"Why are you doing this, Buisson? You know this is a difficult case; you know that we need to arrest this guy and that every article you publish only makes our task much harder."

Buisson suddenly seemed to relax, as though he had led Camille to exactly where he wanted him.

"I offered you a deal, *commandant*. You turned me down; that's hardly my fault. And now, if you–"

"Not a chance. The police doesn't make deals with the press."

A smile creased Buisson's face, and he drew himself up to his full height, the better to look down on Camille from his lofty vantage point.

"You may be a resourceful officer, *commandant*, but you are not a pragmatic one."

Camille stared at the man in silence for a few seconds.

"Thank you for coming in, Monsieur Buisson."

"It's been a pleasure, *commandant*. Any time."

The real pleasure came with the evening papers. By 4 p.m., *Le Monde* was rehashing Buisson's article. By the time Camille called Irène an hour later to ask how she was, she informed him the story had been on the radio news. Deschamps did not even bother to telephone him, and this was most definitely not a good sign.

Camille keyed in "Philippe Buisson journalist."

Louis leaned over his shoulder to look at the screen.

"What's all this in aid of?" Louis asked as Camille clicked on a link that styled itself the "Who's Who of French Journalism."

"I like to know who I'm dealing with," Camille said, waiting for the site to load. Camille whistled.

"Well, well, well, the little shit is an aristocrat, did you know that?"

"No."

"Philippe Buisson de Chevesne, no less. Ring a bell?"

Louis thought for a moment.

"Probably related to the Buissons de la Mortière, don't you think?"

"Oh, no question," Camille said. "You took the words out of my mouth!"

"An aristocratic family from the Périgord, they were ruined during the Revolution."

"*Vive l'égalité!* So, what else do we have here? Studied journalism in Paris. Worked for *Ouest-France*, did some stringing for provincial dailies, did a stint with France 3 Bretagne before moving to *Le Matin*. Never married . . . no surprise there. Then there's a list of his articles and features. It seems pretty up to date! Look, there's my name right at the top."

Camille closed the window, then shut down the computer. He checked his watch.

"Maybe you should think about heading home," Louis said.

"Camille!" Cob said, sticking his head round the door. "Can I borrow you for a minute?"

3

"These are the initial search results for Ballanger's list."

Cob had entered key data from the synopses written by Ballanger and his students into the police database of cold cases and run a search going back ten years. The first results threw up only five cases with similarities to the plots of crime novels. The list was made up of columns detailing the case number, date, the investigating officer, and the date on which the case had been archived for lack of evidence. In the last column, Cob had put the title of the relevant novel.

Camille put on his glasses and scanned the essential details:

» June 1994—Perrigny (Yonne)—Farming family murdered (two parents, two children)—Possible inspiration: Truman Capote—*In Cold Blood.*

» October 1996—Toulouse—Man shot dead on day of his wedding—Possible inspiration: William Irish—*The Bride Wore Black.*

» July 2000—Corbeil—Woman's body recovered from a river—
Possible inspiration: Émile Gaboriau—*Le Crime d'Orcival.*

» February 2001—Paris—Police officer gunned down during
holdup—Possible source: W. Riley Burnett—*Little Caesar.*

» September 2001—Paris—Police officer commits suicide in his
car—Possible inspiration: Michael Connelly—*The Poet.*

"Okay, here's what I came up with in the second search," Cob said,
tapping at his keyboard, "when I was looking for those 'logical
inconsistencies' of yours. Jesus, that was a challenge!"

After a moment, a spreadsheet appeared listing thirty-seven cases.

"Now, if we discount murders committed in the heat of the
moment," Cob said, clicking his mouse, "and those where there's no
obvious premeditation, we have twenty-five. Of these, seven cases
seem to be the work of multiple assailants. That's the second list. Of
the remaining eighteen, we can rule out nine of the victims on the
basis that either there is clear financial motive, or the victim was
elderly, or the woman involved had known sadomasochistic incli-
nations. That leaves us with nine."

"Good."

"That's this list here."

"Anything interesting?"

"Not sure."

Camille glared at him.

"What do you mean, you're not sure?"

"There aren't really any logical inconsistencies in these cases. At
least, not in the sense you mean. Obviously there are unknown factors, but there are no bizarre crime scenes, no weird weapons, nothing that tallies with what we're looking for."

"That remains to be seen. Élisabeth," Camille said, turning to
look up at her. "What do you think?"

"We pull the case files from the archives, spend the night going through them with a fine-toothed comb, and review the situation again first thing tomorrow."

"Okay, go for it," said Camille, picking up the list as it spooled from the printer and handing it to her.

Élisabeth hesitated, then glanced at her watch and looked at him questioningly. Camille rubbed his eyelids for a moment.

"Okay, go home, Élisabeth. I expect to see you first thing. You and rosy-fingered dawn."

Before he too headed home, Camille sent an e-mail to Dr. Crest suggesting copy for the next classified advertisement: "What about your earlier works? C.V."

Tuesday, April 22

1

The team had already gathered in the squad room when Élisabeth strolled in at 8 a.m., pulling a trolley on which were stacked the cold case files: fourteen thick folders that, comparing them against Cob's list, she sorted into two piles of nine and five.

"Where are we at with Lesage?"

"The *juge* has given the green light," Louis said. "For now, she says, there's 'insufficient evidence' to bring him in for questioning, but the *brigade financière* has given Cob everything he needs to go through the Lesages' personal bank accounts, assets, and mortgages with a fine-toothed comb. We'll have to see what he comes up with."

Cob was already at his computer crunching numbers. Having arrived at some ungodly hour, he had commandeered the computer allocated to Fernand—who could barely make out the screen by noon—and connected it to his existing network. By now he was completely hidden behind a bank of monitors, his fingers flitting across the array of overlapping keyboards that made him resemble a church organist.

Camille looked thoughtfully at the piles of dossiers, then surveyed the team. Sifting through so much evidence would require a trained eye, someone who could work quickly: Mehdi didn't have the experience. As usual, Maleval had shown up looking like a poster boy for the morning after the night before; he wouldn't have the necessary concentration. Camille didn't even consider asking Fernand, whose breath already exuded the delicate scent of ethanol.

"Okay, Élisabeth, Armand, Louis . . . you're with me."

The four pulled up chairs and sat around the desk on which the case files were stacked.

"These are files of unsolved cases that have bizarre or unusual elements that seemed to be at odds with what is known about the victim and might indicate that the killer was recreating a scene from a crime novel. I admit that the theory is far fetched, so we shouldn't waste too much time on it. What we need to do is write an outline summary of each case—two pages, tops. We'll pass on these outlines to Professeur Ballanger and his students, and they ought be able to tell us whether the cases correspond to any books they're familiar with. They're expecting us to deliver by the end of this morning."

Camille thought for a moment.

"Louis, could you fax this document to Jérôme Lesage? Let's see how he reacts. If we can summarize these cases by noon, they should be able to get to work straight after lunch."

He rubbed his hands together, like a starving man about to sit down to a bang-up meal.

"Let's get to work. We want this finished by twelve."

2

Attn: Prof. Ballanger

Nine unsolved murder cases that we believe *may* have been inspired by crime novels. The victims include six women, two men, and one child and were committed within the past ten years. We at the *brigade criminelle* need to carefully cross-check the salient facts of the cases with novels on which the murders may have been based.

Case 1—October 13, 1995—Paris—The dismembered body of a 36-year-old black woman is found in her bath.
Unusual elements:
1—After dismemberment, the limbs and torso of the victim were redressed in a man's clothes.

Case 2—May 16, 1996—Fontainebleau—A 38-year-old sales rep dies from a bullet wound to the head in the forest of Fontainebleau.

Unusual elements:
1—The gun used by the killer was unusual—a Colt Woodsman .22.
2—The clothing worn by the victim did not belong to him.

Case 3—March 24, 1998—Paris—Pregnant woman, 35, disemboweled in a warehouse.
Unusual elements:
1—A funeral wreath found at the scene bore the inscription "To my dear parents," although the victim, an orphan, was brought up in a children's home.

Case 4—September 27, 1998—Maisons-Alfort—The body of a man, 48, is found in a garage inspection pit. Cause of death: heart attack.
Unusual elements:
1—Statements from three independent witnesses confirm that they saw the victim, a pharmacist's assistant in Douai, at his place of work at the approximate time of death.
2—Death took place three days before the corpse was moved to the garage where it was found.

Case 5—December 24, 1999—Castelnau—A 9-year-old girl is found hanging from a cherry tree in an orchard 20 miles from her home.
Unusual elements:
1—The victim's navel had been cut out using a box cutter prior to death.

Case 6—February 4, 2000—Lille—The body of a 47-year-old homeless woman is found. Cause of death: hypothermia.
Unusual elements:
1—The victim's body was discovered in the cold storage unit of a derelict butcher's shop. The refrigeration unit was powered by a cable connected to a streetlight.

Case 7—August 24, 2000—Paris—The naked body of a woman is found in the bucket of a dredger on the banks of the canal de l'Ourcq. Cause of death: strangulation.
Unusual elements:
1—The victim had a fake birthmark (inside left thigh) drawn using indelible ink.
2—The victim's body was covered in a layer of fresh silt taken from the canal, though dredging had not yet begun at the site and the machine had not recently been in operation.

Case 8—May 4, 2001—Clermont-Ferrand—The body of a 71-year-old childless widow is discovered. Cause of death: two bullets were fired into the heart.
Unusual elements:
1—The body was discovered in a 1987 Renault Mégane, for which a Certificate of Destruction had been issued six years previously.

Case 9—November 8, 2002—La Baule—A woman, 24, strangled.
Unusual elements:
1—The body was discovered on the beach fully dressed and covered in a layer of dry ice from an industrial fire extinguisher.

3

By early afternoon, the team was working on Cob's second list. Louis was assigned the case in Perrigny, Élisabeth was dealing with Toulouse, Maleval the officer who had been gunned down in Paris. Armand was working on the Corbeil case, and Camille was looking into the suicide of the police officer in Paris.

The good news was that there was no news. There were not enough parallels between the cases and the novels suggested by Professeur Ballanger. It was abundantly clear that their killer was painstaking about even the smallest details, but each of the cold cases they examined deviated significantly from the novels that might have inspired them. Louis was the first to finish, in less than three quarters of an hour ("No way," he muttered solemnly), closely followed by Élisabeth and Maleval. Camille then added his folder to the pile with a sigh of relief.

"Everyone want coffee?"

"There'll be no coffee for you," Armand said, as he shuffled into the squad room looking apologetic.

In the sudden silence, Camille brought his hands together and rubbed his eyes. Everyone else stared at the pale figure of Armand.

"I think you'll want to call the *divisionnaire*, and Deschamps, too, probably . . ."

"What's up?"

"It's this book, *Le Crime d'Orvical.*"

"Orcival," Louis corrected him quietly.

"Orvical, Orcival, I don't give a damn how you pronounce it, but I can tell you that it's an exact copy of the Corbeil murder. Down to the last detail."

At this moment Ballanger called Camille.

With his free hand Camille went on rubbing his eyelids. From where he was sitting he could see the corkboard on which were pinned the photographs of the crime scenes in Courbevoie (the severed fingers arranged like the petals of a flower), Tremblay (the dismembered body of Manuela Constanza), and Glasgow (the pitiful body of Grace Hobson). He struggled to catch his breath.

"Any news?" he asked Ballanger warily.

"Nothing that altogether corresponds to any novel we're familiar with. One of my students thought the March 1998 case, the one where the pregnant woman is disemboweled in a warehouse, sounded similar to a book I've never heard of. It's called . . . *Shadow Slayer* by someone named Chub or Hub. Never heard of him either. I had a look online, but I couldn't find it. Presumably out of print. And there's something else, *commandant*: the case of the sales rep murdered in Fontainebleau forest. That rings a bell. There are one or two details that don't quite match up, but it sounds a lot like *The End of the Night* by John D. MacDonald . . ."

4

Louis brought Camille confirmation that Cob had submitted the new ad, which would go up on the *Nuits Blanches* website the following morning. Camille stopped him as he was about to leave.

"Louis, I'd like to know what's going on between you and Maleval."

Louis was immediately poker faced, and Camille knew that he would get nothing out of him.

"Men's business?" he goaded, hoping for some kind of reaction.

"It's not exactly business, more a little . . . difference of opinion."

Camille stood and walked over to him. Whenever he did this, Louis deliberately made himself smaller, perhaps trying to make up for the difference in their heights or to show some sort of solidarity. Whatever the reason, it was a gesture that Camille found both touching and infuriating.

"I'm going to say something, Louis, and I'm only going to say it once. If whatever is going on has anything to do with work-"

"Absolutely not."

Camille studied him for a moment.

"I don't like the sound of this."

"It's private."

"Personal?"

"Private."

"I'd better go—Le Guen is waiting for me." Camille turned back to his desk.

Louis walked off, and Camille watched him to see which hand he used to push back his bangs, but could no longer remember which gesture meant what. He stood for a moment, brooding, called Cob to check how things were going, then headed for the stairs.

5

Late in the day, Le Guen finished reading the two memos hastily typed up by Camille. Leaning back in his desk chair, he gripped the document, hands resting on his ample paunch. While he waited, Camille mentally played back footage of the two cases that had recently emerged, as far as he had been able to reconstruct them.

The first memo detailed the "admittedly loose similarities" Ballanger had discovered between the 1950s American novel *The End of the Night* and the murder in Fontainebleau.

On May 16, 1996, while walking through the forest in Fontainebleau, Jean-Claude Boniface and Nadège Vermontel had come upon the body of a man who had been shot through the head. The dead man was quickly identified as Roland Souchier, a plumbing and bathroom fittings salesman. Ballistics had determined that the bullet had been fired from a .22 automatic, of which there were few in France. The weapon did not appear on the police database. The victim's wallet was missing. The possibility that this might simply be a mugging was given further credence when a withdrawal was made later that day with one of the stolen credit cards at a gas station

nineteen miles south of the crime scene by someone caught on
camera driving Souchier's car.

The detectives on the case had been struck by two details: the first
was the use of a Colt Woodsman, a rare American .22 semiautomatic
sporting pistol that had not been manufactured since the 1970s.

The second curious fact related to the victim's clothing. He was
found wearing a blue polo shirt and a pair of white moccasins.
When she came to identify the body, his wife pointed out that he
had never worn such items of clothing; in fact, in her statement she
said that she "would never have allowed him out wearing clothes
like that."

"Personally, I don't think it holds together," Le Guen muttered.

"I rather agree."

Once again, they compared the details of the crimes with the
excerpts Ballanger had faxed over from John D. Macdonald's novel,
which had been published in France in 1962.

Page 128:
   There was a pile of rocks twenty feet from the car. [. . .] The man
stood by the open door of the car. He rubbed his neck and winced. He
was maybe thirty-five. [. . .] He wore a light blue sports shirt, sweaty at
the armpits, and gray slacks and black-and-white shoes.

"A little further on, it talks about the killer," Camille said.

He aimed again. The pistol made its little crack. A little black hole
appeared high in Beecher's forehead, slightly off-center toward the left.
His eyes came open, and the can fell off. He took one step to spread his
feet wide, as though to brace himself. And then he went down easily,
breaking the fall.

"Yeah," Le Guen grumbled, grimacing.

The two men sat thinking for a moment.

"You're right," Camille said, "it doesn't add up. Too many details
are different. The book specifically states that the victim was stabbed

with 'a little knife' and that he had 'on the little finger of his right hand, a heavy lodge ring': there was no sign of a ring on the body at Fontainebleau. In the novel, a cigar butt and a fifth of bourbon are found at the crime scene. There was nothing like that, and no sign of Italian tiles having been smashed against the rocks. It doesn't match."

Le Guen was staring into the distance. The silence that ensued had less to do with the fact that the case that they had just decided was still cold, and more to do with another that seemed more troubling.

"As for the Corbeil case," Le Guen said, "I think we need to talk to the *juge*."

Jean-François Richet was not on vacation, but being a rep allowed him a certain amount of free time, especially in July. He suggested to his sixteen-year-old son Laurent that they have a day out and go fishing on the Seine. It was July 6, 2000. Usually it was Laurent who found the perfect spot to set up, but on this particular day he never had the time to look. Hardly had he taken a few steps than his father heard him cry out, his voice choked with fear: floating near the riverbank was the body of a woman. She lay in the shallows, her face half buried in the mud, wearing a gray dress spattered with blood and silt.

The *gendarmes* from Corbeil were on the scene twenty minutes later. The investigation was efficiently led by Lieutenant-Colonel Andréani. In less than a week they had turned up everything that there was to know, which was nothing much.

The victim, a Caucasian woman of about twenty-five, had clearly been subjected to a brutal beating, in the course of which she had been dragged by the hair, as evidenced by bald patches on her scalp from which clumps of hair had been ripped. Analysis confirmed that the killer had hit her with a hammer. The autopsy, carried out by a Doctor Moneir, determined that the victim had died, not from beating, but from twenty-one stab wounds. There was no sign of sexual assault. In the victim's left hand was a scrap of gray fabric. Time of death was estimated to be approximately forty-eight hours before the body was discovered.

Andréani soon discovered that the woman was one Maryse Perrin, resident in Corbeil, who had been reported missing by her parents four days earlier and had not been seen since by her coworkers or her friends. The twenty-three-year-old hairdresser lived at 16 boulevard de la République, in an apartment she shared with her cousin, Sophie Perrin. Everything about her was predictable: she went to the hair salon every morning by bus; she was popular at work; on weekends she and her cousin went out to fashionable clubs, where she flirted with boys and had even slept with one or two of them. There was nothing out of the ordinary except for the fact that she had left home on Sunday, July 7, at about 7:30 a.m. wearing a white skirt and blouse, a pink jacket, and flat shoes. She was found four days later, wearing a gray dress and half buried in the mud. The case was never solved. There was no evidence as to how she ended up in the Seine, or where she had been between the time she left home and the moment she met whoever had murdered her.

Detectives had noticed a number of unusual elements in what was otherwise a run-of-the-mill case. Given the level of violence, it seemed strange that there were no signs of sexual assault. The pathologist confirmed that Maryse Perrin had last had sex quite some time earlier, long enough earlier to be clinically impossible to estimate, but it was certainly a matter of weeks. In her second interview, Maryse's cousin confirmed that for several weeks she had not gone out, having recently broken up with a long-term boyfriend. The boyfriend, Joël Vanecker, a post office worker, was interviewed and immediately eliminated as a suspect.

The strangest element was the gray dress in which the victim was found. Since the girl had already been missing from home for two days by the time she was murdered, it was surprising to discover that she had changed her clothes. Detectives could find no explanation for why, when she was found, she was wearing a dress made in the 1860s. Indeed, the fact that it was an antique dress only emerged later. Initially, the victim's cousin, her parents, and her friends simply found it odd that Maryse was wearing a ball gown, not simply because she did not own one, but because it was so unlike her style.

Puzzled by how threadbare and damaged the dress was, something that could not be explained by the amount of time the body had spent in the water, the forensics team sent it to a clothing expert, who, from the nature of the fabric and the way in which it was made, determined that the dress dated from the mid-nineteenth century. The buttons and lace trimmings made it possible to estimate a tentative date of 1863—give or take two or three years.

Various experts were called upon to value the dress; it became clear that this was not some ordinary crime. In dumping his victim in the river, the killer had also thrown away a dress worth at least three thousand euros. The only theory suggested was that the killer had not been aware of its value.

Inquiries were made at shops selling secondhand and vintage clothing, though the limited number of officers working on the case meant that only those shops in the local area were canvassed. After several weeks the investigation had gone nowhere.

That the girl had been "found wearing a gray dress" was not merely a turn of phrase in the officer's initial report: she had not been wearing it when she was murdered. She had been wearing other clothes when she was beaten and stabbed, and only some thirty-six hours later was she dressed in the ball gown. Here, too, there was an unusual element: the killer had not simply thrown the body into the river; he had carefully, almost delicately positioned the girl, attentive to every fold of the dress and to how deeply her face was buried in the mud. Everything about the scene suggested a meticulousness and a painstaking care utterly at odds with a killer who could have brutally stabbed her two days earlier.

The investigating officers had been baffled.

Now, thanks to *Le Crime d'Orcival*, a novel by Émile Gaboriau first published in 1867, which Professeur Ballanger pointed out was among the earliest crime novels, the unusual elements in the case no longer seemed so mysterious. Like the Perrin girl, Gaboriau's victim, the Comtesse de Trémorel, was blonde and blue eyed. There could be no doubt that the key details of the murder scene—the positioning of the body, the dress Maryse was wearing, the scrap of fabric clutched in her left hand—perfectly mirrored key details in the novel. The most telling detail of all was that the dress had been made during the period in which the novel was set.

"There's no fake fingerprint," Le Guen said. "Why would the guy leave a fingerprint on his other victims and not this one?"

"He didn't start 'signing' his work until the Glasgow murder. Since then, he's signed all of them. Which means we know about all the murders since then—well . . . that's the good news."

"So now all we have to worry about are the ones still to come," Le Guen muttered as though to himself.

6

Irène had made herself an herbal tea.

Sitting in an armchair in the living room, she gazed out at the rain that had been lashing the windowpanes since early evening with a steady insistence.

They had eaten a light supper. For a month now, Irène had not had the energy to cook and only prepared cold cuts, since she never knew what time they would sit down for dinner.

"Perfect weather for a murder, darling," she said thoughtfully, holding the cup in both hands as though to warm herself.

"What made you say that?"

"Oh, it's nothing . . ."

Camille picked up his book and came and sat by her feet.

"Tired . . ."—"Tired?"

They had said the word at precisely the same time.

"What do you call it when that happens?"

"I don't know. Subconscious communication, I suppose."

They sat for a moment in silence, each engrossed in their thoughts.

"You're bored, aren't you?"

"I have been lately. I find time passes slowly."

"Is there anything you'd like to do tomorrow night?" Camille asked halfheartedly.

"I quite like the idea of giving birth . . ."

"Remind me to grab my first aid kit." Camille had set down his book and was idly flicking through its pages, gazing at Caravaggio's paintings. He stopped at a reproduction of *Mary Magdalene in Ecstasy*. Irène leaned forward so she could look over his shoulder. In the painting, Mary Magdalene's head is thrown back, her lips parted, her hands clasped at her breast. Her mane of red hair tumbles over her right shoulder, emphasizing her bosom; her left breast is barely covered. Camille liked this portrait of womanhood. He leafed back several pages and studied Caravaggio's depiction of Mary in *Rest on the Flight into Egypt*.

"Is it the same woman?" Irène said.

"I'm not sure."

Mary was bent over her child, her hair an even deeper red that seemed almost purple.

"I think she's having an orgasm," Irène said.

"No, I think Saint Theresa is the one who has the orgasm."

"They all look like they're having an orgasm."

Magdalene in ecstasy, Mary with her child. He did not say as much, but when Camille looked at them he thought of Irène. He could feel her behind him, heavy and warm. The importance of Irene's appearance in his life was incalculable. He reached over his shoulder and took her hand.

Wednesday, April 23

1

She was the kind of woman about whom there is nothing to say; neither beautiful nor ugly, almost ageless. The face is familiar, almost recognizable, like an old school friend. Forty-something, favoring clothes that are depressingly utilitarian, Christine Lesage sits facing Camille, hands clasped discreetly over her knees, a female carbon copy of her brother. Is she afraid? Is she overwhelmed? It is difficult to tell. She stares fixedly at her hands. Camille believes he can detect in her a tenacity that verges on the absurd. Though physically she bears an uncanny resemblance to her brother, it is clear that Christine Lesage is made of stronger stuff.

And yet there is something lost about her; from time to time her eyes dart about the room as though she is out of her depth.

"Madame Lesage," Camille begins, setting his glasses on the desk, "you know why you're here."

"I was told it's about my brother."

Her voice, which he is hearing for the first time, is high, shrill even, as though she is defending herself against some accusation. The way she tenderly says the word "brother" speaks volumes. A maternal reflex almost.

"That's correct. We're curious about him."

"He's got nothing to be ashamed of."

"That's something I'd like to discuss, if you don't mind. I would be grateful for any insights you might have."

"I said all I have to say to the other officer."

"Yes." Camille nodded to the report lying on the desk. "But that's precisely my point—you don't seem to have much to say at all."

Christine Lesage clasps her hands over her knees once more. As far as she is concerned, the interview is over.

"We are especially interested in your trip to the United Kingdom. In . . ." Camille slips on his glasses and briefly consults the report. "July 2001."

"We weren't in the United Kingdom, *commandant*, we were in England."

"Are you sure about that?"

"Aren't you?"

"No, actually, I don't believe you were . . . at least not for the whole of your trip. You arrived in London on July 2, is that correct?"

"Possibly."

"Definitely. Your brother left London for Edinburgh on the eighth. That would be in Scotland, madame. Which is in the United Kingdom. His ticket confirms he returned to London on the twelfth. Is that correct?"

"If you say so . . ."

"And you didn't notice that your brother was absent for five days?"

"You said from the eighth to the twelfth . . . that's four days, not five."

"Where was he?"

"You said it yourself: he was in Edinburgh."

"And what was he doing there?"

"We have a contact there. As we do in London. My brother likes to visit our suppliers if he gets the chance. It's . . . business, if you like."

"Your contact there is a Mr. Somerville," Camille said.

"Mr. Somerville, that's right."

"We have a little problem, Madame Lesage. Mr. Somerville was interviewed by the police in Edinburgh this morning and he confirms that he saw your brother, but only on the eighth. According to him, your brother left the city on the ninth. Could you tell me where he was between the ninth and the twelfth of July?"

Camille realizes right away that this is news to her. She gives a suspicious, resentful scowl.

"Sightseeing, I assume," she says finally.

"Sightseeing. Of course. He took a tour of the Scottish highlands: the lochs, the castles, the ghosts . . ."

"Spare me the platitudes, *inspecteur*."

"*Commandant*, if you don't mind. Would his curiosity perhaps have taken him as far as Glasgow, in your opinion?"

"I have no opinion on the matter. Nor can I speculate on what he could possibly have been doing there."

"Murdering young Grace Hobson, perhaps?"

A calculated gamble on Camille's part. Such stunts have paid off in the past. But Christine Lesage does not seem the least bit disconcerted.

"Do you have proof?"

"Are you familiar with the name Grace Hobson?"

"I read about her in the papers."

"To recapitulate: your brother leaves London to spend four days in Edinburgh, he stays only one day, and you have no idea what he does for the other three days, is that what you're saying?"

"More or less, yes."

"More or less?"

"That's right. I'm sure that he will have no trouble pro-"

"We shall see. Let us jump to November 2001, if you don't mind."

"Your colleague already ask-"

"I know, Madame Lesage, I know. I simply need you to confirm what you told him, then we'll say no more about it. Tell me about November 21."

"Do you remember what you were doing two years ago in November?"

2

"I am not being asked the questions here, Madame Lesage, you are. Tell me about your brother. Does he travel much?"

"*Commandant*," Christine Lesage says in the long-suffering tone of one addressing a small child, "we run a business. Antiquarian and secondhand books. My brother buys and sells; he visits private libraries, he buys books at auction, he offers valuations, he buys from colleagues and sells to them; obviously he can't do all that from behind the counter of the bookshop. So, yes, my brother travels a great deal."

"Which means you never know precisely where he is . . ."

"Don't you think we might save some time? If you could just tell me-"

"It's very simple, Madame Lesage. Your brother called us and gave us information about a crime."

"This is what he gets for trying to help . . ."

"We did not ask for his help—he offered it. Spontaneously. Generously. He informed us that the murders in Courbevoie were inspired by a novel by Bret Easton Ellis. He seemed extremely well informed. His information proved accurate."

"It's his job."

"Killing prostitutes?"

Christine Lesage blushes to the roots of her hair.

"If you have evidence, *commandant*, I'm listening. Though we both know that if you had any evidence, I wouldn't be here answering your questions. Can I go now?" she says, making as if to get up.

Camille stares at her intently. Meekly, she abandons the half-hearted gesture.

"We were granted a warrant to examine your brother's desk diaries. He is a very meticulous man, very organized. I have officers going through his meetings and appointments over the past five years. Until now, we have queried only a handful of entries, but it's astonishing how many inaccuracies we've discovered, for such a methodical man."

"Inaccuracies?" Madame Lesage seems surprised.

"Yes, the diary says he was in such and such a place . . . when in fact he wasn't. He has recorded meetings that never took place. That sort of thing. He claims to be with someone when in fact he is not. So we can't help but wonder."

"Wonder what, exactly, *commandant*?"

"Wonder what he has been doing with his time, obviously. What he was doing in November 2001 while a twenty-three-year-old prostitute was being hacked in two, what he was doing earlier this month when two other prostitutes were dismembered in Courbevoie. Does your brother frequent prostitutes?"

"You are an odious little man."

"What about *him*?"

"If that's all you've got on my brother–"

"In point of fact, Madame Lesage, those are not the only troubling questions concerning your brother. We have also been wondering what he does with his money."

Christine Lesage gives the *commandant* an incredulous look.

"His *money*?"

"Well, your money, as it turns out. Because from what we understand, your brother manages your fortune."

"I have no 'fortune'!"

She spat the word as though it were an insult.

"Well, you have a stock portfolio, and you own two apartments in Paris that are currently rented out, plus the family home. And perhaps now would be a good time to mention that we've sent a team of officers to your house."

"To Villeréal? May I ask why?"

"We are looking for two bodies, Madame Lesage. One large, one small. But we'll come back to that. We were discussing your fortune."

"I have entrusted my brother with managing my financial affairs."

"Then I'm afraid I should tell you that it may not have been a wise decision . . ."

Christine Lesage stares at Camille for a long moment. Surprise? Suspicion? Anger? He cannot read what is in her eyes. He quickly realizes it is nothing more than steely determination.

"Everything my brother did with my money was authorized by me, *commandant*. Everything. Without exception."

3

"So what have you got?"

"To tell you the truth, Jean, I have no idea. They've got a pretty weird relationship, these two."

Jérôme Lesage is sitting bolt upright in his chair, adopting an attitude of calm composure. He is going to show he is not a man to be duped easily.

"I've just had a chat with your sister, Monsieur Lesage."

Despite his resolve to show no concern, Lesage's face flinches perceptibly.

"Why her?" he says, as if requesting a menu or a train timetable.

"The better to understand you. The better to *try* to understand you."

"She's backing him tooth and nail. It'll be hard to drive a wedge between them."

"Hardly surprising, I suppose. They're a couple."

"Of sorts. But more baffling."

"All relationships are baffling. All my marriages certainly were."

"We're having a little difficulty accounting for your movements, you see? Even your sister, who knows you better than anyone–"

"She knows only what I choose to tell her."

He folds his arms across his chest. As far as he is concerned, the subject is closed. Camille elects to remain silent.

"Would you kindly tell me what it is you have against me?" Lesage says at last.

"I have nothing against you. I'm conducting a criminal investigation, Monsieur Lesage. I have the issue of a number of dead bodies to account for."

"I should never have helped you, not even that first time."

"But you couldn't help yourself."

"That's true."

Lesage seems surprised by his own response.

"When I read the reports of the Courbevoie murders, I was proud to have recognized Ellis's novel," he continues thoughtfully. "But that doesn't make me a killer."

"She defends him; he protects her. Or vice versa."

"What have we got, Camille? Cards on table, what exactly have we got?"

"For a start, we've got the unaccounted-for gaps in his schedule."

"I'd like you to talk me through the time you spent in Scotland."

"What do you want to know?"

"What you did between July 9 and July 12. You arrived in Edinburgh on the eighth, had a meeting that day, and didn't reappear until the twelfth. What were you doing in the meantime?"

"Sightseeing."

"And has he been able to account for these gaps?"

"No, he's playing for time. He's waiting for us to come up with evidence. He knows that as things stand there's nothing we can do. And they both know it."

"Sightseeing? Where?"

"Here and there. I traveled about. Like most people on vacation."

"Most people don't murder young girls while they're 'traveling about' on vacation, Monsieur Lesage . . ."

"I didn't murder anyone!"

For the first time since the start of the interview, the bookseller's tone becomes heated. Being openly contemptuous of Camille is one thing, but to risk seeming like a killer is something else entirely.

"I didn't say you did."

"No, you didn't. But I can see that you're trying to finger me for murder."

"Do you write books, Monsieur Lesage? Novels?"

"No. Never. I'm a reader."

"A voracious reader."

"It's my job. I don't criticize you for hanging around with murderers."

"It's a pity you don't write novels, Monsieur Lesage, because you have a vivid imagination. Why do you invent fictional meetings in your desk diary, with people who don't exist? What do you do during these so-called meetings? Why do you need so much time, Monsieur Lesage?"

"Sometimes I need a breath of fresh air."

"You seem to get rather a lot of fresh air. Do you visit prostitutes?"

"Sometimes. No more than you, I expect."

"Then there are the discrepancies in his finances."

"Significant sums?"

"Cob is going through the books now. There are tens of thousands of euros involved. Almost all cash payments. Five hundred here, two thousand there. It all adds up."

"How long has this been going on?"

"Five years at least. We don't have authorization to go back further than that."

"And the sister didn't notice?"

"Looks that way."

"We're going over your accounts. I think your sister is in for a surprise..."

"You leave my sister out of this!"

Lesage looks at Camille as though for the first time he has let slip a detail that might be considered personal.

"She's not a well woman."

"She seemed hale and hearty to me."

"She's suffered from depression ever since her husband died. That's why I brought her to live with me. It's quite a burden, believe me."

"One for which you reward yourself handsomely, from what I've seen."

"That's between her and me—it doesn't concern you."

"Can you think of anything that doesn't concern the police, Monsieur Lesage?"

"So, where have we got to?"

"Well, the thing is, Jean, we've got a bit of a problem..."

"We'll come back to that, Monsieur Lesage. We have all the time in the world."

"I have no intention of staying here."

"That will not be your decision to make."

"I want to see a lawyer."

"Of course, Monsieur Lesage. Do you think you need one?"

"I think anyone dealing with people like you would need a lawyer."

"Just one question. We sent you a list of unsolved murders. I was most intrigued by your reaction."

"What reaction?"

"Precisely. You did not react."

"I had already told you I had no intention of going on helping you. So how do you think I should have reacted?"

"I don't know. You might have spotted the similarities between one of those cases and *The End of the Night* by John D. MacDonald, for example. But perhaps you're not familiar with the book."

"I'm perfectly familiar with it, Commandant Verhœven." The bookseller suddenly loses his temper. "And I can tell you right now that the case you're referring to does not relate to *The End of the Night*. There are too many discrepancies. I checked it against the book."

"So you *did* check? Well, well. It's a pity you didn't think it pertinent to pass on that conclusion to me."

"I have already given you help. Twice. And look where it got me. So from now on–"

"You gave the same 'help' to the media. Twice. For good measure, I suppose."

"I've already explained that. My comments to the journalist do not constitute a statutory offense. I demand that you release me immediately."

"Even more surprisingly for a man of your erudition . . ." Camille carries on as though he has not heard. "Among the eight cases, you did not recognize a classic like Gaboriau's *Le Crime d'Orcival!*"

"You clearly take me for an imbecile, *commandant*."

"On the contrary, Monsieur Lesage."

"Who said I didn't recognize it?"

"You did, in so far as you failed to mention it."

"I recognized it immediately. Anyone would have—anyone except you, obviously. There's a great deal I could have told you."

"A problem? Don't you think we've got enough problems as it is, Camille?"

"I was thinking the same, Jean; they just keep coming."

"So what's the problem this time?"

"What, precisely, could you have told us, Monsieur Lesage?"

"I'd rather not say."

"That only makes you look all the more suspect, and you're already on rather shaky ground."

"I talked to him again about our list of unsolved murders. At that point, he clammed up. But you know how it is, we all have our pride."

"What exactly is it that you would rather not say?"

"No comment."

"Oh, come on," Camille goads him. "You're dying to tell us."

Lesage glowers at him with unconcealed contempt.

"One of your cases . . . the girl whose body was found in the dredger."

"Yes?"

"Before she was murdered, had she been wearing a swimsuit?"

"I believe so, judging by the tan lines on her body. What are you trying to tell me, Monsieur Lesage?"

"I think . . . I think it's *Roseanna*."

4

Périphériques, expressways, boulevards, canals . . . so many tragedies and crimes, so many accidents and fatalities occur on busy
thoroughfares. To the naked eye, things are constantly moving,
never stopping; but anything thrown here disappears without a
trace, as though sucked down by the waters of a river. The list of
curious objects that do turn up is endless: shoes, aerosols, clothes,
money, pens, cardboard boxes, dog bowls, and gas cans.

Even corpses.

August 25, 2000. The Department of Public Works dispatches
a bucket dredger to clear silt and debris from the canal de l'Ourcq,
scooping foul-smelling mud into a barge.

A crowd soon forms—fishermen, pensioners, neighbors, and
passers-by—on the Pont Blériot, the bridge above the lock.

At 10:30 a.m. the engine roars and splutters, belching exhaust
fumes as black as soot. The collection barge floats like a dead fish in
the middle of the canal. A few minutes later the crane is in position
beside the barge. The gaping maw of the scoop is trained on the
bridge where a dozen people are watching the operation. Standing

next to the crane, Lucien Blanchard, the foreman, gives the signal to the operator, who flips the lever. There is a dull, metallic rasp. The huge bucket lurches violently. Still facing the bridge, it inches toward the water.

The bucket has been lowered barely a meter when Blanchard suddenly notices a commotion among the people on the bridge. They are babbling to each other, pointing to the bucket. Three or four people shout something to him, flailing their arms. As the bucket hits the water, the people shout more loudly and Blanchard realizes that something is wrong. Without quite knowing why, he yells to the operator to stop. Half submerged, the bucket comes to a halt. Blanchard stares at the bridge, trying to work out what the people are shouting. One of the men at the front mimes pulling on a rope and Blanchard assumes they are telling him to raise the bucket. Irritably, he tosses away his cigarette. He is a foreman, not used to being interrupted in his work. He is uncertain what to do. Now everyone on the bridge is imitating the first man, pumping their hands and yelling, so finally he gives the order. The bucket emerges from the water, sways for a moment, then hangs, motionless. Blanchard steps forward, gestures to the crane operator to bring the bucket closer, so he can see what is going on. As soon as he sees what is inside, Blanchard realizes the magnitude of the problem. In the bucket, half buried in black sludge, is the naked body of a girl.

Early statements described the woman as being between twenty-five and thirty. Camille spread out a dozen large photographs on his desk. Even in life, it was clear she had not been particularly beautiful. Her hips were broad, her breasts small, her thighs flabby. She looked like a rough draft, as though Nature had put her together without really paying attention, combining elements of large and small: a broad backside and the dainty feet of a Japanese girl. The woman must have been using a tanning bed: analysis of the epidermis indicated her coloring was unlikely to have come from natural sunlight. Distinct tan lines indicated that she had been wearing a bikini. There were no obvious signs of violence to the body apart from a red scratch extending from the waist to the hipbone. Traces of cement indicated that the body might at one point have been laid on a concrete surface. Her face had been softened by time spent in muddy water. She had thick, dark eyebrows, a wide mouth, and shoulder-length brown hair.

Led by Lieutenant Marette, the investigation determined that the woman died of strangulation after being subjected to depraved sexual abuse. Although the killer had been savage, the body had not been mutilated or dismembered. The victim had been raped and sodomized and then strangled.

Camille was making slow progress through the case file. From time to time he looked up, as though trying to commit the information to memory before moving on, as though hoping it might trigger some insight. Nothing came. The case file was crushingly sad. It told him nothing, or almost nothing.

The autopsy report did little to enhance his mental picture of the victim. She was about twenty-five, five foot six, weighed 128 pounds, and had no distinguishing marks or scars. The tan lines left by the UV light indicated that she had worn sunglasses and sandals as well as a bikini. She was not a smoker and had never borne a child or had a miscarriage. Though neat and well groomed, it was evident that she did not worry unduly about her appearance. There was no indication that she had been wearing jewelry that might have been taken by the killer, and she was not wearing nail polish or any other form of makeup. She had eaten about six hours before her death. Her last meal included beef, potatoes, and strawberries, and she had drunk a considerable amount of milk.

The body had been half buried in the silt for some twelve hours before being discovered. There were two points that intrigued the investigating officers, two unusual details for which the report offered no conclusions beyond what was self-evident.

The first was that the body had been discovered, partially covered in mud, lying in the bucket of the dredger. The presence of mud in the bucket was surprising, since the body had been placed there before dredging began. The bucket had been lowered into the canal, but it had not gone deep enough to account for the mud.

The only possible conclusion—however implausible—was that the killer had dumped the mud into the bucket after putting the body there. What motive could a killer have had for doing such a thing? Lieutenant Marette offered no answer; he simply drew attention to the anomaly.

On closer consideration, the entire crime scene seemed curious. Camille tried to picture it in his mind, considered every possible solution, and concluded that the murderer would have been faced with a bizarre problem. After hoisting the body into the bucket of the crane (which, according to the report, was suspended about five feet above the ground), he would have had to scoop mud from the canal (samples of the mud conclusively proved its provenance) and then poured it over the body. The quantity of mud involved would have required the killer to make several trips, assuming he was using a household bucket or something of the kind. The investigating officers at the time were undecided as to what this ritual might mean.

Camille felt a strange tingling down his spine. This detail was unsettling. He could see no logical reason why the killer would have done what he did—unless he were recreating a scene from a book.

The second peculiar detail was something Louis had highlighted in his summary report: an unusual mark on the body of the victim. At first glance, it looked like the sort of birthmark one might find on any body. Indeed, initial reports had described it as such. The investigation had been done in haste. Photographs had been taken at the scene, the usual overview and close-up shots, the usual measurements. The body had only been properly examined after it arrived at the mortuary. According to the autopsy report, the "birthmark" was in fact a fake. About two inches in diameter, with a brownish pigmentation, it had been applied using a paintbrush and common acrylic paint. The shape was vaguely animal. Various detectives—according to the dictates of their subconscious—had favored a pig, or perhaps a dog. One of the team well versed in zoology—an officer named Vaquier—had gone so far as to imagine a warthog. The "birthmark" had been painted over with a clear, matte varnish containing a drying agent of the kind used for finishing paintings. Camille considered this detail carefully. It was a technique he himself had used when working with acrylics. Later he had given them up in favor of oils, but he still remembered the varnish he used, the heady solvent fumes, at once pleasant and sickly, which could provoke crippling, crushing headaches if used—as it said on the label—over prolonged periods. To Camille, this could mean only one thing. The murderer had wanted to ensure that the "birthmark" was not washed away while the body was submerged in the mud and water.

At the time, a search on the missing persons database had produced no result. The victim's description had been widely circulated, but nothing had been forthcoming. The victim had never been positively identified. The police investigation, despite meticulous work by Lieutenant Marette, had also led nowhere. Both paint and varnish were commonly available and so did not constitute a lead. As for the mud in the bucket, it remained unexplained. The case had eventually been closed for lack of evidence.

5

"For God's sake, how exactly are you supposed to pronounce them?" Le Guen said, staring at the names Sjöwall and Wahlöö.

Camille did not reply, he simply opened the copy of *Roseanna* and read aloud:

"Page 14: 'Death by strangulation,' thought Martin Beck. He sat and thumbed through a bunch of photographs that Ahlberg had dug out of a basket on his desk. The pictures showed the locks, the dredger, its bucket in the foreground, the body lying on the embankment, and in the mortuary . . . he saw her before him as she looked in the picture, naked and abandoned, with narrow shoulders and her dark hair in a coil across her throat . . . She was . . . 5 feet, 6½ inches tall, had gray-blue eyes and dark brown hair. Her teeth were good and she had no scars from operations or other marks on her body with the exception of a birthmark, high up on the inside of her left thigh about an inch and a half from her groin. It was brown and about as large as a 10-øre coin, but uneven and looked like a little pig . . .'"

"Okay . . . ," Le Guen murmured.

"'She had eaten three to five hours before she died,'" Camille carried on reading, "'. . . meat, potatoes, strawberries and milk . . .' and earlier in the book: 'It was a woman. They laid her on her back on a folded tarpaulin out on the breakwater. The deck man . . .' No, forget that, here's the bit I was looking for: 'She was naked and had no jewelry on. The lines of her tan made it apparent that she had sunbathed in a bikini. Her hips were broad and she had heavy thighs.'"

6

Together, Louis and Maleval assembled all the information on the canal de l'Ourcq murder. The stumbling block in the investigation stemmed from an inability to identify the young victim. All records and databases had been scoured; no effort had been spared. Seeing the figure of Cob half-hidden by his computer monitors at the far end of the room, Camille could not help but reflect on the paradox of a young girl disappearing without a trace in a society that was now so comprehensively surveilled. Catalogues, lists, inventories, all the most significant details of our lives documented, every telephone call, every movement, every payment traceable; only a very few lives, by a series of quirks and coincidences that are little short of miraculous, elude surveillance. A woman of twenty-five who presumably had parents, friends, lovers, and employers had disappeared without trace. A month could pass without a friend becoming concerned that she had not called; a year could go by without a boyfriend, once so in love with her, worrying that she had not come back from a trip. The parents who received no postcards, whose telephone calls went unanswered, had given the victim up for dead long before she actually died. Unless the victim had been a loner,

an orphan, a runaway, so angry with the world that she had severed
ties with everyone she knew. Perhaps, even before she died, she had
given them up for dead.

Louis had written a summary of the cases on a flip chart—though
this was hardly necessary. In a few short days, each had developed
with a rapidity that made it difficult for anyone to keep up.

» July 7, 2000: Corbeil, *Le Crime d'Orcival* (Gaboriau)
  Victim: Maryse Perrin (23)

» August 24, 2000: Paris, *Roseanna* (Sjöwall & Wahlöö)
  Victim: ?

» November 21, 2001: Tremblay: *The Black Dahlia* (Ellroy)
  Victims: Manuela Constanza (24), Henri Lambert (51)

» April 6, 2003: Courbevoie: *American Psycho* (B. E. Ellis)
  Victims: Évelyne Rouvray (23), Josiane Debeuf (21), François
  Cottet

"The team watching Lesage's house in Villeréal haven't come up
with anything yet," Louis said. "They've done a brief search of the
grounds of the house, but they say it would take months to search
it thoroughly."

"Christine Lesage is back at home now; I dropped her off earlier,"
Maleval said.

Things had to be particularly grim for Élisabeth not to nip outside for a quick cigarette. Fernand had briefly absented himself,
tottering off with a dignified gait. When he vanished this late in
the day, he generally wasn't seen again until the following morning.
Armand did not seem unduly irritated; he had managed to bum his
colleague's last pack of cigarettes and had enough to tide him over
until he found a fresh victim.

Two teams—Mehdi with Maleval, Louis with Élisabeth—
proceeded to cross-reference the information they had on Lesage

with the details of the cases at hand. The first team pored over Lesage's schedule, the second over his accounts. Armand, with some help from Cob—who was furiously multitasking to deal with queries from all three teams—reviewed the five cases in the light of information given to him by his colleagues. It would take several hours to complete this complex task, but it would be crucial to the success of the next day's interrogations. The stronger the connections, the easier it would be for Camille to put pressure on Lesage and perhaps even get him to confess.

"On the financial front," Louis said, laying his hands flat on the desk and nodding to each file in turn, "there are a lot of withdrawals, but the dates don't make a lot of sense. We're trying to work out how much money would have been needed at each stage of the crimes. In the meantime, we're making a list of suspicious withdrawals and deposits. This is complicated by the fact that Lesage has a variety of revenue streams. There are stocks and shares sold or cashed—we have no way of knowing the capital gains involved—cash sales through the bookshop, acquisitions and sales through libraries, other antiquarian booksellers, and at auctions. His expenditure is even more complicated. We may need to bring in an expert from the *brigade financière*."

"I'll call Le Guen and ask him to get in touch with Deschamps, in case we need to submit a request."

Cob, meanwhile, had requested a third computer, but having no space on his desk, he was now forced to get up every five minutes to update the searches he was processing.

Maleval and Mehdi were both children of the digital age and rarely made their notes longhand. Camille found them huddled together at a monitor, cells glued to their ears so that they could make calls as soon as they found contact details for Lesage's business associates.

"Some of the diaries go back a long way," Maleval said while Mehdi was on hold to someone. "We're having to ask people to check their old diaries and call us back. It's a pretty lengthy process. Especially since-"

He was interrupted by Camille's telephone ringing.

"I've just had the *divisionnaire* on the phone." It was Juge Deschamps. "He's told me about the murder on the canal de l'Ourcq–"

"Where the victim was never identified." Camille finished the sentence for her. "I know . . . it complicates things."

They talked for a few minutes about the best way forward.

"I'm not optimistic that our little tête-à-tête via the classified ads will go on much longer," Camille said in conclusion. "Right now, our man is getting the publicity he's always dreamed of. But I'm guessing we won't hear from him again after the next ad."

"What makes you say that, *commandant*?"

"At first it was just a hunch. But now I'm sure of it. Unless I'm mistaken, we've now identified all the cold cases. He's got nothing more to tell us. Besides, it's become a routine. He'll get bored; he'll get suspicious. Any routine necessarily involves risk."

"Well, right now we have a new case. What do we do next? The media are going to be baying for our blood tomorrow."

"Well, mine, at any rate."

"You've got the press snapping at your heels, I've got the *ministre de la Justice*. We all have our crosses."

Juge Deschamps's tone was very different from what it had been at the start of the case. Oddly, the more the investigation flagged, the more obliging she appeared to become. It was an ominous sign, and Camille made a mental note to have a word with Le Guen before he went home.

"Where do things stand with this bookseller of yours?"

"His sister seems determined to give him an alibi for every day of the year. I've got the whole team preparing for tomorrow's interviews."

"Are you expecting to hold him for the full twenty-four hours?"

"I'm hoping I can get an extension."

"Well, it's been a long day, and it doesn't look as if tomorrow will be any shorter."

Camille glanced at his watch. Immediately he thought of Irène. He told the team to call it a night.

Thursday, April 24

1

Le Matin, early edition:

PANIC AT THE BRIGADE CRIMINELLE.
TWO NEW TOMES FROM THE
BACKLIST OF "THE NOVELIST"

The Novelist keeps detectives guessing

The killer responsible for the double murder at Courbevoie on April 6 last is also suspected of having murdered Manuela Constanza, the young girl whose body was discovered hacked in two on a landfill in Tremblay last November. When, some days ago, it was confirmed that in July of last year, he murdered Grace Hobson in Glasgow, in a homage to *Laidlaw*, a novel by the Scottish novelist William McIlvanney, the death toll of his "literary achievements" rose to four victims, all of them young, all of them "executed" in carefully staged scenes that are as gruesome as they are macabre.

Today, we can reveal the existence of two further cases.

The killing of a 23-year-old hairdresser stabbed more than twenty times is a meticulous reconstruction of a scene from *Le Crime d'Orcival*, a classic nineteenth-century detective novel by Émile Gaboriau.

The discovery of another young woman, in August 2000, who was strangled after being subjected to horrific sexual abuse is the recreation of a scene from *Roseanna*, a crime novel by Swedish authors Sjöwall and Wahlöö.

In total, five novels have served as a pretext for this monstrous killing spree. Six young women have been murdered, each of them in vicious and bewilderingly violent ways.

The police—clutching at straws as the body count rises—have been reduced to attempting to contact the killer through the classified advertisements of an obscure magazine. Their most recent advertisement: "What about your earlier works . . . ?" demonstrates the ghoulish admiration the *brigade criminelle* seem to have for this butcher.

In recent developments, Jérôme Lesage, a Parisian bookseller, has been held for questioning and is now the prime suspect in the case. His sister, Christine Lesage, interviewed yesterday by the *brigade criminelle*, and devastated by her brother's arrest, angrily commented: "Jérôme was the person who put the police on the right track when they were at a loss, and this is how they repaid him! Given that they do not have a scrap of evidence against my brother, our lawyer has demanded that he be released immediately."

It would seem that the police have no hard evidence to implicate this convenient suspect; furthermore, their grounds for arrest amount to a series of trivial coincidences that any one of us might have experienced.

How many other murders have gone unnoticed? How many more innocent young women will be murdered, tortured, raped, or brutally executed before the police manage to arrest the killer?

These are the questions we cannot help but ask.

2

Despite his smug self-assurance, Jérôme Lesage clearly had not slept a wink. His face paler, his posture more stooped, he sat down with a stiff formality and stared at the table, hands tightly clasped to hide a faint tremor.

Camille took his seat opposite him, laid a file on the table and next to it a sheet of paper on which he had scribbled some indecipherable notes.

"We've taken a closer look at the entries in your desk diary for the past few months, Monsieur Lesage."

"I want a lawyer." Lesage's solemn, peremptory tone could not quite disguise the anxious quaver in his voice.

"Not just yet, as I have already told you."

Lesage glared at him as though steeling himself for a challenge.

"If you could simply explain these matters for us," Camille said slapping the file with the flat of his hand, "we can let you go home."

He slipped on his glasses.

"First, your schedule. Let's just have a look at the last few months, if you don't mind. Let's pick a month at random—December 4, you had a meeting with a Monsieur Pelessier, who also runs a bookshop. Monsieur Pelessier was not in Paris on the date in question, so he did not meet with you. On December 17, 18, and 19 you were supposedly at an auction in Mâcon. No one remembers seeing you there; indeed you did not register for the sale. In January, on the eleventh, you've noted a meeting with Madame Bertleman, who had asked for a valuation. She did not meet with you until the sixteenth. January 24, you apparently went to the Cologne Antiquarian Book Fair for four days. There is no evidence you set foot in the city. On the–"

"Please . . ."

"I'm sorry?"

Lesage was staring at his hands. Camille, trying to remain detached, had his nosed buried in his notes. When he looked up, Jérôme Lesage was a very different man. The smug facade had been replaced by a terrible weariness.

"It's my sister," he said, his voice almost a whisper.

"What about her? You pretend to go away on business to keep your sister happy, is that it?"

Lesage merely nodded.

"Why?"

Lesage did not reply and Camille drew out the awkward silence for a long moment before stepping into the breach.

"Your . . . absences are frequent but erratic. What is incriminating is that so many of them correspond with the dates on which young women were murdered. So you can hardly blame us for being curious."

Camille gave Lesage a moment to think.

"Especially since these dates also coincide with substantial withdrawals from your bank accounts," Camille began again. "Let's see . . . in February and March of last year, you sold shares from a portfolio your sister had authorized you to administer. In fact, it's rather difficult to keep track of your activity in the stock market. But at least forty-five hundred euros' worth of shares were sold. Might I ask what you did with the money?"

"That's a private matter," Lesage snapped, suddenly looking up.

"It ceased to be private from the moment we realized that you were making sizable withdrawals during periods when someone was planning a series of murders that required substantial sums."

"It wasn't me!" Lesage roared, thumping his fist on the table.

"Then kindly explain your movements and the substantial withdrawals from your various accounts."

"The burden of proof rests with you, not with me."

"Let's ask the investigating magistrate about that and see what she says . . ."

"I don't want my sister to f-"

"Yes?"

Lesage seemed very suddenly to be exhausted, beaten.

"You don't want her to find out that you haven't been working as hard as you claimed, that you've been squandering her money, is that it?"

"Just leave her out of this. She's very fragile. Leave her in peace."

"What is it that you don't want her to find out?"

Faced with Lesage's obstinate silence, Camille heaved a long sigh.

"Okay, let's start again." Camille peered at him over the rims of his glasses. "On the date Grace Hobson was murdered in Glasgow you have no alibi, having last been seen in Edinburgh. Edinburgh to Glasgow is a short hop. So at the very time that Grace-"

Louis had entered the interrogation room so soundlessly that Camille did not notice him until he leaned down and whispered:

"Could you step outside for a minute? You have a call. It's urgent."

Camille got slowly to his feet, staring at Lesage's bowed head.

"Monsieur Lesage, either you can provide a convincing account of your movements—and I'd suggest you do so as soon as possible—or you cannot, in which case I have some rather personal questions to put to you."

3

Irène had taken a tumble on the rue des Martyres. She had mis-judged the curb. Passers-by rushed to help. Irène told them she was fine as she lay on the pavement, clutching her belly with both hands, trying to catch her breath. The owner of a delicatessen called the ambulance, and some minutes later, the EMTs arrived to find her sitting, legs splayed, in the shop where the owner's wife was regaling anyone who would listen with details of the accident. Irène had no memory of what had happened; she felt only a nagging anxiety, and a dull ache spread gradually through her body.

"Would you ever shut your trap, Yvonne," the deli owner pleaded. "We know what happened."

He had offered Irène some orange juice, and she cupped the glass in her hands like a sacred relic, without taking a sip.

The paramedics laid her on a stretcher and, with some difficulty, managed to clear a path to the ambulance.

Camille, out of breath from racing up the stairs, found her in bed on the second floor of the Clinique Montambert.

"Are you all right?"

"I fell," Irène said simply, as though her mind could not quite absorb this obvious yet unbelievable fact.

"Are you hurt? What did the doctors say?"

"I fell."

Staring up at him, Irène began to cry quietly. Camille took her in his arms. He would have cried himself were it not for the fact that in that moment her face looked just as it had in his dream when she said, "Can't you see he's hurting me?"

"Are you hurt?" Camille said again. "Are you in any pain?"

But Irène kept crying, holding her stomach.

"They gave me an injection."

"She needs to rest: she's still in shock."

Camille turned. The doctor looked like a first-year medical student. He had small round glasses, hair a little too long, and the lopsided smile of an overgrown teenager. He came to Irène's bed and took her hand.

"You'll be fine, won't you?"

"Yes," Irène said through her tears. "Yes, I'll be fine."

"You had a little fall, that's all. And it gave you a scare."

Camille, relegated to the end of the bed, felt excluded. He choked back the question on the tip of his tongue and was relieved when the doctor continued.

"The baby didn't care much for all that commotion. He's a little uncomfortable right now, and I think he might be in a hurry to find out what it was all about."

"You think so?"

"I'm sure of it. I think he might be in a great hurry. We'll know more in a couple of hours." The doctor smiled. "I hope you've got his room ready."

Irène looked up anxiously.

"Will he be all right?"

"Three weeks premature is nothing to worry about."

Louis called Élisabeth and asked her to come to Camille's apartment. They arrived together, as though synchronized.

"So?" Élisabeth smiled. "You'll be a father soon?"

Camille had not quite managed to collect himself. He hurried between the bedroom and the living room, trying frantically to gather some things for Irène, only to promptly mislay them.

Élisabeth, who was calmer and more organized, swiftly located the little suitcase Irène had packed some days before, which contained everything she would need for a stay in hospital. Camille was astonished, though Irène must have mentioned the suitcase; she had probably even shown him where it was, just in case.

"There we go; I think that's everything."

Slumped on the sofa, Camille let out a long breath, then looked up gratefully at Élisabeth and smiled awkwardly.

"Thanks, that's really sweet," he said. "I'll take it to her."

"Maybe Élisabeth could do it?" Louis suggested. He had just come back from getting the mail.

All three of them stared at the envelope he was holding.

4

Dear Camille,

So nice, as always, to see your advertisement.

"Your earlier works . . . ?" you ask. I expected rather more subtlety on your part. Even so, I can't bring myself to hold it against you: you are flailing and floundering in a labyrinth of my devising—one from which you will be freed when and as I decide—you are flailing, as I said, but I know that you are doing your best. Indeed, I would go further, Camille: no one could do better.

Even so, I have to say that your recent advertisement was a little presumptuous. How naive! At the risk of stating the obvious, I shall write to you only about the cases you have identified so as not to spoil my surprises. Otherwise, where would be the fun? And I can tell you I have many more surprises in store.

So, Glasgow. You have not asked me about Glasgow, but I can tell that you are *dying* to know. The process was simple. McIlvanney's magnificent novel gives most of the details of the case, whose sophistication you will have noted. He mentions that the book was inspired by a real-life murder. I adore those loops that perfectly fuse literature and life.

I noticed Grace Hobson in the doorway of the nightclub as I parked my rental car. I chose her without a second thought. That childlike face, those slender hips obviously destined to thicken by her thirties: she was a living embodiment of that troubling and wistful city. It was already late, the street long since deserted when I saw her step out onto the pavement, nervous and hesitant. I had not expected such a stroke of good fortune. I had planned to follow her, to track her movements, learn her habits and later abduct her. I had not planned to stay long in Glasgow, but still I did not expect her to offer herself to me so freely. I got out of my car, map of Glasgow in hand, and asked her for directions I did not need in an English I hoped was gauche and charming. I smiled awkwardly. We were outside the nightclub and I did not wish to stand there for very long. And so, as I listened to her explanation, frowning as though trying to decipher her fluent, rapid English, I steered her toward the car. We laid the map on the hood. I told her I needed to get a pen from the glove compartment. I left the car door open. Then, pulling her roughly toward me, I pressed to her face a rag I had liberally soaked in chloroform, and a moment later, we were on our way. I drove cautiously through the empty streets while she slept peacefully, trustingly. I did something I had not planned to do. I raped her there in the back of the car. She woke with a start as I entered her, just as described in the novel. I was obliged to put her back to sleep. I strangled her then, while still inside her. Together we were united in sensual pleasure and in death, which, as you know, are one and the same.

I had to return to my hotel to fetch the tools I needed. I remembered to take her panties.

Your Scottish colleagues have undoubtedly shown you the photographs of the little scene I staged in Kelvingrove Park. Without wishing to boast, I would like to hope that William McIlvanney, who lives in Glasgow, felt a satisfaction equal to my admiration for his work.

Laidlaw was the first work I decided to sign. I did so because I was weary of police officers who appeared utterly incapable of recognizing my artistry. I realized I had to put someone on the right track, that I had to leave a sign that would connect my homage to *Laidlaw* with my future works. I considered a number of distinct approaches. Leaving a false fingerprint on the body struck me as the most satisfying solution. Actually, though I was concerned I might not be equal to the task, I was already deliberating a tribute to Ellroy's novel in which a fingerprint is brazenly applied to the body. In leaving this distinctive mark, this signature, I nurtured the hope that, if not the police (who, aside from your good self, Camille, are brutish dolts, if truth be told), the aesthetes, the true aficionados, might discover my art and come to appreciate its true value. Besides, the fingerprint left on Grace Hobson's toe did not in any way despoil the magnificent tableau I succeeded in creating in Kelvingrove Park. Everything was in its rightful place. It was, I like to believe, as perfect as it could have been.

I know that by now you have also discovered the wonderful novel by our Swedish friends. Reading *Roseanna* was a revelation, you know? Thereafter, I forced myself to read other works by these twain. Alas, none afforded me the truly vertiginous pleasure of that first volume.

What is so magical about the book? Therein lies another mystery. There is a stillness to it akin to the still waters of the canal de l'Ourcq; very little happens. It is an extended game of patience. The detective, Martin Beck, at once sullen and appealing, is utterly unlike the miserable detectives of so many American authors and the dreary, pedantic investigators of too many French writers.

Obviously, transposing *Roseanna* to a French setting, as I did, was a daunting challenge. The scene had to be rendered in a manner that was convincing, so that the finished work would be imbued with the atmosphere of the original. To achieve this, I used all the means at my disposal.

You can well imagine my joy, Camille, indeed my jubilation, on the morning of August 25 when, standing amid the crowd of onlookers on the bridge above the lock, I watched the bucket of the crane swing toward us like a theater curtain rising, heard the man leaning on the railing next to me shout, "Look, there's a woman's body in there!" The news trickled through the little crowd like a flame along a powder trail. Imagine my delight!

My young recruit . . . I am sure you will have noticed that she was a perfect likeness for Roseanna: the same heavy, graceless body, the same delicate limbs.

Sjöwall and Wahlöö are maddeningly elusive on the precise cause of Roseanna's death. We are told only that it was "death by strangulation in conjunction with gross sexual assault." We learn: "The culprit was brutal. Signs of perverse tendencies." This obviously gave me considerable freedom. The authors, however, are precise on one point: "There wasn't that much blood." These, then, were the elements I had. The most disconcerting was the passage that reads: "She could have received some of the injuries after she was already dead, or at least unconscious. There are things in the autopsy statement that suggest it could have happened that way."

Obviously, there was the "red scratch" extending from the waist to the hipbone, and how was one supposed to interpret that?

I decided on a scratch made using a small block of concrete I fashioned in my cellar. I truly believe the authors would have admired the simplicity of this solution. Otherwise, I strangled her with my bare hands having sodomized her using a shoehorn which, I believe, conveniently ruptured the mucous membrane but spilled little blood.

The trickiest part was, of course, in creating the false birthmark. Forensic analysis will no doubt have told you that I used the most commonly available products. In fact I had to search long and hard before finding an animal stencil that matched Roseanna's birthmark. Unlike your good self, I am not an accomplished artist.

I took the body to the canal de l'Ourcq using a rental car. Do you know, Camille, I had waited almost a year for the municipal authorities to dredge the section of the canal I had chosen as my location? Bureaucracy can be so infuriating. My little joke, Camille, you know me by now.

I assume that at this stage you must be seething with impatience to know the answer to the question you have been asking yourself since you first reopened this case: "Who was Roseanna?"

In life, Roseanna was called Alice Hedges. She was a student or something of the sort (please find enclosed her I.D. so that, should you have a moment, you can trace her family in Arkansas and pass on my thanks for their daughter's collaboration). An important, not to say key, element of this work was that the victim should not be identified too quickly since, in the novel, the crucial mystery is that of the victim's identity. Roseanna is, first and foremost, the story of this quest, and it would have been ridiculous, indeed indecent, if you had managed to identify her immediately. I met her on the Hungarian border six days previously. She was hitchhiking. My initial conversations with Roseanna apprised me that she had not been in touch with her parents for more than two years and had been living alone prior to embarking on a European jaunt, of which none of her friends were aware. This made it possible for me to create the minor masterpiece that, to my great pleasure, has at last been acknowledged.

Doubtless you find me rather garrulous. As might be expected, there are few people to whom I can talk about my work. From the time when I first realized what the world required of me, I have been tirelessly doing its bidding with little hope of conversation. God, how ignorant the world is, Camille. And how evanescent. How rare are those things that truly leave their mark. No one understood what I wanted to give to the world, and there were times, I confess, when I was angry. Times when I forbore, more tirelessly than you can possibly imagine. Forgive the platitude; anger is a poor counselor. I found myself compelled calmly to reread the classics; only in their company could I find the strength to persevere until some elevation of the soul stilled the rage within me. Months and months passed before I abandoned any thought of being other than I am. It was an arduous struggle, but I prevailed, and finally I have been rewarded. For the dark shadows of that period were followed by the dazzling light of revelation. I do not use the word lightly, Camille, I assure you. I remember as though it were yesterday. My rage against the world suddenly fell away, and I knew what was required of me; I realized my purpose, understood my mission. The unparalleled success of crime fiction clearly demonstrates the visceral need people have for death. And for mystery. People frantically seek out such imagery not because they need images, but because this is all they have. Aside from sundry wars and the gratuitous butchery provided by governments to assuage their unquenchable thirst for death, what do they have? Images. Mankind seeks out images of death because he desires death. It is a thirst only the artist can slake. Writers write about death for those who dream of death; they write tragedies for those who yearn for tragedy. And always the world clamors for more. The world is not content merely with stories; it thirsts for blood, for actual blood, not fictional gore. Humanity does its best to justify its desires by transfiguring the real—surely it was to this mission of appeasing the world with images that your mother, a brilliant artist, devoted her career?—but the desire is insatiable, unanswerable. The world wants what is real, what is true; it wants blood. Between the transfiguration that is art and brute reality, there must surely exist some narrow way for those with enough compassion for humanity to wish to sacrifice themselves. Oh, Camille, I do not think myself a savior. Nor a saint. I am content simply to make myself heard; if everyone did likewise the world would be more bearable and much less disagreeable.

Remember the words that Gaboriau puts in the mouth of Commandant Lecoq? "There are people who have a passion for the theater. It is not unlike my own passion. But I cannot understand how people can take pleasure in the shoddy fictions, which are to real life as a tallow candle is to the sun. Being more jaded and more difficult to please than the public, I demand genuine comedies, actual tragedies. Society, that is my theater. My actors laugh truly, or they weep genuine tears." It is a passage that has always deeply moved me. My actors, too, have wept real tears. I have a special affection for Alice, who played my Roseanna, as I do for Évelyne in my restaging of Bret Easton Ellis, because both wept magnificently. Both were gifted actresses, more than equal to the roles in which I cast them. My faith in them was rewarded.

As you will no doubt have sensed, our correspondence must come to an end. I am confident that sooner or later we will pick up this conversation from which both you and I have learned so much, but that time has not yet come. I must complete my "oeuvre," and that demands total concentration. I know that I will achieve my goal. You can have faith in me. I must put the finishing touches to the monument I have toiled so meticulously to build. Only then will you realize that my creation—so carefully planned, so skillfully crafted—is fit to rank among the masterpieces of this nascent century.

I beg to remain, Sir, your humble and obedient servant.

5

"I saw the doctor again. He's surprised I haven't been having contractions."

"I'm not." Camille smiled. "The little guy is hanging in there. He's perfectly comfortable where he is, and I don't blame him."

He could hear Irène's smile over the phone.

"So what happens now?"

"I've just had an ultrasound. The baby waved—he sends his love. If I don't start contractions in the next couple of hours, they'll send me home, and we'll wait until he's good and ready to join us."

"How are you feeling?"

"My heart is aching. I had a terrible scare. I think that's the only reason they kept me in."

Camille felt his own heart ache. There was such need, such pain in Irène's tender words, that it cut him to the quick.

"I'll come in."

"There's no need, darling. Élisabeth was very sweet . . . remember to thank her from me, okay? She stayed here for a bit, and we had a chat even though I knew she had places to be. She told me you received another letter. Things can't be easy for you right now, either."

"It's tough. But you do know I'm with you in spirit, don't you?"

"Of course I know. I'm not worried."

"Right now, he's still in the picture. The fake entries in his diary, the mysterious withdrawals . . . there's a lot of disturbing evidence."

"And you think he might have sent the letter before he was arrested?"

"It's possible."

That afternoon, Juge Deschamps was wearing a jacket and pants of excruciating ugliness, a gray ensemble trimmed with ruffles that looked like a cross between a three-piece suit, a pair of overalls, and a flamenco dress. The woman's eyes, however, were as keen and intelligent as ever; Camille could well imagine the troubling effect she had on men.

She was holding the latest letter from the Novelist, scanning it quickly for a second time, attentive to the smallest detail.

"And you've released the sister?"

"All that matters right now is keeping the two of them apart," Le Guen said. "She's willing to back up everything he says. Blind faith."

"She'll be hard pressed," Camille said. "It's not enough to say he was with her when he wasn't. We have a great deal of evidence that it will be difficult to refute."

"From what you've said, it sounds to me like he's spooked."

"If he really is a twisted psychopath, we can't rely on how he seems. If he's spent years living a double life, deceiving his sister, then he's had a lot of practice. I'm going to need a little help from Dr. Crest. We'll have to use a room with an observation booth, so he can watch."

"I think you're right. Once the custody limit expires, we can't keep them isolated. But he could be extremely dangerous. If we do have to release him, do you have the manpower to keep him under tight surveillance, *divisionnaire*?"

Le Guen held up the rolled-up newspaper he had been clutching since the start of the meeting.

"The way things have been going, I don't think I'll have a problem allocating the necessary resources," he said grimly.

Deschamps made no comment.

"He makes threats in the letter," Le Guen said. "Now, that might be nothing; it might just be a trick. It may be that he doesn't have a plan."

Deschamps clicked her tongue, still staring at the letter.

"It's hard to imagine that a man who could devise such an intricate plan wouldn't have an endgame. No, I think it's a crucial piece of information," she said, looking up at the two men. "In his twisted way, he's a man of his word. He does exactly as he says. He has done since the start. And what really concerns me"—she glanced at Camille—"is that this plan was worked out long ago. He has known from the very beginning where this is leading."

"And we don't," Camille said.

6

Louis took over the questioning of Lesage, followed by Maleval and then Armand. Each had his own tactics, and the contrast between the interrogation methods of the four men had frequently produced results in the past. Louis was scrupulous, urbane, his interviews were subtle; he took time formulating his questions, as though all eternity stretched before him; with the patience of a saint he listened to every answer with unsettling attentiveness, always leaving some doubt as to his interpretation. Maleval, true to his training as a judoka, worked in short, swift bursts. He was often casual, even friendly with the suspect, eager to gain his trust. He could be immensely charming, only to voice all of a sudden some callous conclusion, pounce on a glaring inconsistency with the same force he would once have used to pin an opponent to the judo mat. Armand . . . well, he was Armand. Hunched over his notes, rarely looking at the suspect, asking pedantic questions, jotting down every answer, constantly reverting to minor details, he could spend an hour dissecting a single incident, ferreting out the merest inaccuracy, the most trivial evasion, gnawing away at the same bone until he had picked it clean. Louis's questioning was sinuous, Maleval's was straight, whereas Armand's approach was a spiral.

By the time Camille arrived, Lesage had already spent an hour with Louis, and Maleval had just finished his interrogation. The two were comparing notes at a desk together. Camille headed straight for them but was waved over by Cob from behind his bank of monitors.

"Bad news?" Camille said.

Cob leaned his elbows on the desk, resting his chin in his cupped hands.

"Worse than bad."

They stared at each other for a long moment, hesitant. Then Cob reached out, took a page from the printer, and held it out to Camille without looking.

"I'm so sorry, Camille," he said.

Camille scanned the page, a long column of numbers: dates, times. Then he looked up and stared at the computer screen in front of Cob.

"I'm so sorry . . . ," Cob said again as he watched Camille walk away.

7

Camille strode across the office and, without stopping, tapped Louis on the shoulder as he passed.

"You, with me."

Louis glanced around him, puzzled, then quickly got to his feet and followed Camille, who was heading for the stairwell. The two men did not exchange a word as they crossed the street to the brasserie where they sometimes went for a beer together at the end of a shift. Camille took one of the tables on the glassed-in terrace and settled himself on the moleskin bench, leaving Louis the chair with its back to the street. They waited in silence for someone to come take their order.

"Espresso," Camille said.

Louis gestured to indicate that he would have the same. For a while he kept his eyes fixed on the table, furtively glancing at Camille, until the waiter finally set down their drinks.

"Exactly how much does Maleval owe you, Louis?"

Before Louis had a chance to deny it, Camille had brought his fist down on the table so forcefully that the coffee cups rattled and people at the neighboring tables turned to look. Camille did not say another word.

"A bit, I suppose," Louis said after a while. "I mean, it's not a fortune."

"How much?"

"I don't know exactly."

Camille angrily raised his fist again.

"About five grand."

Camille, who was still not used to thinking in euros, mentally calculated that this was almost thirty-five thousand francs.

"What's his deal?"

"Gambling. He's been on a losing streak; he owed a lot of people money."

"So how long have you been playing the banker, Louis?"

"Not long, honestly. He'd borrowed small amounts before, but he always paid me back. Admittedly, he's been borrowing a lot more recently. Last Sunday when you came round to my place, I'd just given him a check for fifteen hundred euros. I told him it was the last time."

Camille did not look at him. He had one hand in his pocket, and with the other he toyed nervously with his cell phone.

"Listen, this is a personal matter," Louis said calmly. "It's got nothing to do with . . ."

He did not finish the sentence. He scanned the piece of paper Camille had just handed him, then laid it flat on the table. Camille's eyes were welling with tears.

"Do you want my resignation?" Louis said at length.

"Don't leave me in the lurch, Louis. Not now."

8

"My hands are tied, Jean-Claude, I have no choice but to sack you."

Sitting opposite Camille, Maleval blinked rapidly, desperately looking around for something to lean on.

"It kills me to have to do it . . . it really does. Why didn't you just come talk to me?"

Staring at Maleval's hunched figure, Camille saw in a flash what lay ahead, and it pained him. Unemployed, up to his neck in debt, Maleval would have to "muddle through"—that ghastly formulation reserved for those who have long since ceased to be able to.

Cob had printed out the list of calls made from Maleval's cell to the journalist at *Le Matin*. It detailed only those made since April 6, the date on which the Courbevoie victims had been discovered. The first call had been made at 10:34 a.m. It was the earliest that anybody could have known about it.

"How long has this been going on?"

"Since the end of last year. He got in touch with me. At first, I just threw him a few crumbs of information, and that seemed to be enough."

"And then you started having trouble making ends meet, right?"

"I lost a lot of money, yeah. Louis helped me out, but that wasn't enough, so–"

"You realize I could haul in Buisson for bribing a public official," Camille growled with barely suppressed rage. "I could have the little fucker strip-searched in his fucking newsroom."

"I know."

"And you know that I won't, but only for your sake."

"I know," Maleval said gratefully.

"We'll keep it low key. I'll have to call Le Guen, but I'll fix things so that it's handled as discreetly as possible."

"I'll go home–"

"You'll stay here! You'll go when I tell you to and not before, got it?"

Maleval nodded.

"How much do you need, Jean-Claude?"

"I don't need anything!"

"Don't fuck me around! How much?"

"Eleven grand."

"Jesus Christ!"

Several seconds passed.

"I'll write you a check."

Then, seeing that Maleval was about to protest, Camille said calmly, "This is how things are going to play out, Jean-Claude, okay? First, you clear your debts. We can worry about repayments later. As for the disciplinary procedure, I'll make sure it's as swift as possible. If I can, I'll persuade them to let you step down, but you know that decision is not in my power."

Maleval offered no thanks; he merely nodded, staring into the middle distance as though at this moment he had just grasped the enormity of his downfall.

9

When Armand eventually emerged from the interview room into the open-plan office, the atmosphere was palpably leaden. Cob was toiling away in silence. Louis, barricaded behind his desk, had not raised his head since he came back with Camille. Mehdi and Élisabeth, sensing the sudden change of mood and unsure how to interpret it, were whispering to each other as though in church.

Louis took charge of debriefing Armand and cross-referencing data from all the interrogations.

At 4:30 p.m., Camille had still not left his office when Louis knocked on his door. He slipped in quietly when he heard that Camille was on the telephone. Engrossed in conversation, the *commandant* did not even look up.

"I'm asking you as a favor, Jean. Given the shitstorm the case has stirred up in the media, we can't risk this getting out. The whole thing would explode, and there's no way of knowing where it would end."

Louis waited patiently, his back to the door, feverishly pushing back his bangs.

"Fine," Camille said. "Think about it and get back to me. But whatever you decide, I want you to call me before you do anything, is that okay? Okay, speak later."

Camille rang off, picked up the receiver again, and dialed his home number. He let it ring for a while, then hung up and dialed Irène's cell.

"Let me just call the hospital," he said distractedly. "Irène must have been discharged later than she expected."

"Can it wait?" Louis said.

"Why do you ask?" Camille picked up the telephone again.

"It's about Lesage. There's some new information."

Camille replaced the receiver.

"Enlighten me."

10

Fabienne Joly. Thirty-something, freshly scrubbed and dressed in her Sunday best. Short blonde hair. Glasses. Utterly ordinary, and yet there was something about her Camille could not quite put his finger on. Something sexy. Was it the sensible blouse, whose top three buttons were open to reveal her cleavage? Or was it the coy modesty with which she crossed her legs? Setting her handbag down next to her chair, she stared hard at Camille; clearly she was not someone to be easily intimidated. She clasped her hands over her knees and seemed prepared to endure the silence for as long as necessary.

"You realize that everything you say will be taken down and recorded in a statement for you to sign?"

"Obviously. That's why I'm here."

Her voice, a little husky, further added to her charm. She was the kind of woman people seldom notice, but those who do cannot take their eyes off her. A pretty mouth. Camille suppressed the urge to trace it, to sketch her portrait on his blotter.

Louis remained standing next to Camille's desk, taking notes on his pad.

"In that case, can I ask you to repeat for me the statement that you gave my colleague?"

"My name is Fabienne Joly. I'm thirty-four. I live at 12 rue de la Fraternité in Malakoff. I'm a bilingual secretary, currently unemployed. And, since 1997, I have been Jérôme Lesage's lover."

As she came to the end of the little speech she had rehearsed, she seemed to lose her composure.

"And . . . ?"

"Jérôme worries a lot about his sister. He's convinced that if she found out about our relationship, she'd fall back into the crippling depression she suffered after her husband died. He has always wanted to protect her. And I accepted that."

"I don't quite see . . . ," Camille began.

"All the things that Jérôme has been unable to explain concern me. I know from the papers that you took him in for questioning yesterday. I suspect he refused to tell you anything that he considers, well, compromising. I know he invents business meetings so that we can be together. To keep it from his sister, you understand."

"Yes, I think I'm beginning to understand. Though I'm not convinced it is sufficient to explain-"

"To explain what, *monsieur le commissaire*?"

Camille did not correct her.

"Monsieur Lesage has refused to give any account of his movements and-"

"When?" the young woman interrupted.

Camille glanced at Louis.

"Well, in July 2001, for example, Monsieur Lesage went to Edinburgh-"

"Absolutely, on July 9. Actually he arrived on the afternoon of the eighth. I arrived to join him on the late flight the following day. We spent three days touring the Highlands, and then Jérôme went back to London to join his sister."

"It's all very well for you to tell us this, Mademoiselle Joly. But given Monsieur Lesage's situation, I fear that your sworn statement will not be enough."

The young woman swallowed hard.

"I realize this is going to sound ridiculous . . . ," she began, blushing.

"Please," Camille prompted. "Go ahead."

"Maybe it's the overgrown schoolgirl in me, but I keep a record . . ." She reached into her handbag and pulled out a large scrapbook whose romantic nature was underscored by its pink cover decorated with blue flowers. "I know it's silly," she said with a forced laugh. "I write down everything that seems important. The days on which I see Jérôme, the places we visit. I paste in train tickets and plane tickets, cards from the hotels we stay at, menus from the restaurants where we eat."

She offered the scrapbook to Camille, but quickly realizing that he was too short to reach across the desk, she turned and handed it to Louis.

"At the back of the scrapbook you'll see I keep track of the expenses. I don't want to be indebted to him, you understand. The rent he pays on my apartment in Malakoff, the furniture he bought for me, everything. This is my current notebook. I have three more."

11

"I've just had a visit from Mademoiselle Joly," Camille said.

Lesage looked up. Hostility had given way to anger.

"You really stick your nose into everything, you c–"

"Stop that right now," Camille warned. Then, more calmly, "Language like that could well constitute a statutory offense, and that I'd prefer to spare you. We intend to analyze the evidence Mademoiselle Joly has given us. If we consider it probative, you will be released."

"And if not?" Lesage said defiantly.

"If not, I plan to charge you with multiple counts of murder and refer your case to the public prosecutor. You can explain yourself to the investigating magistrate."

Camille's anger was more feigned than real. He was accustomed to being shown some respect and was irritated by Lesage's manner. *I'm too old and too set in my ways to change now*, he thought.

The two men sat in silence for a moment.

"About my sister," Lesage said in a more civil tone.

"Don't worry. If the evidence is found to be convincing and coherent, it's covered by judicial confidentiality, meaning it will not be divulged. You can tell your sister whatever you please."

Lesage looked up, and for the first time, Camille noticed something akin to gratitude. He went out into the corridor and gave orders for Lesage to be taken back to his cell and given something to eat.

"I'll put you through to the maternity unit."

This time, Camille had called from the open-plan office. He had been resisting the temptation to call the hospital, preferring to leave another message on the answering machine at home.

"Do you know if she had her cell with her?" he asked Élisabeth, cupping his hand over the mouthpiece.

"I gave it to her. I brought it in with the suitcase. No need to panic."

This was exactly what he had feared. He said nothing, simply nodded.

"No," came the woman's voice at the other end of the line. "As I told you earlier, Madame Verhœven was discharged at around four o'clock. I have the register here in front of me . . . she left at 4:05 p.m. precisely. Why, is there some problem?"

"No, no problem. Thanks," Camille said without hanging up. He was staring into the distance. "Thank you again. Louis, get me a car; I need to go home."

12

At 6:18 p.m., Camille was scrambling up the stairs to their apartment, cell still pressed to his ear. He was still expecting Irène to answer as he pushed the half-open door. Curiously, he could hear her cell ringing in the distance, and ridiculous though it seemed, he kept his own to his ear as he stepped through the doorway and headed for the living room. He did not call out, did not shout "Irène, darling?" as he often did when he came home and she was in the kitchen or bathroom. He listened. By now the call had gone through to her voice mail. As Camille listened to this greeting, whose every syllable, every inflection he knew by heart, he moved through the living room. Irène's suitcase, the neat little suitcase she had packed ready for the clinic, was lying on the floor, contents spilled everywhere. Nightdress, toiletries, clothes.

"You've reached the voice mail . . ."

The table had been upturned, and books, magazines, even the wastebasket were strewn across the rug as far as the green curtains, one of which had been ripped from the rail.

"... *of Irène Verhœven. Here you are, calling me, but sadly I can't pick up right now* ..."

Cell still pressed to his ear, gripped by a muted panic, Camille went into the bedroom, where the bedside table had been over-turned. Drops of blood formed a long path that led him to the bathroom.

"*It's little things like this that remind you that fate is foolishness* ..."

There was a small, a tiny pool of blood at the end of the bathtub. Everything from the shelf beneath the mirror had been scattered onto the floor and into the bath.

"*Please leave a message and I'll get back to you* ..."

Camille raced back through the bedroom and the living room and stopped dead in the doorway to the study. Lying on the floor where it had been tossed, Irène's cell whispered softly, "... *as soon as I can.*"

Standing frozen in the doorway, staring at the floor, Camille dialed a number without even realizing, hypnotized by Irène's voice.

"*Speak soon.*"

His own words were still echoing in his head—"Call me back, darling, call me back, please . . ."—when he heard Louis answer.

Only then did Camille fall to his knees. "LOUIS!" he howled, his voice clotted with tears. "Louis, come quickly. Please, Louis, you have to come . . ."

13

Within six minutes the *brigade criminelle* had arrived in force. Three squad cars, sirens keening, shrieked to a halt outside. Gripping the banister, Maleval, Mehdi, and Louis took the stairs four at a time with Élisabeth and Armand following behind. Le Guen, panting, brought up the rear, stopping on each landing to catch his breath. Maleval kicked the door open and rushed into the apartment.

They knew what had happened the moment they entered and saw Irène's eviscerated suitcase on the floor, the curtain dangling from the rail and Camille slumped on the sofa, clutching his cell phone, staring around as though seeing the place for the first time. Louis knelt next to Camille and pried the phone from his hands as slowly and as gently as one might pry a toy from a sleeping child.

"She's gone . . . ," Camille said, utterly devastated. With a bewildered look, he nodded toward the bathroom.

"There are traces of blood in there."

The sound of footsteps echoed around the apartment. Maleval grabbed a dishcloth from the kitchen and began carefully opening doors one by one while Élisabeth put in a call to *l'identité judiciaire.*

"No one touches anything!" Louis roared, seeing Mehdi opening cupboards with his bare hands.

"Here." Maleval tossed him another dishcloth. "Use that."

"I need a forensics team down here, NOW . . . ," Élisabeth said and rattled off the Verhœvens' address.

"Here, give me that," Le Guen said, flushed and breathless, snatching the phone from her. "This is Le Guen. I want a team from *l'identité judiciaire* here within ten minutes. Prints, photos, trace evidence, everything. And I want Team 3 down here, too. Every last officer. Tell Morin to call me immediately."

Then, fishing his own phone from his jacket pocket, he punched in a number, his expression grim.

"Divisionnaire Le Guen, put me through to Juge Deschamps. Well, get her off the phone and get her to call me back. Right now."

"The place is clear," Maleval muttered, coming back to stand next to Louis.

A roar came from Le Guen. "Which bit of 'right now' don't you fucking understand?"

Armand sat on the sofa next to Camille, elbows on his knees, staring at the floor. Camille, who had collected himself somewhat, got slowly to his feet, and everyone turned to look at him. What was going on in his head and in his heart at that moment even Camille would never know. He glanced quickly around the room, looking at each member of his team in turn, and something whirred into action, something born of discipline and rage, of professionalism and powerlessness, some heady combination that can stir in the best of men the worst of impulses and which, in others, sharpens the senses, hones the vision, and triggers a brutish single-mindedness. Something that might be called terror.

"She left the hospital at 4:05 p.m.," he said, his voice so low that the team shuffled imperceptibly toward him, listening intently. "She obviously came back here." Camille nodded toward the suitcase everyone had been cautiously circling. "Élisabeth, you check out the rest of the building," he said suddenly and grabbed the dishcloth Maleval was still holding.

He went over to the desk, shuffled through the papers, and took out a recent snapshot of himself and Irène taken on vacation the previous summer. He handed it to Maleval.

"We'll need copies. There's a copier in my office. Just press the green button."

Maleval hurried into the study.

"Mehdi, you and Maleval go downstairs and ask around outside. She's well known in the neighborhood, but take the photo anyway. Irène is highly pregnant so he could not have taken her without arousing suspicion. Especially if she's . . . injured or something. Armand, you take a copy of the photo and go back to the clinic; check at reception and with every department on every floor. As soon as the rest of the team get here, I'll send backup. Louis, you go back to the *brigade*, coordinate the various teams, bring Cob up to speed, and make sure he keeps a line free. We're going to need him."

Maleval came back with two copies of the photograph and gave the original back to Camille, who stuffed it into his pocket. Everyone disappeared in an instant, the thud of their footsteps echoing in the stairwell.

"You all right?" Le Guen said, coming over to Camille.

"I'll be fine once we find her, Jean."

Le Guen's cell rang.

"How many officers have you got on shift?" he asked Morin. "I'll need all of them. Yes, all of them. I want them down here now. You, too. At Camille's . . . You're telling me . . . Now get your ass in gear."

Camille took a few steps and knelt once more before the open suitcase. With the tip of a pen, he gently lifted a piece of clothing and let it fall, then stood up and crossed to the ripped curtain and stared at it for a long moment.

"Camille," Le Guen said, walking over to him, "I need to tell you something . . ."

Camille whipped around. "Let me guess . . ."

"Look, you know what I'm going to say . . . Deschamps is categorical, we have to take you off the case. I'll have to ask Morin to take charge."

Camille nodded slowly.

"Morin's a good officer. You know him. It's just that . . . you're too personally involved, Camille. It wouldn't be right."

From outside came another wail of sirens.

Engrossed in his thoughts, Camille did not even flinch.

"You need someone else to take over the case, that's what you're saying, right?"

"I'm sorry, Camille, but yes. We need someone who's not so involved. It's not that I don't trust–"

"In that case, I want you, Jean."

"What . . . ?"

The stairwell rumbled with the beat of running footsteps, the door flew open, and Bergeret was the first into the apartment. He came and shook Camille's hand and said simply:

"We'll be in and out before you know it, Camille. I've got every available forensic officer on the case."

Before Camille could even reply, Bergeret had turned and was giving orders to his team even as he strode through the rooms. Two techs set up floodlights, and the apartment was bathed in a blinding glare as they were trained on the areas to be examined first. Meanwhile, three other technicians wordlessly shook Camille's hand, pulled on latex gloves, and opened their field kits.

"What the hell are you talking about?" Le Guen turned back to Camille.

"I want you on the case. It's well within the rules, and you know it, so don't try to talk me out of it."

"Look, Camille, it's been too long since I was a serving detective. I don't have the reflexes, you know that. It's crazy to even ask me."

"It's either you or it's no one. So?"

Le Guen scratched the back of his neck, then stroked his chin. His eyes belied any notion that he was thinking. They flashed with stark terror.

"No, honestly, Camille, I don't th–"

"It's you or no one. Are you up to taking the fucking case or not?" Camille tone was peremptory.

"Look . . . I don't know . . . I swear, I don't think–"

"Yes or no?"

"Yes, but . . ."

"But *what*, for fuck's sake?"

"Okay, fine, I'll do it. And, while we're on the subject, screw you!"

"Right," Camille said quickly. "So you'll take the case. Problem is, you've got no hands-on experience, your reflexes are shit, you'll be completely out of your depth."

"Jesus Christ, Camille! Isn't that what I just said?" Le Guen yelled.

"In which case," Camille looked him in the eye, "You'll need to delegate to an experienced officer. I accept. Thanks, Jean."

Le Guen did not even have time to react before Camille turned and strode away.

"Bergeret! Let me show you what I want you to do."

Le Guen stuffed a hand into his pocket, dug out his cell, and dialed.

"Divisionnaire Le Guen. Put me through to Juge Deschamps. Right now."

Waiting for the call to be connected, he glowered at Camille, who was deep in conversation with the boys from *l'identité judiciaire*.

"Crafty little bastard," he muttered.

14

Morin's team turned up a couple of minutes later. In order not to disturb the techs, a quick briefing was held on the narrow landing, which had room only for Le Guen, Camille, and Morin. The five remaining officers perched on the lower steps.

"I'll be leading the investigation into the disappearance of Irène Verhœven. Having consulted with Juge Deschamps, I'll be delegating policy decisions to Commandant Verhœven. Any comments?"

The tone in which Le Guen conveyed this news brooked no criticism. An awkward silence followed, one that Le Guen deliberately allowed to drag on to reiterate his determination.

"They're all yours, Camille," he said at length.

Camille gruffly apologized to Morin, who held up his hands in resignation; then the two of them divided up the teams and everyone headed back down the stairs.

The technicians from *l'identité judiciaire* raced up and down several floors carrying aluminum equipment cases, field kits, and a large trunk. Two officers stood on the landings above and below Camille's apartment, keeping track of the neighbors' comings and goings. Le Guen posted two more officers on the street outside the front door.

"Nothing," Élisabeth explained. "Between 4 p.m. and now, only four apartments were occupied. Everyone else is at work."

Camille stationed himself on the landing, toying with his cell phone, and turning back every now and then to stare at the wide-open doorway of his apartment. Through the frosted glass window intended to allow a little light into the stairwell, he could see the fitful ballet of blue lights from the squad cars parked on the street.

The apartment building was about 60 feet from the corner of the rue des Martyrs. Construction work to lay new pipes had made the opposite side of the street impassable for more than two months, and though the workers had long since finished the stretch in front of Camille's building and were now digging a thousand feet away, where the street joined the boulevard, barriers preventing parking opposite the building were still in place. Though no work was being done on this stretch of road, it was used as a parking space for bulldozers and dump trucks and for three trailers where tools were stored, one of which also served as a makeshift canteen. Two police cars were parked sideways on the street to cordon it off. The remaining squad cars and the two vans from *l'identité judiciaire* had made no attempt to park and were now lined up in the middle of the street, attracting the attention of passers-by and the residents of neighboring buildings, who leaned out of their windows.

Camille had never especially noticed before, but now, as he stepped out onto the pavement, he took a long moment to consider the street and the roadworks; he crossed the street to study the alignment of the barriers, turned to look back at the doorway to his building, glanced to the end of the street, then up to the windows of his apartment, then back to the barriers.

"Of course . . ." And then he ran to the corner of the rue des Martyrs while Élisabeth, clutching her bag to her chest, struggled to keep up.

He knew the woman though he could no longer remember her name.

"Madame Antonapoulos," Maleval said, gesturing to the shopkeeper.

"Antanopoulos," the woman corrected him.

"She thinks she saw them," Maleval went on. "There was a car parked outside the building, and Irène got in."

Camille's heart began to hammer; the pounding echoed in his head. He almost clung to Maleval for support but instead closed his eyes and dispelled the teeming images from his mind.

He asked the woman to recount the scene. Twice. What she had seen could be summed up in a few words, confirming what Camille had suspected some minutes earlier as he surveyed the street. At about 4:35 p.m., a dark-colored car had pulled up outside the building. A tall man, whom she had only glimpsed from behind, got out and moved one of the barriers so that he could park without holding up the traffic. When she had looked out at the street again, the back door of the car was open. A woman was getting in. The shopkeeper had only seen her legs as the man helped her into the car before closing the door. She had been distracted for a moment and when she looked again, the car had gone.

"Madame Antanopoulos, can I ask you to go with my colleague?" Camille said, nodding toward Élisabeth, "We're going to need your help. We need you to remember."

The shopkeeper, who felt she had said all she had to say, looked at him in surprise. This eventful afternoon would provide enough gossip to last her for weeks.

"And you," he said to Maleval, "I want you to go from door to door all the way down the street. And I want you to track down the road workers. They knocked off early. Get in touch with the contractor. And keep me informed."

15

Bereft of officers, since they were all out working on the case, the squad room seemed as though it were in a state of suspension. Behind the bank of monitors, Cob went on with his search, poring over maps of the city, lists of public works contractors and the register of employees at the Clinique Montambert and relaying information to the various teams.

Louis and a young officer Camille did not recognize had already completely rearranged the room, the noticeboards, the flip charts, the case files. Louis was sitting at a vast table on which he had laid out all the open files, and half the time he spent on the phone, passing on information to the various officers working the case. He had called Dr. Crest the moment he got back to the *brigade criminelle* and had asked him to join them as soon as possible. Crest would no doubt have his own agenda, and was probably worried about the support Camille would need in the hours ahead.

As soon as Camille arrived, the doctor got up and with great gentleness went to shake the *commandant*'s hand. Crest's face was like a mirror; in that calm, attentive expression Camille saw himself, the deep lines and the dark circles etched into his face by terror, his whole body taut and rigid.

"I'm so sorry . . . ," Crest said in a calm voice.

The words Camille heard were different, futile. Crest returned to his chair at the end of the table, where Louis had cleared a space for him to lay out the three letters from the Novelist. In the margins of the photocopies, Crest had scribbled notes, arrows, and footnotes.

Camille noticed that Cob had added to his panoply of equipment and was now wearing a hands-free headset, so that he could talk to officers who called without having to stop typing. Louis came over to suggest something, but seeing the grim expression on Camille's face he balked.

"We've got nothing yet," he said. The hand moving to push back his bangs stopped, hovered in midair. "Élisabeth is in an interview room with the shopkeeper. She doesn't seem to remember any more than what she told you earlier; nothing has come back to her. A man, about six feet tall, wearing a dark suit. She doesn't know the make of the car. There's a gap of about fifteen minutes between when she saw him park the car and when it disappeared."

"And Lesage?" Camille said, thinking about the interview room.

"The *divisionnaire* had a word with Deschamps, and I was given orders to release him. He left about twenty minutes ago."

Camille looked at his watch: 8:20 p.m.

Cob had drawn up a rapid report on what each of the teams had been doing.

At the Clinique Montambert, Armand had learned only that Irène had apparently left by herself and of her own free will. To set his mind at rest, Armand had taken the details of the two nurses and two attendants on duty at the time. He had not been able to speak to them because by now they had finished their shift, but four teams had been dispatched to their homes to question them. Two of the teams had already called in to say that no one remembered seeing anything unusual. The door-to-door inquiries on the rue des Martyrs had turned up nothing either. Other than Madame Antanopoulos, no one had seen anything. The man she saw had moved in a cool, calm manner. Cob had traced contact details for a number of the roadworkers, and three teams had been sent to talk to them. So far there was no news.

Shortly before 9 p.m., Bergeret arrived in person to bring the preliminary results from the scene. The man had not used gloves. Aside from those belonging to Irène and Camille, they had found a number of as yet unidentified fingerprints.

"No gloves, nothing, he took no precautions. He doesn't give a shit. It's not a good sign."

Immediately realizing what he had just said, Bergeret looked flustered.

"Oh, God, I'm sorry . . . ," he muttered.

"Don't worry about it," Camille said, patting his shoulder.

"We ran the prints through the system right away." Bergeret struggled to find the words. "The guy's got no police record."

It had not yet been possible to reconstruct the scene entirely, but a number of facts had emerged. Given his recent slipup, Bergeret was now weighing every word, sometimes every syllable.

"It's likely that he rang the doorbell, and your w . . . and Irène went to answer it. We think she had just set down her suitcase in the hall when . . . well . . . we think . . . we're fairly sure it was a kick that–"

"Listen," Camille interrupted, "we're not going to get anywhere at this rate. Not you, not me. So, let's just refer to her as 'Irène,' and for the rest, just give it to me straight. A kick . . . where?"

Relieved, Bergeret went back to poring over his notes and did not look up again.

"He must have struck Irène the moment she opened the door."

Camille felt his heart lurch into his throat. He clapped his hand over his mouth and squeezed his eyes shut.

"I think it might be best," Dr. Crest intervened, "if Bergeret gave the details to Monsieur Mariani. In the first instance."

Camille was not listening. His opened his eyes again, let his hand fall from his face, and got to his feet. As the three men watched, he walked over to the drinking fountain, drank two glasses of ice-cold water, then came back and sat next to Bergeret.

"He rings the doorbell. Irène answers. He kicks her. Do we know exactly how it happened?"

Bergeret looked wildly to Crest for approval, and seeing the doctor nod, he continued.

"We found traces of bile and saliva. She obviously felt queasy and doubled over."

"Is there any way of knowing where he hit her?"

"No, there's no way we can tell."

"And then?"

"She must have run back into the apartment, probably to the window. She was the one who pulled the curtain down. The man ran after her and knocked over the suitcase, which popped open. There's no sign that either of them touched the contents. Then Irène would have run into the bathroom, which is where we think he cornered her."

"The blood on the floor."

"A blow, probably to the head. Not particularly severe, but enough to stun her. She bled a little, either when she fell or as she was struggling to get to her feet. It was Irène who knocked all the things off the bathroom shelf. After that, we don't know exactly what happened. All we know for certain is that he dragged her to the door. We found heel marks from her shoes on the wooden floor. The man had a look around the apartment. We assume he did this just before he left. He was in the bedroom, the kitchen; he touched a number of things."

"What things?"

"He opened the cutlery drawer in the kitchen. We also found his prints on the window catch and on the handle of the fridge."

"Why would he do that?"

"He was nosing around, waiting for her to come to. His fingerprints were found on a glass in the kitchen and on the tap."

"Did he use it to bring her round?"

"I think so; I think he gave her a glass of water."

"Or threw it in her face."

"No, I don't think so. There was no sign of water being spilled. No, I think she drank it. We found a number of Irène's hairs; we think he had to hold her head up. After that, we don't know anything. We swept the stairwell, but it was pointless. Too much traffic, too many people coming and going; we found nothing useful."

Rubbing his forehead, Camille tried to imagine the scene.

"Anything else?" he said finally, looking up at Bergeret.

"Yes, we have a number of hair follicles belonging to the intruder. He has short light-brown hair. We've sent them down to the lab. And we know his blood group."

"How?"

"Irène must have scratched him while they were struggling. We found traces in the bathroom and on a towel he must have used to wipe himself. Obviously, we cross-checked against yours just in case. His is O positive . . . it's pretty common."

"Short brown hair, blood type O positive, what else?"

"That's it, Camille, we haven't be-"

"Okay, thanks. Excuse me."

16

When all the teams had arrived back at the *brigade*, there was a general debriefing. The results were meager. At 9 p.m. it seemed as though they were no further advanced than they had been at 6:30. Crest had studied the last letter from the Novelist and for the most part confirmed what Camille knew already or what he had intuited. Le Guen, enthroned in the only armchair in the squad room, listened gravely to the psychological profiler's report.

"He enjoys toying with you. He weaves a little suspense into the beginning of the letter, as though this is a game. A game both of you are playing. This further confirms what we suspected at the start."

"That this is personal?" Le Guen said.

"Indeed," Crest said, turning to him. "I think I can see what you're getting at, but I wouldn't want you to misinterpret. In my opinion, this didn't start out as a personal grudge. In other words, I don't believe we're dealing with an offender previously arrested by Commandant Verhœven or anything like that. No, it's not personal in that sense. It *became* personal, probably from the moment he read the first classified ad. The fact that the *commandant* adopted an unorthodox approach, signed the ad with his initials, gave his home address."

"I've been such an idiot," Camille muttered to Le Guen.

"There's no way anyone could have known, Camille." The *divisionnaire* preempted the psychologist's response. "Besides, what difference would it have made? It's not as though people like you and me are difficult to track down."

For a brief instant, Camille reflected on his rashness, on the arrogance of acting as he had, of having himself made this case personal, as though he could take the killer on, man to man. He thought again of the conversation in Juge Deschamps's office when she had threatened to take him off the case. Why had he been so determined to prove himself? A pathetic piece of point scoring that had cost him much more than a defeat.

"He knows what he's doing," Le Guen went on. "He's known from the start, and no matter how we handled things, it wouldn't have changed anything. We know that because he says it here in black and white: '*you are flailing and floundering in a labyrinth of my devising—one from which you will be freed when and as I decide.*'"

"I know, I get that part, but it never occurred to me that he intended to target me, to target Irène."

"I'm not sure it would have occurred to me either," said Crest. Though his tone was conciliatory, Le Guen and Camille could clearly detect a hint of reproach. This last letter had not been passed on to the doctor until late in the day. Too late.

"The most important part of the letter is the last section, the one where he quotes at length from Gaboriau."

"Where he talks about his goal, his great monument, I know."

"You see—and this is where I might surprise you—I don't believe it."

Camille turned to stare at the doctor, as did Louis, who was now sitting next to Le Guen.

"The thing is, it's too obvious. He overdoes it. In acting terms, you'd say he's hamming it up. Some of the phrasing is deliberately pompous."

"What are you saying?"

"I'm saying he's not insane, he's simply warped. He's playing a role for your benefit, the role of the deranged psychotic who can't tell the difference between fantasy and reality, between fiction and fact, but I think that's just one more ploy on his part. He's nothing like the character depicted in his letters. Oh, he wants you to believe he is, but that's a different matter."

"Why would he do that?" Louis said.

"I've no idea. The long digression about the needs of humanity, about art transfiguring reality, is so mannered it's almost a caricature. He's not saying what he thinks; he is pretending to think these things. But I couldn't tell you why."

"To throw us off the scent?" Le Guen said.

"Perhaps. Or perhaps he has some higher reason."

"Such as?" Camille said.

"Perhaps it's simply part of his plan."

The various case files were distributed to the team. Two officers were assigned to go through each case, to start again from the beginning, examine every scrap of evidence, every statement. At 9:45 p.m., maintenance arrived to install four more telephone lines and three more computers, which Cob quickly hooked up so that they were all connected to the database on which he had stored all available information. The room hummed as Camille's team fielded questions from the newly assigned officers as they came across some fresh detail.

Camille, Le Guen, and Louis studied the whiteboard, reexamining each of the major lines of inquiry, Camille feverishly checking and rechecking his watch. Irène had been missing now for almost five hours. Everybody in the room knew the statistics relating to abductions.

On the whiteboard, at Camille's request, Louis wrote up a list of all the locations (Fontainebleau, Corbeil, Glasgow, Tremblay, Courbevoie); next to it, a list of victims (Maryse Perrin, Alice Hedges, Grace Hobson, Manuela Constanza, Évelyne Rouvray, Josiane Debeuf);

and finally the list of dates (July 7, 2000; August 24, 2000; July 10, 2001; November 21, 2001; April 6, 2003). The three men stood staring at these lists, searching desperately for some connection, floating theories that came to nothing. Dr. Crest, who had been sitting on his own in silence, reminded them that the Novelist was working to a warped literary logic, and it might be worth considering the books he had copied. Louis jotted down another list (*Le Crime d'Orcival*, *Roseanna*, *Laidlaw*, *The Black Dahlia*, *American Psycho*), but this did not seem to help.

"We're not going to find anything here," Le Guen said. "This is a list of his 'earlier works.' He's moved on."

"No, he hasn't," Camille insisted. "He's moved on to the next novel. The question is, which one?"

Louis went to fetch Ballanger's list, made enlargements of the pages on eight-by-11-inch sheets, and pinned them on the corkboard.

"That's a lot of books . . . ," Crest said.

"Too many," Camille said. But there has to be a novel on that list—or maybe it's not on that list—a novel that . . ."

He trailed off for a moment and thought.

". . . a novel that involves a pregnant woman. Louis?"

"There isn't one."

"There has to be one!"

"I don't see it."

"There has to be," Camille roared, ripping the original list from Louis's hands. "There fucking has to be!"

He scanned the document and handed it back.

"It's not on that list, Louis, it must be on the other one."

Louis stared at Camille.

"Oh, Christ, I forgot . . ." He rushed to his desk and dug out the copy of Ballanger's original list Cob had printed out. In the margin, in Louis's elegant handwriting, were notes on each of the titles.

"It's there," he said finally, handing Camille the piece of paper.

Reading through Louis's notes, Camille had a flashback of his conversation with Professeur Ballanger: "*One of my students thought the March 1998 case, the one where the pregnant woman is disemboweled in a warehouse, sounded similar to a book I've never heard of. It's called . . .* Shadow Slayer *by someone named Chub or Hub. Never heard of him either."*

Meanwhile, Louis brought up the list of suspicious cases that had been given to Ballanger to analyze.

"Yes, I realize it's late, Professeur Ballanger . . ."

Louis turned away and quickly and quietly explained the situation.

"I'll hand you over . . . ," he said, proffering the phone to Camille, who briefly reminded him of their earlier conversation.

"I remember, but as I told you at the time, I've never heard of the book. In fact, the student in question didn't seem entirely sure either. It was just a suggestion. There's nothing to say that-"

"I need that book, Professeur Ballanger, I need it right now. Where does he live, this student of yours?"

"I have no idea. I'd have to check the student records. They're in my office."

"Maleval!" Camille shouted, ignoring Ballanger on the other end of the line. "Take a car, go and fetch Professeur Ballanger, and take him to the university. I'll meet you there."

Before Camille had time to respond to the *professeur*, Maleval was racing for the door.

Cob had already identified some thirty possible warehouses, which Armand and Élisabeth carefully marked up on a map of Paris. Each address, each location, together with whatever details Cob had been able to unearth, were scrutinized. They drew up two lists. The primary list detailed those warehouses that were remote and had been derelict for some time; the second list was of those locations that seemed less likely but nonetheless fitted the criteria.

"Armand, Mehdi, you take over from Cob," Camille said. "Élisabeth, divide the rest of the group into teams. I need them checking out every one of these locations, starting in Paris, then gradually moving out through the suburbs. Cob, I need you to track down a book for me by someone called Hub or Chub or something like that. *Shadow Slayer*. An old book, probably out of print. I don't have any other details. I'm going to the university; you can reach me on my cell. Come on, Louis. Let's go."

17

At night, only two streetlights bathed the facade of the university in a pallid yellow glow. Behind the tall windows of the lobby, they could make out the two staircases leading to the upper floors. Now deserted, the building looked like an ocean liner run aground. As Louis skidded to a halt in front of the main doors, another car roared out of the darkness from the far end of the driveway. Roused by the sirens and the lights, the security guard appeared inside, holding a large dog on a leash. Maleval, leaving Ballanger to extricate himself from the backseat of the car, had already run to the front entrance and pressed his I.D. card against the glass. The guard immediately produced a bundle of keys and bent to unlock the door.

Camille briefly shook Ballanger's hand. The man seemed dazed by the circumstances and slightly panicked after the frantic drive with Maleval at the wheel.

"Thanks for coming," Camille said, breaking into a run.

"You're welc-," Ballanger began. While Maleval explained the situation to the security guard, Louis and Camille took the left-hand staircase, followed by the *professeur*, who was fumbling for his own keys. Less than a minute later, the three men burst into the little office and Ballanger rushed over to a filing cabinet, opened one of the drawers, and flicked through the files beginning with "G."

Camille's cell rang.

"It's Cob. No luck, I'm afraid, I haven't found anything on the book."

"That's impossible," Camille barked.

"I've run it through 211 search engines and databases! Are you sure about the reference?"

"Hang on, I'll pass you to Louis." Ballanger had just handed him a file labeled "Sylvain Guignard," pointing to the home phone number. Camille swapped his phone for Louis's and dialed the number. A sleepy, bewildered voice on the other end grunted hello.

"Sylvain Guignard?"

"No, this is his father. Do you have any idea what time it is?"

"Commandant Verhœven of the *brigade criminelle*. I need to speak to your son, right now."

"Who did you say?"

Camille repeated more slowly and added, "Put your son on the line, Monsieur Guignard. Immediately."

Camille heard footsteps and whispered voices; then a young, clear voice came on the line.

"Is that Sylvain?"

"Yes."

"Commandant Verhœven, *brigade criminelle*. I'm here with Professeur Ballanger. You did some research work for us, remember?"

"Of course, it was about-"

"You mentioned a book he wasn't familiar with, one you thought might be relevant, by someone called Hub or Chub—do you remember?"

"Yes, I remember."

Camille glanced down at the file. The boy lived in Villeparis. Even if they were quick . . . He checked his watch.

"Do you have a copy of this book?" he said. "Do you have one there?"

"No, it's an old book; I just remembered . . ."

"Remembered what?"

"Something about the case. It rang a bell."

"Now, listen to me, Sylvain, a pregnant woman was kidnapped this afternoon in Paris. We have to find her before . . . It's possible that this woman could be . . . I mean . . . She's my wife."

Having uttered these words, Camille swallowed painfully.

"I need that book. I need it now."

For an instant, the young man on the other end of the line was silent.

"I don't have a copy," he said finally. "I must have read it about ten years ago. I'm sure of the title—*Shadow Slayer*—and the name of the author is Philip Chub. But I can't remember who published it. I'm racking my brains, but I don't remember. All I remember is the cover."

"What was on the cover?"

"It had one of those stock pulp fiction covers, an overwrought illustration of terrified women screaming with the shadowy figure of a man in the hat looming over her, that kind of thing."

"Plot?"

"A man kidnaps a pregnant woman, I remember that; it struck me because it was very different from other stuff I was reading at the time. It was pretty horrific, but I don't remember the details."

"Setting?"

"A warehouse, I think, or something like that."

"What kind of warehouse? Where?"

"I honestly don't remember. But I'm pretty sure it was a warehouse."

"What did you do with the book?"

"We've moved three times in the past ten years. I couldn't tell you where it got to."

"And the publisher?"

"No idea."

"I'm going to send someone round to talk to you right now, and I want you to tell him everything you remember, got that?"

"Yes, I think so."

"It's possible that in the process of talking about it, you'll remember something, some detail that could help us. In the meantime, I want you to stay put. Try thinking about the physical book itself, where you were and what you were doing the first time you saw it. It can help to jog your memory. Take notes. My assistant is going to give you some phone numbers, and if you remember anything—anything at all—you call me immediately, is that clear?"

"Yes."

"Good," Camille said, then before swapping phones again with Louis, he added, "Sylvain?"

"Yes?"

"Thank you. Do your best to remember. It's important."

Camille telephoned Crest and told him to go to Villeparis.

"The kid seems intelligent, and he wants to help. We need to win his trust, see if anything comes back to him. I'd like you to go."

"I'll set off now," Crest said calmly.

"Louis will call you on another line to give you the address, and he'll arrange a car and an officer to drive you."

Ballanger was now sitting behind his desk, intently following the various conversations. Louis, who had just finished his call, was pacing in front of the *professeur*'s bookshelves.

Camille punched a number into his phone. Though no one seemed to answer, he let it ring.

"Jérôme Lesage." The voice sounded petulant and irritable.

"Monsieur Lesage? Commandant Verhœven. I can understand why you might be reluctant to help us."

"Can you indeed? If you're looking for help, I suggest you go elsewhere."

Louis turned to Camille, tilting his head to one side, alert to every flicker in his expression.

"Please, listen to me. Please . . . ," Camille said. "My wife is eight and a half months pregnant . . ." His voice faltered. He swallowed hard. "She was abducted from our apartment this afternoon. It's him, I know it; he did this. I have to find her."

There was a long silence.

"He's going to kill her." Camille choked. "He's going to kill her."

And for the first time this thought, on which he had been brooding for hours, suddenly seemed so real, so tangible, so inevitable that he almost dropped the telephone and had to lean against the wall for support.

Louis did not move; he was still staring at Camille's face as though looking through him. His expression was frozen, only his lips trembled.

"Monsieur Lesage . . ." Camille finally managed to utter the words.

"How can I help?" the bookseller said, his tone somewhat perfunctory.

Camille closed his eyes, overcome by a wave of relief.

"A novel. *Shadow Slayer*. By Philip Chub."

Louis, meanwhile, had turned back to Ballanger.

"Have you got a French-English dictionary?" he asked in a leaden voice.

Ballanger got to his feet and stood next to Louis at the bookcase.

"I remember the book, yes," Lesage said finally. "It was published back in the '70s or the '80s—late '70s I think. Bilban were the publishers; they went bust around 1985. No one bought the backlist."

Louis laid the Harrap's dictionary Ballanger had just given him on the desk. He turned to Camille, who was ashen. Camille stared back, his heart hammering in his chest.

"I don't suppose you have a copy?" he asked Lesage, without thinking.

"I'm just looking . . . No, no, I don't think so."

Louis looked at the dictionary, then back to Camille, mouthing a word Camille could not make out.

"Where would we find a copy?"

"That kind of book is difficult to track down," Lesage said, "It was published in a cheap edition; the books themselves were cheap. No one really collects or keeps them. You stumble across them from time to time. It's really just a matter of luck."

Still staring at Louis, Camille asked, "Do you think you might be able to get hold of it?"

"I'll look into it tomorrow." The moment he uttered the words, Lesage realized how callous they sounded. "I'll, um, I'll see what I can do."

"Thank you," Camille said, then, holding the phone at arm's length, "Louis?"

"Chub . . . , " Louis said, "In English, it's the name of a fish."

"And . . . ?" Still Camille stared at him.

"In French it's *chevesne.*"

Camille's mouth fell open and he dropped the telephone which clattered to the floor.

"Philippe Buisson de Chevesne," Louis said. "The reporter from *Le Matin.*"

Camille whipped round and looked at Maleval.

"Jean-Claude, what the fuck have you done?"

Maleval shook his head, staring up at the ceiling, his eyes welling with tears.

"I didn't know . . . I didn't know."

18

No sooner had the squad cars pulled up outside the building on the boulevard Richard-Lenoir than the three men were racing up the stairs, Maleval leading Louis and Camille by several steps.

Camille peered over the banister, but saw nothing but the rising curve of the stairwell and the staggered landings of the five floors. Reaching a yawning doorway seconds after he heard the gunshot Maleval used to blow the lock, Camille saw a shadowy hallway lit only by a single lamp. Drawing his own gun, Camille stepped in slowly. To his right, Louis was advancing, his back to the wall; to his left he saw Maleval disappear into the kitchen, only to immediately reappear. Camille gestured for him to help Louis, who was kicking open doors and quickly taking cover. Maleval moved swiftly toward them. Camille found himself standing in the doorway to the living room. He put his head around the door and glanced to left and right, suddenly, inexplicably, convinced the apartment was empty.

He gazed at the windows overlooking the boulevard. From where he stood on the threshold, the whole room was visible. It was all but bare. Groping for the light switch, he heard the soft thud of footsteps and sensed Louis and Maleval behind him. He flicked the switch, and a table lamp glowed faintly. The three men stepped into the room, which immediately seemed much larger. There were anemic patches on the walls where pictures had been taken down; two or three cardboard boxes—one of them open—were piled next to the windows, and beside them was a ladder-back chair. The floor was polished parquet. Camille's eye was caught by a ramshackle table and next to it another chair.

They holstered their guns as Camille moved toward the table. There was a sound of footsteps from the landing, and Maleval rushed back to the door. Camille heard whispered voices. The only light in the room came from a lamp placed on the table whose lead ran along the wall to the socket next to the fireplace.

On one corner of the table lay a red cardboard folder whose bulging contents strained against the elastic strap. A single sheet of paper was visible, placed carefully in the center. Camille snatches it up.

Dear Camille,

I'm happy you could make it. The apartment is a little empty, which, I grant, is not very convivial. But you know it is in a good cause. Doubtless you must be disappointed to find yourself alone. You probably hoped to find your charming wife here. But for that touching reunion, you will have to wait a little longer . . .

In a few moments, you will finally realize the vast sweep of my project. Everything will become clear. How I wish I could be there to see your reaction.

As you perhaps suspect, and as you will soon realize, my "masterwork," our "game," was rigged. From the very beginning.

I think I can safely say that we are guaranteed a bestseller. I feel sure people will be falling over themselves to read "our" story. It is already written. You will find it in the red folder on the table. Complete, but for a few finishing touches.

With the infinite patience you have come to recognize, I recreated crimes from five novels. I could have done more, but nothing would have been gained. Five is not a large number, but with murders it seemed adequate. And, oh, what murders! The last will be a fitting culmination, I assure you. Even as I write these lines, your charming wife Irène is on hand, ready to play the starring role. She is a lovely woman. She will be perfect in the part.

The crowning glory of my work was to have written my own perfect murder . . . before recreating murders from the most perfect novels. A magnificent achievement, is it not? In this closed circle, so perfectly contrived, there is something of the Platonic ideal, don't you agree?

What a triumph, Camille! A harrowing, true-to-life tale, a metafiction that recounts the murderous machinations of its own creation . . . Before long, people will be desperate to get hold of this novel by a man no one could abide. They will grovel, Camille, you shall see . . . And you will be proud of me, proud of us, and you can be proud of the delectable Irène, who has been truly marvelous.

Fond wishes. You will forgive me if, on this occasion, I sign the name that will catapult me to fame—as it will you.

Philip Chub

Camille pulled out the chair and sat down heavily. His head was pounding. He rubbed his temples and sat for a long moment in silence, staring intently at the folder. Finally, he pulled it toward him and struggled to open the strap. He read:

"Alice . . . ," he said, looking at what anyone other than him would have called a young girl.

He used her name as a sign of complicity but could not make the slightest dent in her armor. He looked down at the notes scribbled by Armand during the first interview: Alice Vandenbosch, 24.

He flicked through the loose pages:

"It's carnage," Louis said in a strangulated voice, struggling to find the words, "It's a bloodbath. But not the usual kind, if you see what I mean . . ."

"I don't see, Louis, not really."

"It's like nothing I've ever seen in my life . . ."

He grasped a sheaf of pages between thumb and index finger and turned them over.

> Mama is working with reds. She applies liberal quantities—blood reds, carmines, reds dark as night.

He flicked forward.

> The victim, a Caucasian woman of about twenty-five, had clearly been subjected to a brutal beating, in the course of which she had been dragged by the hair, as evidenced by bald patches on her scalp from which clumps of hair had been ripped. Analysis confirmed that the killer had hit her with a hammer.

Camille suddenly flipped the whole manuscript over, and read the words on the final page:

> The only light in the room came from a lamp placed on the table whose lead ran along the wall to the socket next to the fireplace.
>
> On one corner of the table lay a red cardboard folder whose bulging contents strained against the elastic strap. A single sheet of paper was visible, placed carefully in the center. Camille snatches it up.

Dazed, Camille turned toward the far end of the room where Maleval was posted, while Louis went on reading over his shoulder. He grabbed a sheaf of pages and began reading through them, skipping over passages, stopping here and there, pausing for a moment to think before reading on.

Camille could not think; his mind was flooded by a surging tide of violent images.

Buisson's "masterwork," his book.

A novel that was an account of Camille's investigation.

It felt as though he were banging his head against a brick wall.

How much of it was true? How would he ever disentangle truth from fiction? One thing, however, was certain: Buisson had murdered at least seven people. Most chilling were the five murder scenes inspired by five different novels. They tended inevitably toward a grand finale, a sixth murder inspired by his own novel, *Shadow Slayer.*

A murder yet to come.

The perfect crime.

In which Irène is to play the leading role.

How had he put it? "The crowning glory of my work was to have written my own perfect murder . . . before recreating murders from the most perfect novels."

He has to find her.

But where is she?

Brigade criminelle, 10:45 p.m.

The red cardboard file lies on the desk. Gutted. Armand has taken the contents to be photocopied.

Everyone is standing, from behind his desk Camille looks around at the assembled officers. Only Le Guen is seated, nervously chewing on the end of a pencil, using his potbelly as a support for the pad on which he is idly taking a few notes. He broods, he listens, and he stares intently at Camille.

"Philippe Buisson . . . ," Camille begins. He covers his mouth with one hand and clears his throat. "Buisson is still out there. He still has Irène with him. What we need to know is where they are, what he plans to do. And when. That's a lot of unknowns, and we have very little time."

Le Guen can no longer detect a trace of the blind panic he saw etched onto Camille's face when he arrived two minutes earlier. He is no longer Camille; he is Commandant Verhœven, the focused, resolute senior officer of the *brigade criminelle*.

"The manuscript we discovered at his apartment is a novel written by Buisson. It gives his imagined account of our investigation.

This is our primary source. But as for what he plans to do next, there is a second source, one we don't have: the novel Buisson published under the name Chub, which contains the scene detailing–"

"Are we sure of that?" Le Guen says without looking up.

"If what we already know about the plot is true, then yes: a pregnant woman murdered in a warehouse."

He glances at Cob, who has emerged from behind his bank of computers for the briefing. Next to him, Dr. Viguier, buttocks perched on the edge of a desk, legs stretched out, arms folded in front of him, is listening attentively. He is not looking at Camille, but at the other members of the team. Cob shakes his head and says, "We've still got nothing on the book."

Armand comes back with five sets of photocopies. Meanwhile, Maleval has been shifting his weight from one foot to the other for almost an hour, as though he is in desperate need of a piss.

"There'll be three teams," Camille says. "Jean, Maleval, and I will go over the manuscript with Dr. Viguier. Armand will lead a second team looking into likely warehouses in the Paris region. I realize it's a thankless task since we've no way of narrowing it down, but we have to make do with what we've got. Louis, I want you to look into Buisson's background: relationships, acquaintances, anything you can dig up. Cob, you carry on trying to track down a copy of Philip Chub's book. Any questions?"

There are no questions.

Two tables are pushed together, Camille and Le Guen sitting on one side, Maleval and the psychologist on the other. Armand, who has picked up Cob's most recent list of warehouses from the printer, is going through the names with a pencil, crossing out those visited by the two teams out in the field, who immediately move on to the next address he gives. Louis is already on the telephone, the handset wedged between shoulder and chin, leaving his hands free to type. Cob, factoring in the newest piece of information—that Chub's novel was published by Éditions Bilban—has search engines running on every computer.

As he settles down to work, Le Guen arranges to have two squad cars on standby. He also alerts RAID and, seeing that Camille has overheard, gives a fatalistic shrug.

Camille knows Le Guen is right. Should they find any solid evidence they'll need a rapid response unit, and RAID are the professionals. Camille has seen them in action, the tall black-clad men with so much body armor they look like robots and so much equipment it seems impossible they can move so swiftly and silently, the technical officers who use thermal imaging and global positioning to scan the terrain and formulate every plan with military precision. RAID descend like the wrath of God Almighty.

The moment the *brigade criminelle* comes up with an address, RAID will take over. For better or worse. The strategy worries Camille a little, it seems somehow incongruous to pit the meticulous precision of RAID against the meticulous precision with which Buisson has orchestrated this whole affair. Buisson has had too much of a head start. For weeks now, perhaps for months, he has been carefully devising this plan, this *thing* with the patience of an entomologist. For all their helicopters, their tear gas grenades, their night vision scopes, their PGM Précision Hécate rifles, the elite marksmen of RAID will be shooting into the clouds.

Camille is about to say all this to Le Guen but bites his tongue. What is the alternative? Is he planning to rush in and save Irène with the service revolver he has only ever fired during his yearly firearms test?

Having opened Buisson's "novel" at page one, the four men find that they read at different speeds and in different ways. Viguier, an experienced psychologist, skims the text, his eyes attentive to detail. He turns the pages at a steady rhythm as though driven by some unalterable momentum. He is not looking for the same things as the others; he focuses immediately on the portrait Buisson pens of himself. He studies the style of the narrative, treats the people as characters in fiction.

Everything in this text is fiction, everything except the dead girls.

As far as Viguier is concerned, the rest of the text is Buisson himself: this is how he sees the world, how he refashions reality. He tries to discern the ways in which Buisson has manipulated the facts to fit his vision of the world—not the world as it is, but as he would like it to be. Three hundred pages of pure fantasy.

Le Guen, for his part, is tenacious. Slow to read but quick to grasp, he has opted for the technique that best suits his way of thinking. He begins at the end and works his way back, chapter by chapter. He takes few notes.

No one seems to notice that Maleval has not turned any pages. He has been staring at the first page for endless minutes. While Viguier, in a low voice, gives some preliminary thoughts, Maleval feels a desperate need to get up, to go over to Camille, to tell him . . . But he does not have the strength: for as long as he does not turn the pages, he feels safe. He is on the edge of an abyss; he knows this. Just as he knows that any minute now someone will give him the push that propels him into the void. He needs to take the initiative, take his courage in both hands, search for his name, verify that the expected cataclysm is imminent. That the trap into which he fell is about to snap closed. He needs to act now, to make a decision. But he cannot move; he is petrified.

Camille, his face expressionless, leafs briskly through the pages, skipping whole passages, scribbling notes here and there, going back from time to time to check a detail. He skims the scene in which Buisson imagines Camille's first meeting with Irène, obviously it is nonsense. What can Buisson know about his first meeting with Irène? What was this shit about a TV program? "It was a straightforward affair. He married Irène six months later." It was indeed straightforward. It was pure fantasy on Buisson's part.

Just as a drowning man apparently sees his life pass before his eyes in a fraction of a second, Camille sees the real story play out in his head. A Sunday morning. The gift shop in the Louvre. A young woman looking for a book on Titian—"It's for a present"— she dithers, looks at one book, then another, sets both down and finally selects a third. The wrong one. And little Camille Verhœven unthinkingly blurts out, "You shouldn't get that one, if you don't mind my saying." The young woman smiles and immediately she was Irène, her smile stunning yet simple. And it was "his Irène" who said "Really?" in a tone of mock deference that demanded an apology. And so he apologizes, introduces himself, says something about Titian that he hopes is not pretentious, but it is, since he feels he is something of a connoisseur. He stumbles over the words. It has been a long time since he blushed. He blushes. She smiles. "So you think this is the best one?" He has too many things he wants to say; he tries come up with some pithy turn of phrase that encapsulates his fear of sounding like a snob and his embarrassment at recommending the most expensive book and finally splutters "I know it's the expensive one . . . but it *is* the best." Irène is wearing a dress with buttons all the way down the front. "You mean it's like buying shoes, then? Except that in this case it's Titian." Irène smiles. It is her turn to blush, mortified at having lowered the tone. She confesses that she hasn't set foot in the Louvre in more than a decade. Camille cannot bring himself to tell her he comes almost every week. Nor can he bring himself to tell her, as she heads for the till, that he would rather not know who her gift is for, that he usually comes on Sunday mornings, that he realizes there is only a one-in-a-million chance that he might see her here again. At the counter, Irène signs the credit card slip, leaning down, peering myopically. Then she vanishes. Camille turns back to browse the bookshelves, but his heart is no longer in it. A few minutes later, tired and overcome by a sudden melancholy, he decides to leave. He is dumbfounded to see her once more, she is standing beneath the glass pyramid reading a brochure. Camille turns, trying to find his way, stares blankly at the innumerable signs that point in every possible direction. He passes close to her. She sees him, she smiles at him, he stops. "So, do you know any good books about finding your way around museums?" she says with a smile.

Camille is already focused on the next passage.

Looking up, Camille sees Maleval, hands resting on the cardboard folder, staring at Le Guen, who is ruefully shaking his head.

"Camille," Le Guen says without looking at him, "I think we may need to have a word with our friend Maleval."

Camille finishes reading:

"My hands are tied, Jean-Claude, I have no choice but to sack you."

Sitting opposite Camille, Maleval blinked rapidly, desperately looking around for something to lean on.

"It kills me to have to do it . . . it really does. Why didn't you just come talk to me? . . . How long has this been going on?"

"Since the end of last year. He got in touch with me. At first, I just threw him a few crumbs of information and that seemed to be enough . . ."

Camille lays his reading glasses on the table. He balls his fists. When he turns, his barely suppressed fury is so apparent in his expression that Maleval starts back on his chair, and Le Guen feels obliged to intervene.

"Okay, Camille, let's deal with this in an orderly fashion. Maleval?" He turns to the young officer. "Is it true what he's written?"

Maleval splutters that he doesn't know, that he hasn't had time to read everything, that he needs to check . . .

"To check what?" Le Guen says. "Were you or were you not feeding this man information?"

Maleval nods.

"Okay, I'm going to have to place you under arrest."

Maleval's mouth, like that of a fish out of water, forms a perfect O.

"Aiding and abetting a murderer who has killed seven times— what were you thinking?"

"I didn't know," bleats Maleval. "I swear I didn't–"

"That bullshit excuse might work on the *juge*, but right now it's me you're talking to!" Camille shouts at him.

"Camille . . . ," Le Guen interrupts.

But Camille is not listening.

"This guy you've been feeding information for months has kidnapped my wife. You remember Irène, Maleval? You've always been fond of Irène, haven't you?"

Even Le Guen does not know how to break the silence that ensues.

"She's a sweet woman, Irène," Camille continues. "She's eight months pregnant. What did you have in mind for the christening present? Or have you already spent the cash?"

Le Guen closes his eyes. When Camille gets into a rage . . .

"Camille . . ."

Camille's anger spirals; the torrent of words keeps coming, the furious invective feeding on itself.

"That whole sympathetic, forgiving *commandant* thing, it's only in novels. Personally, I could cheerfully put my fist through your face. But right now, we're going to hand you over to Internal Affairs: after that it's the public prosecutor, the investigating magistrate: you'll be remanded, you'll be tried, and I will be the star witness. You'd better pray that we find Irène safe and sound, Maleval. Because I plan to make you pay for this, you fucking shit!"

Le Guen pounds on the table. And just then the nebulous thought he has been racking his brains to apprehend, emerges.

"Camille, we're wasting time."

Instantly, Camille falls silent and looks at him.

"We'll deal with debriefing Maleval. You need to get back to work. I'll call Internal Affairs."

He pauses.

"It's for the best, Camille. Trust me on this."

Le Guen is already on his feet, determined to prevail though the outcome seems moot. Camille is still staring hard into Maleval's eyes.

Finally, he gets to his feet and leaves the office, slamming the door behind him.

"Where's Maleval?" Louis says.

"He's with Le Guen." Camille struggles to say as little as possible. "They shouldn't be long."

He doesn't know why he says this. It is like a slip of the tongue. Time is slipping away, and still they have nothing concrete to go on.

When news arrived that Irène had been kidnapped, everyone expected to find Camille devastated, helpless; instead they find Commandant Verhœven straining at the bit.

Picking up the manuscript again, he sees Irène's name. How had Buisson known so precisely the things Irène complained about, how alone she felt, how abandoned? Perhaps all unhappy couples are alike. And all journalists.

It is past 11 p.m. Louis is still completely calm and even looks impeccable still, not a wrinkle in his shirt and—despite rushing around all day—there is not a scuff mark on his gleaming shoes. Almost as though he nips off to the bathroom now and then for a spit and polish.

"Philippe Buisson de Chevesne, born September 16, 1962, in Périgueux. There was a general in Napoleon's army named Léopold Buisson de Chevesne; he fought at Jena. The title and the estate were granted by imperial decree."

Camille is no longer really listening. If Louis had found anything concrete he would have led with that.

"Did you know about Maleval?" he asks out of the blue.

Louis looks at him. He is about to say something, but bites his lip. Finally, he makes up his mind.

"Know what?"

"That he's been leaking information to Buisson. That he was the one who kept him updated on the progress of the investigation. That it's thanks to Maleval that Buisson has always been one step ahead of us."

The color drains from Louis's face, he slumps back in his chair. Camille realizes that he had no idea.

"It's here in Buisson's 'novel,'" Camille says. "Le Guen was quick to spot it. Maleval is being interviewed right now."

There is no need to say any more. Louis's keen intelligence quickly figures out the rest; his eyes dart around the squad room; his lips are parted as though he is about to say something.

"Is it true that you lent him money?"

"How do you–"

"It's right here in the book, Louis, it's all in here. Maleval must have confided in him about it. You see, you're a hero, too; we're all heroes. Isn't it great?"

Instinctively, Louis glances toward the interview room.

"He's not likely to be much help." Camille can read his thoughts. "I'm pretty sure Maleval knows only what Buisson decided to tell him. He was playing him from the start, long before the Courbevoie murders. Buisson anticipated everything. Maleval was well and truly fucked over. And us with him."

Louis stares at the floor.

"So anyway," Camille says, "what were you saying?"

Louis reads from his notes, but his voice now is a barely audible whisper.

"Buisson's father . . ."

"Louder," Camille shouts as he walks over to the drinking fountain.

Louis raises his voice. He sounds as though he, too, might shout, but he restrains himself. His voice quavers.

"Buisson's father is an industrialist. His mother is from Lanquais; her maiden name was Pradeau; she owned a lot of property in her own right. Buisson went to school in Périgueux, though he wasn't much of a student. There's a record of him spending a short period in a clinic in 1978; I'm having someone look into that. The financial crisis of the early '80s hit the Buisson family pretty hard. In 1980, Buisson goes to the university to study literature, but he soon drops out. He decides to study journalism instead and finally graduates in 1985. His father has died the year before. From 1991, he's working freelance, and he joins *Le Matin* in 1998. There's nothing of any significance before the Tremblay murder. His articles attract a lot of attention; he gets promoted to editor responsible for social issues. His mother died two years ago. Buisson is an only child, and he's still single. The family's fortune is no longer what it once was. Buisson sold the business, held on to the properties he inherited; he had a healthy stock portfolio with Gamblin &

Chaussard, and the rent from the properties brought in six times his salary at *Le Matin*. Over the past two years, he's liquidated his portfolio of stocks."

"What does that tell us?"

"That he was planning ahead. Aside from the family home, Buisson sold off everything. These days his entire fortune is in a Swiss bank account."

Camille clenches his jaws.

"What else?"

"To know about his friends, acquaintances, his daily routine, we'll need to ask around, but that doesn't seem relevant at this stage. The media are going to be all over us, and we'll be spending too much time fielding reporters."

Camille knows Louis is right.

The list of warehouses Buisson is likely to be using is almost exhausted.

At 11:25 p.m. Lesage phones.

"I haven't managed to get in touch with as many colleagues as I'd hoped," he tells Camille. "I only have business numbers for some of them, in which case I've left messages. But right now, I can't manage to track down a copy of the book. I'm sorry."

Camille thanks him.

One by one the doors are closing.

Le Guen is still in the interview room with Maleval. Everyone is exhausted.

Viguier has spent more time than anyone studying the "novel." Camille has seen him stifling a yawn. The plump little man who is only a few months from retirement has spent almost five hours poring over Buisson's manuscript, and he looks ready to collapse, but despite the dark circles his eyes are still keen, and he still speaks eloquently and lucidly.

"There are a lot of discrepancies between the text and the facts. I assume Buisson would call that the 'creative instinct.' In the 'novel,' he calls me Crest and shaves about twenty years off my age. We have three officers called Fernand, Mehdi, and Élisabeth, none of whom have a surname: one is alcoholic; one is second-generation Arab; the third is a woman in her forties. A broad cast of characters, something for everyone. Then there's a student called Sylvain Guignard; in the book, he's the one who tells you about Chub's book rather than Professeur Didier—whom he calls Ballanger."

Clearly Viguier, like Camille himself, could not help but check to see how he was described. Here they sit before the distorting mirror of literature. What truth does it tell to each of them?

"His portrait of you is striking," Viguier goes on, as though Camille had spoken aloud. "It's flattering. You come across as an intelligent and decent man—isn't that how most people would like to be seen? There is a great deal of admiration, which is in keeping with the letters and with the writers he admires. We've known since the start that Buisson's murderous rage is rooted in a strong *antipathy* toward authority, toward the figures of the Father. He sneers at authority and yet admires it. The man is a walking contradiction. He has chosen you to symbolize his struggle, and that is undoubtedly why, through Irène, he wants to hurt you. It's classic cognitive dissonance. He admires you, but he wants to destroy you. In doing so he hopes to rebuild his sense of himself."

"Why Irène?"

"Because she's there. Because Irène is you."

Still ashen, Camille stares down at the manuscript in silence.

"The letters he transcribes in the novel are the same letters he sent you, right down to the punctuation. The only thing he has made up is the supposed profile he published in *Le Matin*. As for the rest of the text—though it would be useful to study it more closely—a number of major themes are immediately evident."

Camille leans back in his chair and glances up at the clock he is pretending to ignore. "He's going to carry out the very crime he wrote about in his novel, isn't he?"

Viguier does not seem disconcerted by this sudden change of subject. He calmly sets down the papers he is holding and looks at Camille. He weighs his words with care. He wants to be certain that Camille understands what he is saying. To the letter.

"We've been looking for a logic to his crimes. We have now found it. He wants to recreate the crime he wrote about long ago in his novel *Shadow Slayer*, and in doing so, he will complete this 'novel' he left for us to find. Unless we can stop him, this is what he intends to do."

Tell the truth. The whole truth. Hide nothing. Confirm what he already knows. Camille can see what the doctor is doing, knows it is the only way.

"However, there are a several things we do not know, which might be more . . . reassuring," Viguier adds. "Until we find his earlier novel, we cannot know where or when he has planned for the murder to take place; we have no reason to suppose that it will take place now or in the next few hours. The scenario he is playing out might involve holding his victim captive for a day, two days or longer, we don't know. The facts we have are difficult enough to deal with, there's no point adding to these concerns with speculation."

Viguier leaves a long silence. He does not look at Camille. He waits for his words to sink in. Then, abruptly deciding that he has paused for long enough, he continues his explanation.

"There are two types of fact, Camille. Those he foresaw, and those he invented."

"How can he have foreseen so many things?"

"That is something you will only find out after you arrest him." Viguier jerks his chin toward the interview room. "From what I gather, he had an inside source. But it's also clear that he will have rewritten sections as events played out—a sort of reportage. He needed his 'fiction' to be as close as possible to reality. There must have been several points at which your actions surprised him, but he foresaw those surprises, if I can put it like that. He knew he would have to adapt his story based on your reactions, your plans, and that is what he did."

"Which passages are you thinking of in particular?"

"Well, we can assume, for example, that he didn't expect you to contact him through the classified ads. That was a clever touch on your part. He probably found it exciting. In a sense, he probably thinks of you as a coauthor. 'You will be proud of us,' he said in his letter, remember? But what is most striking is the accuracy of what he did anticipate. He knew that you would be able to make the link between one of his crimes and the book on which he based it; he knew you would doggedly follow that lead even if you had to go it alone. You are not a stubborn man, *commandant*, but he clearly knows you well enough to understand that on certain points you are . . . inflexible. You act on your hunches. And he realized he could use that. He also knew that, sooner or later, someone would make the connection between the name Chub and his actual surname. His whole strategy depended upon it. He knows you rather better than we might have expected, *commandant*."

Le Guen stepped out of the interview room, leaving Maleval alone for a few minutes. The stroll, a tried and trusted interrogation technique. Leave the suspect to stew, come back, let another officer take over, come back again, make it impossible for him to predict what will happen next. Even suspects, or indeed police officers who are familiar with the technique, cannot help but be unsettled by it.

"We're going to shift into high gear, but–"

"What?" Camille interrupts.

"He knows less that we might have hoped. Buisson got more out of Maleval than Maleval managed to get on Buisson. At first, he fed him little bits of information on minor cases. Buisson slowly groomed him. Small sums of money for trivial scraps of information. Almost a stipend. By the time the Courbevoie murders came up, Maleval was primed and in position; he didn't suspect a thing. He's not the brightest crayon in the box, your Maleval."

"He's not *my* Maleval," Camille snapped, picking up his notes.

"Whatever you say."

"The publishing house Bilban was set up in 1981 and went bust in 1985," Cob explains. "Back then, obviously, the Internet didn't exist as such, so there's no trace of them online. Even so, I've found references to their catalogues on antiquarian booksellers' sites and compiled a list of titles. You want to take a look?"

Without waiting for a reply, Cob printed off the list.

A hundred or so books published between 1982 and 1985. Airport novels. Camille scans the titles. Spy novels: *Agent TX is Missing*; *Agent TX and the Abwehr*; *King, Queen, Spy*; *Requiem for a Spy*; *Codename: Ocean*. Crime novels: *Trouble in Malibu*; *Brass Bullets and Blond Bombshells*; *In a Dead Man's Shoes*. And romantic fiction: *Beloved Christelle*; *A Heart So Pure*; *To the End of Love* . . .

"Bilban specialized in buying up out-of-print novels and republishing them under new titles." As always, Cob did not look up at Camille while he spoke but just carried on typing.

"Do you have the names of the owners?"

"Only the managing director, Paul-Henry Vaysse. He had shares in a bunch of publishers, but he ran Bilban himself. He was the one who filed for liquidation. There's no sign of him working in publishing again between 1985 and 2001, when he died. I'm trying to track down the others."

"I've got it!"

Camille rushes over.

"At least I think I have. Hang on . . ."

Cob's fingers flit nimbly from one keyboard to another; on the bank of computer screens, pages scroll.

"What the hell is it?" Camille says impatiently.

Le Guen and Louis have come to join them, and the rest of the team are already on their feet. Camille manages to suppress a gesture of irritation.

"Get back to your work; we can deal with this."

"It's a list of people who worked for Bilban. I don't have them all, obviously, but I've managed to track down six of them."

On the screen is a spreadsheet with six columns: name, address, date of birth, social security number, date of employment, date of redundancy. Six lines.

"Okay." Cob pushes his chair back and massages the small of his back. "I don't know what you want to do next."

"Print this off for me."

Cob nods to the machine, where four copies have been printed out already.

"How did you track them down?"

"It would take too long to explain. And it wasn't strictly above-board. There was a little black hat work involved, if you know what I mean." Cob looks warily at Le Guen, who simply picks up a copy of the list and pretends he has not heard. The three officers read in silence.

"I'll print out the rest," Cob says, staring at the screen.

"What rest?" Camille says.

"Their full history."

The printer whirs into action. Six pages showing every known detail on the six employees. One died earlier in the year; another seems to have vanished into thin air.

"What about him?" Louis says.

"I can't find any trace of him," Cob says. "He's completely vanished. There's no way of knowing what happened to him."

Isabelle Russell, born 1958, joins Bilban in 1982, but she works there for only five months. Camille crosses out her name. Jacinthe Lefebvre, born 1939, worked with the company from 1982 until it went into liquidation. Nicholas Brieuc, born 1953, joins the company at the outset and leaves in 1984. Théodore Sabin, born 1924, also joins in 1982 and stays with the company until it goes bust. Retired. Camille quickly calculates: he would be seventy-nine. Last known address: a retirement home in Jouy-en-Josas. Camille crosses him out.

"What about these two?" Camille says, indicating two names he has circled, Lefebvre and Brieuc.

"I'm already on it," Cob says.

"Do we know their job titles at Bilban?" Louis says.

"No, I haven't been able to find that out. Here we go, Jacinthe Lefebvre, retired, lives in Vincennes at 124 avenue du Bel-Air."

Pause.

"And Nicholas Brieuc, currently unemployed, 36 rue Louis Blanc, Paris X."

"You call the first one, I'll take the second," he says to Louis as he dashes for the phone.

"I'm so sorry to disturb you at such a late hour . . . Yes, I understand, but even so, you'd be well advised not to hang up. This is Louis Mariani calling, from the *brigade criminelle*."

Meanwhile, Brieuc's phone rings and rings.

"And your name is . . . ? So your mother is not there?"

Without thinking, Camille counts the rings, seven, eight, nine . . .

"Which hospital is she in, if you don't mind my asking? Yes, of course, I understand . . ."

Eleven, twelve. Camille is about to hang up when he hears a click. Someone has picked up at the other end, but he cannot hear a voice.

"Hello? Monsieur Brieuc? Hello?" Camille shouts into the receiver. "Can you hear me?"

Louis, meanwhile, has hung up and slides a piece of paper across to Camille: Saint-Louis Hospital. Palliative Care Unit.

"Jesus Christ! Is there anyone there? Can you hear me?"

There is another click followed by the dial tone.

"Right. I'll need two officers to come with me," Camille says, getting to his feet.

Le Guen signals to two of the officers, who reach for their jackets and follow Camille as he dashes for the door, only to run back, jerk open his desk drawer, grab his service revolver, and leave.

It is 12:30 a.m.

The two motorcycle officers drive much faster than Camille, who does his best to keep up. In the passenger seat, Louis nervously pushes back his bangs. The two officers in the backseat are silent, focused. The wail of the sirens is interrupted by piercing whistles from the motorcycles. At this hour, there is little traffic. They take the rue de Flandres at seventy-five miles an hour, the rue du Faubourg Saint-Martin at seventy. Less than seven minutes later they come to a violent halt on the rue Louis Blanc. The outriders have already cordoned off both ends of the street. The four officers leap from the car and sprint toward number 36. Back at the *brigade*, Camille did not even register which officers Le Guen dispatched. He quickly realizes they are two young men, younger than he. The first stops for a second to glance at the names on the mailboxes and mutters, "Fourth floor, left." By the time Camille reaches the landing, the two officers are already hammering on the door and bellowing: "Police! Open up!" And immediately a door flies open— but not the one they want, the one opposite. An old woman pops her head out and peers at them, then swiftly retreats. They hear another door bang upstairs, but otherwise the building is silent. One of the officers draws his pistol, looks from Camille to the lock, then back to Camille. The other officer is still pounding. Camille stares at the door, motions for everyone to step aside, and studies the lock, trying to calculate the trajectory of a bullet fired through a door at point-blank range in an apartment whose layout is unknown.

"What's your name?" he asks one of the officers.

"Fabrice Pou-"

"And you?" he cuts him off and glances at the other officer.

"Bernard."

Fabrice cannot be more than twenty-five and Bernard fractionally older. Camille looks back at the door, crouches a little, then, standing on tiptoe, he stretches his hand out, the index finger extended, to indicate the angle of the shot. He checks that the officers have understood, then steps aside and nods to the taller of the two, the one called Bernard.

The officer steps forward, extends his arm, and is gripping his service revolver with both hands when there is the sound of a key turning in the lock. Camille pushes the door open. A man of about fifty is standing in the hallway wearing boxer shorts and a rumpled T-shirt that had once been white. He looks drunk.

"Wha's goin' on?" he grumbles, staring at the revolver pointed at him.

Camille turns and motions to the officer to put away his weapon.

"Monsieur Brieuc? Nicholas Brieuc?"

The man reels and totters; the stench of alcohol on his breath is overpowering.

"This is all we need," Camille mutters, gently pushing the man back inside.

Louis flicks on the lights in the living room and opens the windows wide.

"Fabrice, go and make some coffee," Camille says, steering Brieuc toward a worn-out sofa. He turns to the other officer. "You, stay here with him."

Louis is already in the kitchen running the faucet; it is some time before it runs cold. Meanwhile, Camille is opening cupboards looking for a receptacle of some sort. He finds a salad bowl and hands it to Louis, then heads back into the living room. The apartment is not a ruin, merely dilapidated. The walls are bare; the green linoleum floor is strewn with filthy clothes; there is a chair and an oilcloth-covered table, on which are the remnants of numerous meals. In a corner, a television flickers, the volume on mute. Fabrice strides over and turns it off.

Slumped on the sofa, the man has closed his eyes. His face is sallow and unshaven; a three-day beard, stippled with gray, encroaches on his high cheekbones; his bare legs are thin and bony.

Camille's cell phone rings.

"So . . . ?" It is Le Guen.

"The guy's completely shit faced," Camille mumbles, staring at Brieuc, who shakes his head heavily.

"You need a team?"

"There's no time. I'll call you back."

"Hang on . . ."

"What?"

"I've just had a call from the force in Périgueux. The Buisson family house is empty—in fact, it's been gutted. Not a stick of furniture left, nothing."

"Bodies?"

"Two. Buried maybe two years ago. He didn't take much trouble to hide them; the grave is on a hill just behind the house. There's a team working to exhume them right now."

Louis holds out the bowl of water and a faded dishcloth. Camille takes the cloth, soaks it in the water, and presses it to Brieuc's face. The man barely reacts.

"Monsieur Brieuc, can you hear me?"

Brieuc's breathing is erratic. Camille soaks the rag again, wrings it out, and presses it to the man's face. Tilting his head, he sees there are maybe a dozen empty beer cans stashed down the side of the sofa. He takes the man's wrist and checks for a pulse.

"Okay," he says. "Is there a shower in this hovel?"

Brieuc doesn't scream. The two officers prop him in the bathtub while Camille runs the faucet, checks the temperature, then hands the shower hose to the taller of the officers.

"Shit!" Brieuc wails as water streams down his face, his threadbare clothes clinging to his scrawny frame.

"Monsieur Brieuc?" Camille says. "Can you hear me now?"

"Yeah, yeah, I hear you, fuck sake . . ."

Camille nods to the officer, who lays the shower head in the bath. It continues to spray water over Brieuc's feet, and he lifts them in turn as though wading through a river. Louis grabs a towel and hands it to Brieuc, who twists and slumps over the side of the bath. Water drips from his sodden T-shirt onto the floor. He pisses into the bath, soaking his boxer shorts.

"Bring him back in here," Camille says, heading into the living room.

Louis has already searched the rest of the apartment: the kitchen, the bedroom, the wardrobes. He is now rummaging through the drawers of the Henri II sideboard.

Brieuc sits shivering on the sofa while Fabrice goes to fetch a blanket from the bedroom. Camille draws up a chair and sits facing the man, and for the first time they stare at each other. Slowly, Brieuc comes to and finds himself surrounded: two men are looming over him menacingly; another is rummaging through the drawers of the sideboard; and the fourth man, sitting on a chair, is studying him coldly. Brieuc rubs his eyes and, suddenly panicked, struggles to his feet and tries to push past, knocking Camille off the chair so that his head slams against the floor. Brieuc has barely taken a step when the officers grab him and pin him to the ground. Fabrice puts a foot on the back of the man's neck while Bernard twists his arms behind his back.

Louis rushes over to where Camille is gingerly exploring the bruise on his temple.

"Get the fuck off me!" Camille growls, waving his hand as though shooing a wasp.

He struggles to his feet, then kneels down next to Brieuc. His face is pressed to the floor, he is having trouble breathing.

"Now you listen to me," Camille says, barely controlling his rage. "Let me explain . . ."

"I . . . I didn't do anything . . . ," Brieuc manages to say.

Camille lays a hand on the man's cheek, then nods to Fabrice, who leans all his weight on his right foot. Brieuc howls.

"I said listen to me! There's not much time."

"Camille . . . ," hisses Louis, but he is not listening.

"My name is Commandant Verhœven," he explains, "and right now there's a woman out there dying." He takes his hand from the man's face, crouches lower, and whispers. "And if you don't help me, I swear I will kill you."

"Camille . . . ," Louis says, louder this time.

"Now, you're welcome to drink yourself to death," Camille speaks in a low growl that causes everything in the room to shudder, "but not until I've left. First, you're going to pay attention, and you're going to give me some answers. Am I making myself clear?"

Unbeknownst to Camille, Louis has signaled to Fabrice, who has gently removed his foot. Still, Brieuc makes no attempt to move; he lies on the floor, face pressed into the green linoleum; he stares at the little man kneeling beside him, and in his eyes he sees a strength of will that terrifies him. He nods.

"We pulped everything."

Back on the sofa, Brieuc is allowed a can of beer and drains half of it in a single gulp. More alert now, he listens as Camille succinctly explains what is happening. He does not understand everything, but he nods vehemently, and that seems to satisfy Camille. These men are looking for some book. This is all Brieuc manages to take in. Bilban. How long did he work in the warehouse at Bilban? Brieuc struggles to think. It was a long time ago. Was he working there when the company went bust? What happened to the stock? From Brieuc's face, it is evident he is wondering why it matters what happened to a heap of shitty novels. Why it seems so urgent. And what the fuck he's got to do with any of this. He tries to concentrate, but he can't make head nor tail of it.

Camille does not attempt to explain. He sticks to simple questions, careful not to let Brieuc stray from the point. "All we need are the facts. Where are the books now?"

"We pulped the stock, all of it, I swear. What else were we supposed to do? The books were shit."

Brieuc raises the can to finish his beer, but Camille deftly grabs his arm.

"In a minute!"

Brieuc looks around for support, but he sees only the grim faces of the three other officers. He feels a surge of panic and begins to tremble.

"Stay calm," Camille says. "We can't afford to waste any more time."

"But I already told you–"

"Yes, I get it. But no one ever gets round to pulping everything. Publishers have stock all over the place; sometimes returns come in after the books have been pulped. Try to remember."

"We pulped everything," Brieuc mumbles vacantly, staring at the beer can in his trembling hand.

"Okay," Camille says, overcome by an immense weariness.

He looks at his watch: 1:20 a.m. He feels cold, suddenly. Looking around he sees the windows are still open wide. He places his hands on his knees and gets to his feet.

"We're not going to get any more out of him. Let's go."

Louis tilts his head as if to say that it's probably for the best. Fabrice and Bernard head down the stairs, elbowing their way past neighbors who have come to see what is happening. Camille brings a hand up to his face. It feels as though the bruise on his temple has swollen. He steps back into the apartment. Brieuc is still sitting on the sofa, dazed, cradling his beer can. Camille goes to the bathroom, where he stands on the wastebasket so he can see himself in the mirror. There is a large bump on the side of his head which has already started to turn blue. He runs the cold water and splashes water on his face.

"You know, now that I think about it, I'm not sure . . ."

Camille whips round to find the pitiful figure of Brieuc standing in the doorway, his boxer shorts sodden, a tartan blanket around his shoulders, like a refugee from some disaster.

"I think I brought back a few boxes for my son. He wasn't interested. They're probably still in the cellar, if you want to have a look."

The car hurtles dangerously through the empty streets. Louis is at the wheel this time. With all the swerving, braking, and accelerating, and the constant shriek of the sirens, Camille cannot read. His right hand grips the door handle, and every time he attempts to let go to turn the page, he find himself thrown forward or sideways. He manages to make out a word or two. The letters seem to dance on the page. Since he didn't have time to put on his glasses, everything is blurred and he has to hold the book at arm's length. After a few minutes of fruitless effort, he gives up and clasps the book against his knees. On the cover, a young blonde woman is lying on what looks like a bed. Her blouse is open to reveal a glimpse of her breasts and her swollen belly. Her arms are stretched out behind her head as though she is trussed. Her face is a mask of terror, her eyes are rolled back, her mouth open in a silent scream. Camille lets go of the door handle for a second and turns the book over. The back cover copy is white against a black background. He cannot make out the tiny print.

The car veers right and stops outside the *brigade criminelle*. Louis brutally yanks the handbrake, plucks the book from Camille's hand, and rushes up the stairs ahead of him.

The photocopier churns out hundreds of pages and, after an interminable interval, Louis reappears with four sets of copies in identical green folders to find Camille pacing the squad room.

"The book runs to"—Camille flicks to the back of a folder—". . . 250 pages. If we're going to find something it'll probably be at the end. Let's say after page 130. Armand, you start there; Louis, Jean and I will start at the end and work back. Doctor, could you take a look at the beginning just in case? We don't know what we're looking for. The smallest detail could be important. Cob, I need you to drop what you're working on. Everyone else, when you find a search term that seems significant, shout over to Cob so everyone can hear, got it? Right, let's go."

Camille opens the folder in front of him. Scanning the last pages of the book, his eye is drawn to certain paragraphs, he skims them quickly, resisting the temptation to read, to make sense of the text he knows he needs to search. He pushes his glasses up his nose.

As he crouched down, Matthéo could just make out Corey's body sprawled on the floor. Acrid smoke caught in his throat and he coughed violently. He lay on the floor and began to crawl. Holding the gun made crawling impossible. He struggled to engage the safety catch and slipped the revolver back into its holster.

Camille turned two pages.

> It was impossible to tell whether Corey was still alive. He didn't seem
> to be moving, but Matthéo could not see clearly. His eyes were sting-
> ing. In a . . .

Camille checks the page number then flicks back to page 181.

"I've got some character called Corey," Louis calls out to Cob
without looking up. He spells the name. "But I haven't got a first
name yet."
    "The girl's name is Nadine Lefranc," Le Guen shouts.
    "There have to be three thousand girls by that name," Cob mutters.

> Page 71: Nadine left the clinic just after four o'clock and headed for the
> supermarket parking lot, where she had left her car. From the moment
> she saw the ultrasound, she had been trembling. Suddenly, the whole
> world seemed beautiful, even the leaden skies, the chill air, the grimy
> streets . . .

It has to come later, Camille thinks, leafing rapidly through the
loose pages, catching a word here and there, but nothing that seems
relevant.

"I've got some cop called Matthéo, Francis Matthéo," Armand says.
    "He mentions an undertaker's in Lens, near Calais," Le Guen
calls, "Dubois et Fils."
    "Slow down, guys," Cob grumbles, typing as quickly as he can.
"The search results give me eighty-seven people named Corey—a
first name would be helpful."

> Page 211: Corey took up position next to the window. Wary of being
> spotted by a passer-by, though the area was almost deserted. He had
> been careful not to clean the windows, which were encrusted with a

decade's worth of grime. Outside, in the faint glow of the only two streetlights that still worked, he could see . . .

Camille flicks back a few pages.

Page 207: Corey sat in the car for a long time, studying the derelict buildings. He checked his watch: 10 p.m. He went over his calculations in his mind and came to the same conclusion. Allowing time for her to dress, to go downstairs, to find her way here given her state of panic, Nadine would arrive in about twenty minutes. He opened the window a crack and lit a cigarette. Everything was ready. As long as . . .

He had to go back further.

Page 205: It was a long, low building at one end of a narrow road about a mile and a quarter from the outskirts of Parency. Corey had . . .

"The town is called Parency," Camille calls out. "Actually, it seems to be a village."

"There's no undertaker called Dubois in Lens," Cob says. "I've got four companies called Dubois: plumbers, accountants, a garden center, and a company that makes tarps. I'll print off the list."

Le Guen got up and went to the printer to collect the pages.

Page 221: "Tell me anyway," said Commissaire Matthéo.

Christian did not seem to hear.

"If I'd known . . . ," he said in a whisper, "in the . . ."

"The girl works for a lawyer named Pernaud," Armand says, "with an office on the rue Saint-Christophe in Lille."

Camille stops reading. Nadine Lefranc, Corey, Matthéo, Christian, undertakers, Dubois, he mentally repeats the names but nothing comes to him.

Page 227: Finally, the young woman regained consciousness. She turned her head and saw Corey standing next to her; he was smiling at her strangely.

Camille feels cold sweat trickle down his back; his hands begin to shake.

"It was you?" she said.

Suddenly panicked, she tried to get to her feet only to find her arms and legs bound firmly. The ropes were so tight, they cut off her circulation; her hands and feet felt like ice. She wondered how long she had been here.

"Sleep well?" asked Corey, lighting a cigarette.

Nadine began to scream, thrashing her head from side to side. She howled until she had no air left in her lungs, and when finally she stopped, breathless and hoarse, Corey had not batted an eyelid.

"You're very beautiful, Nadine. You're so beautiful . . . when you cry."

Still pulling on his cigarette, he laid a hand on the young woman's swollen belly. She shuddered at his touch.

"And I am sure that you will be still more beautiful as you die," he whispered with a smile.

"There's no rue Saint-Christophe in Lille," Cob says, "And there's no lawyer called Pernaud."

"Fuck it," grunts Le Guen.

Camille looks over at him and at the folder he is holding. Le Guen is also reading the last section of the book. Camille returns to his own copy of the novel.

Page 237: "Pretty, isn't it?" said Corey.

Nadine could barely manage to turn her head. Her face was horribly swollen, her eyes now narrow slits that barely let in light; the bruises had already turned a purplish yellow. Though the cut on her cheek had stopped bleeding, thick, dark clots of blood still dripped from her mouth and trickled down her neck. She struggled to breathe, her chest rising and falling fitfully.

Corey rolled up his sleeves and stepped toward her.

"Well, Nadine, don't you think it's pretty?" He nodded to something at the foot of the bed.

Through the blur of tears Nadine could just make out a wooden cross set on an easel. It was about twenty inches wide and looked like a smaller version of a church crucifix.

"It's for the baby, Nadine," he said in a tender whisper.

He pressed his thumbnail so hard into the base of Nadine's breast that she howled in pain. He traced a line down to her pubis, the sharp nail digging a furrow in the taut skin of her belly as the woman screamed hoarsely.

"We'll take him out through here," Corey said softly as his nail dug into her, "A bit like a Cesarean, though you're not likely to be alive to see him afterward, but I promise you he'll be beautiful, your baby, when he's crucified. Christian will be happy. His own little Jesus . . ."

Camille springs to his feet, grabs the pages, and frantically leafs back through them. "The cross . . . ," he mutters. "The easel." Page 205, nothing, 206, nothing, 207. He scans the page and stops. There it is:

Corey had put a lot of thought into choosing the place. The building, which for years had been a warehouse for the nearby shoe factory, was the perfect location. Latterly it had been used as a studio by a ceramicist, and was left derelict when she died . . .

Camille whips around and finds himself face-to-face with Louis. Feverishly, he flicks back through the pages.

"What are you looking for?" Le Guen says.

"If he mentions . . ." Camille does not look up; the pages flash past. Suddenly his mind feels utterly clear.

"The warehouse," he says, brandishing the sheaf of pages. "He says it's an old studio. An artist's studio. He's taken her to Monfort, to my mother's old studio."

Le Guen grabs his phone to call the rapid response unit, but Camille has already pulled on his jacket and grabbed his keys and is dashing for the stairs. Louis marshals everyone and begins to give orders. Only Armand remains seated, staring hopelessly at the folder in front of him. The officers divide up into teams. Le Guen barks into his phone, explaining the situation to the senior officer at RAID.

Just as they are heading for the stairs, Louis's eye is caught by the one still, fixed point in all this chaos. Armand is sitting silently in front of his folder. Louis frowns and looks at him questioningly.

Running his finger under a sentence, Armand says dully, "He kills her at 2 a.m. precisely."

All eyes turn to the clock on the wall. It is 1:45 a.m.

Camille reverses the car as Louis jumps into the passenger seat, and they set off. As the boulevard Saint-Germain flashes past, both men are imagining the same thing: the woman bound to the bed, beaten, screaming, as a thumbnail traces a line across her belly.

As Camille floors the accelerator, Louis glances at him out of the corner of his eye. What is going through the *commandant*'s mind right now? Maybe, behind this mask of cool determination, he can hear Irène screaming his name; maybe as he swerves to avoid the car stopped at traffic lights on the avenue Denfert-Rochereau he can hear her voice, as, white knuckled, he grips the steering wheel so hard he might snap it in two.

Louis has a mental image of Irène screaming as she realizes she might die here, bound and defenseless, a grim sacrifice.

Surely Camille's whole life has telescoped to that single image of Irène with blood trickling down her neck as he heads down avenue du Général-Leclerc at a frightening speed. *Don't get us killed now,* Louis thinks, though it is for Irène's life rather than his own that he fears.

The deserted streets streak past, racing back into the darkness of this night that might seem beautiful but for the horror that is unfolding. The keening sirens break the silence as the car exits the city by the Porte d'Orléans and pierces the sleepy suburbs like a stiletto, weaving between the cars and taking a turn so fast it almost pitches onto two wheels and hits the curb. *It's just a bump,* Louis thinks, although it feels as though the car has left the road and is flying. *Are we going to die here? Has the devil come to take us, too?* Camille pumps the brake; the tires screech. To their right, cars speed past. Camille swerves, accidentally grazing one, then another; there is a shriek of metal, a shower of sparks joins the flashing lights that strobe the darkness; the car rears, swerving wildly down the dark road. It veers dangerously close to the parked cars, clips one, rebounds and clips another, gouging paintwork, splintering wing mirrors while Camille applies the brakes, wrestling with the steering wheel and trying desperately to stop the car careering out of control. Finally, it comes to a shuddering halt, mounting the pavement at the intersection near Plessis-Robinson and hitting a barrier post.

The sudden silence is deafening. The siren has died; the rotating light has become detached and is dangling by a side window. Camille, who was thrown against the door, has hit his head and is bleeding profusely. A car glides slowly past, eyes gawk, then it drives off. Camille passes a hand over his face, and it comes away daubed with dark blood. His back aches, his legs ache, he is stunned from the collision. He struggles painfully to sit up straight, then gives up and slumps back in his seat. He tries to catch his breath, then makes a second attempt. Next to him, a half-conscious Louis rolls his head from side to side.

Camille shakes himself, lays a hand on Louis's shoulder, and shakes him gently.

"I'm fine," Louis says, coming round. "I'll be fine."

Camille scrabbles for his cell, which must have fallen from his pocket. He gropes under the seats, but it is too dark to see. Nothing. Finally his fingers encounter something—his service revolver—which he manages to retrieve by contorting himself. He knows that in a quiet suburb, the noise of the collision will bring men stumbling into the street and women to their windows. He leans against the door, shoves hard, and it opens with a piercing shriek of metal. He swings his legs out and stands up. He is bleeding badly but cannot work out where he has been hurt.

He stumbles around the car, jerks open the passenger door, and puts a hand on Louis's shoulder. Louis shrugs that he is okay, so Camille leaves him to collect himself and goes to rummage in the trunk, where he finds a rag to wipe his forehead. He stares at the bloody scrap of cloth, his fingers feeling for the gash just below his hairline. Studying the car, he sees that all four doors are damaged, as are the rear fenders. Only now does he realize that the engine is still running. He puts the flashing light bar back on the roof and notices that one of the headlights is broken. Camille slides behind the wheel again, glances at Louis, who nods as the car reverses off the pavement. The relief at realizing the car is still functioning is so great, it is almost as though there never was a crash. Camille puts the car into first gear, accelerates, shifts into second, and a moment later is once again hurtling through the dark suburbs.

The clock on the dashboard reads 2:15 a.m. when Camille finally slows. They are approaching an intersection where roads fork left and right, running along the edge of the forest. Camille drives straight on, brutally accelerating, as though determined to drive through the dark bank of trees in the distance. He drops the bloody rag he has managed to keep pressed against his forehead, takes his gun from the holster, and sets it between his thighs. Louis does likewise, then sits forward and grips the dashboard with both hands. The needle of the speedometer is touching seventy-five when Camille finally brakes about a hundred yards from the lane that leads to the studio. The dirt track is rutted and potholed, and Camille would usually drive very slowly. The car weaves to avoid the deepest holes, but jolts and shudders over others. Louis hangs on. Camille turns off the light bar and brakes as soon as he sees the shadowy building plunged in darkness.

There is no car outside. Maybe Buisson decided to park out of sight, behind the studio. Camille switches off the headlights, and it takes his eyes a moment to adjust to the darkness. The front of the one-story building is dominated by the large picture window on the right. The place looks deserted. Camille feels a pang of doubt. Could he be wrong? Could Buisson have taken Irène somewhere else? Perhaps it is the darkness and the eerie silence of the forest stretching away behind, but the studio looks suddenly ominous. Though they do not speak, both men are wondering why there is no light on. They are thirty yards from the door. Camille cuts the engine and allows the car to coast the rest of the way. He brakes gently, as though afraid to make a sound. Still staring straight ahead, he gropes for his revolver, opens the door slowly, and climbs out of the car. Louis finds that his door is stuck, and when he manages to shoulder it open, it makes a dull grating sound. The two men stare at each other, about to say something when they hear a muffled, erratic thwocking. In fact there seem to be two different sounds. Camille creeps toward the building, his gun cocked; Louis stays several paces behind. The door is closed; there is no sign of anyone having been here. Camille looks up, then tilts his head to listen to the pulsing hum, which seems louder now. He turns with a puzzled look, but Louis is staring at the ground, trying to focus on the sound which he cannot identify.

In the instant that both men finally recognize the droning whir, the helicopter rises above the treetops, banks quickly, and hovers above the studio as powerful spotlights illuminate the roof and the surrounding trees in a blinding glare. The noise now is deafening, a wind whips, and dust whirls in eddies. The tall trees surrounding the clearing rustle and sway. The helicopter wheels for a moment, and the two men instinctively crouch and find themselves pinned to the ground not far from the door.

The helicopter dips, its skids almost touching the roof, and the ear-splitting roar of the blades makes it impossible even to think.

The rush of air is such that they cannot look up and have to huddle to protect themselves. Only now do they see the source of the second noise they heard—three huge black vehicles with tinted windows roaring up the lane toward them. The SUVs move in perfect formation, oblivious to the confusion, tires bounding over the rutted track.

They are briefly blinded by the searchlight mounted on the first vehicle. The helicopter suddenly wheels again, training its spotlights on the rear of the building and the surrounding woodland. Spurred on by the sudden irruption of the rapid response unit and still dazed by the thunderous roar, the wind, the whirl of dust, and the searchlights, Camille turns toward the building and breaks into a run. The long shadow cast by the spotlight on the van behind him shrinks with every step as Camille summons his last ounce of strength. Louis, who has been right behind him, suddenly veers off to the right. Camille reaches the porch in seconds, scrambles up the woodworm-riddled steps, and swiftly fires two bullets into the lock, causing the door and the frame to splinter. He shoves the door open and steps inside.

Barely has he taken two paces when he slips on something viscous and falls heavily on his back, flailing for something to grab on to. Behind him the door bounces off the wall and slams shut. For a second, the studio is plunged into darkness, but since the lock is shattered, the door swings slowly open again. The spotlight on the SUV suddenly picks out a wide board set on trestles and the supine figure of Irène, her hands bound. Her face is turned toward him, her eyes open, her expression frozen, her lips parted. Her belly is no longer swollen, but furrowed with rolls of flesh.

Just as he feels the tremor of heavy boots pounding on the wooden steps behind him, just as the shadowy figures of the RAID officers fill the doorway, Camille turns his head, and through the shadows fitfully illuminated by flashes of blue light, he sees a cross that seems to hover in the air and on it, a small, dark, almost shapeless figure, its arms spread wide.

EPILOGUE

Monday, April 26, 2004

Dear Camille,

A year. One year already. Here, as you can imagine, time is neither swift nor slow. Here the time that trickles in from the outside world is so deadened once it reaches us that we wonder whether it passes for us as it does for others. Especially as my position is less than comfortable.

Ever since your lieutenant chased me through the woods in Clamart and shot me in the back in a cowardly fashion, causing irreparable damage to my spinal cord, I am confined to the wheelchair from which I write this letter.

I have become inured to it. Indeed, there are times when I am grateful, since my condition affords me privileges other inmates are denied. I receive greater care and attention than others. I am not expected to perform demeaning chores. It is a small blessing, but in here, every little thing counts.

In fact, I am much better than I was at first. I have settled in, as they say. My legs may be useless, but my other faculties are in perfect order. I read, I write. In short, I live. And, gradually, I have carved out a niche for myself. Indeed, I can say that, contrary to what one might expect, I am envied. After so many months in the hospital, I finally arrived in this establishment to discover my reputation had preceded me, something that ensured me a certain grudging respect. Nor is that the whole story.

It will be a long time before I go on trial, though it scarcely matters to me, since the verdict is a foregone conclusion. Actually, that is not quite true. I am looking forward to the trial. Despite the law's interminable delay, I am confident that my lawyers—you cannot imagine how the vultures squeeze me dry—will finally succeed in securing publication of my novel, which, given all that has been written about me, is bound to get great publicity. It is destined to be an international best seller whose sales can only be enhanced by a protracted trial. In the words of my editor—that mangy cur—it will be good for business. We have already had offers for the film rights, which will give you some idea.

I felt it only right, while I await the next flurry of articles, features, and profiles, to take a moment to pen you a few words.

Despite my precautions, events did not unfold as perfectly as I had hoped. This is regrettable, given that I came so close. Had I simply adhered to the timetable (one that I drew up, I acknowledge), had I been a whit less confident about my plan, I would have disappeared as I intended the moment your wife breathed her last, and I would now be writing to you from the little paradise I had planned and would still have the use of my legs. It appears, after all, that there is some justice. That must be a comfort to you.

You will note that I speak of my "plan" rather than my "masterwork." I have no further need of that pretentious verbiage that served only to further this plan, those grandiose delusions in which I never for a moment believed. Making you believe that I was "charged with a mission," "swept along by something greater than myself," was no more than a novelistic trope. And not, I'll grant, the most original. Happily, I am nothing of the sort. Indeed I was somewhat surprised that you embraced the idea. Once again, psychological profilers have proved their mettle, and once again they have been found wanting. No, I am an eminently pragmatic man. And humble, too. In spite of my creative urges, I was never under any illusion about my talents as a writer. Nonetheless, borne along on the wave of scandal and the horrified prurience that violent tragedy arouses, my book will sell millions, it will be translated, it will be adapted; in the annals of literature, it will endure. These are things I could never have attained through my talents alone. I simply sidestepped the obstacles in my path. I shall have earned my fame.

As for you, Camille, the future seems less certain, if you will forgive my saying so. Those close to you know what sort of a man you are. A man far removed from the Camille Verhœven I described. In order to comply with the rules of the genre, I felt obliged to flatter, to indulge in a little hagiography. Readers expect such things. But in your heart of hearts, you know that you are no match for the character I created.

Neither you nor I are the people others imagined us to be. Perhaps, after all, we are not as different as we might like to think. In a certain sense, did we not both kill your wife?

I will leave you to ponder that question.

You remain, Sir, *my* humble servant,

P. Buisson

ACKNOWLEDGING DEBTS

Irène was my first novel. Since I owe almost everything I am to literature, it felt natural to begin by writing a novel that was a homage to crime fiction. In fact, I made this the subject of my novel, since *Irène* is the story of a killer who reenacts murders ripped from the pages of crime novels.

I began with Emile Gaboriau's *Le Crime d'Orcival*, one of the great precursors to the detective novel. And having paid my debt to history, I decided it was impossible to begin Camille Verhœven's investigation with anything other than *The Black Dahlia* (1987), James Ellroy's masterpiece. There is crime fiction before Ellroy and crime fiction after. Knowing the man himself is a great admirer of Hammett and Chandler, I took the liberty of taking inspiration from him.

American Psycho was a tremendous shock to the reading public. Bret Easton Ellis raises so many moral questions with such intelligence, such skill. Though not considered a crime novel, this defining work deftly addresses readers' ambiguity toward the very violence that is an essential "pleasure" of crime fiction. Yet many criticized the visceral brutality in *American Psycho*, as though the purpose of such fiction is to exorcise our hyperviolent societies, but to remain within "reasonable limits."

Laidlaw, by William McIlvanney, was among the most devastating revelations for me as a reader. Laidlaw is a haunting, wounded figure, and the backdrop to his investigation of Jennifer Lawson's murder is a novel of great social and political depth. I was privileged to meet McIlvanney recently, and it brought tears to my eyes.

John D. MacDonald's groundbreaking *The End of the Night*, following four murderers all the way to the electric chair, is a dazzling and utterly original achievement. In *Irène*, the false trail it inspires is a mark of my genuine admiration.

Sjöwall and Wahlöö's *Roseanna* is a novel with few peers: a slow, deliberately measured book in which, though nothing seems to happen, the reader is held spellbound. Evoking it within the pages of my own book, I pay tribute to Maj Sjöwall and Per Wahlöö, two truly great writers.

These acknowledgments would not be complete without acknowledging the debt I owe to Christopher MacLehose, who, in publishing my work, has brought me to an international readership.

And my sincere thanks to Frank Wynne, an outstanding translator, to whom this book, and all the others, owes much. This novel rather more than the rest.

PIERRE LEMAITRE, 2014

TRANSLATOR'S NOTE

The French judicial system is fundamentally different from that of the United States. Rather than the American adversarial system, in which police investigate and the role of the courts is to act as an impartial referee between prosecution and defense, in the French inquisitorial system the judiciary work with the police on the investigation, appointing an independent *juge d'instruction* entitled to question witnesses, interrogate suspects, and manage all aspects of the police investigation. If there is sufficient evidence, the case is referred to the *procureur*, the public prosecutor, who decides whether to bring charges. The *juge d'instruction* plays no role in the eventual trial and is prohibited from adjudicating future cases involving the same defendant.

The French have two national police forces: the *police nationale* (formerly called the *sûreté*), a civilian police force with jurisdiction in cities and large urban areas, and the *gendarmerie nationale*, a branch of the French Armed Forces, responsible both for public safety and for policing towns with populations of fewer than twenty thousand. Since the *gendarmerie* rarely has the resources to conduct complex investigations, the *police nationale* maintains regional criminal investigations services (*police judiciaire*), analogous to American local police crime scene investigation units, and also oversees armed rapid response units (*RAIDs*), analogous to American special weapons and tactics (SWAT) units.

GLOSSARY

BRIGADE CRIMINELLE—murder squad; combines elements of the American homicide division and major crimes unit; responsible for investigating murders, kidnappings, and assassinations

BRIGADE FINANCIÈRE—fraud squad

COMMANDANT—chief of detectives

COMMISSAIRE DIVISIONNAIRE—police chief; has both administrative and investigative roles, plus full police powers

CONCOURS ADMINISTRATIFS—administrative exams for police promotions

ÉCOLE NATIONALE SUPÉRIEURE DE LA POLICE—France's national police college

GENDARME—member of the local police

L'IDENTITÉ JUDICIARE—forensics department of the *police nationale*

JUGE D'INSTRUCTION—the "investigating judge," a role somewhat similar to that of an American district attorney; responsible for determining if a case should go to trial

PÉRIPHÉRIQUE—inner ring road circumscribing central Paris, linking the old city gates, or *portes*—e.g., Porte de la Chapelle, Porte d'Orléans

PROCUREUR—the public prosecutor, the one who decides whether to bring charges after the *juge d'instruction* has decided there is sufficient evidence to refer a case for possible trial

RAID (RECHERCHE, ASSISTANCE, INTERVENTION, DISSUASION)—a special
   operations tactical unit of the French National Police, analogous
   to American special weapons and tactics (SWAT) units; assists
   in kidnappings and hostage situations

PIERRE LEMAITRE was born in Paris in 1956. He worked for many years as a teacher of literature before becoming a novelist. He was awarded the 2013 Crime Writers Association International Dagger for *Alex* (MacLehose Press, 2012), and for his literary novel *Au-revoir là haut* he is the 2013 winner of the prestigious Prix Goncourt.

FRANK WYNNE is a translator from French and Spanish. His translations include works by Michel Houellebecq, Marcelo Figueras' *Independent* Foreign Fiction Prize-shortlisted *Kamchatka*, and *Alex* by Pierre Lemaitre.